STANDS A SHADOW

COL BUCHANAN

Praise for *Farlander*

"A strong, impressive debut novel and a series worth keeping an eye on. Kudos to Buchanan!"
—*RT Book Reviews* (4½ stars, a Top Pick)

"The writing is mature, the action sequences gripping and suitably bloodthirsty, and there's a plot twist or two. . . . A vivid, impressively detailed work."
—*Kirkus Reviews*

"Two pages into *Farlander* I was hooked. . . . I'll certainly be reading the next book, for I have a feeling that it's going to be even better. Nice one, Mr. Buchanan."
—Neal Asher, author of the Polity books

"An impressively imagined war-ravaged world."
—*Publishers Weekly*

"Col Buchanan weaves a tapestry of characters embodying youthful inexperience, military adventurism, jaded professionalism and wisdom, and the excesses of temporally expressed religious fanaticism into a fast-moving novel that, for all its fantasy elements, explosively addresses the universal questions facing any society."
—L. E. Modesitt, Jr., author of *Scholar*

"*Farlander* is until the last page a well-done Novel of Education; since the education is that of an assassin, it's an exciting read as well as a thought-provoking one. Only at the conclusion does Col Buchanan show who is *really* being educated, which makes this a truly exceptional book."
—David Drake, author of *The Legions of Fire*

TOR BOOKS BY COL BUCHANAN

Farlander
Stands a Shadow

Stands a Shadow

THE HEART *of the* WORLD

—Book Two—

Col Buchanan

A TOM DOHERTY ASSOCIATES BOOK
NEW YORK

This is a work of fiction. All of the characters, organizations, and events portrayed in this novel are either products of the author's imagination or are used fictitiously.

STANDS A SHADOW

A Tor Book
Published by Tom Doherty Associates, LLC
175 Fifth Avenue
New York, NY 10010

www.tor-forge.com

Tor® is a registered trademark of Tom Doherty Associates, LLC.

ISBN 978-0-7653-6661-0

First published in Great Britain by Tor, an imprint of Pan Macmillan, a division of Macmillan Publishers Limited

First U.S. Edition: November 2011
First U.S. Mass Market Edition: August 2012

Printed in the United States of America

0 9 8 7 6 5 4 3 2 1

For my brothers

The good man and the evil man are
but one man, standing as
shadow between day and night.

ZEZIKÉ

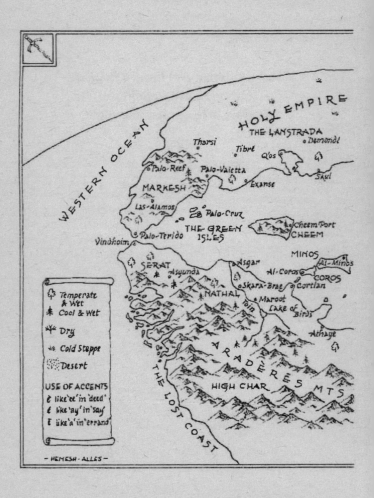

WESTERN OCEAN

HOLY EMPIRE
THE LANSTRADA
Tharsi
Tibré
Demonidl
Q'os
Palo-Reef
Palo-Valetta
MARKESH
Exanse
Saul
Las-Alamos
Palo-Cruz
Cheem Port
Palo-Terido
THE GREEN ISLES
CHEEM
Vindhoim
MINOS
SERAT
Asgar
Al-Minos
Asyunda
Al-Coros
COROS
Skara-Brag
Cortlan
NATHAL
Maroot
Toin
Lake of
Birds
Athage
ARADERES MTS
HIGH CHAR
THE LOST COAST

Temperate & Wet
Cool & Wet
Dry
Cold Steppe
Desert

USE OF ACCENTS
ē like 'ee' in 'deed'
é like 'ay' in 'say'
è like 'a' in 'errand'

— HEMESH · ALLES —

Stands
a Shadow

The Shining Way

It was like being at sea, this plain of grasses that stretched to the brink of the horizon and beyond; the eyes filled with sky wherever they looked. In the milky brightness of day the twin moons hung lonely and high, the smaller of the two a pale white, the larger a pale blue, each cupped in darkness and clearly spherical in form; reminders, to any observer with knowledge or imagination, that the world of Erēs too was a monstrous ball tumbling through the nothingness, and that they were spinning with it.

'Thank the Fool there's no wind today,' remarked Kosh, sitting poised in the saddle of his prized war-zel. 'I haven't the stomach for another burning.'

'Nor I,' replied Ash, and tore his gaze from the far moons, blinking as though returning to himself and the world of man. The air lay thick and hot today, shimmering above the stubby grasses that stretched between the two armies. The heat waves were causing the dark, glittering massif of enemy riders to loom with an unreal closeness.

Ash clucked his tongue as his own zel tossed its head again, jittery. He was a lesser rider than Kosh, and his zel was young and still untested. Ash had not given this one a name yet. His previous mount, old Asa, had fallen with a ruptured heart in their last skirmish just east of Car; a day in which the smell of roasting meat had hung like a pall above their fighting, while the enemy Yashi were burned alive in the great wind-driven conflagration

Ash and his comrades had sent gusting into their ranks. Later, his soot-stained face streaked with tears, he had mourned for his dead zel as much as for his comrades fallen that day.

Ash bent forward and stroked his young zel's neck with a gloved hand. *Look at that pair*, he tried to communicate to the animal by thought alone, eying the still form of Kosh and his trusted mount. *See how proud they look together.*

The young zel skipped once on its hind legs.

'Easy, boy,' Ash soothed, still stroking the muscular neck of the animal, flattening the grain of its coarse hair, black as pitch between the bands of white. At last the zel began to settle, began to snort the fear from its lungs and calm itself.

Leather creaked as Ash straightened in his saddle. Beside him, Kosh uncorked a waterskin and took a long drink. He gasped and wiped his mouth dry. 'I could do with something a little stronger,' he complained, and pointedly offered none to Ash. Instead he tossed it back to his son, his battlesquire, standing barefoot next to him.

'You're still sore at that?' asked Ash.

'You could have left me some, is all I'm saying.'

Ash grunted, leaned between their mounts to spit upon the ground. Blades of tindergrass popped and crackled as they absorbed the sudden moisture. It was the same all across the plain; a constant background noise could be heard – like uncooked rice raining down on far shingles, as the secretions of the two armies wrought a chorus of similar minute reactions from the grasses beneath their feet.

He looked right, over the head of his own son and battlesquire Lin, the boy standing there in his usual quiet absorption. Along the line, other mounts were prancing edgily beneath their riders' attentions. The zels could smell the enemy war-panthers in the odd scrap of breeze, leashed within the distant ranks facing them in this nameless spot in the Sea of Wind and Grasses.

The People's Revolutionary Army were outnumbered today. But then they were always outnumbered, a fact that hadn't stopped them from learning how to win against an enemy overly reliant on grumbling conscripts and the established hierarchical forms of warfare as laid out in the ancient Venerable Treatise of War. Today, the confidence of the old campaigners was apparent as they waited for the fighting to begin. This was it, they all knew, the big throw of the die; everything that either side could muster had been committed to this final confrontation.

A cry rose up and spread along the ranks; General Oshō, leader of the Shining Way, cantering on his pure black zel, Chancer, past the lines of the Wing, the men who today would anchor the left flank of the main formation. A lance bobbed upright in his hand, a red flag trailing from it above the dust that coiled from his mount's hooves. An image was stitched across the cloth: one-eyed Ninshi, protectress of the dispossessed. It was snapping and fluttering like a flame.

Oshō rode with the easy grace of a man taking an early morning ride for the pleasure of it, as confident as the rest of the veterans of the Wing. Their strategy for this battle was a sound one, and it had been proposed by General Nisan himself, overall leader of the army and military hero of the revolution. They had voted overwhelmingly in its favour when the army had held its general assembly during the night.

With the main body of their forces acting as bait for the overwhelming numbers of enemy Pulses, and with feints to the flanks designed to entangle the overlords' predictable Swan's Wings, the real killing stroke would be delivered by the heavy cavalry of General Shin's Wing, the Black Stars, hidden in the long grasses to the south-west, directly behind the position of the Shining

Way. With every Wing of the enemy engaged and ensnared in the action, they would sweep around long
and fast, and in all the confusion take the centre of the
enemy from behind, hoping to create the type of rout
they had seen countless times before.

'Today is the day, brothers!' General Oshō roared
with passion. 'Today is the day!'

Men raised lances and hollered as he passed by. Even
Ash, not one for outward displays of enthusiasm, felt a
rousing of pride as the men cheered and pumped their
fists in reply. His son was one of them.

A plume of dust rose around the general as he drew
his war-zel to a halt. With dancing steps he turned the
mount to face the far ranks of the enemy. At the sight of
them the zel snorted and swiped its tail. Together, Oshō
and Chancer waited as silence fell.

'By the Fool's balls I hope he's right,' grumbled Kosh
with a nod to their charismatic leader. 'It's time we
brought these boys home to their mothers, don't you
think?'

It was a question hardly needing a reply.

Around them, ranging through the ranks, the daojos
whipped at the rumps of zels and shouted for the men
to draw tighter in their formations, reminding them of
their orders and the basic preparations for the fight.

'I hear the overlords offered a casket of diamonds to
any general willing to turn tail.'

Ash flicked a grassfly from his cheek. '*Phh*. When
haven't they tried to buy us out? Today is hardly different.'

'Ah. But today is the day.'

They both chuckled, their throats hoarse from the
smoke of the pipes and the campfires of the night before.

It was true, what Ash had said. In the early days of
the revolution, when the People's Revolutionary Army
was little more than a rag-tag force lacking confidence,
cohesion or any notable victories to call its own, the
overlords had offered each fighter in the army a small

fortune in unchipped diamonds if they would desert to the other side.

Some had defected to the overlords' ranks – a great number in fact. But those who had refused the offer, who remained to fight on despite the sudden impossibility of their position, had found an unexpected strength in their collective refusal to sell out to those who would own and exploit it all. Amongst the ranks, where many had become demoralized by hunger, bitter losses, and the constant threats of capture or death, a renewal of spirit came upon them all, a sense of righteous brotherhood. It was the true beginning of the cause. From that time onwards, slowly but surely, they had begun to turn back the tide.

'It does feel like an end to things, don't you think?' Kosh asked.

'One way or the other,' Ash replied, glancing down at his son.

Lin was unaware of his scrutiny. The boy supported the upright bundle of spare lances in his hands, and the spare wicker shield upon his back. His eyes were wide with a fourteen-year-old's sense of wonder. Specks of reflected sunlight shone in his dark pupils, the whites bloodshot from the heavy drinking of the night before. The boy had sat up late around one of the campfires, joking and throat-singing with the older battlesquires of their Wing.

A different person, Ash now thought, to the half-starved urchin who had stumbled into their base-camp two years ago, having run away to join his father as his battlesquire. The boy's bare feet had been shredded from a trek that most grown men would have baulked at.

And for what? For the love and respect of a father who could no longer tolerate the sight of him.

Ash felt a sudden kindling of pain in his chest; a sense of overwhelming shame. In that moment he felt the need to touch his son, to reassure him with the press of a hand, as he had with the zel a few moments before.

He lifted his gloved hand from the pommel of the saddle and reached out with it.

Lin glanced up. Ash gazed down upon the heavy brows and the turned-up nose that reminded him so much of the boy's mother, and of her family, whom he'd grown so much to despise. Features that seemed not in any way to be his own.

His hand stopped halfway towards the boy, and for several heartbeats they both stared at it, hovering there, as though it represented everything that had ever stood between them.

'Water,' Ash muttered, though he wasn't thirsty. Without comment, the boy hefted up the bulging skin.

Ash took a sip of the tepid, stale water. He rolled it about in his mouth, swallowed a trickle, spat the rest out again. Where it fell the tindergrass hissed and crackled. He returned the skin to Lin and straightened in his saddle, angry at himself.

'They come,' announced Kosh.

'I see it.'

Across the entire enemy front, a roiling carpet of dust began to rise into the air. The Yashi trotted forwards in their formations, high banners bobbing from the backs of riders, flying the colours of Wings and their shifting locations of command. Horns sounded; windwhirls wailed like calls to the dead, the sounds washing slow and rhythmic over the ranks of the People's Revolutionary Army. Ash's zel snorted, becoming lively again.

On this flank alone, the overlords' forces numbered twenty thousand at least, a deep mass stretching to the right towards the haze of the battle line's distant centre. Their black armour soaked up the harsh daylight; helms bobbed with tall feathers. Sunlight sparkled from thousands of metal points, a bright dazzle amidst the dust raised by the advancing army, as the hooves of their zels crunched the tindergrass of the plain into pieces fine as powdered talc.

Before the advancing Yashi, clouds of moths and flies

rose up from the short grasses, and birds too in their thousands. They rushed over the heads of the People's Revolutionary Army in a great crying wave of flapping wings, so many in number that the air cooled for a moment in their shadow.

Below, the zels snuffled and rolled their eyes as a hail of loose feathers and guano droppings fell upon them. Lin hefted the wicker shield over his head to protect himself. Others along the line did so too, so that it appeared as though they were sheltering from sudden missile fire. Jokes sounded from the veterans, laughter even, the rarest of sounds this close to a fight.

Ash wiped his forehead clear and surveyed the hardened men of the Shining Way, this Wing of the army in which he had fought for over four years now; an old veteran himself now at the age of thirty-one. The Wing numbered six thousand in mounted infantry. They wore simple leather skullcaps tied down around their ears, white cavalry scarves knotted around black faces and wooden goggles to mask their eyes from the sunlight. Many of their armoured coats had long ago been painted with stripes of white like the zels the men lived and fought upon, and ornamented with the teeth of their enemy as lucky charms. Squinting, peering beyond these men, Ash could make out the great curve of the rest of the army, this great conglomeration of Wings.

He wondered how many would return to their families and their old lives if they won here today. The revolution had become a way of life to them over the years, bloody and cruel as it was. The People's Army was a home and family to them all. How would they cope with giving up the freedom of the saddle, the bonds they had formed with each other, the highs of action, when they returned to their farmsteads and their regular, mundane lives armed with nightmares and faraway stares?

He supposed he would find out himself. If they won here, and Ash and Lin survived, he would return with his son to the northern mountains and their lofty village of Asa, to their homestead and his wife whom he hadn't seen in years; try to forget the things they had seen and done in the name of the cause. Yet he would miss this life too. In so many ways, he knew he was better at this than he had ever been at supporting a family.

Ash could feel the prayer belt wrapped tight like a linen bandage around his abdomen, its ink-brushed words pressing against his sweating skin. Within its bounds he carried a letter from his wife delivered to him only a week before. Her words, carved into a thin sheet of leather, had pleaded once more for his forgiveness.

'Father,' said his son by his side as the enemy grew nearer. The boy was holding aloft one of the lances, his face slick with sweat. Ash took it, and the shield too. On his left, Kosh's son did the same.

'Are you ready?' Ash asked his son, not unkindly.

The boy frowned, though. He leaned and spat in the same way as his father sometimes did. 'I'll stand, if that's what you mean,' he declared maturely, but he said so in a voice still unbroken with age. There was anger in his tone, at the perceived insinuation that he might run on this day, like he had in his first real battle, overcome by it all.

'I know you will. I only ask if you are ready.'

The boy's jaw flexed. His stare softened before he looked away.

'Stay in the rear, close to Kosh's boy. Don't come to me unless I signal, do you hear?'

'Yes, father,' answered Lin, and then waited, blinking up at him, as though expecting something more.

The thin leather of his wife's letter felt cool against Ash's stomach.

'I'm glad you're here, son,' he heard himself say, and his throat clamped tight around each of the words. 'With me, I mean.'

Lin beamed up at him.

'Yes, father.'

He turned and sauntered away, and Ash watched

him leave as other battlesquires filtered back through the ranks. Kosh's son joined him, slapping the boy on the back; a joker like his father.

A soft thunder rumbled across the heat of the plain.

The Yashi were charging.

Ash pulled the goggles down over his eyes and the scarf across his face. Beneath him, he could feel the tremor of the ground transmitted through the bones and muscles of his zel. He glanced to General Oshō, as did every other man of the formation. Still the general refused to move.

'With heart,' he told Kosh.

Kosh pulled his own scarf up. Some kind of awkwardness kept his gaze clear of Ash. One way or the other, they would probably never fight side by side like this again; comrades, brothers, crazy fools of the revolution.

'And you, my friend,' came Kosh's muffled reply.

They gathered their zels' reins tighter in their fists as General Oshō levelled his warhead at the approaching enemy. Ash lowered his own lance.

Oshō's zel sprang forward.

As one, the men of the Shining Way followed him with a roar.

CHAPTER ONE

Beneath the Gaze of Ninshi

Ash awoke with a groan, and found that he was drenched in freezing sweat and shivering beneath a sky full of stars.

He blinked in the darkness, wondering where he was, who he was, experiencing a moment of delicate affinity with the All.

And then he saw a smear of light track high above him. A skyship, its tubes trailing blue fire across the face of Ninshi's Hood, her one eye glimmering red as she watched the ship and Ash and the rest of the world turning beneath her.

Q'os, Ash remembered with a sudden sensation of sickness in his stomach. *I'm in Q'os, on the other side of the ocean, at the spitting end of the Silk Winds, thirty years in exile.*

The remnants of his dreams vanished like so much wind-blown dust. He let them go, the fading tastes and echoes of Honshu. It was a loss of something irreplaceable, but it was better that way. Better not to dwell on these things while he was awake.

The light of the skyship faded slowly on its course towards the eastern horizon. It diminished in the hazy air above the city, occasionally blocked from sight by the dark, towering shape of a skysteeple. In the starlight, Ash saw his breath coil from his open mouth.

Damn it, he thought as he pulled his cloak tighter about his neck. *I need to piss again.*

Twice already he'd awoken in the night; once with a

straining bladder, the other time for no apparent reason at all. Perhaps there had been a distant shout in the streets below, or a spasm in his aching back, or a gust of cold wind, or he'd simply coughed. At his age, everything woke him if he wasn't thoroughly sodden with alcohol before he attempted to sleep.

Grumbling, the old Rōshun assassin cast the cloak aside and clambered to his bare feet, his joints popping loud enough to be heard in the still air of the rooftop.

The roof was a flat expanse of gritted pitch, and the grit felt sharp beneath the soles of his feet. It was little better to lie on, even with a spare cloak laid flat for bedding. He turned and looked at the tall prominence of concrete that rose at the centre of the grey, starlit space: a concrete cast of a great hand, its forefinger pointing skywards. Ash rubbed his face and stretched and groaned once more.

He didn't make use of the gutter that ran around the foot of the roof-edge parapet, or any of the small drainage holes in each corner of the roof, clogged green with algae. He didn't wish to betray his presence to someone in the streets far below.

Instead, he padded to the southern side of the roof as the city of Q'os lay silent all around him, the curfew still in place since the death of the Holy Matriarch's only son. He lowered himself onto the adjoining rooftop with a throb of complaint from his bladder. This roof was flat and tarred too, though it was interrupted by the raised triangular skylights that served the luxury apartments beneath them. Each was pitch dark, save for the nearest.

The widow, Ash thought. *Up again in the middle of the night.*

Ash stood relieving himself in his usual spot, while he peered into the candlelit warmth of the apartment below. Through the sooty glass he could see the lady sitting at the dining table in a cream woollen nightshift, her white hair tied back with a bow. Her delicate, wrinkled hands were poised with knife and fork over a small plate of food as she chewed with deliberate care.

Four days now Ash had been on his rooftop vigil, and each night he had observed this woman eating by herself without any servants in sight; sitting in the chill black hours next to the empty head of the table, staring off into the depths of the candle flame before her as she ate, her knife or fork occasionally striking the plate with a harsh ring that to Ash sounded, for some reason, of loneliness.

He'd created a story for this night owl in his curiosity. A young woman of privilege once, a great beauty, married off to a man of high status. No children, though – or if there were, then long flown from her life. And the husband, the master of the house, carried off by illness perhaps in his prime. Leaving her with only memories, and a bitter lack of appetite save for whenever dreams of the past awoke her.

Or perhaps she's also wakened easily by her bladder, Ash thought, and grunted, and considered himself an old fool.

A tinkle against the glass alerted him to the fact that he'd swung around too much in his curiosity, and was now splashing over a corner of the skylight. The flow ceased abruptly as the woman glanced up.

Ash held his breath, not moving. He was fairly certain she couldn't see him in this light; though for a curious instant he almost wished that she could.

She looked down at the table again, returned her attentions to her meagre meal. Ash shook himself dry, wiped his hands on his tunic. He nodded a silent goodnight to the woman and turned to make his way back.

Just then, a flicker of the candlelight caught his eye. A large fire-moth, alight with its own inner glow, bobbed around the candle flame as though in courtship. The flame fluttered against the briefest of touches. Ash and the widow both stared transfixed as the creature became ensnared in the flame. A wing stuck fast to the melting wax of the wick. The wing curled and crisped and ignited; the other beat a frantic rhythm as the moth's body caught fire, and the other wing too, until the creature was a struggling form burning alive in a miniature, crackling pyre.

Ash looked away, a bitter taste in his mouth now. He couldn't bring himself to look back a second time. Instead, he scrambled up the brickwork of the wall as fast as he could, as though to escape the sudden images flickering unwanted at the edges of his vision.

They came anyway. As he rolled over the parapet, for an instant he saw nothing but a young man struggling on a different pyre. His apprentice, young Nico.

Ash sucked in a breath of air as one might do from a sudden, sharp knock. His gaze rose to the Temple of Whispers, the towering shadow wrapped by ribbons of windows lit from within. She was in there somewhere, the Matriarch, mourning her own loss; most likely in the Storm Chamber at its very peak, itself brilliantly illuminated. It had been lit like that for the last four nights Ash had been watching.

He blew into his hands and rubbed them together for warmth. Always he felt the cold more these days. He noticed that his left hand was trembling, though not his right one. Ash clenched it into a fist as though to hide the shaking from himself.

After a moment he sat down on his bedding and made himself comfortable before the eyeglass perched there on its tripod, aimed resolutely at the Storm Chamber. He lifted the skin of Cheem Fire and pulled the cork and took a short pull from it. *For the cold*, he told himself. *To help me sleep.* He tossed the skin next to his sword, which rested upright against the concrete hand, and the small crossbow with its double strings removed to keep them safe from the weather. He squinted into the eyeglass. Caught a vague passing of a silhouette in the wide windows of the Storm Chamber.

Ash wondered how much longer he would have to

wait like this, perched above the city of two million strangers at the very heart of the Empire of Mann. He was anything but an impatient man; Ash had spent the greater portion of his life sitting and waiting for something to happen, for an opportunity to present itself. It was a Rōshun's main occupation when not risking his life in the final violent stages of vendetta.

Somehow, this waiting felt different to him. It was no Rōshun vendetta after all. He was isolated here, without support, without even a home to return to if he saw this personal act of revenge through to its end. And his condition was clearly deteriorating.

He had been surprised when the loneliness had first settled in amongst his grief, his guilt. It had come on that first evening he'd found himself alone in the city of Q'os, after Baracha and Aléas and Serèse had left to return to the Rōshun monastery in Cheem, the vendetta completed against the Matriarch's son, his own apprentice dead by her orders. It had been a long night that, huddled in his cloak upon the safest vantage he had been able to find of the Temple, this playhouse rooftop, with a bleak desolation falling upon him.

Ash lay back and pulled the cloak across his stiff body. He rested his head on a boot and locked his fingers across his stomach beneath the coarse cloth of the cloak. It was the first clear night so far in his vigil. Already the twin moons had set in the west, while overhead the Great Wheel turned as it always turned, as slow and fluid as a tide. To the right, low in the sky, hung the constellation of the Great Fool, with the sage's feet hovering close over the earth. Above and further to the right of it, Ninshi's Hood continued to watch over it all.

He found himself gazing at the stars that formed the face within the hood. Most of all he stared at the single eye shining hard with its ruby light, the Eye of Ninshi. It was like no other, that star. At times, it vanished entirely from sight while its companions continued to burn, only to return several hours later, slowly brightening as before.

To see the wink of Ninshi's gaze, the old Honshu seers maintained, was to be absolved of your very worst wrongdoings.

Ash gazed at the Eye unblinking. He stared long and hard enough for his own eyes to begin to sting and glimmer in their sockets, though still he stared, willing the star to disappear.

He failed to notice his hand reach up for the clay vial of ashes that hung about his neck, and grasp it tightly.

—CHAPTER TWO—

Ché

'The family hearth, friends, kinships . . . these are nothing more than the collective denials of the weak in response to the fundamental truth of our existence: that each us is driven by the impulses of self-interest, and nothing more.

'Hence why the weak abhor accusations of selfishness. Why always they will offer charity and goodwill when it suits them. Why with great conviction they will talk of the spirit of a just society.

'Yet take these people. Oppress them. Starve them. Strip them of their notions of solidarity until they are truly exposed to the real.

'Then choose one. Tell him he may save himself if he kills another. Offer him a blade.

'Watch as he takes the knife from your hand and performs the deed.'

*

The Diplomat Ché raised a hand to his mouth to stifle a bored yawn, and for a moment heard the words from the Book of Lies squashing down to nothing in his ears. Beside him, the nearest Acolyte regarded him through the holes in her mask. He stared back at the woman, coolly, without blinking, until she turned away.

Lazily, Ché looked around at the great windowless chamber filled with smoke and gaslight, and to the roof unseen in the vaulting space that rose hundreds of feet above them – so that here, within it, the mood was that of being at the bottom of a well. His attention settled on the sea of shaven heads gathered here on the eve of the Augere el Mann, the hundreds of priestly officiari of the Caucus, listening attentively to the holy words of Nihilis, the first Holy Patriarch of Mann.

Ché couldn't say if he believed in these teachings any longer, or if indeed he even respected the notion of *belief* itself – for what was it in the end, save for seeing the world how you really wished to see it, through personal experience and inclination and opinion? Rarely did it seem to bring you any closer to the truth, save by chance or by self-fulfilling prophecy; more likely it led into realms of delusion, of blinkered fanaticism.

Instead, Ché liked to remind himself of the opening line in Chunaski's forbidden satire, 'The Sea Gypsies': *Beliefs are like assholes, for everybody has one.*

He folded his arms and shifted the weight on his feet so that he leaned back against the cool mosaic of the wall. It had been a long day, and still there was no end in sight. All he wished for was to be done with it, so he could get home to his apartment and relax in the comfort of his own company.

Ché sought out the one face he was meant to be watching tonight. The assembly of priests filled the floor in seven thin wedges of seating: five for each of the cities of the Lanstrada, the Mannian heartland, with Q'os in the very middle, and another two for the regions of Markesh and Ghazni on the outer edges. The man he was looking for, Deajit, sat amongst the faction from the heartland city of Skul, several tiers behind the single chair that was positioned at their apex, where the High Priest of Skul, Du Chulane, was positioned in isolated silence facing the central podium to the fore. He couldn't see the man for a moment, but then a priest tilted his head to whisper into his neighbour's ear, and Ché caught a glimpse of him. The eyes of the young priest were downcast and hooded, as though he was half asleep or deep in contemplation.

Ché sighed, relaxing even further into his slouch. He was hardly out of place here, observing from the perimeter of the chamber, where lesser priests stood between the occasional Acolyte guard, and others came to and fro through the doorways at the back of the room. Each year the Caucus came together in this place during the week of the Augere. Always the assemblies were held at night, a nod to the old ways of Mann, when once it had been nothing more than a secret urban cult plotting to overthrow the Q'osian dynasty. Always they went on until just before dawn.

A rumble of rising thunder; hundreds of feet stamping as the sermon drew to a close. Officiari took the opportunity to leave their seats for refreshments. Others hurried to return. Deajit remained seated as a new speaker took to the podium, a man who announced himself as a tax officiari from Skansk. Deajit sat up in his chair as though suddenly interested.

The new speaker launched himself into a passionate discourse concerning the failing crops in Ghazni. The boom years of intensive farming and overly irrigated fields in the eastern region had finally resulted in a crash in productivity. To maintain revenues, insisted the speaker, they would need to raise taxes for the new year and cut what public expenditure they could. It was enough to rouse another chorus of stamping feet.

Ché found that he was absently scratching his neck again, just beneath the right ear, where it still throbbed with a fast pulse not his own. It was the pulsegland implanted under the skin, responding to the same gland of a fellow Diplomat elsewhere in the chamber. Already, several times, he had studied the faces of the various priests and wondered who it might be, or indeed if there was more than one of them. But there was no way to know, save for approaching each and every person in the room, and so he stopped his scratching, and tried to ignore it as best he could, though his stare continued to roam.

Ché turned inwards instead, letting his thoughts drift to pass the time.

He thought of his plush new apartment in the southern Temple district, recently handed to him upon his return from his mission in Cheem; a reward from the Section, it seemed, for his recent show of loyalty. He thought too of the two young women, Perl and Shale, whom he'd been courting these last few months for sex and the pleasure of their easy company. Like a cat toying with a piece of string, he considered which one he would call on next for an evening of entertainment.

Movement caught his eye. It was Deajit, rising from his chair at long last. Ché watched without turning his head as the young priest ambled to the doors at the rear of the chamber.

He pushed himself from the wall and strode after him.

*

In the bustle of the main corridor, the beat of Ché's pulsegland slowed almost imperceptibly. He spotted Deajit ahead, the priest helping himself to a glass of wine from one of the banqueting tables that lined both sides of the hall. Attendants stood along the tables, explaining the more exotic items displayed there. Deajit sampled a small spoonful of lobster meat, then tried a mouthful of jellied marrow from a snow mammoth. He nodded his head in appreciation.

Ché paused, and sought the cover of an alcove containing a bronze life-sized statue of Nihilis. With the First Patriarch's strikingly dour features looming over him, features more famous now than when he had been alive, Ché removed a small vial from a pocket in his robe. He unscrewed the lid and tilted it upside down with his forefinger upon the opening. Carefully he closed it again, then dabbed the wet finger across his lips. For a second, the scent of something faintly noxious came to his nostrils, and then it was gone.

Deajit was wandering into one of the side rooms along the main hallway, glass still in his hand. Passing a table, Ché snatched up a glass of wine too, and followed him inside.

A viewing gallery ran around the upper half of the room. Ché stopped at the rail where he could see Deajit in the corner of his eye, then looked down on a smaller conference taking place below. A few dozen priests were in attendance, most of them strikingly young. Their faces were keen as they listened to a man speaking before a tall mosaic map of the Empire. The priest appeared to be discussing the two-handed approach to governance.

Deajit sipped his wine and listened to the talk below. A few other priests lingered in the gallery, watching or muttering quietly amongst themselves. Ché remained where he was. He was careful not to touch his own wine, or indeed to lick his own lips.

Of their own volition his eyes flickered over the details of the map, for he was a lover of such works.

He observed the preponderance of white that represented the nations under Mann dominion, a whiteness that had spread across most of the known world like an encroachment of glacial ice. Then he studied the warmer pinks of those who still stood against it: the League of Free Ports in the southern Midèrēs, isolated and alone; Zanzahar and the Alhazii Caliphate to the east, sole suppliers of blackpowder from the mysterious, secret lands of the Isles of Sky; the smatterings of small mountain kingdoms in the Aradères Mountains and High Pash.

He knew he would soon be venturing to one of those

nations shaded in human pink, where he would be accompanying an invasion, of all things, to aid in the defeat of a people whom the Empire had branded their most dangerous of enemies; though Ché suspected it was more to do with their grain and mineral wealth than any real threat they might pose, not to mention their arrogant defiance against the ideology of Mann. Still, it would be a chance to escape the confines of Q'os, all its fanaticism and paranoia and games of power that were the life blood of the imperial capital, and all the petty little tasks of murder that had remarkably become his life.

Ché looked to the window that ran along the far wall at the level of the viewing gallery, gazing out north over the slumbering metropolis of Q'os. A few skyships ranged over the scene, their propulsion tubes leaving trails of fire and smoke across the starry skies. Below them lay the island city, a great handprint of glittering lights and manmade coastline pressed upon the black quilt of the sea.

Ché traced the outline of the island-sized hand, until his attention came to rest on the First Harbour – that stretch of water between the thumb of the island and its forefinger, where pinpricks of night-lamps glimmered in the darkness; the fleet that would carry him off to war as soon as the command was given.

'As Nihilis taught us,' the speaker below him was saying, 'and as we have practised and refined over the years of our expansion, to rule absolutely is to rule on the one hand with force, and on the other hand with consent. People must become complicit in their own submission to Mann. They must come to understand that this is the best and truest way in which to live.

'This is why, when the order first seized Q'os in the Longest Night, it disposed of the girl-queen and the old political parties of nobles, yet still maintained its democratic assembly. And this is why the citizens of the heartland and the Middle Empire vote for the High Priest of their city, and those lesser administrators of their districts, in an act which we call the hand of complicity, the hand that allows the people a small say in the governing of their own lives, or at least the appearance of it. This is the secret of our success, though it is hardly a secret. This is what allows us to rule so efficiently.'

Ché's lips twisted at that. He knew it took more than the two-handed way for Mann to maintain its grip on the known world. He was a Diplomat after all, part of the third hand, the hidden way. As were the Élash, those spies and blackmailers and plotters of coups and counter-coups. As were the Regulators, the secret police; those who watched the masses for signs of dissent or organization, and who claimed everything a crime that ran contrary to the ways of Mann.

He noticed that Deajit too was smiling as he listened. For an instant Ché felt the vaguest of connections with the man. Perhaps he was also involved in the third hand. For the first time he wondered what he had done to deserve such a fate as this, for his handler had said nothing save what needed to be done.

But then Deajit turned and stepped towards the doorway, and it was time.

Ché took a step forwards so that the priest brushed past his arm. In a flash, Ché grabbed the man's wrist and spun him around so that they faced each other. A look of shock crossed the priest's blunt features.

Without warning, Ché planted his lips against those of Deajit, smearing them together in a harsh kiss.

The priest shoved himself backwards with an angry gasp. He glared at Ché, and from the wrist he was still gripping Ché felt a shudder run through his body. 'You should not betray the trust of your friends so freely,' Ché told him quietly, as instructed, and released his grip. His own heart was beating fast.

Deajit wiped his lips with the back of a hand and retreated from the room with a single glance cast back at Ché.

For several moments he waited as those around him nervously avoided his eye. He turned his back on them, and took another vial from his pocket, and emptied some of the black liquid into a cupped palm. He washed his lips clean then rubbed his hands too. With the last of it he rinsed his mouth then spat it onto the floor.

In the corridor outside, Deajit was nowhere to be seen.

Like that, he cast the priest from his mind entirely, as though the young man was already dead.

*

Boom, boom, boom.

The Acolyte lowered her gloved fist from the massive iron door of the Storm Chamber, and stepped back to leave Ché standing alone as it swung open.

Confronting Ché stood an old priest that he did not recognize. He'd heard that the previous portal attendant had been executed for mistakenly allowing the Rōshun into the Storm Chamber during their recent breach of the tower. It was said that the long crawl over the Crocodile had been his fate, and then the slow press of the Iron Mountain.

With a moment's hesitation, Ché stepped through the threshold into the chamber within.

The Storm Chamber was much the same as the last time he had been summoned here, all of – what – one month, two months ago? He couldn't recall. He'd found that his linear memory of time had become oddly scattered since his return from his diplomatic mission against the Rōshun, as though he no longer wished to remember the order of his everyday life. The chamber was empty tonight, though every lamp glowed with a bright, sputtering flame within a shade of green glass.

'The Holy Matriarch will be with you shortly,' declared the old priest, and then he bowed and retreated into a room next to the entranceway. Ché folded his hands within the sleeves of his robe, and there he waited.

The pulsegland had slowed to the pace of his own heart now.

Through the windows that wrapped the circular space, he could see Holy Matriarch Sasheen standing outside on the balcony amongst a small gathering of priests; a tall woman, wearing an uncharacteristic plain white robe, staring out over the rail at the black skies of Q'os as they conversed, their voices muted to murmurs by the thickness of the glass.

Coals crackled in the stone fireplace in the middle of the room, the smoke drawn up through an iron chimney that disappeared through the floor of the bedrooms above it. Next to the fireplace stood another map of the Empire, the same in fact that had stood there during his previous visit: a sheet of paper pinned to a wooden easel, printed with black ink, still marked with the rough pencil strokes denoting proposed movements of fleets for the forthcoming invasion of the Mercian Free Ports. A semicircle of leather armchairs faced this cosy space; elsewhere in the room were other chairs, and long settles covered in throws of fur, and low tables with bowls containing fruits, burning incense, pools of liquid narcotics.

This is where they made it to, Ché suddenly thought. *This is how far the Rōshun made it when they tried again. Right here to Kirkus, her son.*

He could hardly picture it. The Rōshun, one of them a farlander by all accounts, striding through this very room in search of their victim, their route marked by a trail of dead and wounded leading all the way down to the lowest floor of the Temple of Whispers. He doubted if even Shebec would never have made it this far – Shebec, his old Rōshun master, more skilled than any other save for one.

Ash, he thought with an intuitive certainty. *It had to be Ash.*

But then Ché considered it. Was it even possible? Ash would be in his sixties by now if he still lived at all. Could he have managed something like this at such an age?

Whoever it had been, Ché could not help but admire them. He had always been drawn to ventures of risk and audacity, and he found a sly smile creeping onto his face. The Temple of Whispers breached by an army of rats, of all things, and three Rōshun intent on vendetta.

Without warning, deep laughter bubbled in his chest, and he stopped it only by biting his inner cheek until the sensation passed. Ché cleared his throat and composed himself.

The map on the easel drew his eye towards it.

Another venture of audacity that – a sea invasion of Khos no less. Ché glanced through the windows once more at the gathered priests, then found himself stepping up to the map for a closer inspection.

It had been modified with various additions since last he had seen it, though the main details remained the same. Two arrows swept south-east across the sea of the Midèrēs to range along the islands of the Free Ports; two diversionary fleets, both of which had departed the week before to engage the fleets of the Free Ports, hoping to lure any defending squadrons away from Khos. Next to these, in fine pencil marks, were scratched fleet sizes, travel times, other notations. Question marks abounded.

A third arrow ran from the capital of Q'os to trace a sea-course to the far eastern island of Lagos, with more numbers and queries scrawled alongside it. Then, from Lagos, a fourth arrow swept down to Khos – the First Expeditionary Force, the invasion of Khos itself.

He was near-lost in studying the details when Ché realized – with a sudden start – that he wasn't alone in the room.

He glanced across to an armchair so hooded and deep that he'd failed to notice the creature that sat within it: Kira, mother to the Holy Matriarch of Mann.

The ancient crone was asleep, it seemed, her ancient hands folded across the white cloth of her robe. Ché released his breath and peered closer. Glimmers could be seen from beneath her eyelids, two slivers of eyes.

Was she watching him? Had she seen his stifled laughter?

Ché felt the hairs rise on his arms. He was as shocked by his lack of perception as he was by her sly observation of him.

Kira dul Dubois: one of the participants in the Longest Night fifty years before. Rumoured to have been a lover of Nihilis himself; rumoured even to have been involved in his death six years into his reign as the first Holy Patriarch. It was like being in the sights of a silver-snake.

Slowly, he stepped back from the map, hoping as well to move beyond her line of vision. He cleared his throat as he resumed his position in the centre of the floor, and refused to look at the old woman again.

At last the glass doors to the balcony slid open and the priests began to file through the room. A few cast furtive glances in his direction as they left; he recognized one of them as a priest from the sect of commerce, the Frelasé. Behind them came Bushrali himself. Ché had expected the man to be dead by now after failing to uncover the Rōshun hiding in the city. But no, after much political manoeuvring to save his skin, here he was, still alive, still even the head of the Regulators. Perhaps the rumours were true, then; that he held a blackmail dossier on every High Priest of Q'os.

Still, the man had not entirely escaped punishment, Ché saw. He'd been fitted with a Q'os Necklace, an iron collar sealed around his neck, fixed to a length of chain that ended with a small cannonball, which he cradled in his arm as he stepped past. He would be expected to wear the necklace for the rest of his life.

Only Sasheen and a single bodyguard remained outside, the woman lost, it seemed, in her thoughts. Ché felt a draught pressing against his cheek through the open doorway, though he could only faintly hear the city beyond, unusually silent in these recent weeks of enforced mourning. When Sasheen turned and stepped inside the Storm Chamber, she was holding the bridge of her nose between thumb and forefinger as though burdened with a headache. Her bodyguard remained outside, slowly patrolling around the balcony. She approached a stand of steaming bowls and bent to inhale from one. With a gasp she straightened, her face flushing.

Sasheen's eyes flared for a moment when she saw her Diplomat waiting there for her. She moved past to the fire with her hands held out for warmth.

'Is it done?' she asked with her back to him.

'Yes, Matriarch.'

'Then sit. Warm yourself.'

He wasn't cold but he did as instructed anyway, choosing a leather settle before the fire. He maintained an upright pose, his hands folded, breathing deeply, resisting the urge to scratch at his neck. After a moment, the Holy Matriarch left the burning coals and sat down beside him, close enough for their knees to touch.

He could smell the scent of mulled wine on her breath, and realized she was drunk.

The leather of the settle creaked as she folded one long leg across the other, her robe parting along a slit to show the soft cream of her thigh. Compared to her usual attire, the robe was a plain affair, but still it was smaller than it needed to be, so that the cotton stretched tightly over her curves. Below its hem, the nails of her bare feet were painted a vivid red.

'Bushrali tells me they will not come for me, for killing their apprentice.'

'The Rōshun?' ventured Ché.

Her eyes narrowed in annoyance. *Do not play coy with me.*

Ché shook his head. 'It's unlikely. The apprentice

wasn't wearing a seal. It's only on behalf of seal-bearers that they seek vendetta.'

She considered his words; glanced across to the sleeping form of her mother before she next spoke. He noticed then the red welts on the side of her neck, running down beneath the collar of her robe. They looked like the heat tracks left behind after a Purging.

'But this will be personal to them,' she ventured. 'A public humiliation. A murder of one of their young.'

She considers this now, Ché reflected. *Long after the act is done.*

'No, they don't think in such terms. They have a code of sorts. Vendetta is a matter of natural justice for them, or at least a simple matter of cause and effect. They abhor revenge, though. To seek vendetta for their own personal reasons would go against their own creed in every way I can think of.'

'I see,' she said, and her tone was one of lightness, perhaps amused by the idea of such a principle. 'Bushrali said much the same himself. I wanted to hear it from you too: someone who has lived with them, and been one of them.'

Ché could not help but look away at that moment, even though he knew it would betray his sudden discomfort. He almost jumped as he felt her hand pat his leg. Ché met the Matriarch's chocolate-dark eyes, and saw something different in them this time, a softness.

Sasheen smiled.

'Guanaro!' she called out to the room. 'Is it time for breakfast yet?'

The old priest in attendance emerged from the side chamber next to the door. He nodded and went back inside, where Ché could hear gruff orders being given, and the clatter of chopping boards and cupboard doors being opened and shut.

'Some buttered sandshrimps, perhaps!' she hollered after him.

Sasheen settled back, watching the fire in the hearth

before them. Her hand restlessly stroked the leather arm of the settle. 'I have not given you my thanks yet,' came her quiet voice.

'Matriarch?'

'You performed a great service in leading us to the home of the Rōshun. You proved your loyalty to me, and to the order. That's why I requested you as my personal Diplomat in this,' she waved her hand towards the map, 'scheme of ours. You understand?'

Ché offered a shake of his head, and watched her turn to regard him.

'I go forth to war on one of the riskiest ventures we have ever attempted. Once I leave this sanctum I will be as vulnerable as any other. Not only from the enemy, but from our own people. General Romano for instance. He would pluck out my eyes given half the chance. So,' and she smiled once more, a tight fleeting thing, like a confession, 'I will need those around me who I can trust with my life, who I can be certain will follow my commands. Who can get a job done without qualms.'

'I see,' replied Ché.

She did not seem entirely satisfied by his response. Sasheen turned to fix herself a hazii stick from a table next to the settle. 'I've given the general order. We leave with the fleet for Lagos on the morning after next, to join with the Sixth Army in Lagos.'

Ché felt a little flutter of anticipation in his chest. For an instant, he looked at her with the cold eyes of a murderer, hearing the rasping voice of one of his handlers in his mind, telling him what he must do should the Matriarch show weakness or be exposed to the possibility of capture during the campaign.

'You will miss the Augere then,' he said.

'Yes,' Sasheen acknowledged, searching for a match as she spoke. 'All those hours of tedium parading myself to the chattel.'

Smoothly, Ché rose and crossed to the fire, feeling her eyes tracking him. He lit one of the rushes standing in a clay pot on the hearth, brought the burning end of it back to Sasheen, who was indeed watching him with amused interest.

She placed her fingers against his hand to steady the tip of the rush. Her kohl-rimmed eyes flickered up to meet his own, her lips pursed softly around the end of the hazii stick. He felt a pulse in his thighs, his groin.

Stop it, you fool. You know she is this way. Using her charms with those she must rely upon.

He settled himself amongst a cloud of hazii smoke, whilst Sasheen turned back to the door of the side chamber, perhaps drawn by the smell of frying butter. 'Are you hungry?' she asked him. 'I did not bother to ask you.'

The thought of sharing a meal with her, here in this chamber at the top of the world, filled him with a sudden discomfort. 'No, thank you. I've eaten already.'

Sasheen studied him for a lingering moment. She looked at her bare leg and then back to his face. Her hand on the arm of the settle stopped moving; it slapped once, lightly, against the leather. 'You heard, I'm sure, that we caught up with Lucian at last. The Élash snatched him from Prince Suneed's court in Ta'if.'

'Yes. I heard.'

She rose with a soft rustle of her robe and padded across the rug to another table next to the fire. A large, round glass jar sat alone on the tabletop, filled nearly to the brim with a white liquid. There came a sound of glass scraping against glass as she unscrewed the lid with care. Sasheen rolled her right sleeve up to her elbow; leaned forward and took a sniff of the substance within.

'Royal Milk,' she said, without taking her eyes from it. Ché blinked. He'd never seen the Milk before, only knew of its existence, the excretions of a queen Cree from the land of the Great Hush, renowned for its powers of vitality.

The wealth of a small kingdom lay inside that single jar alone.

Even from here, he could smell the liquid over the sweetness of the frying butter and sandshrimps. It was an unpleasant scent, like bile. With care, Sasheen dipped her hand into the white liquid within. She grasped something and began to pull it out; a handful of matted hair.

A *scalp*, Ché thought . . . but then the rest of it followed: a forehead, a pair of closed eyes, a nose, a mouth fixed in a grimace, a dripping chin, a roughly hewn neck. She held this apparition over the jar as the white liquid ran from the severed head and her own hand like quicksilver.

It was the severed head of a middle-aged man, Ché could see as the Milk flowed clear from it. Dark hair turned grey at the temples. A wide full mouth, a long nose, sharp cheekbones and brows.

As the last drop dripped clear of it, Sasheen swung the head over the table and settled it by its ragged neck on the dark surface of tiq.

The face flinched in pain or surprise. Ché stiffened where he sat, his wide-eyed stare fixed on the thing before him. The Matriarch backed away from the head as its eyes flickered open, blinking to clear them, bloodshot and tormented. White Milk spilled from the corners of its lips as it saw Sasheen and glared.

'Hello, Lucian,' she said to the thing.

The head closed its lips, seemed to swallow a mouthful of air.

'*Sasheen*,' the man croaked in a strange, wet voice, almost belching the word.

Ché's eyes darted to the Matriarch then back to the head. It was Lucian all right. Sasheen's one-time famous lover and general, one of the first of the Lagosian nobility to join the ranks of Mann when the island had first fallen to the Empire – before he had betrayed her, by leading the Lagos rebellion in fighting once more for independence.

Ché had witnessed the pieces of his hung-and-quartered corpse hanging in Freedom Square, with the soldiers stationed below them chasing away the hungry crows. He'd thought that had been the end of the man. It seemed though that Sasheen had other ideas for her ex-lover.

The Holy Matriarch turned her back to the head. She smiled at Ché, sudden mischief in her eyes.

Sasheen raised her right hand to her mouth, licked her fingers one by one. Even as Ché watched her do this, he could see the blood rush to her skin, her eyes begin to dilate even further. She finished with a greedy smack of her lips.

'Nothing like it in this whole wide world,' she said breathlessly, and took a step towards Ché, hungry for something.

Once more Ché fought an absurd impulse to laugh. It only worsened as she leaned down towards him, becoming a jostling pain in his chest as she placed her hand against his cheek, pressed her mouth hard against his own. Her tongue darted, parting his lips.

So easy to kill her, he thought, right here and now, if his lips had still been smeared with venom.

The taste of the Royal Milk was like nothing he had ever tasted before. It was neither sweet nor sour, bitter nor salty. His tongue began to sting, and then to go numb, as Sasheen continued to kiss him.

'*Whore*,' came the strange belching voice of Lucian from behind her.

And then the rush of it hit Ché, like a breath of fire blossoming through the blood-ways of his body. It jolted him out of his tiredness in a snap so that his blood surged, pounding, and a sense of weightlessness overcame him, filling him with light instead, and air, and the first real glimmers of lust.

Sasheen pulled clear with a moan, and glanced quite obviously down at his crotch. She whirled away with a satisfied smile.

He gasped, close to losing himself entirely, and sprawled back against the settle as though falling.

Two pulses, he thought distractedly. *I have two pulses in my neck.*

'Ah, breakfast,' she declared, as the old priest entered with a tray of food.

Ché tried to move and then thought better of it. He clung to the settle as though he would fly from it at any instant, while the sounds of Sasheen preparing to eat filtered towards him from far behind.

'What is this?' snapped her voice. 'I can hardly see them, they're so small.'

'Sandshrimps are always small this time of the year, Matriarch. They are still young.'

'What? And they can't be fed up a little? And what's this? Grubby marks everywhere. I suppose the kitchen staff are also too young this time of year to keep the silver clean?'

'My apologies, Matriarch. I'm still training the new replacements in the proper ways. It will not happen again, I assure you. I can have something else prepared, if you wish?'

'And wait even longer? No. You may go.'

Ché looked at the grim face of Lucian glowering at him with his maddened eyes. With a loll of his head Ché looked to his right, where the old woman Kira still sat unmoving.

There was a definite glimmer beneath her eyelids now – those bird eyes of hers staring across the space at Ché as though they could see right through him.

Ché closed his own eyes and soared.

—CHAPTER THREE—

Without Wings

W*hoah*, thought Coya, as a gust of wind buffeted the figure that dangled between the two skyships, and set the man swinging like the pendulum of a clock.

'Hold there!' shouted the startled deck charge, raising a palm to the crewmen heaving away on the secondary line. At once they stopped hauling, and stood there frozen in their positions, watching the swaying figure with the uncertainty of men who'd never attempted this feat before, and were aware of its possibility only because others were telling them of it.

Out there in the gulf of air between the two vessels, bobbing from the line strung between them both, the figure on the wooden chair opened his mouth to shout: '*In your own time, gentlemen!*'

Coya smiled despite his concerns for the man.

'Bring him in, Seday, quickly now,' he told the deck charge smartly, and although Coya appeared young for his twenty-seven years – young even with his body stooped over a walking cane – the men snapped to with the respect of earnest sons for a father, and started to haul on the rope once more.

Just then another gust hit, stronger than the previous one, setting the distant figure pirouetting again on his seat. Coya heard the wind pressing against the silken envelope overhead, saw how the two skyships were drifting from their relative positions. Manoeuvring tubes fired along their sides, at the hurried commands of their captains. Still, the skyships drifted slightly apart, the line playing out on the far Khosian deck. The slack was lost, causing the man to bob even more dangerously beneath its tightening length. With an inrush of breath, Coya leaned forward with his weight on his walking cane and his hand clutching the ebony grip tightly.

To lose this man now could very well equate to losing the entire war.

'Quickly now!' he urged, without taking his gaze from their charge.

The figure was well past the halfway mark and nearing the ship at last. He looked calmer out there than Coya did merely watching from the deck. With his feet dangling over an abyss of several thousand feet all the way to the choppy sea below, he was turning his head to take in the rugged coastline of Minos, and the bay in which the city of Al-Minos lay like a gleaming pearl. Drawing closer, Coya saw his long black hair whip around his wind-reddened face; his hands with their many plain rings; his heavy bear-skin coat covering his great bulk.

Suddenly, Coya felt his pulse grow faster from the sheer anticipation of the Lord Protector's presence.

'Easy, lads,' General Creed boomed as they pulled him roughly onto the decking; and suddenly there he was, towering over them all, feigning an easy nonchalance when in truth Coya saw only exhilaration in his eyes.

The crewmen released the general from his safety harness while Creed clapped a few shoulders for good show. He stepped forward to shake Coya's offered hand.

Coya scented hair oil, and that awful spiced goat's cheese so beloved of these Khosians.

'I'd hoped you were joking when you suggested an underway transfer,' remarked the old general. 'We couldn't have met on the ground, eh?'

Before responding, Coya caught the eye of Marsh, his own bodyguard. Marsh scowled at the gang of crewmen still pressing for a better look at this living legend from Bar-Khos, and shoved them without ceremony towards the rest of the crew gathered on the opposite side of the deck.

'Too dangerous,' Coya admitted when they were at last beyond earshot, while Marsh stationed himself close by, watching everyone on deck through his dark-tinted refractors. His eyes could be seen blinking through the lenses on the back of his head.

'Someone else was hit?'

'Last night in Al-Minos. The visiting League delegate from Salina had the misfortune of being strangled in her sleep. That's eight assassinations in the last two weeks. Which would suggest a coterie of Diplomats is now at large within the city.'

The Lord Protector nodded without expression, keeping his thoughts to himself.

Together they watched as the transfer line was reeled back aboard the Khosian skyship that had borne him all this way from Bar-Khos. The vessel fired its tubes to assume a patrol around the Minosian vessel they now stood upon. In the silence, Coya studied the man's profile in an attempt to judge his present condition. Creed had visibly aged since they'd last met over a year and half before. The greying at his temples had spread into streaks of silver; the lines deeper now around his eyes. All of it from grief, Coya knew from the reports he'd been hearing.

'How are you, anyway?' he asked the Lord Protector. 'I hope your journey was a smooth one?'

'Smooth enough. I only regret that our meeting must be so brief.'

'Yes,' said Coya. 'The Khosian council must fret whenever you are gone from the Shield for so long.' At that they both smiled, knowing it to be true. As their eyes met, unspoken between them lay the question of why Creed was here at all. 'Still, it's good that we can meet for this little while at least. A meal is being prepared for us in the captain's cabin. If you wish, we can retire to some comfort and be out of this wind for a while.'

Creed responded with a look that said he was seldom accustomed to thinking of his personal comforts. He glanced towards Marsh and the many crewmen still watching them, the captain of the ship included. 'I'm too old to be skulking around in fear of a few assassins, if that's your concern,' he said. 'Let's enjoy the fresh air while we talk, and then we can eat.' He paused as he looked at Coya, who was stooped and wrapped heavily against the cold. 'Unless of course it would be better for you . . . to be inside.'

'I'm fine here, if you are, thank you,' Coya replied crisply, and bowed his head politely. The motion caused him pain, as all movements did. Even at his relatively young age, Coya had the arthritic bones of an ancient man. 'Please, at least allow me to indulge you in some chee while we talk.'

Creed welcomed the offer. Within moments the ship's galley boy was standing before Marsh with two steaming leather cups of chee in his hands, the lad's mouth hanging open in wonder, looking between the impressive figure of the Lord Protector and the curious display of Marsh dipping a goyum to sample the chee. With a single tendril dangling in the hot liquid, the fist-sized bag remained the same neutral colour of greyish brown. Satisfied, Marsh allowed the cups to be passed into their welcoming hands.

'How's that pretty wife of yours?' Creed enquired through a waft of rising steam.

'She's well. She sends you her blessings.'

How generous, Coya thought, *to ask after my wife while still grieving for his own.*

'You never did tell me how you hooked her. Blackmail, I'm supposing?'

'No need. She's crazy about me. And I about her.'

'Love then. Mercy help you both.'

Creed's dry wit caused Coya to blink in amusement.

'You must come and stay with us when circumstances allow it. You would like it there. Rechelle ensures the house is filled always with life and other people's children.'

For a moment Coya thought he had said too much. But then Creed replied, with warmth, 'Yes. I would like that.'

They sipped their chee as they stood by the railing gazing down at the vista of land and sea below, the coastline of Minos slowly sliding by as the ship drifted around in the wind.

The city of Al-Minos shone in the afternoon sunlight, the greatest Free Port in all the Mercian islands. Around it swept the arms of the bay, the white beaches darkened by crowds of people and clouds of red kites flying. The cityport was enjoying a festa this week, and even the presence of the First Fleet in its harbour, outfitting for battle, had done little to dampen the holiday spirits of the populace. Coya's wife was down there somewhere in the heaving streets of the city, with his parents and his sisters' many lively children – or perhaps by now they were watching the horse flapping on Uttico beach, and placing bets with their spare chits while wolfing down fresh quaff-eggs from the communal feasting pits.

He felt a pang of regret that he wasn't with them today. Coya had been dearly looking forward to spending the day with his family, of forgetting it all for a short spell at least.

'Zeziké Day,' Creed announced suddenly, as though noticing the kites and the thronged beaches for the first time. 'You know, I'd all but forgotten.'

Coya shrugged. 'You're a Khosian. It's to be expected.'

'We do celebrate the man, you know. Just not quite so fervently as you fanatics here in the west.' He spoke lightly, but as he did so he observed the distant celebrations with something unspoken in his expression, a kind of longing, perhaps. Coya could only imagine what it was like for the man and the rest of the people of Bar-Khos, huddled as they were behind walls unceasingly subjected to bombardment and assault, living day and night on the edge of extinction.

'I'm only chiding, Marsalas. It's hardly as though you haven't enough on your plate already.'

The general straightened and cleared his throat. When he met Coya's gaze, it was from one lonely height to another. 'It must be hard on you also. They must expect a great deal from you, your people. The living descendant of the great philosopher himself.'

'Hardly a burden compared to some.'

Coya desired to change the subject, for he was not comfortable discussing his famous ancestry going back to the spiritual father of the democras. He observed the many warships in the harbour, and was reminded, though he hardly needed a reminder, of the Mannian fleets now heading their way.

'The revolution is one hundred and ten years old this year,' Coya stated. 'One hundred and ten years since we toppled the High King and the nobles who thought they would take his place. Yet I wonder, sometimes, when I'm alone and feeling not quite as hopeful as I should, whether our waking dream of the democras will survive for very much longer.'

'The Free Ports are hardly beaten yet.'

'Come, now. We're not far from it, Marsalas. We hold on by the skin of our teeth. The Mannians strangle our trade routes to the outside world so we are forever close to starving. Zanzahar remains our only life thread, and subsequently exploits us for all the resources that it can. Bar-Khos barely holds the line in the east. League fleets barely hold the line at sea. And in our collective resistance, we become each day a greater threat to the Empire's dominion. Because of us, every morning the world wakes to the knowledge that there are other ways to live than Mann. It is why the Empire loathes us so fiercely. It is why it will not cease until it has defeated us, or is finished itself – and Mann hardly looks as though it's about to fall.'

'It has happened before. Great empires have been

resisted and cast back upon themselves. It can happen again.'

'Yes, of course. And even then, if that were to happen ... would the ideals of the democras still survive, I wonder? Or would we have paid too much for our victory? Would we have too much a taste for war by then, and a need to exact our revenge?'

'After the Years of the Sword, we settled again in peace. We can do so again.'

'We settled because our victory was itself our revenge. We were sated because the nobles had been overthrown. And even then the creation of the democras was a close-run thing. Such times of transition are always chancy, Marsalas.'

Creed listened without expression. 'I've missed our talks,' he declared suddenly, and Coya could only agree with him. He took a sip of chee, feeling himself relaxing into the gentle motions of the ship.

'What news have you heard?' Creed asked him. 'Any movement in Q'os?'

Coya released a hot breath of air. 'Our agents are no further in discovering the timing and destination of the invasion. It would seem to be the best-kept secret in the Empire just now. All we do know is what they can see with their own eyes. The invasion fleet of transports remains anchored in the Q'osian harbour. The men-of-war which left port already have been spotted again by our aerial longscouts. There's no doubt any longer. They are on a course for the western Free Ports. Another sighting arrived this morning of a second possible fleet approaching from the north-east.'

'*Hmmf.*'

'Yes. That was my reaction.'

The general set his cup down on the rail, his hand still clasped around it.

'We need League reinforcements now, Coya. I know a feint when I see one. If the invasion fleet lands in

Khos, we will need our coastal forts fully manned. At present, they can resist little more than a strong wind.'

'Your League delegate still maintains otherwise – you know that, don't you? You have enough men at present, that is what he assures us.'

'*Ach*. What do you expect from Chaskari? He's Michinè. You know how much they fear changing the status quo. Look at how they bind my hands and make us cower behind the Shield, hoping that the Imperial Fourth Army will simply vanish. It's no different with all the Volunteers the League has sent to aid us over the years. The soldiers live amongst our people. The people see how they are, without superiors, without doffing their heads to authority. They remind everyone in Khos that they are members of the League and equal to all as a democras. They remind them how the Michinè are only there at their bidding, that they are leaders given the responsibility of leadership, not of rule. You should hardly be surprised that the Khosian council resists my requests for more Volunteers. That is why I'm asking you personally, as a favour: send them anyway.'

'But, Marsalas, what more can I do? I'm bound hand and foot by the constitution, you know that.'

'Send them anyway. Let us worry about the consequences after the storm has arrived.'

'General. Believe me, I'd dearly love to dispatch every Volunteer that we could, and to do so now. We all would. Khos is our shield and every citizen of the League knows it. But the League cannot meddle in the affairs of a fellow democras, especially not at the request of one man – even if that one man happens to be the Lord Protector of Khos himself. We may only send reinforcements if they are requested of us by your delegate. It's up to you to change your own council's minds on this.'

'I've tried, damn it.'

'Then you must try harder.'

Creed glowered at the cup in his hand. 'What of your

people? They've interfered before in Khosian affairs. They can do so again.'

Coya frowned. 'That was before my time, Marsalas. And we should not talk of these things here. I'm sorry. There's nothing more the League or anyone else could do for you right now. We must wait and see.'

It was an end to the discussion, and Creed breathed loudly through his nostrils and stared at Coya with all the force of his will. Coya held his gaze, not flinching; inside, his body was tense and pulsing. General Creed was like an arrow in flight. When you blocked him, you felt the physical shock of it.

The Lord Protector muttered something, squeezed his fist upon the rail. Coya could only sympathize with the man, though he sensed that they were still skirting the heart of their meeting, the full reason why Creed was here.

'We could have corresponded on this,' he ventured. 'You hardly needed to come all this way in person.'

'No.'

They fell to silence, each buffeted by the wind. *Let him settle his temper first*, Coya decided.

The skyship was turning to windward, bringing the world around with it, so that Minos drifted away to the left and the striking cobalt of the sea filled their eyes. Coya could see a hint of an island chain to the far east, little more than hummocks of rock extending south-east in the direction of Salina. He imagined the loose collection of islands beyond Salina, stretching all the way to distant Khos at its easternmost point over six hundred laqs from where they were now; the archipel-ago of the Free Ports and of the democras, *people without rulers*.

Along with the egalitarian participos of Minos and Coros and Salina, if you took the time to travel the Mercian Isles, you could come across islands that elected councils by lottery and believed in no personal possessions at all, or were based on administrative matriarchies of the old tradition, with simple cottage industries and tightly controlled tariffs on trade, or were free-for-all enclaves like those of Coraxa, fierce individualists living in loose tribes and scattered communities. Even distant mighty Khos was represented in the League, where the last vestige of Mercian nobility, the Michinè, had somehow held on to power following the sweeping years of revolution over a century before – albeit aided by many concessions to the people, and by endless centuries of sieges and invasions that had made the Khosians, as a nation, mutually reliant on those who paid and maintained much of their defences.

The varied democras of the Free Ports, based on the dreams of a political prisoner who had died centuries previously – a philosopher whose blood was running through Coya's veins even as he thought of him now – were the same only in that they shared the common ideals of the League constitution, at least in principle if not always in action, and that they were all part of this unique experiment in rule by the people. It was hardly a utopia they had created here. No one and nothing was ever going to be perfect. But perfect or not, they had fought for a free and fair way of living, without slavery or exploitation of others, and on most islands they had achieved some working approximations of it.

And now this speculation of invasion, ringing in his mind day and night, a jangly disjointed series of anxieties and teetering hopes. It was hard to think of anything else just now. Only last night, Coya had experienced a dream that had caused him to awake in a shaking, sweaty panic.

In his dream, he had imagined the imperial capital of Q'os as a monstrous quivering thing pulsating at the absolute heart of Mann. Its tendrils had flowed outwards across the world of humans in the form of self-fulfilling credence, reaching deep into the minds of people as they slept, and even more so when they were awake; whispers upon whispers that told how life was a vicious competition and nothing more, how human worth was to be found only in those measurable effects of status and materials either gained or given, how man must prey always on man, how those who would be free must first of all enslave. In his dream, the whispers had flowed never-ending until it was all the listeners could do but believe in the words and follow them, and their neighbours the same, and their neighbours' neighbours, so that the needs of the monstrosity were pulsing through them all, and they were inflating with the ugly power of it, becoming the words themselves and making of them a reality – and all the while the monster gorged, and the world itself grew crazed and barren.

All his life, Coya had loathed and feared the tyranny of Mann. And now this impending invasion, these Mannian fleets heading straight for the people of the League with their intentions of conquest; causing him nightmares in the coldest hours of the night.

'There's another matter I must raise with you,' Creed announced, stirring from his own musings. 'Something I can only discuss in person.'

'Oh?'

'If I'm right, and the Mannians invade Khos rather than Minos, then full martial law and all its powers will fall into my hands. I want your people in the Few to know that I will use that power only as intended, in the defence of Khos. Nothing more.'

'Really, Marsalas. Not here.'

'Then where else? Time is short. I need the Few to know that I harbour no plans of becoming a dictator.'

Coya shook his head. 'I would not have supposed it, anyway. Still—' Coya faltered, his mouth open.

Marsh had caught his eye. Something had changed in the stance of the man, a sudden alertness that would have gone unnoticed had Coya not know known him for the better part of his life.

'I'm certain your words will be well received,' he continued as Creed followed his gaze: both of them looking at Marsh, at the bodyguard's hands now reaching beneath his brown leather longcoat for something in the small of his back. 'You have nothing to fear from us, believe me. You are wise enough not to allow such power to ruin you entirely . . . Besides, you know too well the consequences, should that ever occur . . .'

Coya blinked in surprise as Marsh lifted a pistol in his hand and aimed it towards the crew.

The crack of the shot went right through him. He stared in shock at his bodyguard, standing there like some duellist with his right leg extended forwards, his other hand still beneath his coat, a puff of smoke dispelling in the wind from the end of the raised gun. Coya followed the line of the shot and spotted a man toppling backwards onto the deck, while crewmen around him shouted out in surprise or dived for cover. The victim was a monk, he saw, one of the pair of monks who had come aboard to bless this august occasion of their meeting.

Another bang went off nearby, loud enough to burst his heart. Creed shouted something by his side as chunks of debris whistled past them.

A wash of black smoke blew across their position by the rail. He had time enough to see a second monk leaping towards them, something round and black in his hand, and Marsh pulling another pistol from his coat, then firing it, before the smoke engulfed them entirely; and then Coya was sprawled on the deck with a great weight pressing down on him, and another bang tried to squeeze the insides out from him.

When the smoke cleared, Marsh was still standing there with his hands now empty save for a knife. He was turning to track the monk vaulting over the rail to his death.

Coya gasped as the man vanished over the side.

'Are you all right?' asked Creed, patting him down before helping him to his feet.

Coya found his voice again. 'I'm fine, I think,' he said

as he stooped awkwardly for his cane. 'And you?' he asked, as he leaned on it for support and looked up at the general. 'You seem to be bleeding, on your head, there.'

Creed dabbed at his head where a shallow wound ran crimson. The general frowned then turned to look over the rail. Coya was curious too.

Below, a great distance below, a canopy of white drifted down towards the surface of the sea. As the wind carried it in the direction of the coast, he saw a man dangling beneath it, the burned orange of his robes unmistakable.

'These Diplomats,' Creed said, shaking his head in obvious fascination, 'they grow crazier every year.'

—CHAPTER FOUR—

The House on Tempo Street

In sweat, they lay with their lungs heaving and their cries still ringing in their ears, both of them splayed like martyrs on the sodden bed, their bodies glistening in the daylight cast through the tattered, mouldy curtains of gala lace that hung across the open window.

Bahn blinked to clear his eyes. Through the air above the bed the dust motes were dancing as though in play, whipped up by the frantic action of the last hour.

'We make too much noise,' she muttered next to him, but without much concern in her voice, even as a child's yell rang up through the thin boards of the floor, and voices murmured from behind the even thinner wall at their heads.

Bahn could only gasp and wait for his galloping heart to stop racing. He was burning up, and he kicked away the thin blanket that had snared itself around his ankles. He wiped his stubbled face dry, and realized that he'd forgotten to shave that morning.

The room was a cupboard-like space with a triangular, slope-beamed ceiling too low for a man to stand properly beneath. It reeked of dampness, sex, and the spiced smoke from an incense burner sitting beneath the open window. A *perch*, they called this kind of attic room in Bar-Khos; the preserve of prostitutes and street hustlers, or those in hiding from the law.

Bahn looked down at the girl as she rolled against his side and rested an arm across his stomach, her white skin as smooth as paper. Like her face, her small breasts were flushed, and he lay there and enjoyed the sensation of them flattening against his chest while the soft lilt of her voice played in his ears. 'Or rather, *you* make too much noise,' she was saying in her Lagosian accent, and she slid her hand downwards past his stomach, and stroked his downy hair with painted nails.

'You were hardly quiet yourself,' he breathed, and felt his scrotum tighten as her nails explored him further – sweet Mercy, he was responding again already. He could not get enough of this girl.

Absently, Bahn wondered if a shade had possessed him these past days and weeks; one of those spirits of mad impulse that seized hold of lives and spurred them headlong into tragedy with their insatiable needs.

If only I believed in such things, Bahn considered in his usual rational way. He knew that this weakness was his alone to carry. He thought of Marlee, his wife, and felt the usual first flutters of guilt in his stomach, a nausea he would carry with him for the rest of the day. He sighed heavily.

The girl beside him knew that sound by now, and she drew her hand away to leave him in peace. She cradled her head against the nook of his shoulder, her blue eyes fixed on the low sloping beams of the ceiling above them. He observed the spikes of her honey-coloured hair as they bristled against his skin.

'I hardly recognized you, when I first came in,' he told her.

She looked up with those eyes that he still found so mesmerizing.

'Your hair,' he explained, nodding to the ridge of erect hair that ran along the middle of her scalp, like the mating display of some jungle bird. He could smell it, the wax that coated it and made it stiff like that. 'It makes you look like one of those travelling tuchoni.'

'You don't like it? Meqa did it for me. She's half tuchoni herself, or so she tells it.'

'I like it well enough. It's certainly . . . exotic.' Yet Bahn couldn't help but think of the first time he'd ever laid eyes on her, standing on a corner with the other street girls of the Quarter of Barbers, in a thin rain that had plastered her short hair in curls around her head. 'I just thought it suited your name, the way that it was.'

'I still have my curls,' she purred, twisting one with a finger, blinking up at him through her lashes.

'Enough now,' he urged.

'What?'

He said nothing for a few moments. 'Let's just lie here a while. Two people in a room together. I'll still pay for your time.'

She smiled, and it was the first genuine smile she had ever offered him. 'I can do that.'

The girl lay back against his arm. She pursed her lips and blew at a shining dust mote to push it away from her face. Her eyes followed it and Bahn found himself doing the same, tracking its motion through the cloud of swirling specks that filled the room.

The mote drifted over a stack of folded clothing pressed between the bed and the wall. At last it vanished amongst the leaves of a jubba plant in a chipped wooden bowl, where a single blue flower was in late bloom. A Lagosian thing that, to pot plants and bring them indoors, a fashion that had been catching on in the city since the steady influx of refugees from Lagos had first begun; Marlee had even started doing it.

Outside, a crow flapped past the window, making its

ugly calls. For long moments Bahn simply gazed through the curtains of lace, staring at the meagre view of housing tenements under construction on the other side of the yards and communal vegetable plots, the cranes and scaffolding poking up beneath a slab of azure sky. The voice sounded again through the sheet-thin wall behind them; Meqa, bartering with a customer over her price. From below, the sounds of the children continued to rise from the ground floor.

They were a tribe, those fifteen children, and they were ruled only by their mother Rosa, the landlady of the house, who as it turned out was not their mother at all, save for two of them; rather, she was a middle-aged widow with a good heart, who could not help but take in every stray hungry child that she encountered. The children themselves barely seemed to notice the men who clambered up the creaking stairs at the rear of the house at all hours. Bahn, on his handful of recent visits here, had been ignored by them after only a few glances his way – the children too busy shrieking around in the muck of the backyard, fighting over worms and yelling in delight each time they snapped one in half.

It was enough to make Bahn think of his own son and infant daughter, though he chased those thoughts away, quickly, before they could gain any substance.

'It's quiet,' the girl said.

She referred to the silence of the guns at the Shield, half a laq to the south.

Bahn nodded. The Mannian guns had lain silent for more than a week now. It was said that a period of mourning had been declared across the Empire in respect for the death of the Matriarch's son. In return, the guns of the Bar-Khosian defences had followed their example, though purely to preserve their blackpowder.

His voice was wistful as he spoke. 'It was like this ten years ago, before the siege and the war. Just normal everyday sounds of a city.' Bahn sighed once more. 'I wonder if it will ever be this way again.'

'You sound troubled,' she said, and narrowed her eyes as she watched his expression. 'Have you heard something?'

For an instant Bahn felt a tension in his chest, his muscles clamping tight around his heart. In his mind's eye he saw the far sparkle of fires in the distance, like cities burning.

'No,' he lied to her. 'Not that I could tell you, anyway, if I had.' Bahn squeezed her shoulder and tried to ease the tension in his chest by breathing deeply. 'I've too much on my mind, that's all.'

She asked nothing more of him, and simply laid her head upon his beating heart. 'You should not fret so,' she murmured.

'Why do you say that?'

'Because you worry like an old woman. Too much thinking,' and she lifted her head to tap him twice on his left temple.

He forced a smile to his face. 'My mother is the same. Always worrying about something or other.'

She nodded, understanding.

Bahn looked at her fully, sprawled as she was against him; the slight redness of her nostrils from inhaling dross; the bruise on her neck the precise size of his pursed lips. He had been rough on her again.

When had he last given Marlee a lusty bite like that? he wondered. Before their son had arrived, he realized. Before the war, when they had both been young and carefree.

Bahn ran a finger across the smooth skin of her shoulder.

I will feel this guilt either way, he considered.

Without warning he rolled himself on top of her. For a moment there was surprise in her eyes, though it was gone in an instant as he bent and kissed her throat, to be replaced by something unreadable.

*

He was losing it, Curl thought to herself as Bahn departed and the thump of his boots faded on the outside stairs. Curl had seen it before in other siege-shocked soldiers of the city, men ready to snap and run amok through the lives of those around them, tearing and snarling for a way out. They were always the roughest ones, she'd noticed, but Bahn in truth was not so bad on her, more fiercely passionate than anything else, as if he simply needed, in these brief hours with Curl, to forget everything about his present circumstances.

A suicide case, perhaps; hardly a berserker.

She hadn't liked the fear in his voice though, when he had been talking about the guns lying silent. As if he was doomed; as if they were all doomed. She didn't need to hear things like that; let him share those worries with his wife, whose name he kept crying out in the heat of the moment.

Curl rose and slipped her payment into her hidden pouch of coins in the pot of the jubba plant. The pouch held a handful of silvers and a little more in coppers. Not much for all the business she was doing. With the worsening shortage of food in the city leading to ever-higher prices, forcing Rosa to ask for larger contributions to their meals, she was finding it hard to maintain even that small sum from week to week.

Curl poured a jug of water into the clay washbasin. She stood naked on a cotton towel that she laid on the small portion of floor-space before the stand, and washed herself down with a bar of apple-scented soap. Around her, the smoke from the incense coiled about her body and chased away the after-scents from the room. Still, an atmosphere of heaviness remained behind, the man's woes and low spirits lingering on in the quietness. Curl hummed something from her childhood, making the room her own again.

Goosebumps rose on her skin as a cool breeze played through the open window. She dried herself quickly, and smeared a little lemon juice over her legs where the fleas kept biting. She checked her hair in the broken sliver of mirror that leaned next to the washbowl, then slipped into the cotton robe that she wore whenever she wasn't working. Still humming, she slipped the wooden charm back around her neck, and listened to the shouts of Rosa chasing the children from the kitchen.

Rosa rented out all the upper rooms of her house to feed and clothe her tribe of wayward urchins. It made for a curious combination, with their world of playful youth and tantrums seeping always upwards through the cramped, sordid sessions of the working women in their tiny rooms, and the ghostly lives of the hardcore dross junkies, and the gentle madness of the urban hermits and struggling artists who lived alongside them. But it worked somehow, perhaps simply because they had no other choice but to make it work. Rosa kept the rents as low as she was able, and ensured that everyone felt part of an extended family. Against all expectations, there was a warmth in the house, a sense of belonging.

Curl was shaking now, though not from the cold. With care, she gathered her small wooden box from the floor and sat back against the pillows. Inside lay her precious stash of dross, the dusty grey powder held in an envelope of folded graf leaf. Curl poured a line of the stuff along the back of her hand, returned the envelope to the box and laid the box on the bed. She placed the stub of the reed she used for these occasions into her nostril, and held the other nostril shut, and took a deep, sharp inhalation that cleared the dust from the hand in one go.

She rubbed her nose and sniffed and lay against the pillows with a gasp, the back of her throat turning numb already. Her fingers and toes tingled, and the tingling spread to leave heat and pleasure in its wake. The sensation filtered up her limbs, her body, her head . . . until at last, with grace, it reached into her mind.

CHAPTER FIVE

Good Things Come in Life

His head was splitting with pain that morning, and he chewed on a dulce leaf as he stepped between the stalls of a thriving Q'os marketplace, peering out from the wet folds of his hood at a drizzle of rain that fell so fine it kept drifting, losing its direction.

Overhead, the bells of the nearby temples rang out the turning of the hour, sounding brash and overly loud after their dormancy of so many weeks. From the direction of the nearby Serpentine, the early morning chants of the pilgrims could be heard as they headed in a mass towards Freedom Square, celebrating the first day of the delayed festa that was the Augere el Mann, the period of mourning seemingly lifted.

Ash still wasn't certain what he was doing here risking his neck in broad daylight for the sake of a little fresh bread. At the sight of so many people filling the streets the urge had simply come upon him, and no greater compulsion had countered it, so here he was, moving through the press of shoppers, with a scarf wrapped around his face and his hood low over his eyes, the smell of the closest bakery leading the way.

It was with a growling stomach that he found himself waiting his turn before a busy baker's stall. From the leaden skies the rain continued to fall, dripping from the canopy overhead to patter onto his back. Ash cast his eyes around the walls and buildings that circled the market square. He paused to inspect the entrance points at either end of it, and the pair of auxiliaries who strolled around the stalls idly swinging their batons, looking for a reason to use them.

I shouldn't be here in daylight, he told his stomach. *This is reckless even for me.*

An opening appeared before him and Ash squeezed

his way into it, his purse in hand. 'Yes?' asked one of the aproned lads behind the counter.

'Three seeded loaves. The largest you have. And something to carry them in.'

The lad tossed the loaves into a bag of twine netting and held it towards him. 'One-and-a-half marvels,' he informed him. 'Plus a quarter for the bag. That's one-and-three-quarters.'

It was an extortionate price, no doubt a result of the festa and the countless pilgrims, though he handed over two marvels and plucked the bag from the youth's hand.

'That'll be an extra quarter.'

'For what?'

'For providing change.'

Someone shoved into Ash from behind as they tried to get closer to the counter. He shoved back without looking, restoring the inch of space around him. 'You want me to give you a quarter, so you can give me a quarter back in change?'

'I don't make the rules,' the lad said impatiently, already looking to the next customer before him.

Ash blew the air from his lungs. He waved the business away with a hand then pushed his way clear of the stall before he lost his temper with it all. He started back the way he had come, but he saw the two auxiliaries coming that way towards him. Instead he turned and walked for the other entrance at the opposite end of the market, wishing only to return now to the seclusion of the rooftops, where he could enjoy his breakfast alone with his own company.

'*Ken-dai!*' came a shout that stopped him in his tracks. '*Ho, ken-dai!*'

Ash turned swiftly, and instantly spotted a dark face above the passing heads, barely a dozen paces from where he stood; a man from Honshu like himself.

The man was looking down at him from where he sat upon a sedan chair borne by two muscled slaves, a

scented kerchief held to his nostrils like a white blossom. When their eyes met the man raised a hand in
greeting. Ash glanced around, pulling the scarf a little
higher over the bridge of his nose; watched as the figure
clambered down to the ground. His two armoured
bodyguards were already clearing the vicinity by shoving people out of the way.

'*Ken-dai!*' the man exclaimed again in their native
Honshu, while one of his bearers snapped open an umbrella to hold above his head.

Ash replied with a curt nod.

'You're wise to travel about like that. They've been
arresting many of us in the city for questioning.'

Ash said nothing, and there was a moment of awkward silence between them. The stranger was of a similar age to Ash, and dressed in fine robes of Honshu silk.
He was a little overweight, and Ash could not help but
notice the many glittering rings of gold and diamonds
upon his fingers. A silk merchant perhaps, drawn to the
Midèrēs on the silk winds long ago; or perhaps even a
political exile like himself.

'How is the old country?' the merchant asked in obvious hope that he would know.

'I couldn't say,' Ash confessed. 'It's been many years
now since I was there.'

The man's nod was heavy with meaning. 'Yes, such a
voyage as that should be made once in a lifetime. I can't
imagine how these sailors do it, coming back and forth,
playing such odds as that.' He sniffed beneath the dripping umbrella, raised the kerchief to his nose again. As
he did so, Ash saw the tattoo on his left wrist – a circle
with a single eye within it.

'You were with the People's Army?' he blurted.

The merchant saw what he was looking at, then
dropped his hand as though guilty of something. 'What
of it?'

Ash looked at the rich clothes and jewels that he
wore; at the slave holding up the umbrella, hair lank in

the rain; at the other bearer still standing behind the sedan, eyes downcast; at the two armed thugs paid to do his bidding.

'You have fallen far,' Ash drawled.

The man's eyebrows shot up in surprise, levelled again in anger. He looked to one of his guards.

'Grab this one!' he snapped.

Ash was already moving, though, pushing his way through the crowd in the direction of the exit. 'Bring him back here!' he heard the man shout, and then Ash was dashing through a clear space between the stalls, his bag of bread swinging in his hand and people cursing in his wake.

He slowed as he neared the exit; stopped entirely as he found himself trapped by the Thief Toll that blocked it – a line of caged turnstiles with slots for quarters.

He was struggling for his purse when one of the bodyguards made a grab for him through the bars that had sealed him in. The man missed, shook the bars in angry impotence.

The second guard pushed into the adjacent stile, fumbled too in his clothing for a coin as his other hand snaked in through the side grille, groping for Ash's hood.

Ash dropped a whole marvel into the slot, hardly surprised that it was accepted, and broke free from his grasp as he pushed through the stile into the Serpentine beyond.

As far as the eye could see, the thoroughfare was filled with snaking processions of red-robed pilgrims. On the opposite side of the road stood the old quarter of the district, with its winding alleyways and its tilting, top-heavy buildings of stone. Ash dived headlong into the procession, weaving through the pilgrims as he tried to get across. He glimpsed men and woman whipping their bloody backs and breasts in frenzy; others chanting as they sported skewered cheeks, their faces held aloft and ecstatic.

Then he was through them, trotting into the mouth

of a narrow alley with the two bodyguards emerging close behind.

'Clear away!' he bellowed as he picked up speed. He dashed headlong past folk and pilgrim tourists bartering over trinkets and whores, trying to lose himself in the maze of passageways and small plazas that were the guts of the old district.

They were fast, these boys. Even in their boots and their leather armour they were keeping pace with him, pounding along the flagstones of the passageway in single file with their shoulders brushing the walls, whooshing air from their lungs in a manner suggesting they could keep this up all day.

Ash was wondering if he shouldn't pick up his pace a little more, but then he saw the passageway open out ahead of him, and a less taxing option presented itself.

He reached for his sword from beneath his cloak, drew it the instant he was clear of the alley.

In his next two steps he had stopped himself and was spinning around on the ball of his foot, his other leg stretching out so that he was low, extended, his sword pointing in front of him.

In the last instant he adjusted the aim of the tip a fraction, and then the first guard ran straight into the blade, shoving Ash back a pace with the force of his impact. They both grunted, and then the second guard ran into the first one, right into the blade sticking out of his back.

Ash straightened from his stance, the hilt of the sword still in his grip. The two men grimaced and sweated and tried to pull themselves free while Ash inspected their wounds. The first guard looked at him; looked back down at the blade in his side.

'I've avoided your organs,' he told them both. 'Keep the wounds clean and you should live.'

Without warning he jerked the blade free. They sagged to their knees, hands reaching for their sides. People nearby were staring in wonder.

Ash cleaned the blood from his blade on one of their backs, then picked up his bag of bread and trotted away.

*

Ché strolled home feeling light and loose-gaited, the taste of the Royal Milk still lingering on his tongue, his body trembling with the energy of a coiled spring.

His new and exclusive apartment was located in the southern side of the Temple District, that area which surrounded the Temple of Whispers where lesser sky-steeples rose above priestly mansions and apartment blocks and ornamented buildings of entertainment. He walked back through the steady rain listening to the birds singing from the parks and the rooftop gardens, wondering in his elevated mood if they were celebrating the return of life to the city streets, for there was an atmosphere of excitement in the air today, this first day of the Augere. In the streets, children watched the red-robed pilgrims march by in chanting processions, goggling at the numerous races of the Empire, drawn here in record numbers for the fiftieth anniversary of the Mannians' seizure of power.

In his apartment, Whiskers was there already, tidying the large empty rooms in her meticulous way. Ché felt a moment of affection when he saw the woman; after only a few weeks, she had become a welcome detail of stability in his scattered life.

'I leave in the morning,' he announced to the house-slave, even though she couldn't hear him, for she had been rendered deaf by hot oil some time during her captivity. 'Whiskers,' and he waved a hand to catch her eye, 'no need for that now.' But the woman continued to polish the shelving, paying him no mind.

He looked at the slate board that hung about her chest, swinging free as she bent forwards, along with a stub of chalk fixed to a length of string.

He had so far refused to use the board to communi-

cate with the woman, largely because Whiskers refused
to use it herself; as though she preferred to let it hang
there uselessly like an accusation of all that had been
done to her. Instead, he preferred to talk to the woman,
persisting in the hope that some communication might
still pass between them.

Besides, he liked to hear words spoken in the usual
silence of the apartment, even if they were only his
own.

Ché wandered into his bedroom and stared at his
double-sized bed, with its silk covers of maroon taste-
fully chosen to match the pale golds of the wallpaper.
He realized that he was still too energized from the
Royal Milk and the previous night's events to sleep, so
instead pulled off his robe and changed into a loose-
fitting tunic and trousers, and then a pair of soft leather
shoes, which he laced tightly.

'I'm going for a run!' he hollered on his way out of
the door.

*

Ché pounded along the wide, tree-lined avenue of the
Serpentine. He ran with the city's rhythms in his ears,
the local priests calling out through bullhorns from
their temple spires; the calls of hawking cart-merchants
and street dealers; the doleful songs of slave-gangs going about their business. People turned to watch him
pass or to step out of his way, drawn by the simple
spectacle of a man running through the streets. Sweat
beaded his skin, and the rain too. With every footfall he
found his head clearing of all the thoughts that had
been possessing him so compulsively of late; a clarity he
struggled for ever more these days. Ché dodged past
carts and groups of people, light-footed and free.

His usual route was a circuit of streets to the east of
his apartment, an area that was prettified with the
greenery of parks. He turned left at the Getti playhouse
and followed a boulevard alongside the Drowning

Gardens, seeing the rich greens of the trees and shrubs through the flicker of the iron railings, the contrasts of red-robed pilgrims scattered amongst them. In the street, building-sized paintings of the Holy Matriarch snagged his eyes, and the lesser placards for new restaurants, housing developments, brands of alcohol and food; he tried to ignore their simple messages, but the images flashed by and left their impression nonetheless, the smiling white-toothed faces of happy affluence.

Joy Street lay at the end of the boulevard, and next to it his mother's Sentiate temple. Ché had been ignoring his mother of late, unable to bring himself to visit her. He didn't wish to be reminded of what she represented in his life, nor of her role within the order. When he saw the Sentiate tower looming ahead, its scarlet flags raised high today to show that it was open once more for business, his mood began to falter along with his pace.

He turned away before he reached Joy Street, and entered the Drowning Gardens instead.

He followed a straight paved path between the shorn lawns. On the hottest of summer days he would sometimes run in these gardens of glittering pools and broken shadows to escape the clammy heat of the streets beyond. Today, though, he saw that it was a mistake to come here, for the pilgrims were drowning themselves in earnest.

Ché ran past stone pools with pilgrims kneeling all around their rims, heads plunged deep in the water. Occasional bubbles broke the surface, and some flailed their arms without control as they forced themselves to remain submerged; the more dedicated had their arms bound behind them with leather belts. He skirted around attendants of the Selarus, the priests working over prone forms, pumping water from lungs, breathing into mouths, slapping faces to revive them. One pair was carrying a limp form away.

He sprinted even faster, with the effort pulling the breath from him. Ahead was a congregation of dancing pilgrims, so thick he saw no way through them. Ché wasn't in the mood for stopping.

With a feral grin he put his head down and charged into the crowd at full speed, shouldering the men and women out of his way. Like a raging bull he tore his way through the mass of pilgrims as men and women spilled to the ground or pursued him with their shouts of anger.

He emerged on the other side fighting for air. His brow was wet, and when he dabbed it with his fingers they came away red.

Onwards, with the rain gently cleaning the blood from him, the taste of it mingling with the taste of the Royal Milk in his mouth.

*

When he returned to the apartment he realized he'd forgotten to bring any coins with him to get back inside the building. He cursed and pulled the doors in vain, but then the door opened from within – one of his neighbours stepping out – and Ché ducked inside.

He jogged up the stairs and entered his apartment. Whiskers was just crossing the room and she glanced at him with a frown on her reddened features. A whistle was shrieking from behind her.

'Good timing,' he noted as he stepped past the woman, pulling off his clothing as he moved towards the bathroom and the source of the high keen. Whiskers hurried past him. When he entered the bathroom's steamy atmosphere she was already turning off the gas flames beneath a great copper pot fitted tightly with a lid. A jet of steam was shooting from the whistle fixed in the lid, and it died quickly as Whiskers opened a spigot near the bottom of the pot, to release a flow of hot water into the tiled bath sunk into the floor.

Naked, his mood still high, Ché pinched her rump as

he stepped around her, and gave a quick smile in return for the scowl on her whiskery face. 'You're too good to me,' he told her as he stepped into the few inches of water in the slowly filling bath, and lay back and sighed as it rose gently around him. Whiskers eyed him scornfully.

He closed his eyes as his body grew lighter in the water. His skin burned pleasantly, and he heard the woman roll up her sleeves and kneel beside him. Ché sighed long and deeply as she scrubbed him down with a flannel of rough sharkskin and one of the balms his mother had insisted on giving him for his troubled skin. Methodically, she worked on the rashes that covered his body, and he groaned at one point, in something approaching sexual pleasure, at the relief it gave from his constant itching.

This life had its benefits, Ché reflected idly. Not least of all a hot bath every day if he wished for one; no small thing that, in a world where most people were lucky to wash in a basin of cold water with copal leaves for soap.

You're getting soft, he thought, and wondered what his old Rōshun master Shebec would think of him now, if he'd still been alive to see him.

Whiskers cleaned the small cut on his brow, making no enquiries either by gesture or by look. When she finished, she sluiced the water from her hands and left him to enjoy his soak alone. His mind was still clear from his run. He placed a sodden flannel across his face and breathed through its clinging embrace, feeling tired all of a sudden, the effects of the Royal Milk finally fading. Perhaps he'd sweated them out of his body.

Ché yawned and knew he would sleep soon. His thoughts drifted like the steam in the room, and in small measures he allowed them to contemplate the bizarreness of the night now behind him, and what was to come the next morn.

War, he thought with a sudden sobriety. *Tomorrow, I set off for war.*

*

A letter was waiting for him on the table by the front door when he arose in the afternoon from his sleep. Whiskers was gone, returned to her slave quarters in the basement of the building.

He had an aversion to letters. They came bearing only bad news or reminders of responsibilities. Still, he picked it up anyway and opened it.

I hope the new ointment is working. Come and see me, my son. I miss you. Please come.

His mother. The leash they kept on him to ensure his loyalty to the order.

Ché held the letter for a while, not sure what to do with it. In the end he opened the drawer of the table, and took out a plain piece of paper and the stylus and ink. In careful lettering he wrote:

Dear mother. I must leave with the fleet in the morning. No, I do not know how long I will be gone. I will think of you, as I always think of you.

Your son.

He blew on the ink until it was dry, then folded the paper carefully, and scratched instructions for delivery to his mother at the Sentiate temple. He left it where Whiskers would see it.

For a moment Ché considered sending an invitation to Perl or Shale, or even to both of them. But the young women would expect their fair share of pleasure narcotics for the evening, and would expect him to join them in their vices. He didn't feel like being intoxicated tonight, nor most nights for that matter; he didn't like where his mind sometimes went in those altered states.

No, better if he remained inside tonight so that he was fresh for the morning. Besides, some peace to himself would be a luxury in itself. Best to make the most of that too while he still could.

Ché dug out his leather backpack and started to pack for the morning, wanting to be done with it so that he could properly relax. He packed some clothing without any great attention to what he was doing, though when he came to his bookcase he paused, and sat down to give some it proper deliberation.

It was Ché's job to know as much of the world as he possibly could. Hence the shelves held many travelogues and diaries and books of maps, and texts of religion and history. It was this knowledge, Ché sometimes suspected, that really lay behind the sense of distrust he sometimes felt from his handlers; this abundance of learning of other cultures and the ideologies that ran contrary to Mann.

In the end he selected one of the works by Slavo, an account of the Markeshian's travels – imaginary most likely – to the far side of the world and the foreign peoples he'd discovered there. It had been a while since Ché had read that one.

As an afterthought, he turned to his copy of the Scripture lying closed on top of the bookcase. Only once had he actually read the thing in its entirety since his return to his life of Mann. It had been part of his re-education after living all those years as a Rōshun apprentice in the mountains of Cheem, when the spypriests of the Élash had slowly reintegrated him into the ways of the divine flesh, before informing him that he was to become a Diplomat for the Section.

He lifted the thin volume and packed it only reluctantly.

*

In the darkening hours of evening, with the living room lit by gas lamps, Ché sat down in his armchair dressed in a clean white robe, his stomach comfortably full, a modest glass of Seratian wine in his hand, gazing out onto the street below, lost in thought.

His mood of earlier was long gone. Instead, he felt vaguely depressed now that his packing was done and there was nothing left but to wait for morning, the reality of it finally sinking in. This life of a Diplomat allowed him to exist in relative, blessed isolation from his peers. Now, though, for weeks on end, he would be expected to live shoulder to shoulder with his fellow priests, and the Matriarch and her entourage of sycophants. He would have to watch his every step, his every word. Not an easy thing that, not now with his thoughts running ever more contrary to everything around him.

Since Cheem and his betrayal of the Rōshun, a seething anger had been rising within Ché. He could feel it whenever his temper snapped in a dozen little ways during the course of an ordinary day, or when he said things he shouldn't be saying, or when he provoked those of authority with his seeming arrogance towards them, which in truth wasn't arrogance at all, but a nonchalant mental shrug, a lack of caring. It was as though he wished to be challenged on his behaviour, as though he wanted to have it out with the priests at last, regardless of the consequences. A kind of deathwish perhaps, gathering slowly in momentum.

Ché took another sip of the wine, appreciating the soft rasp of bitterness against his palate, the perfect accompaniment to the peppered rabbit he could still taste from dinner. In the kitchen, he could hear Whiskers cleaning the dirty pots and plates.

It had stopped raining at last, and people were stepping out to enjoy the evening entertainments of the streets below. For a while, Ché watched a pimp running his little empire from the corner of the street, the fellow strutting and preening himself beneath the streetlights. When he grew bored of that, he shifted his attention to a group of young men and women sitting on a low wall behind a tram stop, passing hazii sticks amongst themselves, chatting and laughing, warming each other with their companionship. They seemed not much younger than Ché, yet he watched them as though with the eyes of an old man.

At first he didn't notice Whiskers as she emerged into the living area, her hands folded before her, waiting to be relieved for the night. The woman cleared her throat, and he turned and blinked and stared at her tired, sagging face.

Ché had no idea what this woman was really called. Non-indentured slaves weren't allowed names as a rule, save for what their masters chose for them; hence he'd coined her nickname when he'd first been given the keys to this apartment, and laid eyes on the house-slave that came with it, this middle-aged woman with blonde downy hairs on her face and a pair of fierce blue eyes. He knew that she was from the people of the northern tribes, though only because of the colour of her hair, and the blue-ink tattoo he had once glimpsed on her upper arm.

Not much of a life, he'd often thought. Seven days a week at his beck and call with only the late nights truly to herself; and even then, only if she wasn't required in her master's bed. He imagined she had been well used by her previous masters, for she was womanly enough. He'd toyed with the idea himself for a while, before deciding he preferred more consent in these matters.

Behind Whiskers, shadows hung across the apartment in heavy veils that shifted in the gaslight. They hid the clock that ticked its isolated ticks on the far table, and the piles of reference materials stacked against the wall, and the lacquered globe of the world, turned so often it needed oiling again already. Not much else, though, save

for emptiness and bare walls and the sounds of the world
outside it.

'Stay a while longer,' Ché heard himself say to the
woman, motioning with his open hands.

She seemed to misunderstand him, for a little colour
came to her pale features.

Not for the first time, a suspicion crossed his mind
that perhaps Whiskers really could read lips, as many
slaves learned to do after they'd been rendered deaf –
and that she was keeping the fact to herself for reasons
unknown to him.

'No, I didn't mean . . .' He shook his head and looked
away, then noticed the ylang board on the small table
before him. He gestured to it. 'Perhaps you could join
me for a game, if you play?'

Her stare took in his gesturing hand then returned to
his eyes. Pity crossed her features. For an instant he saw
it clearly, and he wondered what caused such an emotion
towards him. The woman remained where she stood.

'Wine?' he asked, holding up the bottle above an
empty glass.

When he looked up, it was to see the look of a cautious animal approaching.

Whiskers settled herself in the chair opposite as she
held the slate board against her chest, then folded her
hands neatly in her lap. He watched her as he poured
out a generous measure of wine.

They played in silence, with the shouts and laughter
from the street muted by the thick panes of window
glass. Indeed she could play, at least enough to make a
game of it at the beginning. Ché went easy on her anyway, wanting to make it last a while. She played along
with that too, an amused awareness in the occasional
glance shot from beneath her thick eyebrows.

With each move she made, she held the slate against
her chest so it wouldn't get in the way as she leaned
forward over the game board. Ché finally pointed at the
thing, catching her eye. 'Please. Take that thing off.'

She blinked at him.

He pointed again, and made a gesture of removing it over her head.

She looked down at the slate, studied it for a moment. Then she pulled it off her with a rough hasty motion, and set in down against a leg of the table.

'Now, how about the rest of your clothes?'

He watched her closely as she watched him. Was there a flush of colour on her face again, just a hint of it?

His curiosity only intensified.

Whiskers took a drink of wine, then deployed three of her pebbles, using them to flank one of his own, picking it up with her calloused fingers to place it next to her other captured stones.

'I leave in the morning,' he said, watching her eyes closely as he did so. 'With the fleet. We go to wage war on the non-believers.' Nothing. No change in her expression.

Ché carelessly drove his black stones against her gathered whites, now huddling for protection in one quadrant of the board. He allowed himself a few mistakes until his offensive stalled and she rallied with her own. She didn't take long with her moves, as though she was hardly taking the game seriously herself. She seemed more interested in the wine.

He refilled her glass, and waited until she'd nearly finished that helping too. When next he caught her eye, he declared: 'I've been told by my handler to kill the Holy Matriarch.' And the words sounded loud in the dim quietness of the apartment.

Her eyes danced wildly, watching him. Ché could feel the sudden charge in the air between them.

'If she runs from battle, that is. Or looks as though she might be captured. It seems they will not allow that. She must win or fall. Nothing else.'

He placed a pebble down, picked up another, placed it next to the first. A third snuggled in behind them. 'Now,

I mostly wonder who my handlers *are*. I wonder who I am really working for after all this time, if they can order the death of a Matriarch.'

Whiskers' face thrust towards him. 'Hush now!' she said with an uneven voice, the tones slightly off. Her hands gripped either side of the table.

For a moment, Ché was startled enough to say nothing. He simply swallowed hard.

'What?' he replied quietly, and gave a toss of his hand. 'You think they're listening in the walls?'

She looked up from his mouth, her chest rising and falling fast; a silent panting. 'You will cause us both harm with talk like this. Why say these things to me?' Her face was so close he could feel her hot breath against his own.

'Because I thought you couldn't understand me,' he said slowly. 'You've been pretending as much since we first met. Pretending you couldn't read my lips.' And he fixed her with a hard, accusing stare.

'I owe you no loyalty,' she snapped back at him with her strange tone of voice. 'I am not your wife, to be telling your woes to. And neither am I your mother.'

At once Ché's mood darkened. It was like a lamp going out.

'I know very well what you are,' he growled, and of their own accord his eyes glanced at the slave collar about her neck.

Her eyebrows arched high. 'Oh? And what is that, if not a slave of a slave, then?' And her gaze darted around the walls of the apartment. 'They afford you a finer cage than the rest of us, that is all.'

Slowly, Ché tipped over the ylang board until the pebbles began to slide one by one onto the wooden floor, where they clattered and rolled as the two players locked stares. As the final pebble settled and silence returned once more, he dropped the edge of the board back against the table with a snap.

Whiskers sat back trembling.

'Are you working for them?' he demanded. 'Do you report to them about me?'

'Who?' the woman replied blankly.

Ché exhaled a long breath of air. He stared long at her, torn inside between anger and anguish.

'Go,' he told her. 'Get out.'

She rose, lifting her slate as she did so. Walked without another word for the door.

'Here,' he snarled as she glanced back, and he corked the half-empty bottle of wine and tossed it into her hands. Her eyes widened in surprise for a moment, but then she composed herself. She took the bottle with her, closing the door behind as she left.

Ché leaned back in the chair, found that he was staring down at the scattered pebbles on the floor – something in the pattern of them he could not quite read.

—CHAPTER SIX—

The Bastards of St Charlos

The fat man guarding the top of the stairs fell into her arms with a groan of surprise. She tottered there against his weight for a few moments like a young wife handling a drunken husband, then helped his body to fold neatly and silently onto the landing.

Swan flicked the blood from her knife, inadvertently scattering some of it across the damp wall. The woman stared at the spatter of droplets she had created, liking the contrast of crimson against the yellowing plaster.

'What are you doing?' Guan asked her as he stopped by her side. 'Are you high?'

'Only a little. Stop worrying, brother. It keeps me sharp.'

Together, the two priests stepped over the corpse and

stopped before the door. A gabble of loud voices came from the other side of it. She could hear a baby crying half-heartedly.

'Please people, one at a time! Milan, I saw you raise your hand first.'

'I only wanted to say, if we do call off this plan of action then we should do it for deliberate reasons, not because we're afraid of what they'll do to us.'

'But, Milan,' came another voice. 'During the week of the Augere? They'll murder us where we stand for disrupting the holy week like that.'

'And who would work the mills and steelworks along the Shambles then?' a woman replied. 'Or do you think they'd be content to lose their profits while they trained a new workforce?'

'Pish!' shouted another. 'In the mills they could turn around a new workforce within a few weeks. That isn't the point here. The point is they're vulnerable during the Augere. All these pilgrims gathered from around the Empire. All these representatives of the Caucus. The whole world is supposed to be celebrating the unity of Mann this week. One big happy Empire, with all of us waving our flags and feeling like we're part of it like the good sheep they teach us to be. And meanwhile, behind closed doors, they make their latest deals for squeezing us even further. No, they won't like it one bit when we show them up by taking to the streets. But if they want to settle quickly, without a bloodbath in front of everyone, they'll have to consider our terms.'

'We aren't here to discuss a revolution, Chops. What if they wait until the pilgrims have left, then burn us all alive in the Shay Madi for sport, like they do with the homeless, and then fill the factories with those poor souls who really *are* true slaves?'

'Then we'd have a real uprising on our hands. Like in our fathers' and mothers' times, when the priests last thought they could take the bread from the mouths of the working people. They must allow us to make a living. Even the priests concede that much.

'Besides, it's fear of what we could lose that has led us here in the first place. All those times we should have stood together and we didn't. And always because they threatened to bring in slaves to replace us, or even to move the factories elsewhere. I work more hours on the presses than I spend at home. So does my wife and our eldest sons. And still we can barely clothe and feed ourselves, let alone make the arrears on our rent, or pay for medicine when the children are sick. We have to do something, for kush sake.'

Swan smiled; not at the words, but at the glib inscription carved in the lintel above the door.

Better to light a single candle than to curse the darkness.

Her brother, loosening his neck muscles by her side, pointed to something in the shadows above the writing. It was a carving of two hands clasped together and entwined in barbed wire.

'They call themselves the Bastards of St Charlos.'

'St Charlos? Never heard of him.'

'No, you wouldn't have,' Guan replied. 'His name was outlawed twenty-five years before we were born. He was a priest of the old religion, back when the city was still a monarchy. He lived and worked here in the Shambles along the east bank. Gave all his money to the poor. Worked to set up these respite houses. They remember him as a saint for it.'

'You see? This is why I'm so glad that you're my clever brother. Otherwise, I'd have to read all those dull books myself. Tell me then, in your wisdom . . . Why do these chattel call themselves *bastards*?'

'Charlos had an eye for the women. It was said that half the children of the district were his illegitimate spawn.'

Swan laughed at that, more loudly than it warranted, while her brother watched her with a bemused frown.

The voices beyond the door fell to a deathly hush.

'Shall we?' she asked him.

'After you.'

Fifty faces were turned to the door as Swan stepped through it. Eyes widened as they saw her priestly robe and her smooth skull; even the crying infant in the lap of its mother blinked at her through its tears.

Swan snapped her fingers loudly, and the infant stopped crying with a startled jerk.

The room was packed from wall to wall with seated men and women, the air thick with the heat of so many bodies pressed so closely together.

How can they sit like this, in each other's stench?

'We're looking for Gant,' her brother declared, loudly. 'Please show him to us.'

Nobody moved. The man standing at the front of the room wrung his hands in dismay.

'Are you Gant?' Swan asked him.

He looked to the others for support, and Swan noticed a few men along the sides reaching beneath their coats for weapons.

'Who wants to know?'

It was a man standing by the shuttered window, his arms folded across his burly chest. He had a pipe in his mouth, and a peaked cap on his head cocked over one eye.

'I do.'

'And you are?'

'They call me Swan.'

'Well, Swan, they call me Gant. And this is a peaceful assembly. We're doing nothing wrong here.'

Her brother snorted. 'I would say that planning dissent amongst your fellow chattel is very wrong indeed.'

Chairs began to scuff against the floor. People were standing, moving back towards the walls. A handful of men were taking up positions around them.

'No trouble,' Swan said with her empty palms raised.

She nodded to the man Gant. 'Good evening to you, then. Or what remains of it.'

Slowly, with caution, they both backed out of the room, their task here complete. Swan took a final glimpse of Gant's curious expression then pulled the door closed behind her.

Instantly, her brother broke a bonding stick in half and used it to seal the door in its frame. The door handle rattled; someone trying to open it.

The voices grew loud again on the other side.

Swan and her brother hurried down the stairwell, racing each other. The Respite House was a tall building with many floors and rooms. Perhaps it had been an hostalio in its time, or one of the famous brothels of the district. People had scattered from the stairs and the landings when they'd first seen the two of them go up. Now, mutters sounded from behind closed doors, children's cries stifled suddenly. Swan broke her own bonding stick in half, and helped Guan close the main exit of every landing as they descended, sealing each one in turn.

Her brother wouldn't meet her eye as they did it.

Outside in the cobbled street, a stinking breeze was blowing down the narrow stretch of the Accenine – the only river on the island of Q'os – and amongst the twisting, diabolical streets of the slums that were the Shambles. The fumes from the nearby steelworks caught in the back of her throat, dark smokestacks pouring their effluence into the evening sky. Guan worked quickly to seal the main front door while Swan thrummed to her inner music, and observed the figures scurrying from the sight of their robes.

She stared at the distant Temple of Whispers above the skyline, a tall, warped sliver amongst smaller sky-steeples. It was more brightly lit than before. She knew that the second night of the Caucus must be starting by now; felt a moment's relief that they did not have to be there again tonight.

Much closer, on the opposite bank of the fast river,

the Lefall family fortress stood in a brilliance of focused gaslights. Barges were filling up with soldiers along the quayside: General Romano's own private troops, shipping down to the harbour for the fleet's departure tomorrow. Swan still had to pack, she recalled, and see to it that her new house-slave understood how to care properly for her animals.

Guan nudged her side, and she returned to the business at hand.

He took out his pistol and stood watch as she lifted one of the unlit brands they'd left leaning against the wall. Swan aimed her own pistol at it and fired.

The oil-soaked wood ignited and a blue-orange flame sputtered in the breeze. Quickly now, Swan ran the torch along the side of the wall, leaving a trail of fire that quickly climbed upwards where they'd splashed it with oil.

She circled the building, leaving her brother where he stood, passing the two other doors they'd already sealed. By the time she returned to him, the entire structure was sheathed by flames.

Banging on the front door now. People trying to get out.

'Remind me again: why aren't the Regulators handling this one?'

'Because, sister, the Matriarch's family owns half the linen mills in the Shambles. No doubt she wanted the job done right.'

The sounds of panic were starting to compete with the roaring of the flames. Shutters were being thrown open across the building, people hanging out amongst spumes of smoke.

'You think this will work?'

'Maybe at least they'll stop banging on about *rights* for a while. To hear their talk, you'd think that rights were handed to each and every one of them when they were born.'

Someone shrieked, and then a smoking body landed

before them with a thud against the cobbles. More people began to rain down; *crack crack crack* went the splintering of their legs.

Swan hopped back as a skull spattered its contents out across the street. She stared at the gory mess in fascination.

A baby was crying close by. She spotted it amongst the moving bodies, still wrapped in the arms of its broken mother. For all she knew, it was the same infant she'd seen in the room at the very top.

'Lucky you,' Swan said to it as she bent down for a closer inspection. To her brother: 'They cry so quietly, these children of theirs. Have you noticed?'

'No,' he replied amidst the screams and the roaring of the flames. 'Let's go.'

She nodded, then left it there bawling; someone else's problem.

*

Pedero glanced behind him as he knocked on the heavy door of tiq. His hand was shaking as it fell to his side, and he felt the wetness of his armpits where they had bloomed as stains against his priestly white robes.

In his belly lay a sense of dread so intense he thought he might throw up from it.

Get a grip on yourself, the spypriest commanded, and took a deep breath, and exhaled, and clenched his fists tightly.

He was admitted into the room by an Acolyte in plain clothing. The man frisked him roughly, his gaze sweeping over Pedero's appearance with displeasure. 'Wait here,' he instructed, then walked the length of the large room to where a wooden stall was fitted against the far wall; a house-slave stood next to the open doorway of the stall with a bowl of sponges in his hand.

Pedero tried to calm himself as he waited in front of the heavy desk. The rest of the space was crammed with various boxes of files still waiting to be unpacked, much

like his own office in the other wing of the building, following the yearly move of the Élash order to its new
anonymous premises. A half-eaten breakfast lay amongst
the documents on his superior's desk. Through a doorway behind the desk, he noticed the heavy travelling
chest on the floor of the other room, sealed tight by a
leather latch and a wrapping of hairy rope.

'Make it quick!' came Alarum's rough voice from his
personal privy. 'I must leave soon for the harbour.'

Pedero's head jerked around at the spymaster's sudden
announcement. 'I have a report for you, sir. I think –
I think it best that you read it.'

'Is that you, Pedero?'

'Yes. Yes, it's me.'

'Well, can't it wait?'

Pedero looked down at the report he clutched in his
trembling hand. The ink of the small, neat handwriting
had smudged in places from the sweat of his fingers. 'I
don't believe so. It's from one of our listening posts. Concerning a Diplomat by the name of Ché. I understand he's
accompanying the Holy Matriarch on her campaign.'

A hand emerged from the open doorway.

Pedero sidestepped towards it, stuffed the document
into the waiting hand without looking. He bowed his
head as he stepped back to a respectable distance, clasp-
ing his own hands behind his back.

After some moments: 'He said this? To his damned
house-slave?'

'Yes, sir.'

A mumble of oaths ensued. Alarum wasn't normally
a bad-tempered man. Since declaring that he was to
accompany the Holy Matriarch as her personal intelligence adviser, though, he'd been waspish with everyone
around him.

'The time stamp is dated for last night. Why am I
only hearing of this now?'

Pedero coughed for air. 'There was some confusion,'
he began, wincing, 'concerning the paperwork.'

'You mean it's been sitting on your desk all this time, and you didn't bother to read it until several moments ago.'

He couldn't deny it. He'd already tried to think of a way that he might push the blame of his own error downwards, but his mind had been gripped by a greater terror just then – sitting there behind his desk with the report trembling in his hand, his mind in a panic at what it had just read, appalled by the knowledge that he was now infected by it, that he couldn't very well *unread* the words and therefore be spared the fate most likely promised by them. *Tear the bastard thing to pieces and burn them*, his thoughts had jabbered in a dizzying moment of hysteria. He'd even stood and turned to the door with that very intention in mind, when he'd noticed Curzon perched behind his own desk across the room from him, peering down his nose above his spectacles; teller of everyone's tales.

Do your job, Pedero had numbly decided in the chill loneliness of the moment. *Brazen it out like you always do*.

A moment of madness, he now considered, standing there in the reality of his decision. Pedero lifted his head high as though offering his throat for sacrifice. 'I'm afraid so, spymaster. With the move, you see . . . we're still getting back on our feet.'

'Excuses, Pedero? I should have you sent to the pain block for a week for this, and you should thank me for being so lenient.'

'Yes, spymaster.'

A long and weary sigh. It was hardly the most reassuring of sounds from this man.

'Tell me. How many hands has this report passed through?'

With those words the blood drained from his face. He could feel it, the sudden coldness of his flesh; like he was dead already. He looked to the Acolyte and the house-slave, but they were avoiding his eye.

'The listener. And myself.'

'The listener's name? I can't make it out here.'

'Ul Mecharo.'

'And the slave woman?'

'Her number is on the report. Top left.'

'I see it.'

Pedero heard something strange from the stall. He realized it was Alarum clacking his teeth together, a habit his superior tended to exhibit when trying to coerce some detail from his memory.

'I know this young man,' he mused through the wall of the stall. 'Or at least I used to know his mother, when I was young. She was a Sentiate back then, still is, I think. Not one of these dead-eyed girls you get now either. No, full of fire and claws this one. Had to stop seeing her after she fell pregnant, though. Couldn't stand the taste of her . . .'

'It does put a rather strong question mark over this Diplomat's state of mind,' Pedero tried. 'He signs his death warrant with such talk, once the Section receives the report.'

'I rather suspect, Pedero, that his death warrant was signed the moment the details of his mission were first disclosed to him. He knows too much now. We must assume the Section will have him killed as soon as his mission is completed, one way or the other.'

Pedero bit his lip, wondering how to press the spymaster further. He had known the man for several years now. Alarum had always demanded frank discussions with his staff, most of all by his own sometimes brutal candour; he considered it a necessary requirement of their job if one was to remain in any way level-headed.

Pedero glanced to the Acolyte and then to the slave, but both seemed to spend their lives here staring unfocused at the floor. He took a step closer to the stall again, almost pressing against it. 'Is it true?' he asked his superior, his voice nearly a whisper. 'What he said, I mean?'

Alarum's response came loud and sudden. 'Leave us,' he commanded, and at last the Acolyte and slave looked at Pedero, then both headed for the door.

'You would really wish to know, if it were?' asked Alarum when they had left.

'I rather have the feeling a noose is around my neck anyway.'

'Oh? Then what of me? Haven't I now laid eyes on this report also?'

'You may be part of it already,' said Pedero, bravely. He knew it was long past the point for caution.

A soft wheeze came from the stall. Pedero decided that it was laughter.

Why is he laughing? What is it in the smallest of ways that could be funny about any of this?

'My superiors, perhaps,' came his voice at last. 'This Diplomat's handlers within the Section, certainly.'

Pedero dabbed his moist lips. He had stopped breathing, it seemed. Just then he found himself thinking of the brick of hazii weed that awaited him in his private chambers back in the Temple District, and the long evening of pleasure he had promised himself with his newly acquired body-slave. He wondered if he would even make it home alive.

It was a hard stare he gave as the document glided through the stall's doorway and came to rest on the floor.

'Bury this in the files somewhere. Say nothing of it to anyone. Is that clear?'

He could have thrown himself at the Alarum's feet, so grateful he felt in that moment. The relief that flooded him was like a flush of sexual pleasure.

'Of course, spymaster,' Pedero replied as he hurriedly bent and scooped the sheet of paper from the floor.

'And – Pedero?'

Breathlessly: 'Yes spymaster?'

'What does this Diplomat look like?'

'I believe his description is in his file.'

'Bring it to me.'

CHAPTER SEVEN

Assassin

Ash failed to notice the batwings flying towards him at first, for they were mere specks in the distant haze above the city.

He was working through a series of stretching exercises beneath the warming morning sky, loosening his muscles and easing the aches of his knees and back in preparation for what was to come, for he knew, deep in his guts, that today she would be coming out from her high raven's nest at long last.

His attention was wholly focused on his movements, and on the sound of his own deep from-the-belly breathing. Ash was paying little mind to the sky, never mind to the noisy streets below him, even though they were thronged with people in their thousands. The early light seemed harsh to his eyes, the onset of another headache, he knew. He hoped it would not be a major one.

It was when he squatted down to stretch his ham and back muscles that at last he spotted them, a formation of batwings gliding low over the rooftops towards the Temple District, ranged across half a laq. He stayed low as one of them soared directly overhead, so close that he caught a glimpse of the rider slung underneath the wing and heard the rattle of metal and harnesses before it was past. It left a little stirring of air that narrowed his eyes.

Ash caught a flash of white in the edge of his vision, off to the left where a building rose opposite the western side of the playhouse. He ducked even lower, and sidestepped across until he was pressed against the parapet for cover. He raised his head slowly and ventured a look.

An Acolyte was moving on the far building, a longrifle perched over his shoulder as he strolled around the rooftop, occasionally stopping to look down on the streets below. Ash turned around, surveying the other nearby roofs on the other side of the playhouse. On many of them, those which were flat, he saw white-robes emerging into the daylight.

Before him, the door began to squeal open.

Ash froze on the spot.

The door of the playhouse roof was located in the great concrete hand that stood at its centre, and on the far side from where he was squatting. Ash glanced to the base of the hand, where his spare cloak lay wrapped around his weapons.

An Acolyte stepped out into view from behind the hand. His back was to Ash, and he held a longrifle fitted with an eyeglass in one hand, and a pistol in the other. The white-robe shifted his balance as though to turn around.

Ash acted without thinking by flinging himself over the parapet.

A moment of vertigo passed through him as he hung by his fingertips from the side of the building. His legs dangled into space above the much lower roofs of the original playhouse below, and the thousands of heads bobbing through the streets. The sounds of the crowds were loud in his ears now, like an ocean removed of all sense of harmony, ragged and crashing against itself.

What am I doing down here? he wondered, as he gripped with all his strength the rough concrete edge of the parapet.

A scrape of feet sounded overhead. He looked up to see the Acolyte looking down at him, only his eyes visible through the mask. A breeze tugged at the edges of the figure's cloak; its curious patterns of silk glimmered in the daylight. In his mind, Ash saw the pyre burning again, and the white-robed Acolytes gathered around it, watching Nico burn.

'Give me a hand there,' Ash said to the man in Trade,

and released the precious grip of his left hand to hold it out for him. It was not a request, but a command.

The Acolyte shifted uncertainly. His eyes darted to the offered hand. Ash could feel the fingers of his other hand starting to burn, knew that soon they would go numb altogether. He thrust his free hand once more towards the Acolyte.

'Quickly there!'

The man laid his rifle down, though he held the pistol steady as he reached for Ash's grasp. Ash pretended he was unable to reach any further with his hand. The Acolyte leaned out to grab it.

Their hands met and clasped together. With a grunt, Ash heaved with all the strength in his arm and pulled the Acolyte forwards, off balance, so that the man toppled over the parapet and fell.

He heard a shout as the Acolyte went past him, and then nothing.

Ash hauled himself up over the parapet. He regained his feet, scanning the surrounding rooftops. No other Acolytes were looking his way. He exhaled long and hard, and glanced back over the parapet. The Acolyte lay crumpled in the rain-gully between two of the playhouse's roofs.

'*Huh!*' Ash exclaimed.

*

He stepped out into the chaos of the Serpentine with his hood pulled low over his face. It was a scene of festa in the wide boulevard and the side streets branching off from it. Many in the crowds seemed intoxicated already, and people waved the red-hand flags of Mann, or garlands of white and red flowers bought from the many flower sellers who had suddenly appeared on every street corner, next to the street merchants selling hot food, alcohol, narcotics. Soldiers were clearing the road and forcing everyone back to the sidewalks. He knew what that meant; knew too why they were flying batwings over the district and so earnestly checking the rooftops.

He jostled through the press, his roll of belongings carried under his arm. He found a clear space in an archway next to a hot-food vendor, from where he purchased a paper cup of hot chee and a wrap of pork meat and peppers, and enjoyed breaking his fast as children shrieked in excitement all around him.

An old mangy-coated dog came up to him, and sat and looked up at his food with drool dangling from its panting mouth.

'Hut,' he said to the dog as he tossed the last third of the wrap into its mouth. The dog wagged its tail across the paving, wolfing down the food in a few swallows. It looked up at him for more, its tail still swinging.

Ash wiped his greasy hands and held them up empty for the dog's inspection. 'No more,' he growled.

The dog lay down. Ash tried his best to ignore it as he leaned against the wall to ease the weight on his feet. There he waited beneath the archway, his eyes cast along the winding canyon that was the Serpentine, towards Freedom Square and beyond, where the Temple of Whispers reared high above a rabble of roofs and chimney stacks. He scratched his unkempt beard and listened to snatches of conversation around him. People spoke of the invasion ships in the harbour getting ready to set sail; of the Matriarch setting off for war. Questions abounded as to where they were destined.

At noon, a great battle-cry rose up from the direction of the square. Minutes later, it was followed by more cheering from further along the Serpentine. Over countless heads Ash spotted a procession making its way along the avenue. Painted red hands swayed from the tops of elaborately carved poles, and beneath them priests rocked to the same rhythm, decked out in their white robes and mirror-masks of burnished silver.

He turned his back to the street and bent low over his roll of belongings. The dog blinked and watched what

his hands were doing as Ash tugged free the crossbow
and locked its arms back into their firing position, glancing over his shoulder to see if he was being observed.
He pulled the double strings back and fitted a bolt into
place, then another, the scent of grease filling his nostrils.

For a moment, he experienced the sense of *wani*; of
having lived this moment before, and then it was gone.

When Ash stood with the crossbow gripped within
his cloak, the van of the procession was already passing
by. He surveyed the balconies across the street filled
with families rejoicing. Above them, Acolytes were positioned on several of the rooftops, studying the scene
below through the eyeglasses of their longrifles.

A roar from the crowd was spreading towards him
like a wave, matching pace with a high palanquin that
moved slowly along the street, near-lost in clouds of red
and white petals, people flinging them from the sidewalks or from the balconies above. He caught a flash of
her, Sasheen.

Soldiers struggled to hold back the crowds that
surged forward for a closer look at the Holy Matriarch,
or, even better, for the Matriarch to lay eyes upon them.

Sasheen looked resplendent today. She stood on a
massive palanquin in the form of a glittering, jewel-
encrusted dolphin, with oversized reins stretching back
from its mouth to a rail she was resting one hand on for
balance. The palanquin was borne on the backs of two
dozen naked slaves, and she swayed slightly as they
marched, her body encased in a contoured suit of white
armour, her golden mask sculpted in her own features.
She was holding aloft a stubby, gilded spear.

The adoration of the crowd heightened as the figure
of the Matriarch turned her masked face to regard them.
People fell to their knees in devotion. Ash witnessed several pilgrims fainting on the spot.

The crossbow was shaking in his hand as he lifted it
up and aimed it at her head.

All of his previous waiting, his long rooftop vigil,

seemed like the blink of an eye now. His chance had
come at last, his chance to lay the boy's torment to rest
within him. Ash tried to steady his aim, intensely aware
that he was about to cross a line that could not be un-
done. He would no longer be Rōshun after this. Even
though he had already cast that role aside by words, this
deed would be the real ending of it.

So be it. I'm dying anyway.

He curled his finger around the trigger, tracking her
as she came directly past him.

Something was wrong. A sheen of sunlight reflected
for a moment off the space around her. Ash hesitated,
squinting, and saw that she was surrounded by a box of
incredibly thin glass. He knew what it was in an instant; the exotic, toughened glass so sought after from
Zanzahar, and brought all the way from the Isles of Sky.
Nothing could pierce it save for explosives.

He lowered his crossbow in disgust, tucking it quickly
inside his cloak again.

Ash rocked back on the balls of his feet. To his surprise his heart was racing. He watched, stunned, as the
Matriarch went by unmolested, his hand squeezing the
grip of the crossbow in impotent frustration.

The dog whined from where it lay by his side. It
prompted him to act. With haste he disassembled the
crossbow and stowed it inside his rolled-up cloak next
to the eyeglass and the sword. He glanced at the Holy
Matriarch progressing along the Serpentine, knowing
that he needed to keep her in sight, to follow until some
opportunity presented itself. He hefted the burden and
turned to pursue her.

The Rōshun pushed on through the crowds, leaving
the dog staring after him.

*

Ash could smell the brine of the sea as he stalked the procession along the winding route of the Serpentine, knowing at last that they were nearing the First Harbour.

Along the sidewalks the crowds were packed so tightly he was finding it difficult to keep up with even the slow pace of the Matriarch's palanquin. It was like a dream of childhood, of trying to hurry through thickets of unyielding bamboo in the height of a storm. As he lost sight of her entirely, he growled and shoved through a group of men into a clearer side street. From there he proceeded by a different route to the harbour.

When he emerged onto the open quaysides, he stopped and took in the fleet lying at anchor there. It looked smaller than when last he had seen it, on the day he had bidden farewell to Baracha and the others on their journey home. The swarms of men-of-war that had previously been harboured there were largely gone now, save for a few remaining squadrons. The rest were heavy transports, the vessels surrounded by scores of rowing boats ferrying last-minute supplies and personnel from the quaysides. In their midst, the massive hulk of the imperial flagship loomed over them all.

He stood there watching helplessly as the foot-slaves bore Sasheen's palanquin across a gangplank, and onto a large barge that awaited them in the water. The rest of the Matriarch's entourage followed, and then the gangplank was pulled onboard, and long sweeps emerged to push the barge away from the wharf. It began to row out towards the flagship.

People brushed past him, though Ash barely noticed their touches. He didn't stir, his eyes filled with the sight of the barge heading out into the deep water of the harbour. All along the quayside the crowds were waving their Holy Matriarch off, shouting blessings on her forthcoming victory. Ash shot a hungry glance about him, seeking some way to follow her: a free rowing boat he could procure, perhaps, or a space on one of the boats already going back and forth between the fleet and the quay.

Chancy madness, he knew, born from his own desperation.

Easy, he said in his mind. *Calm yourself.*

Once more Ash made his way through the press with his bundle of weapons, and found a quieter spot against the brick wall of a warehouse. He looked out to sea, hoping for some inspiration to strike him.

Gradually the crowds dwindled, until it was mostly only those involved in the loading of the fleet who remained. The sun arced higher in the sky, its heat carried away in a breeze that was playing off the water. In ones and twos, the ships of the fleet completed the loading of their stores and set off for the open sea, pulled by their own sweeps or by rowing boats and ropes.

The flagship itself began to depart, drawn towards the harbour mouth by its own minor fleet of small vessels. Ash forced himself to remain seated.

For a while he studied the majority of vessels still at anchor, the lack of movement on many of their decks. He turned his attention to the chaos still apparent along the dockside. Tempers were running high, various captains along with their crews arguing with quartermasters as they tried to procure what supplies they still required.

At this rate, Ash pondered, many of those ships would be setting off in darkness. He leaned back, pulling his hood further down over his face. He crossed his arms and closed his eyes.

Without hurry, the autumn afternoon faded towards the onset of twilight.

*

There was a story told of the Great Fool, that Honshu sage of the Dao who had decried all dogmas, yet had himself become a religion after his own death. Every Rōshun apprentice was taught the story during his training.

While walking in the mountains along the source of the Perfume River, the Great Fool's newest follower, the branded woman Miri, had asked of him: *How does one remain still, great master?*

In reply, the Great Fool had cast a stick into the rushing torrent, and bade his followers to watch as it floated along with the flow.

But I am not a stick of wood, Miri had replied with frustration. *How can I flow with the stream so naturally?*

The Great Fool had tapped her forehead once, lightly. *By allowing your mind to be still.*

It was a paradox that had impressed Ash when he had first heard it as a Rōshun in training, for he'd been in great need of a saviour back then. Cast into exile with his fellow comrades, his family lost to him and with no hope of ever returning home, he had needed, desperately, something with which to tame the bleakness in his heart, and the runaway thoughts in his head that told him to end this life of his that was no longer worth living. And so he had embraced the Rōshun way of stillness, and it had saved him.

There was another story, one the Great Fool had himself used to instruct his followers, which Ash remembered too from that time.

A madman is held in a cage, with a blinded tiger as a companion.

For as long as he can remember, the madman has been walking from one side of the cage to the other, circling the tiger as it circles him, the animal snarling in hunger. For as long as he can remember, he has been leaping aside from its blind attacks, or standing silently in a corner watching it work its slow way around the bars. Never has it stopped this ranging about, so powerful are its desires.

One day, the madman finds he can no longer carry on this way. He stops his pacing. He turns his back on the tiger. He sits down and waits to die.

He falls asleep, or so he assumes – for when he opens his eyes again, all is different.

The door of the cage is hanging open. At long last, freedom beckons him.

The madman steps outside. He sees how everything is one in this place of all-consuming light. He sees how the bars of his confinement have been dividing his vision into narrow vertical slices for all this time. He looks to the tiger still prowling the cage. He sees how he has attached a name to it, and an identity, and a story of all the times they have shared together. He sees too how immature and petty, how strong and noble, the tiger truly is.

It is then that the man steps back into the cage with his earnest companion. The animal wishes to devour him even now; it still fears for its lasting survival.

But it does him no harm, for he is the master here.

He is sane.

It was in this way that Ash was no longer certain of himself. He no longer knew if he was flowing skilfully with the Dao in clear and detached purpose. Perhaps, in his grief, he had lost the Way.

How to know, though? How could he ever know the right way from the wrong way, when everything seemed equally as dark and unclear to him now?

Just breathe and go with it, the Chan monks of the Dao would have said. So Ash inhaled the cool night air deep into his lungs, and exhaled in a single long release all the pressure and confusion that was caught up within him; and from his stillness he launched himself from where he sat, springing up like a man on fire and sprinting through the darkness across the hard paving of the quayside, out onto the wooden planking of a jetty, pounding all the way to the very edge of it, where he leapt with a whoosh of breath and dived headfirst into the sea.

CHAPTER EIGHT

The Breach

The procession of cloud-men walked along the cob-bles with their black robes flapping in the wind and their voices loud as they chanted the solemn words of the death rite. Clatters sounded from the occasional coin dropped into their begging bowls; incense trailed grey and pungent around their shaven heads. In the hands of the oldest monk, following at the very back of their pro-cession, a wooden aeslo clapped together like the jaws of a mouth, beating a slow and steady rhythm that was a jolt to the senses every time that it sounded.

Bahn offered nothing as they passed by. It wasn't that he wished to refuse them a donation; he simply couldn't rouse himself enough to perform the simple act of it. He was standing as though buried ten feet within himself, looking out through a bramble of whispered thoughts in a weariness that had become familiar to him now.

All he desired just then was to skip his duties this afternoon, and catch a rickshaw back to their home in the north of the city, and climb into bed, and pull the blankets over his head, and shut out the world until morning.

He had been plagued with this lethargy for a week now. Achieving sleep had always been a nightly struggle for Bahn, his head spinning with reflections and con-cerns. Yet now, no matter how much sleep he was able to manage, whether three hours of tossing and turning or ten hours of total oblivion, he would still wake feel-ing lifeless and drained.

It was all he could do to watch in dull silence as the monks rustled along the street between the lines of on-lookers paying their respects; and after them, the pale mourners who followed, the small jar of ashes cradled

in a young man's arm, his even younger wife next to
him, barely able to walk without support.

Bahn needed to resume walking again, if only to in-
vigorate his senses. Not wishing to show his disrespect
by rushing past them all, he stepped behind the mourners for a while, trying not to yawn as he watched their
grief from behind.

*

He headed south, through the bustling Quarter of Barbers, that district where Bahn had been born and raised,
along with his two brothers. From there the Mount of
Truth could be seen rising gently over the rooftops to
the west, the hill with a crown of green parkland around
its flattened summit, and a building of white that was
the Ministry of War, where Bahn reported on most days
to his superior, General Creed.

Not today, though. With the lull in the fighting, the
general had taken the opportunity to fly to Minos on a
personal mission of diplomacy, or so he had deigned to
explain it when Bahn had voiced his curiosity. Bahn
hoped he would not be long in returning. It had become
a daily chore of his to field the endless missives from the
Michinè council, demanding to know when the Lord
Protector would be back, why he'd failed to seek their
consent before deserting Bar-Khos and the Shield for so
long.

Bahn had begun to respond with the same stock answer every time. He simply copied it from a carefully
worded page he kept lying on his desk.

He passed a long line of refugees and locals waiting
for their bread rations from one of the council-sponsored
bakeries. It made him wonder if he should buy some
food for the energy it might give him. Bahn had been
eating less lately too, often giving his share of their meagre supplies to Marlee and the children. When he walked
through Hawkers' Plaza, though, the food stalls of the
small bazaar were nearly empty, and what little was on

display bore prices he could hardly justify squandering with his few coins. Better to grab some plain bread and beans from one of the mess tents when he could.

He stopped as he emerged onto the High King's Road, the longest thoroughfare of Bar-Khos, running from east to west along the coastline for the entire breadth of the city. The High King's Road crossed the mouth of the Lansway, the thin isthmus that ran out towards the distant southern continent, and upon which stood the distant ranked walls of the Shield. The road too overlooked All Fools here, the closest district to the Shield and the only civilian area to be found on the isthmus proper, packed now to bursting with refugees. Beyond it lay the canal that intersected the Lansway to connect both harbours, and, beyond that, a line of construction that was a new wall in the making, dwarfed by Tyrill's Wall, which rose as sheer and massive as a cliff, given scale by the occasional small speck of a Red Guard patrolling its crenellated crown.

Reluctantly, Bahn trod towards it.

*

The no-man's land between the walls was churned expanses of planked walkways and sagging field tents, bordered on either side by the sea-walls and ahead and behind by the larger walls of the Shield, so that the space within them contained the acoustics and light of a deep valley trough. The chaos of city life was replaced with orderly discipline and the raw mood of men who fought every day on the top of the ramparts, and below them.

A full army was garrisoned here in these spaces between the foremost two walls of the Shield. Stepping out of a postern gate in the penultimate wall, Bahn found himself in the principal military encampment of the war. Ahead stood Kharnost's Wall. It was the only thing now standing between himself and the Imperial Fourth Army on the other side.

A full chartassa of heavy infantry drilled in formation under the heat of the noonday sun, their step sergeants screeching out commands for the manoeuvres they were expertly practising. He watched as the phalanx of men halted with a stamp of their feet, and the front ranks lowered the glittering warheads of the spears they called charta, and cried out with a collective shout. Red Guards and League Volunteers strode amongst the tents. Specials lingered next to the open-sided towers that perched over the pitheads of the tunnels that ran beneath Kharnost's Wall, where the siege engineers laboured in the dark earth, and the Specials fought when they were needed.

Over by the mess tents, a group of Greyjackets and Volunteers had stripped to their trousers and were playing a game of cross. Colonel Halahan was there, smoking his pipe as he stood in his plain grey uniform, offering the occasional bellow to the men of his brigade, all of them internationals from abroad; Nathalese, Pathian, Tilanian and beyond. Across from him, Halahan's counterpart in the Free Volunteers appeared to be offering encouragement to his own men by way of laughing at their mistakes.

The Volunteers were fighters from Minos and the other islands of the democras. They held nothing back as they gestured and swore at their mocking officer in a manner that always surprised Bahn whenever he came across it; such informality would never have been tolerated within the rigid hierarchy of the Khosian army. Just like the Greyjackets they were competing against, these men had no superiors save for those they most respected; they could even dismiss and replace their officers by a show of hands whenever that respect was lost.

Halahan raised a hand now at the sight of Bahn, and Bahn nodded in response to the old Nathalese veteran. 'Colonel Halahan,' he called out in greeting. 'You look well.'

'You're a bloody bad liar, Bahn,' the old veteran

shouted back, just as one of his men was knocked sprawling to the ground before him, and he was in snarling amongst them all, breaking up a fight.

Bahn was in the shadow of Kharnost's Wall long before he reached it. The guns along the top of the battlements sat silently, but sharp-shooters were taking the odd shot up there.

It was the breach of Kharnost's Wall that Bahn had come to inspect this afternoon, that section which had collapsed in the previous month after it had been undermined by the Imperials, and which had been hard fought over for a week until the defenders had been able to plug it with debris.

It drew Bahn to it now, a pale jumbled wedge filling a broken portion of the great rampart. A makeshift job, he could see even before he reached it. Men and zels laboured to lift blocks of cut stone into place as they built a thin sheath wall to cover the loose filler. Still, they said the rampart would be permanently weakened here.

It had been a while, Bahn realized, since he'd actually mounted Kharnost's Wall and looked to the other side. Not often were the guns so subdued, the air so clear of flying projectiles. Bahn decided to take a look.

He could feel sweat on his forehead by the time he had hiked the long steps to the very top. It was the armour: he'd never learned the knack of carrying its weight properly. On the upper parapet he placed a hand on a crenellation and tilted his helm back to wipe at his brow. A pair of Red Guards cast him a glance then returned to their game of rash; their lieutenant paid him no notice at all, the man was occupied with eyeing the isthmus beyond.

Bahn peered over the battlements himself. He saw dark lines of earthworks, and siege guns still wrapped in their night protections of straw and oiled canvas. Here and there were movements of white, and the odd desultory puff of smoke from one of their snipers.

Behind their lines spread the vast encampment of the Imperial Fourth Army, like a smoky, sleepy city.

We should ask them if they fancy a game of cross, he thought. *We could settle the entire war here and now and get on with our lives.*

Below, on the Khosian side, the game of cross was just finishing. He could see Halahan limping towards the wall as though he intended to climb its steps. Bahn had little wish to talk to the man, or anyone else just then.

He moved on, unconsciously keeping low as he stepped along the parapet towards the site of the breach, feeling exposed at each wind-blown open space between the teeth of the crenellations, and the occasional gaping emptiness where a section of the battlements had fallen away entirely. No one else was walking bent over, though, nor showing the least sign of concern about the odd incoming shot. Bahn forced himself to straighten his back and to walk in a way more befitting an officer.

He stopped as the battlements dropped away altogether, the stonework ragged where the undermined wall had collapsed. Bahn gaped down at the filled-in breach.

The rubble and earth that plugged the gap was a good half-throw across in size. It had been tamped down and floored with loose planking, and a crude barricade of stone blocks had been set across it for cover, although no one was out there just now. The breach itself was no longer visible from the Mannian side of the Shield. It was faced with the same great slope of earth that fronted the rest of the wall, the only defence they had found that could withstand the constant bombardments of cannon.

Still, it was certainly visible from where he stood, and Bahn could not tear his gaze from it. He stared at the broken section of wall as though staring into the depths of himself, feeling some kind of affinity with this weakened mass of stone.

He thought of the note that had arrived from Minos intelligence the week before, suggesting the possibility of an imminent invasion of Khos. He had been bound by duty to keep the news to himself; it was, after all, only a supposition of the enemy's plans. Even Marlee he had kept in the dark, not wanting to cause her unnecessary worries; she had known that something was wrong with him anyway, had noticed the despondent way he carried himself these days. And then the guns on the Mannian side had fallen silent, supposedly as part of the Empire's period of mourning. To Bahn, it had seemed more as if they were catching their breath for the onslaught to come.

Bahn removed his helmet, set it down on a surviving crenellation next to him with a scrape of metal. A cistern was built into the battlements here, filled with rainwater, and he drank a few sips from a cup fixed to it by a chain. Sated, he leaned against the stonework and gazed out over the Lansway, lost in the tumult of his thoughts.

A thunderstorm was trailing curtains of rain across the far end of the isthmus and the crust of hills that stretched away on either side of it: the very tip of the southern continent, and the land of Pathia, now ten years fallen to Mann. His hair blew about in the breeze as birds wheeled high and aimless in the sky above.

He ducked as a shot whined off the stonework near to him. Bahn turned to look at where it had struck, and saw Halahan standing there with the foot of his bad leg propped up on the rubble of the broken battlement, a hand on his raised knee, his other holding the clay pipe in the corner of his mouth, coolly studying a breath of dust drifting from the stonework next to his boot.

The Nathalese veteran leaned and spat on the chalky bullet-strike as though putting out a flame, then spoke to Bahn without turning to him. 'Thinking of some poke?'

Bahn blinked, not understanding his meaning.

'You seemed lost, a moment ago. I wondered if you were thinking of some lass.'

Bahn rose from his crouch and brushed fingers through his hair and fixed the helm back on his head. He was careful all the while to remain behind the protection of the battlements. 'You walk quieter than a mountain lion,' he replied to the Nathalese man, before he realized what he was saying.

Halahan was gracious enough not to glance down at the hinged metal support that wrapped a good portion of his leg, but instead simply met his gaze. A dark humour played in the backs of his eyes, which shone with the dazzling dark blue of setting skies. Bahn had always liked the Nathalese commander of the Greyjacket brigade, had always respected his no-nonsense manner, without guile or self-importance – unlike so many of the other officers he knew within the army.

The colonel had been a priest once, or so he'd heard, though it was hard to see anything of the religious man about him now. Instead there was something windburned about his character, and something lawless.

'I was thinking of that fleet in Q'os,' Bahn confessed. 'I was wondering if it would be setting forth soon, and if so, for where.'

'You were wondering if it would be coming here.'

'Of course. Aren't you?'

Halahan seemed to laugh without showing it anywhere but in his eyes.

'Is the old man back yet?' he asked him.

Ah, thought Bahn.

'No. And the council are flapping my ears off about it.'

'I can imagine. It looks bad on them when the Lord Protector goes off by himself asking for League reinforcements.'

'You think that's what he's doing there?'

'Certainly. Amongst other things. What else can he

do? The council would rather bury their heads in the sand. By the sounds of it they're just hoping the Mannians invade Minos rather than here.'

Bahn offered a shrug, but the motion was lost beneath the shoulder-guard of his armour. 'Maybe they're right, then. Minos could be as much a target. They're being hard hit as we speak.'

'Aye, I've been following the reports. Imperial Diplomats running amok in Al-Minos. The Second Fleet engaged in a battle with sizeable enemy formations.' Halahan sounded as though he didn't believe any of it. 'And the Third Fleet dispatched from our waters to help, it's so bad. Handy that. If you wanted to slip an invasion fleet down here from Lagos unmolested.'

Halahan puffed on his pipe as the wind jostled his long grey hair about his face. It did not seem as though he was discussing the matter of their possible extinction here. Bahn had often wondered about these men who lived through war as though it were an ordinary life to them. How they were able to switch off their imaginations from the worst of fates that could befall them. How they glided through their lives whether in peace or in battle.

He was envious of anyone who exhibited such traits. Bahn never seemed to stop being frightened of the future and the war. And he certainly didn't glide through his life; he trod furtively with his attention darting left and right, always concerned at making a false step or saying the wrong thing. Perhaps he should develop a taste for drinking more, like so many of his fellow officers. Or for the hazii weed, like Halahan always seemed to be smoking. Even now he could smell it in the odd twist of the wind.

A flight of skyships was circling over the city, far above the merchant balloons tethered to their towers, higher even than the wheeling birds. Bahn had dreamed the other night that he and his family had been aboard one of those magnificent flying vessels, heading towards the rising sun in search of sanctuary.

'You know, don't you, that every one of them has a private ship moored in the western harbour. Fast sloops with their crews on standby, in case the Shield ever falls.'

Bahn nodded absently. He listened to the cuff of the wind against his ears.

'Still,' he spoke at last, and his voice sounded fragile, ready to break. 'The feint could be here, don't you think? Minos could be their real target.'

Halahan studied him for a time, the humour gone from his eyes.

The man placed a hand on Bahn's shoulder.

'Better get your head straight, son,' Halahan told him softly. 'They're coming for us all right.'

—CHAPTER NINE—

In the Company of Rats

The ship sped along on its south-easterly course with its sails straining fat with wind and its prow clipping through the rise and fall of the swells. Ché stood by the rail with the salty spray hissing past the hull, the vessel thrumming beneath him as it bore them across the Heart of the World.

To others, he looked as though he was merely taking in the sea air on another day on their journey east. For Ché, it was a form of meditation standing like this, his mind focused on the flow of his breathing and the senses of his body. It was a pleasure to be this way, so much so that a slight unconscious smile curled the corners of his mouth.

He didn't dare do any more than this. Not here, not in the presence of so many of his peers. To squat down now on the main deck in the customary position of a Daoist monk, or a Rōshun for that matter – kneeling with spine erect, thoughtless and still – would be an open challenge to them all. Remarks would be made. Something would be said to him by one of the Mon-barri, threats veiled behind skilful questions of double meaning.

His feet rocking to the gentle swaying of the ship, Ché could see the wheelhouse rising high before him in the mid-section of the ship, a legion of signal flags fluttering from the top of it. Behind him, at the stern of the vessel, the quarterdeck rose three storeys tall, where the stately cabins of the Holy Matriarch were located, along with those of her two generals. Sasheen was up there now, on the uppermost deck, taking in the sea air like Ché himself, though she was seated in a deep wicker chair and wrapped in a heavy fur cloak against the bite of the wind, surrounded by white screens to shield her position. Between the screens, Archgeneral Sparus and young Romano could be glimpsed sitting on either side of her, engaged in conversation and attended by slaves. The Matriarch wasn't looking at them as they spoke. Sasheen was watching the skyship that was passing overhead, one of their birds-of-war guarding the invasion fleet; a scattering of vessels that stretched ahead and behind as far as the eye could see.

He sensed rather than heard the approach of some-one behind him.

'Don't dwell on it,' came the quiet voice of a man. 'It's always much worse than you can imagine anyway.'

Ché felt a moment's irritation, and turned his head to see Guan standing there, the young man of the Morta-rus sect who had come aboard with his sister as part of Sasheen's travelling entourage. The priest stood dwarfed by the ship's great masts and sails that diminished half the sky.

'And what's that?' Ché enquired drily.

'The invasion. You've never been to war, have you?'

Ché simply shook his head.

'I was there with my sister, the last time we invaded the Free Ports. It wasn't a pretty sight.'

'You were in Coros? You hardly look old enough.'

'No. We hardly were. Our father was the commander of the Fifty-Fifth Lights. Bringing us along was his idea of an *education*. And we learned, all right. We learned what a warhead could do to the integrity of his skull.'

His father, Ché reflected. It was rare for a priest to speak of a father; to even know who the man was.

He saw that Guan was waiting for him to ask more, so instead he said nothing. He wished only to be left alone.

It was Guan who broke the silence. 'You don't know what I'm saying, do you?'

'I haven't the faintest idea.'

'Then you're not alone. The people on this ship seem to have no idea of what they're getting into either. These aren't some northern tribesmen that we plan to invade here. Or an army of Lagosian insurgents, for that matter. These are Khosians, with the finest chartassa in all the Free Ports. They've fought off more invasions than most of the southern nations combined.'

Ché was in no mood for horror stories of war today. The man simply wished to show off, to notch himself a little higher than Ché.

'I see. A people to be feared.'

Guan stared hard at Ché, and Ché stared out to sea.

'I'm wondering if you've balled anything lately, Ché? You seem a little uptight.' And Guan smiled suddenly, as though that would make it fine to say these things to him. 'Or perhaps you're getting plenty enough from the Matriarch herself?'

Ché allowed a scowl to show in his eyes.

'You're either a fool or a lunatic, Guan. I think your Mortarus training leads you too close to a worship of death.'

Guan shrugged without care. A fool, then, Ché decided. 'I see you don't deny it.'

Ché turned away from the man, refusing to be drawn into this conversation. He wondered once more if Guan and his sister were not in fact Regulators in disguise, and if Guan was merely playing at being a careless fool. Indeed, Ché had been surprised at this man's insistence in befriending him, had wondered if perhaps he had been tasked with watching Ché during the long voyage to Khos.

Guan sighed as though ridding himself of frustration. 'Have you eaten yet?'

'I'm fine.'

'Later, then. We can share a drink perhaps, and find ourselves another game of cards. It's your turn to lose, as I recall.'

'Perhaps,' responded Ché.

He waited until he heard the man walking away, then gradually relaxed again.

It was often this way with his peers. Even a few moments of simple chatter could seem like a squabble over spilled milk. How could it not be? They had been raised knowing three things above all else in life: their own self-importance, their freedom to pursue every desire, and their voracious need to defeat each other. Always they would look for ways to better him, to manipulate him; it grew tiresome after a while, when all he wanted was some honest companionship. It made him as hostile as they were.

The price, of course, was one of alienation, but Ché had found the alternative to be even worse: alienation from his true self. He felt lost when he was with these people for too long, weakened in his own struggling convictions.

Guan was wrong about one thing. The men and women on board were hardly ignorant of what they were facing. He could feel it all around him, the tension in the air, the quietness.

Ché's gaze roamed up to look at the Matriarch again, the woman still listening to the talk of her two generals. Romano was a dangerous one to bring on this expedition. The young general was the greatest contender for Sasheen's throne; hence, Ché suspected, she had elected to suffer his presence during the campaign, fearing what troubles he might foment during her absence from the capital. But he was to be feared here too, for with him had come his contribution to the invasion force, his own private military company of sixteen thousand men. If it came to it, they would be loyal to their paymasters, Romano and his family, before even the Holy Matriarch herself.

Such a dynamic could only provoke tensions on a long voyage such as this one. Sasheen and Romano despised each other at the best of times, even when they conversed with seeming civility. Ché wondered how long it would be before they were at each other's throats, and before he himself was dragged into it.

He tried to breathe all the nonsense from his head and return to the peaceful state of before. It was no good. His calm mood had been spoilt.

Ché made his way through the sailors and marines and priests on the weatherdeck and headed for the forward hatchway. On his way he passed a squad of Acolytes training naked in the sunshine, serious young men and women much the same age as himself, with a handful of older veterans amongst them. They were taking turns sparring with each other, or limbering up while they waited their turn.

'Watch it,' one of them snapped as he backed into Ché.

For an instant, Ché wanted to grab his arm and break it.

'Eat shit,' he snapped back at him without breaking step.

Before Ché descended the steps he noticed Sasheen eyeing him from her vantage above. She raised a flask of wine in a toast, and he bobbed his head at her, and quickly descended.

*

Blackness smothered Ash for every day and night he lay down there in the bilge of the ship, this fat rolling transport where he'd stowed himself aboard as the fleet had left Q'os harbour. Blackness, and a closeness of air so foul it was hardly fit to inhale, and a battering of noise never-ending: the ballast of sand and loose gravel shifting against the hull; the creaks and bangs of the hull; the splashes of the rats in the darkness – all of it conspired to unhinge him.

Ash had found a space above the slosh of the water on which to lie, a projection of wood near the aft of the bilge, a few feet in width, where he had wedged himself next to his sword. He lived like one of the rats down there, and although he couldn't see the rising and setting of the sun, he knew when it was dawn by the pounding of feet overhead as the shifts were changed, and when it was night by the raucous sounds of laughter and songs.

Like a shy scavenger he stole out in the dead of night to find water and what scraps of food he could to sustain himself, creeping silently through the black spaces of the ship while most of the crew were asleep. Upon his return from these ventures he would sit on his narrow ledge and eat, and what was left he would feed to the small colony of rats that lived down there with him, muttering to them quietly in the darkness. Soon, they stopped trying to eat him in his sleep. Some even began to climb onto his body and huddle there for warmth.

His usual headaches subsided, perhaps due to the lack of any sunlight, which was fortunate, for he'd almost run out of his precious dulce leaves. Constantly he shivered from the dampness, though, and knew it was getting into his chest. His breathing was becoming tight and restricted. He feared he would develop pneumonia.

Ash thought of dying down here in this black hole, and imagined his corpse floating from one side to the other in the rancid bilge water, the rats making good use of him until he was nothing but bones settling loosely upon the ballast. He tried at times to dry his clothes – the leather leggings lined with cotton, the sleeveless tunic – by wringing them out then spreading them against the curve of the hull, but, like his boots, they refused to dry. One night, he took a risk and was lucky enough to steal a heavy oiled cloak from one of the sleeping crew above. He wrapped his naked body in it and hoped it would do.

Occasionally, Ash found himself wondering where the fleet was headed. He recalled seeing a map in the Storm Chamber when he and Aléas had finally breached it, something denoting movements of fleets. He hadn't looked at it properly, though, and try as he might he failed to picture any details now.

Mostly, he just wondered how soon the fleet would reach land. He wasn't sure how much longer he could stand it down here in this bilge that had become his private misery.

Ash was sixty-two years of age, long past the life expectancy of a Rōshun still working in the field. The years had certainly taken their toll on him; his body felt stretched thin and taut these days. His joints ached from arthritis, and his muscles tended to complain whenever he moved too swiftly or demanded too much of them. It took longer for him to heal; even now, the minor knife wound in his leg from the vendetta was still festering, so that daily he had to squeeze the pus from it and clean it out with seawater.

In a way, Ash didn't mind further confinement in this black pit he had crawled into. Within his own depths he felt as if he deserved to be there, that he would gladly suffer an eternity of this desolation if it meant bringing Nico back to the living. Beneath the oiled cloak, he could feel the small clay vial of ashes lying cold and dead against his chest.

CHAPTER TEN

A Matter of Diplomacy

'The Holy Matriarch requests a moment of your time,' cooed Guan, standing there with his twin sister, both watching him with their hooded, arrogant eyes.

Ché gripped the open cabin door a little harder as they all swayed with the violent motions of the ship. All around them, the flagship groaned and complained against the buffeting of the heavy seas. The sister was studying him closely, and he stared back at her, her face as sharp and lean as her brother's, her thin lips slightly parted on one side.

He held his forefinger up. *One moment.*

Ché closed the Scripture of Lies in his hand, making sure they saw it first, then replaced it on his neatly made cot in plain sight. He stepped out into the passageway and followed them.

He was glad of a chance to stretch his legs, despite his usual sense of foreboding whenever he was summoned by the Matriarch. He hadn't ventured out much these several days past, the weather being too poor for dallying out in the open. Today was the worst so far. The ship pitched so steeply from side to side they had to walk with their hands along the walls of the passageway to keep their balance.

One by one they stepped up onto the main deck and bent into the blasts of wind. A gust sent the sister stumbling sideways, tottering with outstretched hands before her brother tugged her by the sleeve back to his side. A wave crashed against the hull and threw a froth of water hissing over the decking, knocking over a few sailors so they went sliding amongst it in their rainslicks.

The three priests wiped their faces dry, and in a line made for the steps that zigzagged up the flank of the quarterdeck, where they started to haul themselves up.

'A little choppy today!' the sister, Swan, called back at him.

Guan looked back too, his expression cool.

The man hadn't spoken with Ché for some days now. Perhaps Guan had finally taken his hint about wanting to be left alone.

Still, there was a look in his eyes; something wounded in them. Not the reaction he would have expected if these twins really were Regulators in disguise. Perhaps he was simply being paranoid after all.

This is why I am without friendships, he thought.

At the door of General Romano's cabin they passed a pair of Acolytes stationed as guards, sheltering as best they could beneath the tiny porch. Within, even over the din of the gale and the waves, the raised voice of Romano could be heard cutting through the laughter of his people. Like many, the young general had been revelling in drink and narcotics since the bad weather had confined them all to their quarters.

On the topmost floor, at the door to Sasheen's private cabins, the three of them stood within the porch as the honour-guards searched them for weapons. The sister was last, and as she was carefully patted down Ché noticed how her brother watched the process with a frown. She ignored his scrutiny, though, looked at Ché instead with her features softened by a delicate smile.

Pretty, he thought, and glanced down at her body without subtlety, her wet robe clinging to it.

'Clear,' said the Acolyte as he finished, and his partner knocked on the door.

Heelas, Sasheen's personal caretaker, beckoned them into the salon, where priests of the entourage lounged in a subdued silence. Heelas led the three of them across to the door of Sasheen's private cabin and rapped a knuckle on it gently, then opened it and passed through without waiting for a response.

The moment Ché entered the room he could feel it, the anger in the air. Sasheen sat on her great chair at the rear of the spacious cabin. She was wrapped in a fur coat over plain robes. Her chest was rising and falling quickly. Ché noticed a broken wineglass at the foot of the wall, and drops of red wine amongst the shattered glass, running one way then the other as the floor pitched from side to side.

Around the Holy Matriarch were gathered those of her inner circle. Her old friend Sool was there, sitting by her side on a cushioned stool, turned half around so she could stare out through the windows at the ragged sea and clouds beyond. Klint the physician was as ruddy-faced as always as he pulled absently on one of his piercings. Alarum, vaguely known to Ché as a spymaster in the Élash, offered a congenial nod of the head, eyes keenly observing him. Lastly, Archgeneral Sparus, the Little Eagle, stood in the centre of the room as though he had just stopped pacing, one eye covered with an eye-patch, the other pinning Ché in its glare.

Ché ignored him and glanced around the room itself. His quick search took in the jar of Royal Milk bracketed on a table behind Sasheen, then stopped at the two bodyguards standing outside on the balcony, huddling beneath their hoods.

'Diplomat,' Sasheen declared with a rueful twist of her lips. She was intoxicated, he could see, though it was only obvious by her reddened cheeks and nose, for the Matriarch spoke with focus. 'I have a task for you, Diplomat.'

Ché bowed his head. 'Matriarch,' he said with false calm.

'I need you to send a message to General Romano. As swiftly as you can manage it.'

Ché stifled the beginnings of a smile. *And so it begins.*

'And what is the tone of this message, Matriarch?'

'A warning only,' rumbled Archgeneral Sparus with a glance to Sasheen. 'His catamite lover should suffice.'

'Make an example of him,' drawled Sasheen. 'A fitting one. Do you hear me?'

Another bow of his head. 'Is that all?'

Sasheen pinched the bridge of her nose, not responding.

'You may go,' replied Sool.

The twin priests accompanied him back outside. Ché hesitated in the shelter of the porch. He looked to the brother and was about to address him when he changed his mind, spoke to the sister instead.

'Any notion as to what this is about?'

She looked amused by his directness. The brother shifted by her side, glanced to the two guards standing behind them.

'Romano has been slandering the Holy Matriarch,' Guan replied before she could speak. 'In his chambers, intoxicated with his entourage.'

'In what way?'

Swan leaned towards him, her piercings dripping water. 'Her son,' she said quietly. 'He's been slandering her son.'

Ché blew an exasperated breath of air from his lips, understanding at last.

*

That afternoon they caught their first sight of Lagos, ill-fated island of the dead.

The bad weather finally settled down, as if it wished to strike a more solemn chord for the occasion; though really it was only that they had sailed into the lee of the island. South they headed towards the harbourage of Chir, with the rest of the fleet tightening up around them. White cliffs rose along the coastline, and green slopes covered by grey flecks that were the famous Lagosian long-haired goats.

It seemed that every one of the thousand souls onboard the flagship now crowded along the rails. Ché watched the Matriarch where she stood on the foredeck, flanked by her two generals and their entourages.

He studied the trio closely, curious as to how they

must feel gazing upon green Lagos, that island of insurrection, its entire population so famously put to the
torch. The Sixth Army, still stationed there, now due
to become part of the Expeditionary Force, had been
led by Archgeneral Sparus when they'd finally put
down the rebellion. And it had been Sasheen herself
who had given the order to kill the majority of the
citizenry in retribution for their support of the rebels,
even against the protests of many within the order itself, horrified by the loss of so much potential revenue
in slaves.

In doing so, the Matriarch had stamped her authority
on the pages of history. She would never be forgotten
for this act of genocide.

Yet now, facing Lagos for the first time, Sasheen offered nothing but stiff-necked formality as she stood by
the rail, while around her, the gathered priests of her entourage seemed more proud than anything else at having
reacquired this most prized of possessions.

Back in Q'os, the news-sheets were filled with stories of the island's *pacification*, and how the land was
now open to immigrants from across the Empire. They
played down the true extent of the slaughter wrought
upon the Lagosians, and blamed them when they did
mention the burnings and the clearances by pointing
out how the rebellion had first begun: as a protest by
the surviving Lagosian nobility, unable to stomach the
continuing losses of their tenanted lands to their new
Mannian masters.

Only a single detail betrayed anything of Sasheen's
inner condition. Beside her, on the rail, she had planted
the living head of Lucian – the first time she had chosen
to display him in such a way in public. The Matriarch
held a palm against its scalp to keep it there, so that the
leader of the insurrection could look upon his desolated
homeland in his own unfathomable silence.

*

Horns sounded from the foremost ships of the fleet ahead. They were approaching the harbour of Chir at last, one of the greatest marvels of the known world. Soon, as they rounded a rocky headland, Ché gazed open-mouthed at the legendary Oreos as it rose impossibly high before him, that colossal arch which spanned the natural mouth of the harbour inlet of Chir, the clouds of mist rolling beneath it.

The cityport of Chir, once rich from its trade in wool and salted meat with Zanzahar, and the former high seat of the Lagosian civilization, sprawled around a rocky inlet that formed the largest natural harbourage in the Midèrēs. The city had constructed the Oreos across its harbour entrance as the grandest of statements to the world. Cast in iron, it resembled a blade bent into a curve so that its flatness cut the wind in two, gleaming a brilliant painted white beneath a sky that had finally broken to reveal the sun.

He'd never before travelled to Lagos or its port of Chir, though he'd read much about them, and of the feat of art and engineering that he now gazed at. The mists were caused by seawater pumped by the motion of the waves into the body of the arch itself, and out through the countless nozzles arrayed along its underside to create the finest of sprays.

On some days, banded colours could be seen within the hazy span of the Oreos. It was common to see four or five or even six rainbows stretching through the spray or reflecting across the surface of water. The *Rainbow Catcher*, the people of Lagos often called it, with affection. Or they had done, when they had still lived here.

Ché could see one now, a bow of vibrant colours like a second archway, and beyond it, tinged by its hues, the sprawl of the city around the banks of the harbour, with imperial ships already at anchor there. He shaded his eyes with a hand and squinted up to the top of the Oreos. He could make out tiny figures up there, white-robed priests gathered along a railing, taking in the sights of the cityport from its high elevation.

Ché would have studied the scene for longer, but his eyes just then caught movement up on the foredeck. It was Romano's catamite, Topo, striding over to the general and the woman in his lap to exchange a flurry of heated words.

Topo whirled away and stamped towards the steps.

With a final glance cast at the approaching Oreos, Ché pushed himself from the rail. He tracked the youth as he returned alone to Romano's cabin, red-faced and shoving past the guards at the door. Ché waited a few moments longer to ensure that no one was joining him, then set about delivering his message.

*

He entered Romano's chambers silently via the rear balcony, while everyone overhead, including the guards, stood on the landward side taking in the sights of the harbour.

In the cabin, with the sounds of splashing water coming from the bathroom, Ché murdered a bodyguard with the slash of a knife across his throat.

He stepped back from the mess as the man collapsed onto the rug.

'Hello?' came a voice from the bathroom beyond.

Ché stood still for some moments while the man gargled blood at his feet. He listened until he heard the gentle splash of water once more from the other side of the door. With a garrotte dangling from one hand, he pushed the bathroom door slightly ajar. Steam escaped around his shaven head.

He looked in to see the man lying in the wooden bathtub, muttering to himself with his eyes squeezed shut. Ché slipped inside, and stopped behind his head as he gripped the garrotte in both fists. He gazed down on Romano's young lover. There were fresh scars over his pale, lean body; scabbed bruises the size of bite marks.

Ché observed the great bronze pot of a water-heater sitting on the stove at the foot of the tub, and knew what he must do.

The young man jerked, and snapped his eyes open as Ché looped the garrotte around his neck and pulled hard on the cork handles.

Brown eyes, Ché noted, near popping out of their sockets; and there, within the glassy pupils, a shadow, Ché himself looming large. The youth snorted and wheezed for air, his face bulging. His hands scrabbled at the garrotte around his throat. His legs flailed in the water spilling in waves over the side to splash around Ché's sandalled feet. The Diplomat maintained his steady pressure. He thought of nothing as he performed the act, though he felt, strangely, a rising sense of anger.

At last, Topo stopped floundering and lay limp in the settling water. Ché maintained pressure for a few moments more, then released the garrotte with a gasp.

Panting, he kicked open the door of the stove beneath the heater and tossed in a log from the wooden bin that sat next to it, then after that as many more as would fit. Then he unlatched the lid of the pot to expose the warming water within. Quickly, he hauled the body out of the bath, with his hands slipping on its slick skin. Ché was strong enough for all his modest height; still, it was an effort to lift the dead weight of Topo into the great pot, to make it fit as the displaced water rose up around it, so he could replace and refasten the lid.

By the time he was finished the flames of the stove were starting to roar. He imagined the smoke tumbling out of the chimney far above his head; hoped it wouldn't draw Romano's early return. He stepped from the bathroom and listened for the sounds of footfalls.

Behind him, the bronze water-heater made a sudden popping sound. Ché stopped.

Another thump sounded from within it.

He's still alive in there.

Ché hesitated, at once caught in a moment of self-doubt. He glanced back through the doorway, struggling with an impulse to rush inside and unlatch the lid and haul the lad out from there.

He fought it down. He'd spent too long at this already.

Ché strode across the main cabin while a faint scream pursued him to the open window. It shook him to hear it; his hands trembled as he clambered out onto the balcony, cursing himself for his own carelessness.

From the bathroom, the scream grew in pitch until it was consumed by the piercing shriek of steam that suddenly blasted through a whistle.

*

In the early evening chaos of the Chir harbour, Ché waited in line before the thronged gantry, impatient to be off the ship so that he could sample some of the attractions of the ancient cityport.

On the other side of the gantry, the dockside was awash with slaves manhandling fresh supplies onto the waiting ships, and a host of newly arrived immigrants from elsewhere in the empire, drawn to the island's sudden land rush now that it was conveniently deserted. Through them all, in stamping columns, the grim, orderly troops of the Sixth Army marched aboard the transports in preparation for the dawn departure, when the newly combined army and fleet of the Expeditionary Force would set sail for Khos.

He was first aware of trouble when he heard the distinct sound of shouting up towards the quarterdeck. He turned instinctively towards Sasheen's quarters, saw that the Matriarch's door was lying open, her honour guard nowhere to be seen.

Ché swore under his breath, then bounded for the steps and the open doorway. He passed the two twins,

Guan and Swan, standing at the top of the stairway with their expressions wholly neutral.

Inside, the guards were struggling with a group of priests who were trying desperately to protect General Romano. The man raved beyond reason, his spit flying towards the Holy Matriarch, who sat in a chair flanked by her two personal bodyguards, watching his fury with a self-satisfied smile. Ché's eyes widened as he saw a flash of a blade in the young general's hand. A priest shouted and tried to grasp it. Beyond them, bizarrely, the severed head of Lucian sat balanced on a table, watching it all with an expression of manic glee.

Footsteps sounded behind him as Archgeneral Sparus marched into the room. He took in Ché and the rest of the scene in a single unhurried glance from his eye.

'I'll kill you for this,' Romano was screaming. 'I said nothing I wouldn't say to your face! Your son was a coward – and you, you are the—' One of his fellow priests hissed and clamped a hand over his mouth. Romano heaved to be free of it while another priest did the same, two hands over his mouth.

Ché stepped aside as the guards forced the struggling group backwards out of the room. Archgeneral Sparus stared at Romano without expression as he was dragged outside, then closed the door behind them.

Clumps and curses on the steps outside. Silence settling.

'He does not mean what he says,' pleaded an elderly priest on his knees before the Matriarch. 'He is intoxicated, and distraught at his loss. He's lost his mind for a while, that's all.'

Sasheen flashed her eyes at caretaker Heelas.

'Out,' Heelas said to the kneeling priest, and lifted him with a tug of his robe to shove him outside after his master.

A wet snort came from the severed head on the table. Lucian was trying to laugh.

'And you,' Heelas snapped as he crossed the room.

'Back in your jar, little man.' Heelas lifted the head in both hands and let it settle back amongst the Royal Milk.

Moments passed without anyone saying a word. They looked to Sasheen, who no longer smiled, but instead glared at the door through which Romano had just departed. Her eyes flickered to Ché. She nodded, gracefully; looked to the rest of the priests still gathered in the cabin. 'I have reason enough, as witnessed by all here, to execute him now and be justified in doing so.'

'Matriarch,' Sool said, bending close to her. 'He will soon calm himself and see his position. That will be the end of it, if you let it end here. He will understand the message given to him. He will submit.'

'It's civil war otherwise,' added Archgeneral Sparus. 'In Q'os, once his family found out, and here, in the fleet, if his men caught wind of it. A third of the Expeditionary Force could turn against us.'

Sasheen's fingernails scratched along the ends of the armrests.

'I will not forget those words,' she said harshly. 'I will never forget what he said to me, about my own son, to my face.'

*

In the absolute blackness the rats fussed around him. Ash ignored the creatures, his ears keen for any sounds above. Every set of footsteps overhead was a story untold to him.

It was his twenty-first day in this reeking bilge, at least by his own rough reckoning. Hours previously, he'd heard the thunderous racket of the anchor being dropped and felt the shudder of it through the timbers of the hull. At once, he'd experienced a sudden urge to climb out of his hole and make his way through the ship to the uppermost deck, so that he could see where it was the fleet had anchored; see too if he could leave the ship for good.

He'd mastered the desire though. He knew he should wait until the silence of the crew heralded nightfall before he stole outside and chanced a proper look.

In the deep hours of the night, when all was indeed silent above him, Ash decided it was finally safe enough to make his move. Fully clothed and with his sword in his hand, he left the bilge as quietly as he could, and carefully made his way up through the bowels of the ship.

The weatherdeck was the most dangerous place for him to be, and Ash crouched low as he finally made his way onto it, checking the positions of the sailors on night-duty to fore and aft. He sucked down a lungful of air and almost groaned aloud from the freshness of it. Clouds blocked most of the stars overhead, but a dim light glimmered off the masts and the furled sails.

He looked about him, blinking at the lights of a cityport that shone through the masts of the fleet. When he turned to seaward, his eyes widened to take in the awesome arch that stood with feet on either side of the harbour opening, and the clouds of barely visible mist at play beneath it.

The Oreos, Ash instantly recognized, and knew they were in Chir, in Lagos, island of the dead.

It was Khos, then. There was no other reason for the invasion fleet to be this far west, not unless they planned to wage a reckless war against the Alhazii and risk losing their supplies of blackpowder. No, they were stopping here for supplies or men, before continuing onwards to Nico's homeland; the boy's mother and his people.

Ash hung his head, and for a long time he didn't move.

CHAPTER ELEVEN

The Old Country

The ship was pitching through heavy weather again. Bilge water swamped his legs as it washed from one side to the other, causing the rats to scurry over him as the hull creaked and banged in distress.

Ash lay in the darkness beyond time and place. In his mind, words formed as though they were being spoken aloud.

He was having a conversation with his dead apprentice.

I don't understand, Nico insisted. *You told me once how the Rōshun don't believe in personal revenge. That it goes against their code.*

Yes, Nico. I did.

Yet here you are.

Yet here I am.

So you are no longer Rōshun then?

He shied away from answering. He hardly wished to dwell on it just then.

You can't bring me back, you know, said Nico. *Even if you kill her, I'll still be gone.*

'I know that, boy,' Ash replied aloud to the black echoing space, scattering the rats from him.

Nico fell silent for a time. Ash rocked with the violent motions of the ship, bracing himself with his hands and feet, trying to calm himself.

Tell me, master Ash, came Nico's voice again. *What was it that you did before you became Rōshun?*

What I did?

Yes.

I was a soldier. A revolutionary.

You never wanted to follow a different path? A farmer, perhaps? A drunken owner of a country inn?

Of course, Ash replied.

Which one?

I am tired, Nico. You ask many too questions.

Only because I know so little about you.

A sudden sharp tilt of the ship pressed Ash against the hull, though he barely noticed it. He spat brine, wiped his face dry, glared back into the darkness.

Before I was a soldier I raised hunting dogs for a time. We lived in our cottage, my wife and son. I tried to be a good husband, a good father, that is all.

And were you?

Ash snorted. *Hardly. I made a better soldier than I ever did a husband and father. I was good at killing. And getting others killed.'*

You're too hard on yourself. I knew you to be much more than a killer. Your heart is kind.

'You do not know me, boy,' snapped Ash. 'You cannot say such things to me, not now, not ever.'

The freezing water washed over his head once again, shocking him into the present. Ash floundered for a moment, puffing his cheeks in and out as he fought for a breath. He clutched the ledge he lay upon and heard the rats squealing in terror. Moments passed as he lay there panting.

He wondered if Nico was still with him.

'Boy,' he croaked.

In the blackness, the sound of the handpumps could be heard drawing water from the bilge up to the decks above. It was hard to talk above the noise.

'Nico!' he shouted.

I'm here, I'm here.

'Tell me something. Anything. Take my mind from these things.'

What would you like to know?

'Anything. Tell me what you wished to be before you became my apprentice.'

Me? I suppose a soldier, like my father. Though I had

a dream of being an actor for a while. Travelling the islands, performing for my living.

Ash sat up, tried to wedge himself tighter against the tilting hull. 'I did not know that,' he confessed.

No. You never asked me.

The bilge water was crashing around as waves now. The rats squealed ever louder.

'You should have left, Nico, back in Q'os,' Ash shouted as he shook the water from his face. 'When you returned that evening and told me of your doubts. You should have left me!'

I know, said Nico. *But I couldn't.*

'Why not?'

A thoughtful silence followed, then a quiet voice that he clearly heard amidst the noise.

Because you needed me.

*

It was a storm, and a bad one. The hull banged with the violent impacts of crashing water, and creaked and groaned as its prow lifted free from the crests of waves then dropped shuddering into the deepening troughs. Stinging seawater poured into the bilge from gaps in the planking above his head. His boots and clothing were drenched through. His cloak was belted tight around his waist, along with his sword.

His ears hurt from the noise of the storm. Through it all, Ash could hear men running and shouting in panic overhead.

He tried to cling to the side of the hull but it was hopeless. Soon he was swirling about with the struggling rats in bilge water that had now risen up to his stomach.

Ash realized how desperate the situation was when he heard the rats pattering up the walls to escape the bilge entirely. Perhaps he should have followed their example, but he wasn't a rat, and he could hardly go unnoticed. Instead he clung to the sides when he could, and washed about when he could not, and vomited from the awful motion of it all and the saltwater he couldn't help but swallow. Like a nightmare, he felt the level of water creeping gradually up to his chest. At last he could stand it no longer. He began to fight his way towards the steps.

It ended more violently than he had expected.

The ship shuddered violently as though it had struck something, throwing him off his feet as he fell engulfed in shifting water.

Ash floundered, righting himself, and then from overhead came the heart-stopping sound of wood being torn asunder, and a thunderous noise like a waterfall roaring towards him, shaking him to the core and terrifying him in that first instant of approach – and then the hatch exploded open and the sea was flooding through it, and Ash was swept up by the boiling surge all the way to the very back of the bilge.

He smashed against the hull, spluttering for air. His arms flailed out, his feet scrabbled for purchase. Ash managed to right himself, and he tried to push his way back towards the steps. It was hopeless, though. The full weight of the sea pressed him back, squeezing him flat against the hull with such force that it was all he could do to gasp for a dry breath of air.

The timbers of the ship began to groan with a different pitch. The ship tilted nose-first, rolled onto her side at the same time.

She was going down.

Ash drew a breath in the last few feet of air between the churning surface and the planks rushing towards his head. The water was freezing, leeching the strength from his muscles. Despite himself, he began to hyperventilate, so that he swallowed air and water.

Ash allowed the brief moment of panic to flood his body with vitality, and then he pinched it off with a practised command of will.

His head struck the planking above. Still the rush of water felt like a slab of rock pressing against him. He would have to wait for the ship to flood before he could swim out through the hatch.

It was no easy realization that, as the rising water finally submerged him.

Even beneath the water he could hear the torment of the ship's hull. Ash clung to his precious lungful of air, and kicked towards the hatchway.

The pressure in his ears increased. He knew the ship had sunk beneath the surface, was dropping now to the seafloor. With increasing haste his hands scrabbled along the planking in search of the hatchway. For an eternity he grasped at wood, unable to find the way out. Again that repression of panic.

His hands groped against emptiness and he pulled himself through it. Something floated against him and he pushed it away. A body, drowned already.

Ash swam towards where he thought the ceiling should be. Objects brushed against him, the sacks and joints of meat that had been hanging there. He pushed through them, found his hands grasping steps; pulled himself upwards through another opening. By memory he knew that he was in the galley passageway now, with steps at its far end leading to the upper deck. He swam with all his strength, his ears throbbing from the increasing pressure that wrapped him like a skin of stone. His lungs were on fire. Another body drifted across his path and he pushed that one aside too. This time it moved – hands jerked out at him, grasping for life. Someone was still alive down here.

Ash broke free from the grip. He reached out, grabbing a face – rubbery lips, a nose, bristly eyelashes, hair. He grabbed a handful of that hair, and with his feet he pushed off hard. An eternity passed as he dragged the flailing sailor along to the end of the corridor. He came to the steps, unmistakable against his touch.

With a final kick, Ash dragged them both clear of the sinking ship.

He opened his eyes a fraction, ignored the stinging pain of the saltwater. He gazed upon an endless darkness; like looking into death.

He had no way to tell which way was up, for light and weight were an absence here. His mouth tried to open for air. Ash clamped his jaw shut, his chest throbbing with a white heat.

This is it, he thought for an instant. *This is it!*

A flash in the distance. Without thinking he turned that way.

It flashed again, making him wince with its brilliance, though it was gone so quickly he was aware of it only as an afterimage in his eyes. It had been distant.

Ash frog-kicked with his remaining strength towards it.

*

His lungs were bursting when he breached the surface, and his throat rasped once for air before he was pulled under again by the sailor's weight. He regained the surface and fought to stay there.

It was night, and rain and waves lashed down on him. Ash pulled the sailor closer, but the man was dead. As lightning broke the darkness he glimpsed a face staring calmly at the sky.

Ash closed the sailor's eyes and released him to the sea.

A wave lifted Ash's body. For an instant he saw the scene laid out before him: a coastline of white cliffs, dark coves, a few pale beaches, a fire burning on top of a hill – and the fleet, strung out across it, thrown into disarray by the raging sea. The ships were making for the shelter of a bay, but some had been blown off course, and seemed in the process of floundering on outlying rocks.

His strength all but spent now, Ash tried swimming for the shore and a beach he could see there. But after only a dozen strokes he had to stop, panting for breath, too tired to carry on. His head slipped beneath the surface. He fought free of it.

Debris was floating all around him. He threw his arm over an upturned stool, found he had barely the energy to cling on to it. The swell lifted him again. He turned his head to see the waves rolling in.

Ash knew there was only one chance left to him now.

He released the stool and started to swim as the next wave came roaring in from behind. For a moment he thought he wasn't moving fast enough to be taken by it, but then he felt his body lift, and with the last few strokes left in him he made one last surge.

The wave caught his legs, pulling them upwards behind him. He pointed his arms straight ahead, raised his chin free from the water as the wave-front rose and curled and carried him towards the beach.

Ash rode it all the way in with a grimace stretching his face, and the blood in his veins singing with exhilaration.

The wave dumped him onto the wet sand, left him there gasping in its hissing retreat back to the sea. Ash coughed to clear his lungs.

He was alive.

*

Captain Jute, commander of Pashereme's coastal fort, peered from the battlements through the lashing rain of the storm and waited for another flash of lightning to illuminate the sea.

'Are you certain?' he asked again of his second-in-command, Sergeant Boson, a shiftless rogue of an individual whom Jute had come to distrust in all things, save for those matters which concerned his own skin.

'As certain as day and night. They're there all right. We'd better be clearing out of here right sharpish too.'

Thunder split overhead, and a bolt of lightning struck the sea out in the boiling bay. The captain hunched forward, clearing his eyes of rain, felt a punch of fear in his stomach as he saw them: ships, hundreds of ships, bob-bing through the swells towards the beaches.

'Sweet merciful Fool,' he uttered, and gripped the stone battlements to steady himself. *An invasion*, he thought, suddenly giddy. *A bloody full-on invasion!*

'Captain?' came Boson's voice through the fog of his shock.

The captain nodded, trying to think straight. He turned to the sergeant, and he couldn't help that his voice trembled a little as he spoke. 'Right,' he said. 'Light the signal fire, and get a bird in the air. We haven't much time, lads.'

'In this weather they might not see the fire, Captain. Better if we head to Olson's fort and pass on the word there, I'd say.'

'Just do it!' bawled Captain Jute.

He turned back to the water of Whittle Bay, which was a smaller, sheltered inlet within Pearl Bay itself. On the slopes on the far side of this natural harbourage, the buildings of the fishing village were dark at this late hour. Jute prayed that someone in the village would spot the signal fire and get them all out in time.

Another flash, and the captain saw that boats had already landed on the beach below, and dark figures were scurrying through the dunes towards the hill upon which the fort stood.

Sweet Mercy, he thought to himself. *There're too many of them. All this time requesting more men for the fort, and now it's too damned late.*

'No way we're holding that many off.' It was Sergeant Boson who spoke, returned from passing out the orders to the men. Jute looked to him, keen for once to hear what he had to say. 'We need to evacuate now, Captain, or we'll be under siege in no time, and with no way of holding them back. You know, don't you, what they do to their prisoners?'

Jute's wide-eyed stare darted towards his men. They

had armed themselves with burning brands from the
guardroom hearth, and were poking life into the signal
fire that stood in an iron dish upon the battlements.
Soaked with spirits, the wood caught well enough despite the wind and the rain. In moments it was blazing
tall.

'Has the bird been sent yet?'

'Just now.'

'And the logs? We must burn them too.'

'In the fire, captain.'

'Very well,' said Jute, and took one last glance at the
advancing figures below. Commandos, he saw, faces
blackened for night work. 'Let's damn well get out of
here then, shall we?'

But when he turned to leave, the sergeant and the rest
of the men were already gone.

'You feckless bastards,' he muttered to himself, and
hurried after them.

*

When Ash came to, he was still lying where he had
washed up on the beach, and crystals of sand caked his
lips and face. It seemed he had passed out momentarily.
The storm continued to rage, and the sea washed against
his legs.

Ash's body was a dead thing sprawled on the sand;
limp, detached from his will, shaking from coldness and
shock. His throat was raw from the seawater he had
swallowed, and he turned his open mouth towards the
rain to catch some of it against his tongue.

It came to him slowly, vaguely, that he would die of
exposure if he stayed here.

Ash groaned as he pushed himself to his knees. Standing was a deliberate process, moving one muscle after
the other until at last he swayed on his feet. His legs
trembled, ready to buckle at any moment.

When our legs are spent we must walk on our will, he

recited in his mind, as the rainbow flicker of exhaustion played around the edges of his vision, and he stumbled onwards.

*

Other shipwrecked survivors were dotted along the beach: sailors, soldiers and camp followers. They walked to and fro as though in a daze, with their feet leaving confused, meandering trails in the sand. Wails of grief added to the high keen of the storm. They were all wretchedly exposed here, from the wind and rain that lashed so thickly it felt as though Ash was breathing water again. He wiped a hand across his face, blinked to see clearly. On his right, people huddled together amongst the dunes; ahead, others were setting off towards the bay.

Once more he wiped the rain from his eyes. The rainbow colours were expanding, creating a tunnel in his vision. He was aware of staggering into the dunes to seek some place to lie down out of the wind. Lightning sheeted overhead – he saw the sloping sand beyond his feet studded with pits from the impacts of rain.

Ahead a woman's voice shouted out in anger, and others joined her. A scream. The laughter of men. The wind shifted and carried away the sounds, and Ash sniffed. His nostrils caught the lingering scent of woodsmoke.

A fire!

On all fours he struggled up the slope of a dune, panting ragged like a dog. At the top he righted himself. His eyes narrowed, taking in the scene below – a group of men, short glints of steel in their fists; a group of women being set upon before a fire.

The hope of warmth and shelter revived Ash momentarily. He focused on what he was seeing, and made out an older woman, wild-haired and defiant, shouting at the men and fighting them off with a length of driftwood. The men – sailors, he thought – seemed only to be sporting with her.

'*Ho!*' Ash shouted, and every face turned to look up at him.

Lightning flashed again. He thought it an apt moment to sweep his blade from its sheath.

With a sudden nervousness the sailors eyed each other and backed away from the women. The older woman dropped the length of wood and gathered her girls around her.

Run, you bastards. I have not the strength for this.

They were waiting to see what he would do next. Ash took a step down from the dune, was hardly surprised to feel his legs buckle beneath him. He was quick enough to get his other foot out in front in time, and to turn his fall into something that approximated a downward rush. In his plummet he held his blade out for balance.

When he collapsed in front of the fire he was relieved to see the backs of the sailors fleeing into the night. He was shivering hard, and another gust flattened the flames across the wood, causing the embers to glow brightly. When the wind subsided, the flames crackled with renewed effort. The heat warmed Ash's soul.

'You,' he croaked to the older woman. 'Have you water?'

The woman ignored him. As he sat up she fussed over her girls, setting them around the fire beneath a stretch of canvas. There were five of them in all, and she talked to them curtly, businesslike, as though she was an old aunt to them. Satisfied, she wrapped a shawl over her head and shoulders and came across to join him. He saw a flask in her hand, which she offered freely.

Her eyes took in the colour of his skin.

'Only rhulika,' she said, settling down next to him and readjusting her dress. 'Good for starting fires and warming the belly. Drink, old farlander. It's the least I can offer you.'

He would have preferred freshwater just then but he drank it down anyway, his teeth chattering against the wooden spout. He swallowed the whole lot in one go, and the alcohol flared in his stomach, sent tendrils of heat threading through his spent limbs.

The flask dropped from Ash's limp fingers. The rush of alcohol crashed against the weight of his exhaustion.

Close to his face, the woman's pale features were reeling in and out of focus, her mouth moving quickly, saying something.

With a groan, Ash toppled forwards and fell through the world.

—CHAPTER TWELVE—

Paintings of Memory

The echoes of his own footfalls bounded ahead of Bahn as he rushed through the endless corridors of the Ministry of War, his hobnailed boots offering little purchase on the polished floors of marble. Bahn slid clumsily as he rounded a corner, regained his footing, and pounded towards the doors of the general's office, too breathless to shout aside the guards standing there at attention.

The two guards took one look at his fevered face and his hands waving them out of his way, surmised that he had little intention of stopping – or indeed, was even capable of doing so in time – and smartly sidestepped out of his way.

Bahn flung himself through the heavy oak doors in a panting burst of drama. 'They've landed!' he declared to the room beyond.

General Creed, standing in the early morning light by the opposite expanse of windows, and facing an easel over which his hand hovered with a brush, inclined his head slightly, but said nothing.

'General,' Bahn tried again. 'They—' But the brush

flicked across the page: once, twice, three times, and Bahn faltered.

Creed inspected the result of the strokes closely, then nodded, and set down the brush.

He turned and took the measure of Bahn in one burning glance. 'Where?' rumbled his heavy voice, and he grabbed up a rag and began to clean his hands with it.

Now that he was required to speak, Bahn found the words sticking in his throat. 'Here,' he managed to say. 'At Pearl Bay.'

'When?'

'Last night. The first birds from the bay forts have started to come in.'

'Numbers?'

Bahn shook his head. 'Conflicting so far. The fleet is still unloading. But by the size of it, at least forty thousand fighting men.'

'Acolytes?'

'Yes. And General, the Matriarch herself is leading them. Some of our rangers spotted her standard flying from the flagship. They also report seeing the standard of Archgeneral Sparus on the beach.'

General Creed tossed the blackened rag onto his desk and sat down in his leather chair. He inclined back and settled his boots on the varnished surface of the desk, with his long legs crossed and his hands clasped loosely, his thumbs toying with each other, his face a flinty cliff.

He takes it well, thought Bahn, whose stomach was still quailing inside.

He'd always supposed that composure was an excellent quality in a leader. Instead, right then, it made him feel like a scared youth.

'Perhaps the death of her son has made her reckless,' Creed mused, though Bahn offered no response, for the general was only thinking out aloud.

Bahn's body wanted to move, to act. In nervous impatience, he gazed out the window beyond the general's head. The Lansway and the Shield were visible from here, and he could even see the encampment of the Imperial Fourth Army, spread across the waist of the isthmus in its neat grid.

The lull in the fighting made perfect sense now. It had been more than an observance of mourning for the Matriarch's son; they had been waiting for the invasion force to arrive, the hammer to their anvil, with Bar-Khos caught in between. Bahn wondered how long it would be before they renewed their assaults on the walls with everything they had.

At the thought of the fighting to come, his gaze turned to the easel and canvas next to the window, and the vision of peace the painting had captured. It was rendered in the minimal farlander style so favoured by General Creed. Rather than portraying the view outside, it was instead a scene from memory; gentle slopes covered in vines, rising towards distant mountains.

Bahn was reminded of a different bereavement, a different loss; the woman whose spirit, in painting these scenes time and time again, the general hoped most of all to recapture. General Creed had been married for thirty-one years when Bahn had first joined his staff as a junior aide. Bahn had met the general's wife Rose only once at a staff function here in the Ministry; a small bundle of a woman, dignified in carriage and softly spoken. She had talked, briefly, of their vineyard on the southern slopes of the lower Alapolas, and of her wish for her husband to come home and visit her more often there. She had seemed lonely, and out of place in the lesser function hall of the Ministry. Bahn had stayed by her side until he'd managed to gain from her a shy smile, then introduced her to his own wife to take his place. The women had connected like two old friends.

Bahn looked away from the painting and saw the general's sharp blue eyes locked on his own. They flickered towards a chair, and Bahn worked his way around it and sat.

'Gollanse!' bellowed the general.

The doors, still open behind Bahn, admitted the general's ancient concierge.

'Call a staff meeting, will you? I want everyone here within the hour.'

'Yes, lord,' replied the old man curtly.

To Bahn: 'Has the council been informed yet?'

'A runner's been sent.'

'And the League?'

'Not as yet.'

The general nodded to Gollanse. 'Dispatch a fast skud to Minos. Carrier birds too. Advise them that recent imperial fleet actions have been a diversion. The real thrust is here, on Khos. We'll need all the Volunteers they can send us.'

'Yes, lord. Is that all?'

'Aye, and be quick about it now, no dallying for biscuits and chee.'

The old man raised an eyebrow, but said nothing as he shuffled from the room.

General Creed tilted his head back, calculating. 'Pearl Bay. That's a good hundred and forty laqs from Bar-Khos, with difficult terrain for the first thirty until they come down onto the Reach. They'll need to take Tume, they can't leave it at their backs. But they'll push hard. Thirteen, fourteen days, maybe, before we start seeing their advance forces here. That's hardly long enough for League reinforcements to arrive in time.'

Thirteen days. I could have Marlee and the children far away from Khos by then.

'We can also expect a renewed campaign against the walls. They'll press us from every quarter now, hoping to break us in between.'

'General . . .' said Bahn, searching for the right words. 'What can we do?'

Creed unfolded himself from his chair. He placed his palms on the desk and rose to tower over Bahn, his eyes dancing. 'Do? We must mobilize every man that we can, as quickly as we can do it. Any man who can still march and fight.'

'You want to meet the Mannians in the field?'

'What – you'd have us close the gates, I suppose, and hunker down behind the walls to await their arrival?'

Yes, that was surely what Bahn would have done. The lesser walls of the city would at least provide them with some advantage against the approaching imperial army. But it was a short-sighted strategy, and Bahn dismissed it even as he thought it. He was merely considering the protection of his family, not any larger picture. *This is why I would make such a poor leader*, he mused.

The general seemed to read his thoughts. 'The lesser walls are hardly the Shield, Bahn. They won't stand long against modern cannon, and I'm fairly certain they've brought a few of those along with them.'

Bahn nodded, rubbing a hand across the back of his neck.

'In the meantime, they'd slash and burn all of Khos from under us. If we sit and wait for them, there'll be nothing left to protect save for this city.'

'But in the field, sir,' he blurted. 'How can we possibly defeat that many?'

'We don't need to defeat them, Bahn. All we need to do is buy ourselves some time.'

Bahn massaged his tired eyes for a moment. It felt as though he was speaking in a different language to the man.

'But, General,' he said, as Creed began to pace back and forth before him. 'Even if we mobilize every Khosian reserve that we can, even if we scrape the barrel, we can only put six or seven thousand shields into the field. Our resources of blackpowder have gone to the navy and the defence of the walls. Our field cannon are few. We don't even have the guns to match them, never mind the men.'

The general stopped before the windows, his hands

behind his back. In the light, his black hair shone with a near-blue lustre.

Whether he was looking at his painting or the silent walls of the Shield, Bahn couldn't tell.

'It's a bad stroke they've given us, I'll grant you that. I'd hardly credit the Matriarch with such imagination. And it's too risky for Sparus to have thought of it. Perhaps old Mokabi has come out of his retirement, then. I sense his flair in this.'

Creed paused, and his head tilted towards the window: at the very instant that he had spoken the name of the retired Archgeneral – the same man who had led the Imperial Fourth Army to the walls of Bar-Khos – a boom sounded from the direction of the Shield.

Another sounded, and then another, until the windows themselves were trembling from the rippling concussions.

The Mannian guns had started to fire on the Shield once more.

—CHAPTER THIRTEEN—

Beachhead

The woman held a mug of chee for him when he woke late the next day. Ash struggled to sit up, his chest feeling tight and sore. Cakes of sand fell from one side of his face as he coughed long and hard into his fist, his eyes watering from the pain of each convulsion.

Through his tears Ash saw that the storm had passed in the night, though a wind still blew strong from the sea. The breeze had dried his clothes and his skin, at least those parts he had not been lying on, and heat wafted over from the small fire next to him.

When Ash stopped coughing long enough to take a

tentative sip of the steaming chee, he found his spirits lifting.

'My thanks for your help,' said the woman on the sand next to him. 'It was timely of you.' She held out a hand to him. 'Mistress Cheer.'

Ash shook it. She had a man's grip, and it was not shy of strength. For a moment the air between them was a passing curtain of smoke, and he peered through it, taking in her features beneath her thick thatch of dark hair. She reminded him of his wife's mother, of all people – Anisa, possessed of that rare attractiveness that seemed to improve with age and stature.

And then the smoke cleared, and Ash saw the curl of the old scar that clove through her upper lip – like a hare-lip, though running up to her face and across her left eye.

'Ash,' he said, somehow still taken by her looks.

She creased her lips with a smile. 'A pleasure,' she told him, and appeared to mean it.

Behind her, the young women she had been protecting the previous night were rifling through a collection of clothes chests. It seemed they were putting together outfits for the day.

Mistress Cheer gathered her skirt above her ankles and stretched her stockinged feet out to the fire with a sigh. 'A fine mess they've made of the landing,' she said with a gesture of her head towards the bay.

'Where are we?' Ash asked over the brim of his mug.

'Khos. In a place called Pearl Bay.'

He'd been right then. Now, no doubt, the army would be heading for Bar-Khos in an attempt to take the city from behind. The boy's mother lived near there, he recalled.

He kept his thoughts to himself as he drank down the chee. The wonderful sensation of warmth in his belly made him realize how long it had been since he had enjoyed a hot drink or a meal. Mistress Cheer squinted at him, taking in the dark tone of his skin. 'What are you – a mercenary? You're a little old for this work, don't you think?'

'Bodyguard,' he said without thinking.

'Oh? And your employer?'

Ash nodded in the direction of the sea.

She blinked quickly, evaluating his meaning, and said, 'Then you're a timely stroke of good fortune, is all I can say. Our own man couldn't swim, though he thought it too unimportant to mention until we were neck-deep in water. My girls are in need of some protection, as you might have noticed.'

They both looked towards the girls she spoke of. He caught glimpses of them beyond the flames as they were dressing; the stretch of smooth calves and thighs; the sway of a heavy breast; lips being painted; a pair of dark-kohled eyes glancing across at him.

Ash looked away and cleared his throat.

Prostitutes, he realized, feeling thick-headed. Here to follow the army during its campaign.

Ash sipped his chee and considered her offer. It would take time to find his bearings here, and to discover a way through to the Matriarch. It could take days, he knew, if not longer. All the while, he would have to keep up with the army.

Ash could recognize a gift of fate when he came across one.

'Pay?' he enquired, though the question was merely for show.

'Oh, we have money. I can pay you campaign rates of ten marvels a day, and meals on top of that when we get ourselves back on our feet.'

'Fifteen,' he said, again for the sake of appearances.

'Agreed,' she allowed him with a gracious nod of her head. 'And thank you, again. Truly. That was a courageous act, stepping in to help us like that in your condition.'

'It was your fire I was really after,' he confessed, but she only smiled as though he was joking.

*

Ash left them to finish their preparations. With his sodden boots perched next to the fire, he went for a swim to clean and wake himself.

The beach appeared even more desolate in the light of day. Wreckage lay strewn in heaps amongst frayed cordage and seaweed; bodies too, the early crabs clambering over whitened skin. Birds shrieked in the air, squabbled over scraps on the sand. Ash saw how the beach curved inwards into the bay itself, where the fleet rode at anchor in the choppy waters, barely diminished, for all the battering the storm had given it. He could see rafts and boats bringing in men and supplies; even cannon poking out over the bobbing gunwales.

The invasion force stopped him in his tracks. The imperial army had established a beachhead on the white sands and the system of dunes behind them. Smoke drifted from a thousand campfires and more, and the ground swarmed thick with figures all the way to the first sloping pastures that rose between the tawny hills. A village lay in blackened ruins on a ridge that overlooked the far end of the bay, a bleak counterpoint to the smouldering fort on the opposite side of the beachhead.

Ash looked for any sign of Sasheen, and almost immediately spotted an army standard of a black raven on a white field, flapping on the beach amongst several others. Try as he might, though, he couldn't see the Matriarch amongst so many.

One step at a time, he thought to himself.

He picked his way through the survivors gathering what they could from the storm wreckage. He stripped at the water's edge, then waded out into the sea with the waves frothing around his thighs. Scrubbing himself, he noticed the bruises on his arms, the black fingerprints where the sailor had clutched him in the sinking ship.

Ash dived into the water and swam for a while, easing the tensions in his muscles. Now and again, he glanced across the beachhead towards the fluttering standard of Sasheen, squinting for a sight of her.

*

The wind was whipping the drying grains of sand from the dunes, and the Matriarch strode through the hiss of it with her eyes narrowed down to slits. Ahead, her body-guards cleared the way of milling soldiers and civilians, while behind her straggled her field aides, hiking up the flanks of the mounds and down into their troughs in a long line of bleached-white robes, a procession that extended all the way back to the churned beach.

Not now, Archgeneral Sparus thought in irritation. *I haven't the time for this now.*

Sparus watched her approach from his position on top of a dune, where he sat on a field chair amongst a gathering of his closest officers. The other men were dressed as he was, in their plain imperial armour of hardened leather, their tattoos of rank clearly visible on their temples. They squatted on the sand around him in a loose circle. A canvas canopy snapped a few feet above his head, and on the ground lay an unfolded map of the island of Khos, across which scratched particles of blown sand.

'One last point,' he continued to his men, hurrying to finish before the Matriarch reached him. 'We know our enemy. We know that Creed is a natural fighter with a reputation for aggressiveness, of going for the throat. And we know that this trait of recklessness has only been constrained over the years by the Khosian council of Michinè. Now, though, that changes. With our presence here, Creed will be afforded full powers under his role of Lord Protector. We can therefore assume that he will come at us with everything he can muster. We must hope for this, in fact. If he does, we may win this campaign even before we arrive at Bar-Khos.'

His officers nodded, knowing all of this already, though aware too of the importance of stating it once more.

They began to stand as Sparus rose from his chair to receive Sasheen, all of them stooped like age-broken men beneath the low flapping roof of their shelter.

She looked well in her suit of white armour, Sparus had to admit. She wore it like a veteran, and watching her approach him now, confident and relaxed in her stride, Sparus had to remind himself that this was her first campaign in the field, her first martial command. That was her mother's influence: Kira had insisted Sasheen be trained in the arts of war. Thank kush the old witch wasn't here with them, though. Kira would have dominated her daughter in that mocking way of hers, and at a time when they needed their Matriarch to be at her strongest. Even worse, campaigns in the field were intimate affairs amongst the officers and leaders of an army. Those around Sasheen would have seen how it truly was: how her mother wished for her to be Matriarch more than Sasheen did herself.

The old general felt his annoyance fade away as he thought of all that; this woman he was fond of, living a life she had been sculpted since birth for, but who, at times, seemed hardly to have the heart for it.

Sasheen shot him a wide smile as she tramped up to their position. 'How are we doing?' she panted over the wind with a voice edged by excitement, and Sparus saw that she was sober for once, her eyes clear of drink and narcotics, yet they shone brightly none the less. It seemed Sasheen was enjoying this venture of theirs, even with her left arm bound up in a sling.

'Please,' Sparus said, stepping forward to give her a hand up. 'Sit down. What happened?'

'It's only a broken arm, Sparus,' she chided, though she accepted his vacated chair readily enough. 'And hardly the only one after last night.'

'Aye, if only broken bones were the worst of it.'

Sparus remained stooped as the Matriarch turned her head to survey the grassy slopes that rose up from the dunes behind them. The fort up there was still smouldering, where Hanno's Commandos had stormed it in the night and fired it in their recklessness. On another hilltop a village smoked in ruins too; the work of the Hounds that one, the veteran skirmishers of eastern Ghazni. Beneath the village, Acolytes were constructing a palisade that would surround the Matriarch's command camp for the night.

When the Matriarch turned back to face him, Sparus finally sat down again, squatting on the sand next to her as his officers did the same.

'How bad is it?' she asked him.

The general was holding a twig of driftwood in his hand. He used it now to point at the map. 'It seems we've landed a dozen laqs or so from where we intended to. We think we're here, in Whittle Bay. The inland approaches are steeper from this position. If we wish to keep to our schedule, we'll have to push the army even harder than we intended.'

'But what of our losses?'

Sparus ran a hand across his bald scalp; scratched at the back of his neck. 'We're missing at least thirty ships from last night, and one of those is a powder ship. Meaning we have a third less blackpowder than we were hoping for. That isn't the worst of it. Most of our heavy cavalry have gone, sunk or blown off course – we don't yet know. And four transports of auxiliary infantry.'

A sudden gust roared through the space, so that they all turned their heads away from the stinging sands. Sparus waited with his one eye closed until it had passed. 'Also, we're still waiting for our air support to turn up. After that storm, though, there's no telling if any of them will.'

Sasheen leaned back and chuckled to herself, a sound wholly incongruous with the tone of his words. 'You make it sound as though we are already doomed, Sparus.

And yet look at us. We are here, sitting on Khosian sands, with an army behind us and a nation awaiting its own downfall.'

Sparus blinked at her, keeping his thoughts to himself. He wasn't in the habit of looking on the bright side. It did you little good.

Besides, the Coros disaster was fresh on his mind today. Nine years had passed since he had last stood on Mercian soil, yet still the memories were raw within him; the chartassa of the Free Ports cutting through the imperial forces twice their number, their ranks ragged from grape and grenades and missile fire, yet not stopping until they had hewn the invading imperial army in two and broken it.

Sparus had only been a minor general then; as had Creed, leading the small contingent of the feared Khosian chartassa. The islands of the democras had won that day, and Sparus would be damned if he was going to let such a disaster befall him again. To be beaten twice would be unforgivable; better to take a knife to his own heart. Sparus was Archgeneral now; Creed the Lord Protector. To defeat Creed here in Khos would seal Sparus's reputation as the supreme general of his time.

Sparus would win this campaign he had been so opposed to commanding, but he would do so not with a hopeful complacency, but in the supremacy of their own logistics and might. This time, they had an army large enough for the task at hand, and an army of veterans at that, not nervous recruits. And he was older, wiser, a better general by far. He'd learned from their mistakes. At his insistence the imperial heavy infantry had developed their own phalanxes of heavy pikemen, capable – he hoped – of taking on the mighty chartassa.

Still, he thought: the loss of so many war-zels in the storm was a heavy blow to the campaign, and before it had even truly started.

'It's always this way, yes,' he said to the gathering,

though he directed his words mainly to Sasheen. 'Always you have a carefully prepared plan that falls to shreds the first moment it engages with reality. That's why we prepare for the worst. And why we will make do with what we have now, as we always make do.'

Sasheen narrowed her kohl-lined eyes. 'Surely there must be some good news too? Something to rouse the army's spirits?'

Sparus looked away for a moment to take in the long stretch of white beach beyond the dunes. It was chaos down there. Half-crazed zels ran amok with their harnesses trailing loose, leaping over scattered boxes of equipment and spilling men out of their way. Squads of infantry wandered around, trying to find their commanding officers; stragglers were still coming in from along the coast, stumbling over the sand like the blind. Sparus had never seen a beachhead in such disarray.

Still, it could have been much worse.

'Good news?' he heard himself say to them all, and tossed the stick in his hand into the wind 'We're still alive, aren't we?'

—CHAPTER FOURTEEN—

An Ambush

The meeting of general staff had ended barely a half-hour ago – for Creed was counting the minutes on his precious waterclock as he sipped on a lukewarm cup of milk – when the doors crashed open for the second time that morning, and in stamped the Michinè in all their righteous anger, their gold and diamond links jingling over the rustle of silk clothing.

Chonas and Sinese were at the front of the crowd, their painted faces pale contrasts to the fervour in their eyes. At the sight of General Creed sitting behind his desk with a cup of milk in his hand, Sinese lost all semblance of self-control.

'You can't do this!' the Minister of Defence hollered over the desk, and shook his cane as though he wished to hit him with it.

Creed settled his cup upon the desk and waved the guards at the door away. 'I can, and I have,' he told Sinese in a level voice, and returned the man's incensed stare without blinking.

Chonas, the First Minister, stepped up from behind and tapped Sinese on the arm. The man glared at the First Minister for a moment, then lowered his cane and backed off with his chest heaving.

'General,' said Chonas as he settled into one of the chairs in front of Creed's desk, and the men behind him blinked in surprise, for it was hardly the place of a Michinè to sit before a common-born, not even if he was the Lord Protector of Khos. The act was not lost on Creed either. He nodded to the composed old man who sat before him, a man he had known for twenty years and more, and whom he respected despite all the differences in opinion between them.

'As Minister Sinese so graciously explained just now, you cannot pursue this plan of yours. We have come to repeal your orders immediately.'

'On whose authority?'

'On the authority of the council!' snapped Sinese, taking a step closer again. 'Or do you forget your station, man?'

The words hit Creed like a slap to the face, enough to feel the blood rushing to his cheeks. The rest of the Michinè held themselves poised and continued to eye Creed with a cool passion. All at once, he felt the potential of violence amongst this gathering.

Ah, he thought wryly. *So the gloves are finally off.*

Creed sat back and casually drew open one of the drawers in his desk. A pistol lay within it, loaded and ready to be primed.

'In case you haven't noticed,' he said to them all, while the windows shivered once more to the sound of the guns on the Shield, 'we've been invaded by an imperial army of Mann. While we stand here bickering, foreign forces stand on Khosian soil. By the terms of the Concordance, as Lord Protector of Khos, I am now in ultimate command of the defences of this island.' He looked hard at Sinese. 'Above even you, Minister. That is the martial law as it's written.'

'I see,' scoffed the Minister of Defence. 'So now you wish to play at being a king, is that your game?'

Creed ground his teeth together to contain his temper. 'I think it is you who forgets your place, Minister.'

'What do you mean by that?'

'Please,' said Chonas, raising a hand to calm them.

Creed continued to glare at Sinese. 'You do not stand in the council chambers now,' Creed told the man. 'You stand in my office, and you would be advised to show some civility, or I shall have you escorted from this building under guard.'

The gathered Michinè exploded with indignation.

'Gentlemen!' said Chonas above the sudden shouts of anger. 'Please! Let us have some order here. Marsalas, we have known each other, you and I, for a great many years now. I respect you deeply, though I may never have told you that before now. All of Khos respects you. Every day the people give thanks to Fate that we have been gifted with such an able general in times as bleak as these. I speak to you as a comrade as much as your First Minister when I say this, so please listen. You cannot go and meet them in the field. You will be outnumbered more than six-to-one, not to mention their advantage in cannon. They will make meat of you.'

Creed sighed. 'Always you think in numbers, my old friend. That is your problem, all of you. You think this is purely a matter of resources and where to put them most efficiently. But you forget what we are, what we have.'

'You think the chartassa alone can save us,' interrupted

Chonas. 'That is what you mean, is it not? The famous Khosian chartassa, feared and respected by our many enemies. The Giant Killer, the Pathians called it. Defeat, the Imperials knew it as in Coros.' Chonas shook his head sadly. 'No, Marsalas. It is you who are mistaken. I may be a tired old politician. Our fighting esprit may be strong. But still the numbers cannot be washed away by some vainglorious gesture of defiance. Yes. The chartassa will make for a fearsome sight on the battlefield. And then they will die, all of them. And Khos will be lost to us for good.'

'What choice do we have?' snapped Creed. 'Let them rape and enslave every town in Khos while we hunker behind the city walls? Is that what you would have us do?'

'No, Marsalas. If we had any viable alternatives, it is not what I would have us do. But it *is* the terrible situation we find ourselves facing. Even now, the Imperial Fourth Army masses on the Pathian side of the Shield for a major attack on the walls. Listen to their guns! Listen! Have you heard such a thunder since the first years of the siege? They will be coming at the walls with everything they have now, and they will not cease this time – while you, you would take half our men into the field on some reckless venture in suicide.'

'You will have General Tanserine, one of the finest tacticians in all the Free Ports, here to lead the defences. And with enough men to hold until our return.'

'And what if you do not return?'

'Then you must hold them off until more Volunteers can arrive from the League.'

'And how will we do that without the reserves you are taking with you? No. We make our stand here in Bar-Khos. What we can spare, we will use to fortify and hold Tume. We will dig in and await aid.'

Creed flexed his jaw. 'If we dig in, we may all be dead before reinforcements have time even to arrive. If we fight them, we can at least buy ourselves some time.

Sweet Mercy, man! The Matriarch herself is here: don't you realize what an opportunity that is for us?'

Chonas bowed his head as though he was no longer listening. On cue, a man stepped from the gathering of Michinè and approached the desk. He wore the stiff bleached garments of a city professional.

'General Creed,' the man announced. 'If I may draw your attention to article forty-three of the Concordance: *At all times, the defence of the Shield must be paramount when apportioning supplies to offensive or defensive operations.*'

'Who is this man?'

'An advocate,' explained Chonas. 'We felt he might be able to shed some light on our differences, should any be remaining.'

'An advocate?'

'What the man is saying is this: we can refuse you blackpowder for those cannon of ours you wish to take into the field. It is written in the martial law.'

Creed was speechless for a moment. 'You would let us meet them without guns?'

'We are rather hoping, without cannon, you will not go at all.'

The First Minister looked at Creed from beneath his bushy brows. He leaned closer, and when he spoke, he did so quietly. 'I know you, Marsalas. You have had enough of sitting in your chair behind the Shield doing nothing for all this time. You wish to have a proper crack at them, for all they have done to us, for the lives they have taken, for your own father who died fighting them abroad. You see this as a last chance to meet them in the open theatre of war and prevail. But it is a grand folly only. I implore you to see this now.'

General Creed sat back in his chair, disarmed by the truth at the core of the First Minister's words.

He was not a person prone to self-doubt, but for an instant he entertained the notion that he was in fact wrong in all of this, and that Chonas was right, that he was leading them all to their downfall. Since hearing of the invasion a few hours earlier, and whilst everyone around him seemed on the verge of losing their heads, Creed instead had found himself thrilled by this sudden development in the war, this chance to make a fight of it.

The Michinè glared at him as he eyed each of them in turn.

It came to him that it wasn't merely their fears that charged this sudden hostility towards him. He was the first Lord Protector in forty years to gain the full rights of his position under the terms of the Concordance – that century-old agreement forged between the Michinè rulers and their military commander. Now the scales had shifted without warning. With invaders on Khosian soil, Creed could do as he pleased with the army, never mind what the Michinè had to say on it. Predictably, these noble-borns were intolerant to such a turn of events, this sudden collective step down in the grand pecking order of power. And so here they were now, come to dispel such notions from him before he had a chance to exercise his new powers properly.

He thought of all the times they had restrained him, had stopped him from taking on the enemy face to face, more concerned with preserving the status quo than in breaking the siege. He looked to Chonas, the Michinè's expression eager beneath the great overhangs of his brows.

Aye, the First Minister might be a good man. But when it came down to it, he was still one of them.

Creed rose slowly to his feet. He was larger than these men before him, not in height but in bulk, and in his own capacity for action.

'I will not stand by and do nothing while good people are put to the sword. My orders stand. We march in the morning.'

He held a hand up to silence them all, and felt a brief moment of satisfaction as their mouths closed again as one. 'Gollanse!' he called out.

His ageing orderly shuffled past the group of Michinè, escorting a man who was also dressed in the clothes of a city professional. He had a leather satchel beneath his arm, and a pair of spectacles on his bland, sharp, clever face.

'Ministers, this is my own advocate, Charson Fay. If you have any legal issues involving my orders then please address them to him. He will construct a case file so that we can all meet together in open session of court upon my return.'

The general closed the drawer with the gun and stepped around the desk. 'Now, if you will excuse me. I have an army to prepare for the march. Good day to you all.'

Creed strode from the room with the murmur of their discontent like music in his ears.

*

'Is it true?' someone shouted at Bahn as he stepped through the gates of the Ministry of War into the crowd of people gathered there. Behind them, horns were blaring from the Stadium of Arms, calling the city's soldiery to action; faint wails between the concussions of the distant guns. Every dog in the city seemed to be barking.

'Have we been invaded, Bahn?' came the voice again as he pushed through the crowd. He saw that it was Koolas, the war chattēro.

Bahn brushed past the man without comment, but Koolas matched his stride as he headed for the path that would lead him down from the Mount of Truth. The war chattēro was sweating even in the cool breeze that ran in from the sea, the man too heavy to make the hike to the summit easily. His great paunch bounced beneath his shirt at the pace Bahn set for them. Still, Koolas had energy enough to laugh incredulously as they walked, and to sweep the curls of his black hair from his face in strands wet enough for it to be raining.

'It's true, then!'

Bahn scowled at him but held his tongue. Koolas made his living by writing news on the war for the copyhouses of the city, and for the proclaimers on the wailing towers of the bazaars. He knew that within an hour the news would be spreading like wildfire throughout the city.

It hardly mattered, he supposed, as they came down off the hill onto the Avenue of Lies. The horns were announcing a full call to arms, and everyone could hear them. The mood in the streets already seemed close to panic. Citizens bawled at each other in their haste to be home or at their local tavernas. Mothers were plucking their children off the streets. All about, he could see Red Guards hurrying towards the Stadium of Arms, and old retired veterans, the Molari, heading for the stadium too, bearing dusty shields and their long chartas bundled in oiled canvases.

'Come on, now,' Koolas said to him amicably enough. 'They already know we're in trouble. All I'm after are some details so their imaginations won't run wild on them. What are we up against here? Is it a raid or a full invasion?'

Bahn held up a hand to wave down a passing rickshaw. The bearer sped past him without stopping, the rickshaw empty of passengers. He swore under his breath as he looked around for another, finally managing to get one to stop for him.

'Olson Avenue,' he told the bearer quickly, and just before he climbed into the seat he made the mistake of glancing back at Koolas just once.

'Fool's balls,' Koolas exclaimed as he caught the look in Bahn's eyes. 'Is it that bad?' He sounded appalled, and for a moment Bahn was reminded that Koolas was more than a simple chattēro after a story, that he was Khosian too, born and raised in the city, with his own friends and family to worry over.

Bahn sagged within his armour. 'One moment,' he said to the rickshaw bearer, and stepped closer to Koolas.

'It's an invasion, that's all we know right now.'

'How many? Which army?'

'Reports indicate it's the Sixth Army from Lagos, with auxiliaries from Q'os.'

The man drew himself straighter. 'How many?' he insisted.

Bahn turned as though to walk away, but paused. 'All I can say is that we're calling up every man we can. We're emptying the jails and stockades of veterans. Even the Eyes.'

'What? Those murderers and lunatics?'

'Any that can still carry a shield, aye.'

'And the council, what do they make of it? I just saw a delegation go inside the Ministry.'

'Does it matter? We've been invaded. It's out of their hands now.'

Koolas rubbed his face ruefully. 'Aye. And I'm sure Creed made that more than clear to them. There's a man with a chip on his shoulder if ever I saw one.'

Bahn scowled, and left before the chattēro could ask anything more of him. He climbed into the rickshaw, and nodded to Koolas as the bearer pulled him past.

He offered the bearer an extra five coppers to make a faster pace of it, and sat back and tried to calm himself as the rickshaw wove between the bustle and traffic of the streets.

In the far north of the city, in a small avenue lined with cherry trees turned bronze by autumn, Bahn climbed down with thanks to the bearer and stepped into the house that had been his family home for seven years now. The rooms were cool inside, everything still. A smell of incense still hung in the air from their small shrine to Miri, the Great Disciple who had brought the Dao and the Great Fool's teachings to the Midèrēs.

His son Juno would be at the schoolhouse today. Upstairs, he heard his infant daughter begin to cry.

Bahn found Marlee in the backyard, turning the soil in their small vegetable patch as though oblivious to the distant horns, yet her movements were quick and frustrated.

'Hey,' he said to his wife as he slid his arms around her waist from behind. Marlee straightened against him, her body tense. 'Can't you hear her?' he asked.

'Of course I can hear her. She's teething again.'

'Need anything?'

'No, we still have some mother's oil left. I daren't give her any more, though.' Marlee turned around and looked up at him. Her smile faltered. 'What is it, Bahn? Why the alarms?'

He heard the sigh escape his lips. 'I haven't long. I should be at the stadium right now helping with the preparations.'

'Preparations?'

He squeezed her arm and could not speak.

'Oh, Bahn,' she said, and her eyes shone moist. 'They've landed here?'

He nodded stiffly.

Ariale wailed even louder from inside the house. Neither of them could find any words to say. Marlee looked to her feet and took a deep breath of air, then looked up again. 'I'll go and settle her,' she said quickly. 'Then you can tell me how bad it really is.'

He reached out to stop his wife.

'I'll go,' he said with a smile of sadness, and left to settle his daughter.

—CHAPTER FIFTEEN—

Enlistment

She had been a child – perhaps four years of age – when her mother had died giving birth to her youngest sister, Annalese. So young in fact that she could hardly recall the experience now, whether it had been day or night, summer or winter, quick or slow; nor even who had been there, and who had not.

Only the few moments before the end did Curl truly remember, and those moments were so fresh in her still that to recall them brought a flush of emotion from her beating heart.

Her mother, pale as moonlight, wasted and bloody on the birthing bed with her gaze fixed distantly on the ceiling above. The dark curls of her hair plastered around the sheen of her complexion. Her chest barely rising as she fought to breathe, a faint rhythm growing fainter. Her nipples, dark and hard on stretch-marked breasts made plump with milk, the wooden charm hanging between them, a dolphin, shaped from unseasoned jupe. The newborn, screeching in the room beyond the open doorway.

In the end, her mother had seemed hardly aware at all as Curl gripped her hand and shed tears over her prone, draining body. Just once their eyes had locked. For a moment, her mother had looked upon her daughter with a blink of recognition. She had gripped Curl's small hand until it burned with pain, and had glared at her as though trying to impart something of meaning in her last moments on this world.

Make the most of this life, my daughter, her eyes had seemed to say to Curl in the years to come. *Follow no path but your own!*

And then she had passed into sleep, and into death, and into the ground.

The years after that were dim too in Curl's memory, as though some shroud of forgetfulness had covered her world. Only glimpses remained.

Her father, silent and spiteful, no longer the man he once had been, losing himself in his work as the local physician. A house without joy or happiness or laughter. Foot-creaks on floorboards; everyone treading lightly. And beyond the confines of their family grief, soldiers passing through the village; priests of Mann shouting

sermons, decrying the old faith; rumours of war and rebellion like thunder in the distance.

At thirteen, her aunt and younger sisters celebrated
Curl's coming of age.

It was her aunt, whispery and wise and subtly beautiful, who had explained to Curl the budding of the
moon's cycles within her body, who had taught them all
how they would some day become women. On that
night of celebration, the woman had made a gift to Curl
of a simple lump of wood. It was a knot from a fallen
willow, she had explained.

'Carve it tonight,' she said, 'when you are alone. Finish it before you sleep.'

'What will I carve?' Curl had asked in wonder.

'Whatever you like, sister's-daughter. Whatever brings
warmth to your heart.'

When the others went up to bed, she sat on the deep
rug in front of the hearthfire, a little drunk on the apple
cider she had been allowed to sample for the first time,
and with her father's smallest carving knife and polish-
ing stone, began to carve the piece of wood in whatever
way seemed most appropriate. Hours passed fleeting; the
fire dwindled until it was only ashes glimmering with the
memory of heat.

She awoke where she had fallen asleep before the
hearth. It was still night. Her aunt was lifting her into
her arms. The woman had wrapped a blanket about her
and was carrying her up to bed. Curl's two sisters slept
soundly in the other bunk.

'What have you carved?' her aunt whispered as she
placed Curl beneath the blankets. Curl opened her hand
to show her.

In her palm lay a simple figurine the size of her thumb,
a woman of plump, fulsome curves. There were few dis-
cernible details in the carving, merely the vague contours
of shape. The breasts were big. The belly swollen.

Her aunt smiled. Kissed Curl's forehead.

'Your mother would have liked that,' she told her. 'It's a fine ally indeed. Now make sure you wear it always, and may it look out for you when you most have need of aid.'

Curl slept, knowing she would remember this day for the rest of her years.

Later, during the coldest nights of deep winter, her father began to visit Curl while her younger sisters feigned sleep across the room.

And so their world changed once more.

For Curl it was a winter of bitter dreams and darkness, marking more loss in their lives, not least of all a father.

In the spring of the following year, they found him hanging by the neck from the rafters of the smokehouse. They stood there, all three of them, gazing up at his gently spinning body clad in his old and handsome wedding garments, his shoes freshly polished, his hair neatly combed across his balding head.

Against his chest hung the wooden dolphin charm once carved and worn by their mother.

*

The morning the soldiers came, Curl was out gathering sixbell in the fields that overlooked the town of Hart, where her aunt had taken them to live following their father's demise.

She was hoping to ward off the chance of pregnancy with the little blue herb, for she was secretly seeing a man in the town by then, a married wagoneer more than twice her age. That morning she wandered far, ranging over the hills in her searching, spending quiet hours slowly filling her pocket.

It was only upon her return that she noticed the smoke filling the sky ahead like storm clouds. Hitching up her skirts, she hurried over the crest of the last hill and gasped in incomprehension at what lay before her.

The town was on fire. White specks of soldiers surrounded it, and they were moving inwards.

The screams of its people fluttered like bird cries on the wind.

Curl thought of her aunt and her sisters down there. She thought of their faces as the soldiers and flames approached them. She doubled over in anguish and thought she would be sick.

Curl hid all day in the grasses, listening to the sounds of the town's folk dying even as she pressed her hands to her ears. At times the shame of her guilt became too much, and she would try to rise as though to go and help them. But each time she froze, unable to move any further. She wept until she could weep no more, and then she grew numb, and silent.

The soldiers left in the fading light, marching out with their wagons loaded high with booty. Behind them, the town was a smoking desolation.

Curl waited another hour before she could bring herself to venture down to the ruins.

Blinded with tears, choking with grief, she was unable to find her family amongst the smouldering pile that had once been their house.

*

She lived a feral existence after that, wandering aimlessly amongst the pyres and ruins of her homeland. Her mind was a little gone by then. Her sense of time stretched into an eternal moment.

One day, Curl was walking along a beach when she sighted the man ahead of her, large and thickly bearded. She retained enough sense to fling herself flat to the ground.

Too late, though, as it happened. The man came to where she lay with her face pressed against the rough grasses of the dunes.

'It's all right,' he said to her gently. 'I won't harm you, girl.'

She looked up into a tired and weather-beaten old face. His voice sounded strange, though it was only that she hadn't heard another's voice for so long.

'Come with me,' the man said, holding out a hand. 'We must leave now.'

Curl climbed to her feet and turned to make a run for it.

Go with him.

At once she faltered in her tracks.

'It's all right,' he said again, taking her carefully by the arm. 'Come now, we need to be gone from here.'

He led her down to a cove and a small beach of shingle. A fishing boat bobbed in the water. Men and women were wading through the waves to climb aboard.

The man led her out into the water. Curl convulsed from the bitter shock of it against her thighs.

'One more!' he hollered to someone already on board, and a few heads turned to acknowledge her. She saw men and women with reddened eyes, hair askew, faces sagging. No one spoke as they helped her into the boat. Curl found a space amongst the bundles of goods and sat down and huddled with her knees pulled up to her chest.

'Is that everyone?' asked the man.

'Aye, skipper,' replied another. 'Now let's bloody well get away from here while we still can.'

Two men pulled on oars, slowly dragging the boat out through the waves of the cove into the breakers beyond. The sail was unfurled, snapping as it caught the offshore wind. After a time they were shooting across the choppy water, with all eyes turned to the distant island behind.

'That fool Lucian and his rebels,' spat a small bald man, glancing about him with a set of black eyes. 'He brought it down on all of us, and damn his soul for it. *Damn your soul, I say!*' he bellowed, shaking his fist at the land.

The rest of the group sat in silence. They continued

to gaze upon their homeland as it faded into the distance.

The old skipper shouted a command. At the rudder, a young lad turned the boat so that the sun wheeled behind them.

The bald man calmed himself by steady degrees, his muttering diminishing until he was silent. He sobbed for a while, the other men looking away in embarrassment. One by one the women began to cry too, though Curl only stared over the side of the boat, still numb.

'You're a lucky girl to stumble across us like that,' said the bald man, his eyes dry now as he shifted across to sit beside her. Curl inched away from his touch. 'Perhaps your ally there was looking out for you, hey?' And he chuckled drily to himself in mockery.

'Leave the girl alone,' snapped the old skipper. The man scowled, but he let her be.

Curl heard the women beside her talking amongst themselves.

'Where are we going?' asked the youngest.

'The Free Ports,' replied the oldest. 'They are free, still. And they are not so hostile to refugees as Zanzahar.'

Refugees. Curl tried the word against her tongue. So that was what she was now. She thought it was a small word for all that it meant.

Curl looked back at the island of Lagos, a mere smudge on the horizon now. In her hand she clutched the piece of wood that was her ally, rubbing it with her thumb as the lean wind cut through her body, piercing her to the heart.

*

'Enough of that, now. I don't want the children hearing you.' Rosa spoke in an exaggerated hush, and bustled to the kitchen door to close it before she returned to folding the children's clothing on the table.

'What?' exclaimed Curl, sitting across from her and watching the woman work. Exasperated, she glanced through the open window at some of the half-wild urchins in the backyard, where they were enacting street robberies for play.

Rosa's movements were stiff and angry. The table rocked whenever the woman leaned any weight on it, so that its legs clattered against the wooden floor and transmitted the urgency of her frustrations. They were alone together. Breakfast had been served long ago, shortly after dawn, and the assorted lodgers had eaten their small portions of gruel with the sound of the guns on the nearby Lansway fuelling their talk of invasion and war. Even now, across the room, the main dining table squatted in silent accusation at Curl. She eyed it with distaste, the filthy oil-cloth that was never removed from it, not even when eating, the debris of used bowls and platters and cutlery of the lodgers. It was Curl's turn this morning to clean up after them all. Try as she might, she couldn't rouse herself to start it.

'I'm only telling you what I've heard,' she said.

'Well, whether we know of these things or not, it won't make a bit of difference to what's happening. We'll know it soon enough if those monsters come tearing over the walls for us. Until then, please, give it a rest. Let us live in some peace while we still can.'

Curl plucked at a loose thread on her linen blouse and held her tongue. It wasn't easy, though, when her blood was still humming from the tail-end of her high, and her mouth wanted nothing more than to flap away in idle chatter.

'I've half a mind to go and volunteer myself.'

A roar of laughter burst from the woman. 'Oh Curl, you do make me laugh!'

Curl found her face flushing red. 'What? I don't mean to fight. But they need people for other things. Cooks and . . . such.'

Rosa stopped laughing and threw a folded nightshirt into the basket on the floor. She picked up the last of the freshly washed nightshirts, her breathing loud. 'I don't know what's got into you today, my girl. You'd better not go saying anything like that to the children. I'll clip you one, I truly will. You'll have the poor things heart-broken with all your talk.'

The door to the kitchen burst open and Misha and Neese came running in. '*Out, out!*' shouted Rosa. 'You're trailing dirt all over the place!' But the girls were brave enough to ignore her for a moment, and they stopped before Curl, and opened their mouths and widened their eyes in feigned surprise, and let out a chorus of screams at the sight of her prominent hair.

'*Out!*' shouted Rosa as they ran back outside again, hollering all the way.

'Very funny, girls,' Curl shouted after them.

Pea was standing in the doorway, her nose running and a thumb held in her mouth. She was new to the house, and still hadn't learned to take Rosa's barks for what they were.

The girl was holding a hand to her small belly. 'I'm hungry,' she said.

'You'll just have to wait,' Rosa told her. 'Now run along, little one.'

As the girl wandered away, Rosa sighed and wiped the back of her hand across her forehead. She stood there framed in the light of the window with her other hand on her hip, looking out at the children in the yard with tender consternation in her eyes.

It softened Curl too to see her like that. She had grown deeply fond of this woman in her time here.

Curl knew she had been blessed all those months ago when she had first arrived in the city of Bar-Khos, and had spotted the sign on the door and knocked upon it in search of lodging. She'd stood there wearing hand-me-downs donated by the volunteers from the refugee camp, feeling lost in a city of this size, lacking the faintest idea of how she was going to support herself; and then the door had suddenly tugged open, and Rosa stood before her with her tired, kind eyes.

Now, like her night terrors come real, the Mannians were coming to destroy her world once again.

'It's just . . .' she ventured. 'I need to feel like I'm doing *something*.'

Rosa turned her head, observed her for a moment with sympathy.

'You could do something useful for me right now, my girl.'

'Oh?'

Her head gestured to the table of dirty platters, a sly humour in her expression.

Curl clapped her hands to her cheeks and blew an exasperated breath of air.

*

The shutters of the window lay open, so that over the grumble of the guns Curl could hear the faint sounds of shouted orders, and the dim beat of marching feet in great numbers. She was sitting on her bed with the small box on her lap, the dross half-unwrapped on its open lid. The sounds outside, though, caused her to set them aside and cross to the window.

There was nothing to see, save for the houses opposite, and a handcart being pushed along the street by an old rag man, some children running past him in silence. No street girls in sight anywhere, she saw. Most likely they were out along the Avenue of Lies, snatching what quick business they could from the troops filtering out of the city towards the marshalling grounds beyond the northern walls.

Curl felt a moment's relief that she didn't have to work the streets any more. She wasn't proud of how easily she had taken to this profession of hers, nor how popular she was amongst the roving clientele of the area. Still, in only a few months of working she'd been able to gain a steady number of reliable customers, enough so that now she could take appointments in her room, and charge all the more for doing so.

She recalled that she was entertaining that evening, that old lech Bostani, with his stench of tarweed and ale and stale sweat, and his pig eyes that seemed dead to everything, even to pleasure. Curl made it a habit to never think of these things in her own time. She retreated back to the bed and placed the open box on her lap once more, and stared down at it unblinking.

The grey dust was something else she was hardly proud of. She'd taken to the stuff much too easily as well, finding in it something that could get her through the long days and the even longer, lonely nights. A dross-addicted prostitute, she thought to herself. Her aunt and sisters would be distraught to see what had become of her. And her mother, her ally . . .

Curl looked away from the box of dross with a sudden glimmer in her eyes.

Why had she even come to Bar-Khos, she wondered? The cityport of Al-Khos had been closer to the northern refugee camp than to here. Yet some compulsion had led her to tramp and hitch rides all the way to the south of the island barefoot and alone, often only escaping trouble by luck or the kindness of strangers.

Curl didn't know why, but some part of her had needed to come to Bar-Khos and the legendary Shield; this city of eternal siege where they had stood and held firm against the forces of Mann, and where they were still doing so, even now, while an imperial army massed on the eastern coast intent on their conquest.

She'd come to like these Khosians and their ways. At first, she'd been distrustful of the aid they had given her party of refugees, freshly arrived in their boat from Lagos. In a short time, though, Curl had realized that this generosity of spirit was an honoured trait amongst these people, and humility too, for all their contradictions of pride and hardiness.

As a people, their moods seemed prone to melancholy, though they were romantics too, so that even their soldiers could be poets and lovers as easily as drunks and suicides. They relished their freedoms yet favoured cooperation and community. They prioritized families and simple, peaceful lives above all else. Those of wealth and power, like their own Michinè nobles, were often spoken of with a kind of bitter sympathy, as if the painted men and women of influence were ill of spirit, warped by their own desires to lord it over others.

Speaking with other refugees living in the area, those who had travelled the Mercian Isles and knew them well, Curl had heard how it was the same with all the peoples of the Free Ports – if not even more so – where people lived with no nobles at all. She still found the notion a hard one to grasp.

Curl glanced back to the dross in her lap. At breakfast, one of the lodgers had said that the imperial invaders were from the Sixth Army. The same men who had laid waste to Lagos.

Curl thought of a town on fire, a pale sky obscured by smoke. Her family's cries lost amongst the tumult of so many others. The tears spilled down her cheeks. For long moments she sat there, shaking and awash with heartache, a wet hand covering her burning face.

When a sob finally forced its way from her chest she sat up straight and shook her head in self-admonishment. She sniffed, and brushed a hand across her cheek as though to swipe away a cobweb.

She looked up at her little shrine to Oreos, a decision somehow made within her.

'Shit,' Curl said.

*

The interior of the Stadium of Arms was larger than she'd imagined from its outer facade of pillars and curving stonework.

As she stood in its main entranceway, pressed against

the side to stay clear of the soldiers rushing past in both directions, she looked on a scene of barely contained chaos. Men in their hundreds occupied the sandy floor of the amphitheatre, where every Fool's Day the zel races were held, and every other day it was used for the training of recruits.

She saw Red Guards and Specials, Greyjackets and Free Volunteers. Many of the older men were dressed in civilian clothing. Some men even wore dirty rags, and were having manacles removed from their ankles. Amongst them all, soldiers ran back and forth humping loads of equipment, which they were piling into mounds scattered across the sand. There seemed no order to it. Yet men bawled commands as though they knew the lie of this land.

Curl pressed even closer to the stonework as a company of Red Guards began to march by in rank and file, some of the men jeering and whistling at her as they stamped past, even though she wore the plain boy's clothes she had been wearing on her arrival in the city. She ducked her head and hurried past, fleeing into the wide arcade that ran beneath the tiers of seating overhead.

A zel was rearing beneath the arches as men tried to hitch a cart to it. Its hooves clattered on the flagging. Blacksmiths hammered away at swords or spearheads; soldiers brushed past without a second glance, or cursed her out of the way. Curl felt her blood beginning to rise at the confusion of it all. She stopped a young man with a quick smile, and asked where she might find the recruiting office.

He thought she was joking at first, but she scowled until he relented. 'On the right,' he said with his glance darting all over her body and a hand flapping vaguely. 'Through the doorway there. Then take the second on your left.'

When Curl followed his directions through a bustling

passageway she found herself standing in a latrine. A row of armoured men were lined against the trough talking and pissing. In an instant a dozen faces were calling out to her in the close confines of the stinking room, while they tried to pierce her eardrums with their whistles. She ignored the flashes they gave her; instead she raised a single eyebrow, and left with a tirade of curses tumbling from her lips.

Curl was hot and flustered by the time she finally found herself at the door to the recruitment office, a room that turned out to be the busiest she had yet seen. She slipped past a man hurrying through the doorway and made her way into the centre of the room, where a heavy desk stood piled with papers, and behind it sat a man who by all appearances was in the midst of a heart attack. His face was redder than any Curl had ever seen before. The sweat flowed off him in ribbons.

'I don't care!' he was shouting to a nervous man hovering by his side, his voice hoarse and strangled. 'If they can march then they go!'

'But their gear is weather-damaged,' the nervous man told him. 'All of it.'

'I don't care! Just do what you need to get them moving!'

Curl waited for him to take a breath before approaching. 'Excuse me,' she tried, then bent over the desk to be heard better, placing her hands carefully so as not to disturb the papers there, or the stylus and the jar of ink. 'Excuse me,' she said more loudly.

The officer turned his rounded eyes on her. She watched them trace a figure of eight. 'What is it now?' he growled. 'You want to kiss a sweetheart goodbye?'

On the desk, her hands screwed themselves into small, tight fists. 'I'm here to enlist,' she told him.

The man opened his mouth and kept it that way. Around him, the silence spread outwards until the room was wholly quiet and every man was looking at her.

'Go home, girl,' he said with a dismissive wave of his hand. 'We haven't need for any more camp whores, believe me.'

Curl seized the inkwell in her hand without thinking. She flung it at the man and watched it bounce off his forehead even as she realized what she had done.

'You little bitch!' he screeched as he clutched his forehead in shock. She found herself picking up the jar for the stylus too, and swinging her arm back to finish the job.

But then a hand gripped her own from behind, and the jar was plucked from her grasp.

She spun around in a hot temper, looking up as she did so. A man towered there in black leather armour, heavily scarred about the face and neck.

'Bad girl,' he said from behind his thick beard. 'You almost took the man's eye out.'

'I was trying to,' she said in a pant.

He laughed, and then the men around him were chuckling too.

'You're serious, about wishing to enlist?'

'This is the recruitment office, isn't it?'

The man looked at the officer behind the desk, then studied Curl for a moment.

'Can you stitch wounds?'

She thought of her father the physician; his scalp wound that had needed stitching once, how he had talked her through it while her fingers trembled.

'Well enough,' she told him. 'I know some medicines too, home folk stuff. Herbs and ointments.'

'Give your details to Hooch over there. Our medicos might make some use of you. I'm Major Bolt, by the way.'

She smiled, opened her mouth to thank him.

'No, don't thank me, girl,' he said, holding up one of his large hands. 'You can curse me in your own time – but just don't bloody thank me.'

CHAPTER SIXTEEN

The Eyes

People seldom remembered what the old fort on the hill had originally been called. They simply knew it now as the 'Eyes', a name that referred to the dirty faces that could always be seen pressing against its thickly barred windows, their desperate glares staring out from their confinement at a world that was passing them by.

The Eyes had long since ceased to be a fort. It stood on a hill in the Fallow District of the city, a brooding presence that overlooked the eastern wall and the houses and workshops of the area. These days it was used solely to hold veterans of the war, those soldiers who were siege-shocked badly enough to have become a danger to themselves or even to others; the Specials in particular, those who fought in the tunnels beneath the Shield.

At times, often when the mood in the city itself was tense, the inmates would call out to the Red Guards stationed atop the eastern wall with jokes or obscenities, or they would shout at the citizens of the district surrounding it, ordinary folk going about their business, too polite to look up at the lunatics on the hill.

That evening, Bahn couldn't tell if anyone was calling out from the windows of the place, for a crowd of Red Guards was causing a din at the wrought-iron front gates of the institution, so that he could hear nothing else but their shouting. He pressed through to the front of the crowd and found that the gates were closed. On the other side of them stood an opposing group of jailers, clad in thick leather aprons and armed with cudgels. They were shouting back through the gates just as vehemently.

'What's going on here?' Bahn hollered to the lieutenant of the squad he now stood amongst.

'They've been ordered by the governor to stop us from entering,' the officer shouted back with a hand cupped over Bahn's ear.

'They know why you're here?'

'Of course. That's why the governor's trying to stop us.'

'All right,' Bahn said. 'Tell your men to give it a rest.'

He turned to face the jailers as the noise began to settle down.

'I am an aide to General Creed, and his order has been clearly given. Now open the gates and stand aside.'

He saw a movement amongst the men, and two of the jailers parted as a grey-haired fellow pushed through to confront him. 'I am Governor Plais,' the man informed him, 'and by the council's authority I am responsible for this institution. I repeat what I have already said to your fellow officer. There are no men fighting fit within these walls. They would not be here otherwise.'

'Governor,' said Bahn, stepping up to the gates. 'Right now, an army of forty thousand Mannians stands on the shore of Pearl Bay. As you can hear, even now the Fourth Army pounds the Shield in preparation for a full-scale assault. We need every man who can fight, whatever his crimes, whatever his state of mind.'

'But these men are disturbed! Dangerous even!'

'Still, the order has been given. Now open the gates.'

For a moment no one moved.

'Open them!' Bahn snapped without patience. He looked at the jailers behind the gate until one of them took a step forwards, and then the rest of them followed, and the gates squealed open, and Bahn and the Red Guards stepped through into the courtyard with the governor protesting in his face.

'The council will hear of this,' he shouted, but Bahn stepped around him and headed for the building entrance.

'I have no doubt that they will,' he cast back over his shoulder.

*

The cell was approached through a long passageway sealed by a series of iron gates cast brown by rust, which shed the odd flake whenever a gate slammed shut and was locked behind them. The walls were damp down here in this silent basement level, where the only light came from the oil lantern carried by one of the jailers.

'But the man is a maniac,' the governor was insisting in his grating voice.

'I know who he is. I fought by his side in the first years of the siege.'

'But he's a convicted murderer, a torturer – he's more likely to kill you than the enemy! Have you lost your mind?'

'He's the only man here I haven't yet spoken to. I'll have a word with him, at least.'

Darkness pressed upon them from all sides. It seemed to follow their little haven of light as they walked in a collective hush along the passageway, the only sounds the dripping of water and the scrapes of their feet against the stone floor. There were four jailers with them, clad in leather aprons and gloves that came up to their armpits, stout clubs dangling from their grips. They were silent, their eyes fixed ahead. They seemed to be steeling themselves for confrontation.

Bahn followed them, not liking the close confines of this place. He couldn't imagine being locked up as a prisoner down here. An hour would have him tearing at the walls to get out.

The door to the cell was made from a solid, fire-hardened slab of tiq wood banded by iron. One of the jailers stepped up and opened the small viewing hatch.

Bahn leaned forward to peer inside.

He saw a candle, burning a halo of warmth in the centre of a small vaulted cell. In its light sat a large naked man, chained by the neck to the wall he leaned his back against, one leg stretched before him, the other bent up and its knee supporting a limp hand; his face was smoky shadow, with two eyes that glowered at those in the hatch with open hostility.

Bull, Bahn thought. *How did I know you would always end up like this?*

He stepped back as the door was unlocked and pulled open by two straining jailers, the hinges protesting loudly.

'Stay behind the chain,' the jailer with the lantern advised Bahn. 'He blinded one of our men a few months back. With his thumbs.'

The man ducked inside with his club at the ready. Bahn stepped into the cell and stopped by his side, his ankles touching a chain that hung slack across the tiny space. He held his helm beneath his arm, and tried to stand tall in his armour and his red cloak.

The prisoner placed his hands upon the collar around his neck, and lifted himself to his feet in all his naked glory, displaying a patchwork of scars across a tensed, muscular frontage. He looped some of the chain over his arm to support the weight of it, a curious gesture, as though he was adjusting some fine robe of office.

You've aged, Bahn thought, as he took in the heavy abuses of the man's face, and the receding hairline at his temples, where a pair of horns were tattooed.

Bahn had indeed fought alongside this man in those first few desperate years of the war, before Bull had been chosen for the heavy infantry of the chartassa. Bull had been crazy even back then; a dangerous and volatile man who enjoyed a fight more than any other Bahn had ever known. It hadn't surprised him when Bull had finally lost his temper once too often and with entirely the wrong person – his superior officer, a fellow whom Bull nearly killed with a single clout, and for the careless mistake of calling him by his real name.

Two years in a stockade had come of it, and a full discharge from the army. After that, Bahn had vaguely followed his rising celebrity as a champion pit-fighter. One of the best in Khos, it was said.

And then the day came when Bahn, along with the rest of the city, heard the news of Adrianos's murder. Adrianos, hero of the Nomarl raid, the last commander to have personally led a successful offensive against the Imperial Fourth Army. The city's hero had been found in several different pieces in his fine apartment just off the Grand Bazaar. He had been gagged and bound and tortured. Parts of him had been flayed.

Next to his carcass, Bull had sat, wearing nothing but blood.

'Hello, brother,' Bahn said to him in a hush.

Bull took a step towards him. 'Bahn?' he asked, incredulous.

'Yes.'

Bull stepped closer, the chain unravelling from his arm as it stretched tight behind him. The jailer at Bahn's side shifted uneasily, weighing the club in his hand. Bull refused to acknowledge him. He remained focused on Bahn, his massive arm held against his stomach, the knuckles of his hand disfigured by swelling, the skin recently torn and bloody. 'What brings you here then, eh? Are you lost?'

His voice rasped as though he hadn't used it for a very long time. 'Speak up,' growled Bull. 'I'm doubting this is a social call. What is it?'

All at once, as Bahn listened to the lilt in the man's voice, and stared into the dark eyes above his sharp cheekbones, he was taken back to the days of the early war, hunkering down behind a parapet as Bull grinned in his face, slapping his back to stop him coughing and enjoying every moment of it, the crazy barkbeating bastard.

'The Mannians have landed in force in Pearl Bay.'

Bull narrowed his eyes, pushed his head forward to scrutinize him more closely.

'I'm here for the veterans. To see if any of you are fit to stand with us.'

'Another judge, then,' Bull spat, half turning away.

'What? You think you've been judged unfairly?'

The chain snapped tight as Bull towered over him. Bahn fought the urge to step back a pace.

'Easy, now,' soothed the jailer as he poked his club into Bull's bare chest.

Still Bull ignored him, stared instead at Bahn. 'No, I suppose I don't. But then neither was Adrianos. You understand? When *I* judged him.'

He sounded anything but insane. Wrathful, certainly. Eager for violence.

'Will you stand with us, and fight for your people?'

'My people?' he asked, incredulous.

'Aye. For the people of Bar-Khos, like your father. And for your mother's people in the Windrush.'

Suddenly, a wide smile creased his face like the gash of a knife. Two of his front teeth were missing, Bahn saw. The rest looked to be rotting. 'I owe no loyalty to anyone, least of all the people of Bar-Khos.'

'Will you fight for us?'

'Is it a pardon. Is that what you're offering?'

'Yes. If that's what it will take.'

'And all I have to do is kill some Mannians in the name of *my people*, is that it? You'll take the slayer into your ranks even if he's a cold-blooded murdering bastard of a barkbeater, is that how it's to be, Bahn?'

For a long moment Bahn swayed in his armour, feeling tired and out of place here.

'Believe me, Bull,' he told his old comrade plainly. 'Where we are going, we'll have great need of men like you.'

CHAPTER SEVENTEEN

Free Enterprise

Mistress Cheer was clearly a woman who knew how to land on her feet. In the space of a single day, amidst the confusion and high emotions of the beach-head, she obtained for herself a wagon and a mule, a cartload of supplies, and enough home comforts to create a small camp for her and her women on the seaward edge of the dunes.

By evening, awnings had been erected over two sides of the wagon and the sand underneath covered in mats of woven grasses. There were stools to sit on, and a fire smoked beneath a hanging kettle and pot, with water and stew warming in them. Mistress Cheer had even procured three tents for them all, which she instructed Ash to pitch not far from the wagon, though far enough for some privacy.

The women relaxed at last, preening themselves in clear view of the men surrounding the camp, squabbling amongst themselves whenever their mistress was beyond earshot. A few casually flirted with Ash, sporting with him over the colour of his skin, the firmness of his old body. He chuckled in pleasure, giving as good as he got.

Ash had overheard that the place itself was called Whittle Bay, a broad cove within the larger sweep of Pearl Bay, which was located on the eastern coastline of Khos. It was a pretty enough location, with its hills to the west and the high peaks of mountains both north and south, and the rocky, gull-covered island out in the greater bay. In many ways the scene reminded Ash of northern Honshu, though it was spoiled somewhat by the stink of the army deployed across the beachhead, and by the closer press of thousands of camp followers, who had accompanied the invasion force all this way to Khos, like Mistress Cheer, in hope of making a profit.

The fleet lay at anchor out in the clear deep waters just beyond the coastal shelf of the cove. Its ships bobbed in tight formation, looking weather-beaten even from here, with spars and masts missing or hanging broken amongst wrappings of sails, some of the hulls listing too far to one side. The work was hardly slackening with the falling twilight. It seemed that a great deal still required unloading before the army could set forth in the morning.

Ash rested as best he could. His cough was worse today. Every now and again his limbs would shake as if from some inner chill, though his clothes were blessedly dry for once, and he kept the oiled cloak wrapped tight about him, and refused to stray long from the warmth of the fire.

Occasionally Mistress Cheer would cast him one of her pointed stares. He would groan to himself and climb to his feet, before wandering around the camp with his sheathed sword in his hand for show, scowling at the soldiers and non-enlisted men camped all around their small oasis of perfume and stockings and girlish laughter.

As the sun finally set, Mistress Cheer put the women to work with sharp claps of her hands and practised words of encouragement. They were hardly the only prostitutes on the beach – far from it – but still, soon enough, a long line of soldiers stretched from their little camp as they waited their turn, drunk and boisterous on this foreign beach far from home. Ash maintained order within the camp itself as the girls took turns leading the clientele into the tents, their business brief.

His mind was barely on the job. To the south, where the ground rose up towards the ruins of the burned village, he could see the palisade and tents of the Matriarch's camp, with her standard flying high. It seemed to call to him each time he turned his attention elsewhere.

There was little trouble with the men that evening. It was late when the women's calls for respite grew loud enough for Mistress Cheer to acknowledge them, and to declare an end to business for the night. A number of drunken soldiers still awaited their turn, but their complaints died quickly at Mistress Cheer's glare and the hard, silent farlander by her side.

Rather than preparing for sleep, the girls set about having a small party instead.

Ash was weary after the long day. He excused himself, and with reluctance left the warmth of the fire, and found a spot on top of a nearby dune and huddled down in his cloak where he could keep an eye on them, but remain alone. With his sword lying by his side, he studied the lights of the distant camp of the Matriarch, the lie of the moonlit land around it. He looked for movement amongst the many fires that were merely glimmers from here. He wished he had his eyeglass with him; even a pair of eyes younger than his own.

Ash coughed once more, spat phlegm, wiped his mouth dry. Clouds were drifting in from the north, ponderous and heavy. More rain on its way, maybe. They would obscure the waxing moons and make a darkness of the land beneath them.

A good night for it, he thought to himself.

'See something of interest up there?'

He smelled her musky perfume even before she sat down on the sand, and fixed her dress over her legs as the coarse seagrass flattened beneath them. Ash looked at Mistress Cheer as she settled a flask of rhulika in his hands.

He nodded a grateful thanks to her, taking a long drink to warm himself.

'Easy. It's the last of it.'

He returned the flask with a brief smile. 'Thank you. It has been some time since I last had a proper drink.'

Behind them, the squeals and laughter of the women rang out from their small, firelit hollow in the dunes. A breeze played through the fringes of Mistress Cheer's hair. She fixed her shawl tighter about her head.

'Tell me again what it was your previous employer did?'

Ash tapped the flask in her hand with a fingernail.

'Alcohol?'

'He shipped a small fortune of it here. Would hardly let me touch the stuff, though.'

It was a poor lie, Ash thought. He couldn't tell if she believed him. Cheer looked away, her eyes dancing with the lights of the campfires. Singing and laughter drifted with the breeze; people elsewhere in the dunes celebrating in high spirits.

Over it all they could hear the rhythmic wash of the sea.

'We're a long way from home,' she said to him sombrely.

Ash gave a slow nod of his head.

She turned to look at him again. 'Some more than others, I suppose. Do you ever miss it – Honshu, I mean?'

'Yes. Sometimes.'

'Of course you do,' she said in what sounded like self-admonishment. 'Of course you do.'

He saw that the cloud mass was nearing the moons now. It would be getting dark soon, dark enough to prowl.

'You know, you have the saddest eyes I think I've ever seen. And I've seen my fair share of them, in my time.'

Ash's forehead wrinkled in a frown. He felt an urge to rise and walk away from the woman and her prying talk. But then she shifted over to press against his side for warmth. He found that he liked the feel of it enough to stay where he was.

She studied his expression, waiting for him to say something. He had no words for her, though.

'Well, I feel my bed calling. Time the girls got some

rest too.' She rose and brushed the sand from her dress. 'Aren't you tired?' she asked, and he heard the heat in her words, the unspoken offer.

His eyes lingered on the curves of her body beneath her dress. He wished very much that he could accept it.

'I think I will stay up a while, and watch over the camp.'

She covered her disappointment by looking down at the sand.

'It's the scar, isn't it?'

'Not at all,' he replied. 'Really. I am just tired.'

She nodded, not believing him.

'Goodnight, then,' she said as she turned away, and trudged down the slope of the dune.

He waited a full hour to be certain the girls and Mistress Cheer were soundly asleep. Some fires continued to burn amongst the dunes, small groups of people talking as sparks rose upwards with the smoke. On the beach, the work parties laboured on through the night with the supplies still being brought to shore.

It was a risk, to leave the women without protection. But a risk he would have to take.

Removing his heavy cloak and picking up his sword, Ash stole out into the night.

—CHAPTER EIGHTEEN—

Surrender and Be Free

'I have to go,' Bahn told his wife as he tied down the last of the equipment to his saddle.

Marlee nodded stiffly. Behind her, in the evening shadows, a man on crutches hobbled past in the otherwise empty street, a flap of skin hanging where his foot had once been. The man was in a hurry, as though pursued by the sounds of the tower horns that wailed across the city to announce the departure of the last of the troops.

'Remember what I said, now. Get a message to Reese. Let her know she can come and stay here with you. Tell her I'm sorry I haven't been to see her.' Bahn suddenly ran his fingers through his hair. He recalled the last time he had seen his sister-in-law; her quiet voice explaining how her son had left the city. 'Sweet Mercy, I haven't even been to ask after Nico. How long has it been now?'

'It's all right,' soothed his wife behind him. 'I'll tell Reese. She'll understand.'

Her words failed to assuage him. Bahn had felt a certain responsibility towards Reese and her son ever since his brother Cole had deserted them.

He cinched the leather strap with a final sharp tug, putting his frustration into it. He inspected his work, then took a deep breath before turning to face his wife.

'Time to go.'

Marlee nodded without expression. She was maintaining her composure for the sake of them both.

He'd felt awkward around his wife these recent weeks. He'd found that in her presence his guilty conscience would often make him think of the girl Curl, and it made him uneasy in his wife's gaze, as though she might somehow see through him.

Now he stared hard into her eyes, unflinching. Marlee clasped her arms around his neck as he held her slim waist in his hands. Their noses touched.

'I love you,' he told her.

'And I love you, my sweet man.'

Her eyes shone with the beginnings of tears.

He held her to him tightly, crushing her against his armour. He did not wish to let her go.

I don't deserve this woman, he thought bitterly.

The children were already asleep inside. Bahn had kissed his sleeping infant daughter on the forehead, had shared a few words with his bleary-eyed son tucked up in bed.

He couldn't shake what he'd seen in the streets on his hasty return home. People had been lining the thorough-fares as columns of soldiers and old Molari marched for the northern gates, cheering them on as they passed by, forcing good-luck charms and parcels of food and bottles of spirits into their hands. Some had cried at the sight of them, old men even, stirred by the determined expressions of the soldiers and the knowledge of what they all marched towards.

We can do this, Bahn had thought as his own emotions soared with the collective spirit of the crowds. *If we stand together we can get through this.*

But then, cutting through the backstreets to make better progress, he had passed countless people rushing with their belongings towards the harbours, hoping to find safe passage off the island, and he had watched them pass with something of envy in his heart.

On the walls, fresh graffiti was painted as though in blood. *The flesh is strong. Surrender and be free.* The work of Mannian agitators, resurfacing in the city now that it was truly vulnerable, and the majority of its forces were leaving.

Standing with Marlee in his arms, Bahn once more felt the urge to grab his wife and shake her and say, *For pity's sake, take the children and find a way out!* But they were words for him alone, for he could never bring himself to say them. Not to Marlee, his pillar of strength, this woman whose father had fallen on the first day of the siege in defence of the city. She would say no, absolutely no, and then she would think less of him as a husband, as a man.

'Look after them,' was all he could say amidst the soft thickness of her hair.

'Of course,' she breathed. 'And promise me you'll be careful.'

'I will.'

And despite their words of reassurance, they kissed long and hard and desperately, as though they would never see each other again.

*

On the still-smouldering hilltop, Ash stood amongst the ashes and debris that were the remains of a small fishing village, and stared down at a line of severed penises laid out in the gloom like a children's forgotten game of half-sticks.

Close by, the charred corpses of their owners lay contorted amid the rubble of a collapsed stable. Ash had glimpsed smaller bodies lying amongst them: children and even infants.

Of the women, there was no sign.

Not for the first time in Ash's long life, it struck him how death smelled the same no matter if it was man, zel, or dog. Ash had seen such things before in his days with the People's Revolutionary Army. The long-running war of his homeland had burned the compassion from many men's hearts. Friends had become unhinged with loss or simply callous and hardened like himself, while those men already tainted with cruelty within had revelled unfettered through a landscape of war where the normal bounds of decency no longer applied.

It had broken his heart the first time he'd witnessed such an atrocity; an anguish almost akin to the heartbreak of a beloved's infidelity, though much worse than that; like a great lie at the heart of the world, suddenly exposed by shocking vivisection.

'This is not your war,' Ash told himself aloud in the darkness of the night.

He almost expected to hear the voice of Nico in admonishment. Those were Khosians lying there in the rubble. The whole country, the boy's family included, faced slavery or the same fate as this.

Nothing came to Ash, though, no voice of conscience or disembodied spirit, only the vague unsettled feeling that he was as much a part of this as anyone, whether he chose a side or not.

*

The brief gap in the clouds closed above his head, and pitch blackness enveloped him. Sheathed sword in hand, face and hands blackened with soot, Ash turned his back on what lay there in the darkness.

He held a finger against a clogged nostril and blew it clear, then stepped beyond the ruins to the edge of the hill, where he lay on his belly on the coarse grass and looked down on the glowing tents of the Matriarch's camp below.

The tents were visible for the lamps that shone within them, and they stood on a rise of ground that was broad and flat on top, surrounded by a palisade of sharpened, outward-leaning stakes, and the black line of a ditch ran around the foot of the position. Behind the stakes, white-robed sentries stood half a dozen paces apart. At their backs, a bonfire crackled in a clear space between the tents. The flames were illuminating the twitching flag of the Matriarch.

Ash ranged outwards with his gaze, taking in the much larger camp that sprawled around the Matriarch's palisade, perhaps a thousand Acolytes or more. They were surrounded in turn by a band of blackness, and he struggled to make out the double picket lines he knew would be positioned there beyond the light. He couldn't see them, though; only the fires that flickered further along the dunes, the main army spread out far and wide.

He snapped his attention back to the imperial enclosure. By the look of it, the entrance lay on the western side of the palisade, but he couldn't see clearly enough from here. He would need to get down there if he wanted a closer look.

*

Over the course of the next half-hour, Ash descended towards the outermost perimeter, working his way around it as he went. He stopped once to take a drink from a brook running down a cleft in the hill. He stopped again when he was on the flat ground to the west and sensed that he was approaching the first line of sentries, the pickets he'd been unable to see from above.

Ash waited until he formed an impression of what was ranged before him; an outer ring of guards spaced widely apart. He could smell them, their musk of sweat and garlic. He could hear them too: a throat being cleared, the rustle of movement as a cloak was drawn tighter against the chill.

When he thought he knew where the nearest two were located, Ash crept forwards carefully through the space between them. It was no more difficult than that.

Ahead stood the inner line of pickets. He could see them silhouetted against the many fires, standing some fifteen paces apart. They were too far out, he thought in his experienced way; more vulnerable here in the backlit darkness where they were visible but could barely see.

At the heart of the camp stood the Matriarch's enclosure. Barbed wire had been stretched in coils between the stakes of the palisade. The ditch below it was invisible from his position; most likely filled with caltrops to impale the soles of unwary feet. At least he could see the entrance to the enclosure better. It was covered by a screen of wood, and while he watched he saw it being dragged aside to allow an Acolyte to pass through.

Ash had a decision to make: whether this was to be a reconnaissance or a full attempt at reaching Sasheen. He'd seen enough to know there was only one way for him to gain access to her enclosure.

He lay down on the cool grass and rested his chin on his hands. Tried to sense the flow of it all. The opportunity was there all right, though it was a risky one. And no telling what procedures the guards were following at the entrance to the enclosure – not from here.

Let us go and find out then.

Ash singled out the closest sentry to him, a form standing alone taking the odd drink from a flask. He judged the size of the Acolyte and thought that he would do.

For another half-hour, Ash crawled towards the figure through the blackness of the night. It was hard work, moving each limb a tiny fraction at a time without sound. It required his utmost concentration. All the while, his troubled chest burned with the pain of breathing so shallowly.

Six feet from the sentry, he froze as a cough nearby broke the stillness. It made Ash want to cough too. His chest convulsed, and he clamped a hand over his mouth and fought the urge until it had passed. He saw the Acolyte turn his head in his direction.

Ash lay pressed against the grass, barely breathing, his eyes closed.

Long moments passed, enough for a passing mosquito to settle on his sooty cheek. He felt the itch of it, but remained so perfectly still that after a moment the insect took off again, without biting him.

He peered through his eyelashes and saw that the Acolyte was looking elsewhere. Ash began to move again. Like a cat on the hunt, he lifted and settled his limbs with a deliberate slowness, closing the distance an inch at a time. Sweat beaded his skin by the time that he was within range.

He lay right at the man's boots.

The white-robe sniffed the air, looking about him. He could scent Ash's sweat.

Ash lunged up and stabbed his thumbs into the man's throat. The Acolyte choked, trying to release a sound; a hand clawed at Ash's face. Ash pressed his thumbs even harder, seeing the white flash of his victim's eyes through the mask.

He helped him to the ground as the man went slack

in his grip. Maintained the pressure of his thumbs until he was certain he was dead.

'Cuno?' came a voice from the darkness to his left.

Ash froze with his hands still around the Acolyte's neck. He caught a scent of the alcohol that had spilled from the man's dropped flask.

He swallowed air and forced a belch from his gullet.

'Aye,' he said in Trade, and waited for a cry of alarm.

'Nothing,' came the voice again. 'Thought I heard something.'

Ash hurried. His victim was larger than he'd first appeared, and as Ash donned the Acolyte's armour and robe they felt much too big on him.

No, he realized. It was Ash who was smaller now. He'd lost weight during the long voyage.

He pulled the cloak over the oversized armour, hoping that would be enough to the hide the ill fit and the curve of his sword. Then he fixed the mask about his face, which covered his scalp too, like a helm. Only once did he glance at the contorted face that had been revealed beneath it; a middle-aged man with a shaven head, his jowls pronounced beneath a hard face. Ash bent and closed the Acolyte's bulging eyes.

The camp was quiet at this hour, with most of the Acolytes asleep, though laughter and music played from the largest, brightest tent within the Matriarch's enclosure. The camp was arranged in orderly squares, and Ash strode along the lanes between the pup tents and dying campfires as though he rightly belonged there, ignoring the occasional Acolyte that walked past him, or hunkered down over some flames.

As he neared the mound of the enclosure the sounds grew louder in his ears. He heard a sharp cry of pleasure, and a bell ringing.

Ahead, an Acolyte was approaching the palisade with a camouflaged scout limping by his side. They stopped at the screen of wood and wire drawn across the entrance. Ash increased his pace a little, rehearsing a few words in his head as he strode towards the entrance himself.

And then his heart skipped a beat, for he saw the Acolyte stop and display the stubbed little finger of his hand to the guards behind the screen.

Ash cursed and faltered in his stride. He watched as the screen was dragged to one side to allow them through.

If he sprinted now, he might just make it through before it was closed again.

And then what? Fight his way through a hundred men?

He felt his chest convulse, and then he erupted into a fit of coughing from behind his mask. He stopped and doubled over, saw the guards at the entrance turn to regard him through the closing screen.

Ash straightened and walked away from the entrance, knowing how suspicious he must look to them. He wanted to hurry. Instead he walked calmly, his pace steady, waiting to be challenged at any second.

'You there!' came a man's voice through the night.

*

Ché looked up as he heard someone call out his name.

It was Sasheen who had called to him, from where she lounged on a couch in total nakedness, save for the grey plaster wrapped around her broken arm. Already, though, her attention had returned to the young woman who kneeled before her on one of the fur rugs, lapping at Sasheen's heavy breast. Sasheen stroked the shaven head of the young aide, and whispered something down to her while she held a small pinchbowl of narcotics near the girl's nostrils.

Klint the physician was walking around the edges of the tent with a joybell in his hand, a bottle of wine in the other. He was ringing the bell loudly each time he heard a cry of pleasure from one of the writhing forms he carefully trod around, all the while chanting wordbindings

of devotion. He stopped before one of the alcoves
in the tent wall, where the head of Lucian sat on a pedestal. The head blinked dully back at him as Klint shook
the joybell in his face, and shouted, grinning, '*Free
yourself, and all you desire you shall have!*' Sasheen
laughed, egging him on. She was in high spirits tonight.
They all were. The First Expeditionary Force had made
landfall at long last, and they were alive, and having
their fill of it.

A shriek cut through the smoky air of the great tent.
Some priests in a far corner were having their way with
one of the freshly caught slaves – their first taste of
Khos, one of them shouted, as he threw a rag of clothing over his shoulder and fell upon the woman.

Ché rubbed his eyes where he sat on a chair in one of
the alcoves, and wondered when the Matriarch would
relieve him for the night. He had never been one for
these *passionestas* of the order. They exposed him in
ways more than merely physical, requiring that he drop
his guard while in the presence of his fellow priests.
Even so, he was becoming aroused despite himself.

The floor around him was like a pool of merging flesh
now, the air so heady with narcotics he was finding it
hard to focus. He listened to the rasp of breaths and
voices, observed the sheen of oil on interlocked limbs,
the flash of eyes, pink tongues, teeth, smiles and scowls,
whispers, genitalia.

All hail the divine flesh, he reflected sourly.

Everyone was there of Sasheen's inner circle and entourage. The two generals, eyeing one another like fighting dogs as they each caressed a slave girl and partook of
dried fruits and wine. Sasheen's caretaker, Heelas, going
down on one of his young studs. Alarum the spymaster,
holding court to a ring of apt listeners, including Sool.

The priests around these figures formed the outer
circles of Sasheen's court, those of lesser status who
vied always to climb higher. At their very edges were the
Matriarch's aides and hangers-on. The twins were there,

Guan and Swan, the brother and sister frolicking with a woman between them.

Around them all, Sasheen's honour guard watched with their scratch-gloves sheathed and resting lightly on folded arms, their stares hidden by smoky goggles.

And who is watching the watchers, he wondered absently, and scanned the priests who also sat around the edges of the tent in the little alcoves, talking quietly or looking on with steady eyes, some too old for this sport, or too weary, or too bored. Three priests of the Monbarri, the fanatics of Mann, sat within an alcove across from him. The largest, seated in the middle of them, wore a lipless scar-mask for a face, his skin etched by acids in a statement of intent that was extreme even for a Monbarri inquisitor.

His eyes were studying Ché from across the tent.

Ché casually stared back at the faceless man. The bodies were pressing closer now, like a tide pressing against him. A head brushed his boot as a pair of lovers heaved before his feet. He placed his sole against the smooth scalp, pushed until they rolled away from him. As he did so, he caught a glimpse of Swan and saw that she was looking at him from afar.

He offered the young woman a nod of his head. She smiled. The moment of connection warmed him, sent a thrill up his spine.

The Monbarri was still watching him from across the room.

Ché decided he needed to clear his head, and rose to his feet in the same moment. He paused to catch Swan's eye, willing her to follow him, then turned and strode to the entrance as the Monbarri watched him leave.

As he stepped outside he took a deep lungful of untainted air. The sentries ignored him – just another priest of Sasheen's entourage. Ché looked to his right, where a bonfire burned high into the night sky. Two Acolytes were throwing another empty wine crate onto it, one of many the priests had already worked their way through.

It was to be expected, Ché supposed. With the success of the crossing and the survival of most of the fleet during last night's storm, the Matriarch and her general staff were in need of venting their tensions. Watching them tonight, feasting and gorging themselves, it had become clear to Ché that until the very moment they had reached land with their forces largely intact, no one had been entirely sure if it was possible.

Ché stepped a little further away from the noise of the tent. He waited in hope that Swan would emerge, while a slight breeze blew down the valley, carrying with it a hint of the winter still to come. They would have to make haste if they were to take Bar-Khos before the first falls of snow.

An Acolyte was escorting a scout through the entrance to the palisade, a weary middle-aged purdah covered in dirt and sporting a limp. His wolfhound was nowhere to be seen. Ché squinted. Behind the messenger and scout, a second Acolyte had been approaching the entrance, though the man had stopped as the screen was drawn across the entrance again, and had doubled over in a fit of coughing, and now was walking off in a different direction entirely.

Odd, thought Ché.

'You there!' Ché shouted to the guards at the entrance. They turned to see who was shouting.

Another shriek broke the night air. It recalled to Ché the sound of a scream from a boiling water-heater, the whistle that had finally obscured it.

Ché's eyes lingered over the retreating Acolyte.

'Never mind,' he shouted to the guards.

He looked back to the threshold of the tent. Swan had not ventured out to join him.

Ché stalked off to his tent alone.

CHAPTER NINETEEN

Old Wants

Ash awoke to an iron-capped boot prodding at his ribs.

He opened his eyes, bleary with what little sleep he'd been able to snatch in the small hours of the night, and felt a warm body pressed against his own.

He tugged the blanket from his face and blinked up at the scowling face of an imperial soldier.

'On your feet, old man.'

Ash groaned and covered his head with the blanket once again. The boot prodded him harder.

He growled and scrambled to his feet, his sheathed sword in his hand. 'What?' he snapped, gaining himself a precious second to take in the situation.

Three soldiers surrounded him. Others were waking people across the dunes to press them with questions. Ash relaxed a little. They didn't know who they were looking for, not by appearance at least.

Even so, all three soldiers were staring at the confident way he held his sword and had their hands resting firmly on the pommels of their own.

'Captain Sanson!' shouted the man with the friendly toecap. Another soldier stepped towards them. He took one look at the old farlander and narrowed his eyes.

'You like walks in the night, old man?'

'Is that an invitation?'

The captain tensed. From the corners of his vision, Ash saw that other soldiers were dragging away a man they deemed to be suspicious.

'He's with me,' came a voice from below. All of them looked down to see Mistress Cheer emerging from the blanket, wiping sand from her flanks as she stood up in her heavy nightdress.

Captain Sanson eyed the woman coolly. 'In what capacity, mistress?'

'He's my bodyguard,' she explained as she took Ash's arm in her own. 'What did you imagine he was?'

'And when did you employ him?'

Her eyes flickered to Ash. 'Two years ago. For all it's got to do with you. What's the meaning of all of this, anyway?'

Captain Sanson ignored her for a moment. He took another long questioning look at Ash, then at the tents where the girls were still sleeping. He bowed his head to Mistress Cheer. 'My apologies,' he told her. 'Some enemy scouts may have been in the area last night. We're making a security sweep of the beach, that's all.' A flick of his hand commanded the others to follow as he strode away.

'My thanks,' said Ash when they were safely out of earshot.

Mistress Cheer shivered in the cool morning breeze, then released her grip on his arm. 'I repay my debts, that's all. Is there something you wish to tell me, Ash?'

'You heard what he said. Enemy scouts.'

She looked away for a moment, then fixed him with a hard stare.

'I noticed you were gone for most of the night, before I came and joined you.'

Ash tightened his lips and looked to the sand at his feet.

Last night, when he'd finally returned from his botched mission, he'd collapsed in exhaustion next to the dead fire of their small camp. Some time later he'd half awakened to find a blanket placed over him, and Mistress Cheer pressing her soft body against his own.

'Be that way, then,' she snapped at him now, and her anger was unmistakable. She took a few steps away before rounding on him. 'I don't care if you were thieving or worse last night. But I can't have a bodyguard I can't rely on to be here when he's needed. Nor a liar whose secrets I can't fathom. I've paid my debt to you. Help yourself to some hot food when the others awake, then I'll give you your coins. But no matter how much I may be fond of you, Ash – if that even be your real name – I think it best that you move on after breakfast.'

It was her loss of trust in him, he could see. She was a woman sensitive to past betrayals.

He cast his mind back to the early hours of the morning. Their long kisses beneath the blanket and the clouds overhead, their slow tender passion. She'd been the first woman Ash had lain with in several years, and it had made him realize how much he missed it; the intimacy, the shedding for a short time of his loneliness.

Knowing there would be no changing her mind, though, he bowed his head low. 'You and the girls – you will be safe?'

'I'm sure we can find another hungry blade for hire somewhere on this forsaken beach. We'll be fine.'

He nodded again, then surprised her by kissing her full on the mouth, her scarred lip feeling strange but thrilling against his own.

'Good luck to you, strange old man from Honshu,' she said as he walked away.

*

Ché returned from the latrine feeling poorly rested after the late night before, but he was thankful not to be hungover like many of the other men and women he passed in the encampment, with their pale faces and bloodshot eyes.

It was a windy day, and the press of it against his face was cool and refreshing. He could feel the new-grown stubble on his scalp rubbing against the hood of his robe; Ché had stopped shaving his head now that he was here in Khos, preparing for whatever mission amongst the population might be required of him. It felt good to have some hair again.

In the open space of ground before the Matriarch's

tent, the spymaster Alarum was cinching a bedroll to the saddle of a zel.

'Going for a ride?' Ché enquired as he stopped and looked up at the spymaster, who this morning resembled nothing more than a local peasant bandit. The priest was dressed in plain civilian clothing; fur-trimmed riding trousers, an outer coat of green wool, a bandana tied across his bald head. He'd removed his facial jewellery, and had replaced it with a single loop of gold in his right ear. Two long curved knives protruded from the thick leather of his belt.

Alarum glanced in Ché's direction with one foot in the stirrup. He hopped a few times and swung his other leg over the saddle, righting himself as the zel snorted and shifted back a step. 'Priest Ché,' he said, tightening the reins in his gloved hands. Behind his mount, a string of two more zels stood loaded with supplies. 'Yes, a spot of fieldwork,' he explained a little breathlessly, a little excitedly.

'Alone?'

'Believe me, I prefer it this way. Much safer.'

The zel became still beneath him, and Alarum placed his hands on the pommel of the saddle and stared down at Ché with an odd, searching expression.

'Tell me, Ché. Has your mother ever spoken of me, perchance?'

'She's spoken of many men. I don't keep track.'

Alarum gathered his thoughts for a blinking moment.

'It's just . . . I knew her once. A long time ago, before you were born.'

'Yes?'

'Yes. And she's a fine woman. Helped me through a difficult time. When you next see her, you must tell her that I ask after her fondly.'

Ché nodded without commitment. He was uncomfortable with this talk of his mother, and as always in moments of discomfort, his hand began to scratch at one of his rashes.

'That skin problem of yours,' observed Alarum. 'You should come and see me when I return. I have ointments that may help.'

'Thank you, but I already have some.' He patted the flank of the zel and stepped back from it. 'Good riding.'

Alarum raised a hand then kicked his zel into a trot, leading the string of extra mounts behind. Ché watched him leave for a few moments, then turned once more into the wind.

Back in his own small tent, he returned the bundle of graf leaves in his hand to the open backpack on the floor, then looked at the field bunk along one wall, and the stool, and the simple wash stand.

He stood and did nothing for a moment, something troubling him.

His eyes scanned the tent, each item at a time, and came at last to rest on his copy of the Scripture of Lies. It lay face down on the bed, where he had left it face up.

Ché opened the leather-bound book and riffled through its pages roughly. A slip of paper spilled out to land at his feet.

He glanced over his shoulder, then bent to pick it up.

YOU KNOW TOO MUCH, MY FRIEND.

The handwriting was unknown to him. No signature adorned it.

Ché crumpled the note and stood and looked outside. He returned to his bunk and sat down with the piece of paper in his fist, pondering.

At last he stuffed the note into his mouth, and began to chew.

*

That morning, the First Expeditionary Force set forth for war.

Behind it, a contingent of soldiers, merchants and slave porters remained on the filthy sands of the beachhead, tasked with bringing in the rest of the supplies and transporting them forward to the army. The fleet would leave after that, bound for the safety of Lagos. It was too exposed here without adequate squadrons of men-of-war, and the closer harbourages of the southern mainland remained too much of a risk while the Mercian convoys ranged back and forth to Zanzahar for their vital trade. At least the army had some air support at last, for three imperial birds-of-war had finally limped in to rejoin them. The rest were still missing.

For the majority of the Expeditionary Force it was a slow start, and it required most of the morning for everyone, including the camp followers, to begin their march. Draught animals had to be fixed to carts and coaxed into pulling over terrain that seemed to include no roads; herds of livestock and zels needed shepherding up the wide valley floor.

Ahead of the vanguard, light cavalry roved the countryside, searching for enemy contingents and civilian targets to fire and plunder. It was easy work, though, for the highlands of eastern Khos were lightly populated and defended, and those who did live here had mostly hidden themselves in the rocky fastnesses of the region. Further inland, the elite purdah scouts ranged with their great wolfhounds at their sides, employing their usual methods of stealth to remain undetected. They were scouting the path that the army would need to take through the highlands in order to reach the Tumble-downs and the Cinnamon River, which it would then follow downwards into the Reach.

From the main body of the Expeditionary Force, skirmishers fanned outwards to form mobile flanks of protection for the slower troops moving in columns. The light infantry, the predasa, were at the van of the main procession, multinationals from all corners of the Empire, clad in bright cloaks and leather armour, their shields and helms slung from their backs, tramping a rough path through the grasses and heather as they marched. Behind them came the predoré, the heavy infantry, the core of the army, most with the lighter complexions of Q'os and the Lanstrada, accompanied by carts bearing bundles of pikes wrapped in oiled canvas. Behind those came the Acolytes, chanting quietly as they went, the few thousand voices adding a curious harmony to the stamp of so many feet; working to a rhythm that matched the sway of the palanquin that bore the Matriarch in their midst.

In the churned mud at the very back of the column, the carts and civilians of the baggage train stretched noisy and chaotic: blacksmiths with portable forges, wild-haired hunters from the hinterlands, animal herders and their herds, pistoleered rancheros on their fast zel ponies, meat merchants and butchers, slave traders and slave porters, stitchers, carpenters, merchant venturers, private military companies, healers, surgeons, professional scavengers, poets, prostitutes, astrologers, historians . . . everything one would expect to find in the wake of an imperial army bent on conquest.

And so the ponderous inertia of such a huge force was set into motion, and stubbornly maintained for the next three days as it snaked upwards into the rugged hill country of eastern Khos, following whatever tracks the purdahs had marked out for it.

The army camped in the places its scouts chose for it during the day. The soldiers erected their pup tents and made fires from whatever scarce wood they could forage; the Acolytes put up the larger tents of the Matriarch's encampment before surrounding it with the stakes of the palisade, which they bore with them on heavy wagons. The camp followers made do with what they had or what they could find.

It was bitterly cold here at night in the high country, and often as not Ash huddled beneath his cloak without the luxury of a fire, for what little fallen wood there was amongst the scraggly forests of yellowpine was usually scavenged early for the needs of the army. For food, he used the coins Mistress Cheer had paid him – a more than generous amount for all the work he'd done for her – and purchased what he needed from the many small food merchants that accompanied the army. The rates were extortionate, of course. Soon, he had to dip into the hidden purse slung beneath his leather leggings.

He would have grumbled more if he hadn't seen how the soldiers of the army itself were exploited in much the same way. Like Ash, they had to buy food using their own pay, and did so either in bulk from the merchant venturers of the baggage train, or from the countless food vendors who swarmed around them every meal-time like scavenging flies.

Ash marvelled at an army that did not feed its own men. He wondered how it could possibly work, until he overheard an exchange between a soldier and a bored prostitute, in which the man was trying to pay her in rotten apples. His wages were too low to sustain him on the march, he explained, and so he was already in debt to his superior officer. Once they sacked a town or won a battle he would be on his feet again, for plunder and slaves were divided amongst the men after the officers received their cut.

It was profit, Ash came to appreciate, that drove many of these men onwards, much like the camp followers themselves, for those few followers he exchanged words with told similar tales: bad debts to landowners and moneylenders; an inability to find anything but seasonal work in regions clogged with slaves. They were desperate, and in their desperation had sold what they had left and had paid to come here in droves.

Ash mainly walked alone during the long marches through the hill country. He went by his original cover story of a bodyguard whose employer had drowned during the storm. He seldom needed to use it, though. Mostly, he came and went throughout the baggage train as he liked, always making certain to keep his distance from Mistress Cheer and the girls, but it wasn't difficult in such a multitude, and he saw them only once during the first days of the march. Mistress Cheer had hired a new man, a rangy youth in a brown woollen cloak who used his sword to chop wood.

Ash kept to himself, speaking to few but listening to many. All the while, his eyes hungered for a glimpse of Sasheen.

—CHAPTER TWENTY—

Juno's Ferry

The settlement of Juno's Ferry lay to the south of the Windrush forest, that myth-wrapped woodland that spanned the central region of Khos. In the summer months, the boughs of the trees would sway in the warm *asago* that blew in from the east bearing sands from the far Alhazii desert, and in the colder seasons would clatter instead in the occasional storm of the *shoné*, gusting across the breadth of the Midèrēs all the way from the northern continent; a wind said to cause depression and madness for those who lived in its path.

To the east, the great swathe of the Windrush was naturally bounded by the mighty Chilos, the sacred river of Khos. Known for its cleansing properties of mind and spirit, the Chilos was also renowned for never freezing over even in the depths of winter. Its source came from the hot springs of Simmer Lake, site of the ancient floating town of Tume, and as its waters wound their slow way south towards the Bay of Squalls, they cooled only gradually.

On a widening stretch of the Chilos, the twin settlements of Juno's Ferry sprawled along both banks like inverse reflections of each other. On the western bank could be seen the fort and encampment of the Khosian elite reserves, the 'Hoo', named after their battle cry, two thousand heavy infantry in all. Next to them ranged the temple complexes with their stone bathing areas and their bronze bells that rang out the hour; deep tones that rolled across the flat waters of the river. Countless camps sprawled between the temples. Thousands of devotees washed away their transgressions in the turgid flow.

In contrast, the eastern side was a ramshackle place of smoky tavernas and zel dealers and wagon shops, a staging post for travellers and merchant caravans, a place of commerce. It was here, on the eastern bank, that the Khosian army had camped for the night, bedding down on the edge of the civilian settlement. The flat-bellied ferries continued to ship men and equipment across the river in darkness.

Like many of the men, Bull stood naked and thigh-deep in the river, his feet sunk into a sandbar as he scrubbed himself clean. Men were whooping all around him from the chill of it, though the water was hardly as cold as it should have been. A few of the army's monks washed alone in devoted silence, the silent cloud-men of the Dao who would bless them before battle in the name of the Great Fool. Bull threw a handful of water over his bare chest and watched as it shed off him with tiny sparkles of blue. Wherever it splashed against the slow-running surface, the froth burned with the same ghostly light before it faded away; the strange effect of Calhalee's Tears, legendary figure of Simmer Lake to the north, from which these waters gained not only heat but these enchanting, eerie properties.

He'd stood in this river once before, as a boy, when his father had brought him here with his younger brother at the insistence of their mother. Then as now, Bull had felt invigorated by the cleansing waters of the sacred river, but nothing more. Perhaps its spiritual properties were all nonsense; or perhaps whatever it was that tainted his spirit was too deep to be washed away by what little faith he possessed.

To the north, on the other side of the river, the forest could be seen as a wall of trees standing black and still beneath the stars. Sharp knocks were sounding from within the tree line, like giant birds pecking holes in their trunks. They were the alarm signals of the Contrarè, the free-spirited hunter-gatherers and occasional brigands of the forest. Bull imagined them standing there with their goad faces and their clothes of woven bark, watching them cautiously.

His mother had been one of the Contrarè, before she'd married his father, a skins merchant from Bar-Khos, and had moved with him to the city to start a family. Bull had known little about her people, save for the tales told to him at his bedside, and the songs she'd sung when bathing him, and the little superstitions she'd carried with her from her previous life in the forest – like the sign of protection she made at the rumble of thunder and the flash of lightning. Still, his accent bore some of his mother's voice in it, and his skin was particularly swarthy and his eyes were narrow above high cheekbones. As a boy, people had known what he was – a barkbeater – and many had treated him like a dog because of it.

He was reminded of those hard, painful days of youth as he turned and saw how the soldiers were avoiding the flow of the river directly downstream from him. Now it wasn't because he was a dirty barkbeater. Now it was because he was the slayer, the killer of their hero Adrianos.

Bull didn't mind, or so he told himself anyway. Since an early age he'd raged against the jests and cruel indifference of his peers. He'd fought tooth and nail to gain the respect of these Khosians, first as a street brawler and then as a soldier in the Red Guards. Now at least they no longer looked down on him. Aye, now they feared him.

Besides, he was free at last, and that was all that Bull cared about just then. In truth he'd been ready to lose his mind in the confines of that buried cell. Yet here he was, standing thigh-deep in the Chilos river, with the stars bobbing on its surface and Calhalee's Tears glowing all around him, the scents of the deep forest strong in the night air. If these were to be the last days of his life, Bull could hardly ask for more than this.

He sluiced a last handful of water over his face and shook his hands dry, his disfigured knuckles cracking loudly, ruined after all those years of pit-fighting. For a few moments longer, his eyes lingered on the distant forest. He'd never ventured further than the trading posts along its fringes, yet it was part of him. It was in his blood.

What's stopping you? Bull asked himself, and could not fathom the answer.

*

The men of his chartassa file sat around the fire, talking amongst themselves and passing around a skin of wine. Bull said nothing to them, for he knew they wouldn't heed him. Indeed, as he stood there against the heat of the fire, sweeping his skin dry with his hands, they ceased to talk entirely, and none would look his way.

Bull scowled and wandered off to one of the nearby wagons, his bundle of equipment under an arm and his backpack over his shoulder. Away from the warmth and light of the fire he dressed quickly, though he left his armour balanced against the wagon next to his sheathed shortsword. He pulled the cloak about him and sat with his back against one of the wheels, then searched around in his pack until he found the small vial of mother's oil. He dabbed a little on his finger, and ran it around his gum where his back teeth were throbbing again, all the while eyeing the men huddled around the fire.

They're frightened, thought Bull to himself. *They know they march to their slaughter.*

He thought of the battle that lay ahead at the end of

their march, and felt the fear of it inside him too. The sensation thrilled him; made him feel that he was alive.

Bull drew his new sword from its sheath, and inspected the watermarks along the gleaming steel of the blade. It was Sharric steel, cast here in Khos, the finest in all the Midèrēs. He contented himself with sharpening the edge of it with the finer side of his whetstone.

In the light of a nearby campfire, he spotted General Creed walking past, conversing with the colonel of the Greyjackets. Bahn followed a few paces behind, looking as pensive as he had the first day Bull had ever met him, all those years ago on the cold marshalling grounds between the walls, with the first two walls of the Shield already fallen, the third likely to be next, the men shattered, their morale lower than any time before or since.

Bahn saw him now and gave a curt nod of his head, though Bull noted how he did not pause, did not share with him a few words.

Bull stared coldly back as the man walked beyond the light of the fire.

Behind the departing figures, young Wicks came stumbling towards him as the lad guzzled wine from a flaccid skin. Wicks tripped and rolled on the grass, then climbed to his feet again as though nothing had happened. He was alone too, though that seemed a matter of choice for Wicks.

He noticed Bull in the shadows and flopped down next to him. 'Hey, champ,' Wicks panted as he offered Bull the wine. Bull shook his head. He no longer trusted himself with alcohol, not since the day he'd gone to the home of Adrianos and butchered him like a stag.

Wicks settled himself with exaggerated care by his side, resting his back against the wagon wheel. 'All this bloody marching,' he muttered as he massaged a foot. 'My soles are killing me.'

'This is nothing. You're lucky we're not pushing even harder.' Even as Bull spoke he felt the ache of his own feet and back, and knew they would only worsen before they got better. He was in poor condition after a year in the cell, never mind that he'd tried to maintain his condition.

'Nothing, he says. And me with my feet in tatters.'

In the distance Bull heard a roar of men, the second time now he'd heard them. 'What *is* that? Is there a fight?'

'Aye. They're at it again, the Greys and the Volunteers. Two bare-knuckle champions this time.'

Wicks looked about him with his large eyes sparkling in the firelight. He was bored, Bull could see. The lad wanted some mischief to occupy himself for a while. It reminded Bull of his own restless boredom.

Bull sighed, and took the skin of wine from the young man; allowed himself one long satisfying pull from it before tossing it back.

'You know, I saw you fight once. The time you became champion of Bar-Khos.'

'I hope you bet on me to win.'

'I wish I had. But I thought you were just another contender like the rest of them. You lost me a full purse of stolen coins that night. Though I'll say it was worth it, just to see you fight. I thought you were going to kill him in the end.'

'I was. If they hadn't stopped me.'

'I can't believe it's really you. The real thing, right here in front of me. The greatest fighter in all of Khos. Unbelievable.'

Bull swept the whetstone along the edge of the blade, ignoring the lad now. It had been a long time since a stranger had offered their admiration to him. Once, he had relished such praise, had felt validated in every way by the respect of so many.

Now it was only a reminder of how fickle most people really were.

'They're talking about us again,' said Wicks casually with a nod to the fire. The men around it were trading words in low voices. Old Russo, the veteran of Coros, cast a one-eyed glance in their direction.

His accusing stare caused Bull to grind his rotten teeth together. He felt the satisfying throbs of pain deep inside them.

'Find yourself a whore yet?'

'No,' Bull admitted. 'None of them will touch me.'

'They probably think you'll strangle them where they lie.' Wicks laughed drunkenly at the thought of it.

'Don't laugh at me, boy. I'll have your eyes out if you laugh at me.'

The lad seemed to sober up for a moment; his grin faltered. Wicks sprawled onto his back, surprising himself with a belch. 'You can't take a joke, champ. That's your problem.'

Bull felt momentarily chastened by his words. He knew the young man was right.

He couldn't help but like this lad. Wicks reminded him of his younger brother: feckless and afraid of no one. He'd been one of the few to approach Bull and converse with him during the march so far; a thief playing at being a soldier, he'd told Bull, as he showed him the branding scar on his wrist, told him how he'd been released from a military stockade on the day the army had marshalled outside Bar-Khos.

Bull looked at the wineskin in his hands and said, 'I thought you were skint. Have you been thieving again?'

'I went swimming,' he told Bull. 'Over by the temples. If you go when the sun's still up you can see the coins lying along the riverbed.'

'You fool,' growled Bull. 'It's bad luck to steal people's offerings. You want to bring a curse on your head?'

Wicks waved his hand. 'What difference does it make? They throw the coins away and never see them again.'

There was no point trying to explain it to him. The lad simply had no concept of tradition or belief.

Again that roar of throats in the night. It sparked a decision within him.

Bull climbed slowly to his feet.

'Where are you going?' Wicks asked in sudden interest.

'To pick a fight,' he told him as he cast his cloak aside. 'Want to come?'

'Wait a minute,' said Wicks, and tried unsuccessfully to get to his feet. Bull had to help him up in the end. 'We should pool our coins. I'll lay the bets for you.'

'Wicks,' Bull said with a grin that split his face from ear to ear; and then the smile vanished in a flash. 'You really think that anyone's going to bet against me?'

*

Bahn was walking a little easier tonight. The pains in his calves and back from riding all day were no longer excruciating, as they had been on the previous nights of the forced march, for he was finally getting used to the saddle again. They were covering almost twenty laqs a day at their present pace. It was as hard as General Creed dared to push the army, for they still had days of travel ahead of them. The Lord Protector wanted the men fighting fit once they engaged.

In front of Bahn the general and Halahan strolled side by side. They were in good spirits tonight, having reached Juno's Ferry on schedule, where the army had joined the two thousand men of the Hoo. The mood of the men too seemed especially boisterous. They had crossed the Chilos, and now faced a march through the lands of the Reach, hell-bent on closing with the enemy. Tonight the reality of their situation was beginning to hit home. They were in need of some distractions.

Bahn could smell the hazii weed from Halahan's pipe as they walked. Tonight he would have welcomed a proper pull on a hazii stick. Now that they had crossed the Chilos, he too had felt a sense of cold reality coming over him.

'They're approaching Spire, according to our scouts,' Creed was saying before him. 'Following the Cinnamon as we expected. In a day or two they'll be entering the Silent Valley. We'll engage them there, before they reach Tume. If it goes badly for us we can fall back to Tume and regroup.'

'Vanichios will be glad to see you,' Halahan drawled, causing Creed to shoot him a dark look.

Bahn recalled the name. There was history between the general and the Principari of Tume, though his recollections were vague on the subject. Something about a duel.

'The reserves from Al-Khos,' Halahan ventured from beneath the wide brim of his straw hat. 'Do we know when they'll reach Tume?' His crippled leg was causing him to limp more than usual this evening, a result, he had said, of his knee playing up in the falling temperatures.

'If they're pushing hard enough, they should be halfway there by now. That is, of course, if that fool Kincheko doesn't dither around.'

'You think he will?'

Creed gave a shake of his head. 'Who knows with that fool? He might linger for a day or two just to show his contempt for my orders.'

'It was a greater fool who made him Principari of Al-Khos in the first place.'

'Aye, well Michinè blood is thicker than wine.'

A squad of Specials, just arrived in from the ferry, tramped by burdened with their backpacks and arms. They nodded in turn as they stepped past the general in a ragged line. One of them knew Bahn, an old friend of his brother Cole. The man surprised him with a warm embrace and words of good luck, before hurrying to catch up with his squad.

'What's going on over there?' Creed had stopped, and was studying a crowd of men gathered in a clearing next to the river. The men were Volunteers and Greyjackets mostly, cheering and jostling each other as they watched two men stripped to the waist slugging it out.

A detachment of Red Guards was attempting to break them up, led by an officer on zelback, though some Volunteers shouted the officer away, jeering at him and spooking his zel by waving their hands at it. The animal reared, almost tossing the rider from the saddle. Other Volunteers were stepping in to try to defuse the situation. Bahn saw the general's eyes narrow.

'Look at them. Always disregarding discipline at the first opportunity. This is why we Khosians have the finest chartassa, and they do not.'

Halahan chuckled by his side. 'They're only having their fun while they still can.'

'Fun? It isn't fun they need, Colonel.'

'Oh, come now, once it's morning again and we're back on the march, they'll be as tame as kittens.'

Creed snorted.

They walked on, the general showing his face to the men and seeing for himself how they fared. He spoke to some of the animal handlers in the corrals where the war-zels were quartered, and to the quartermaster as he flustered over the supplies being ferried across. He even stopped at one of the skyships that had landed for the night, asking the crew if they needed anything, careful not to show them his frustrations at the lack of skyships accompanying the army; a mere three of them and a handful of small skuds, hardly adequate for controlling the skies.

Amongst the Hoo, the men of the elite chartassa, Creed sought out Nidemes, the colonel who had fought with Creed in Coros. Creed talked with the small quiet man alone for a time, while Halahan smoked his pipe and leaned on his knee while he talked with some of the men, veterans all of them; and Bahn blinked across the flames at heavily scarred soldiers with hard eyes, who sat wrapped in their purple cloaks, saying nothing.

'He's worried,' Creed told Halahan when they continued onwards. 'He wanted to know our plan of attack.'

'What did you tell him?'

'The truth. That I'm still thinking on it.'

Halahan chuckled drily, and the sudden sound of it irritated Bahn.

'These men face an army of forty thousand,' he heard himself say. 'And you laugh because you haven't a plan yet.'

Halahan plucked the pipe from his mouth and flashed his mocking eyes at him. 'And I'll be there with them, won't I?'

Bahn closed his mouth in exasperation.

'What's bothering you, Bahn?' asked the general. 'Spit it out, man.'

Bahn lowered his tone of voice. 'It just seems to me, General, that we're marching into certain defeat here, and that you're both happy enough to be doing it.'

Creed started walking again, more briskly now. The other two strode after him.

'Nothing is ever certain, Bahn,' Creed snapped over his shoulder.

'No. But you can always consider the odds.'

'*Pff*. Odds? We lost those a long time ago.'

His voice was rough with anger, and Bahn had no wish to push him any further. When all was said and done, he still had every faith in this man.

Bahn had fought on the Shield in those early days of the war, after all. Back then, General Forias had still been Lord Protector of Khos, that decrepit nobleman who had gained his role through family connections. Even before the siege had begun, when the Mannians had first taken Pathia to the south and refugees had flooded towards Bar-Khos, it had been General Creed, not dithering Forias, who had ordered the gates to be opened so they could gain sanctuary within.

For the first year of the siege, Forias had commanded the defence of the city, and the Khosians had reeled as the walls had fallen one by one. Old Forias hadn't been entirely inept in his role as Lord Protector: he had ordered the slopes of earth to be piled against the surviving walls to ward off the constant barrages of cannonfire, and at times had even fought on the walls himself next to the men, risking his neck with the rest of them. But still, he lacked the charisma and bravado that was needed most of all in those dark days of plummeting morale. He simply hadn't been a warleader who inspired hope in the people. Public protests were made against him. Mass calls for his resignation. Still old Forias, backed by the Michinè council, refused to step down.

When the news came that the Imperials had invaded distant Coros also, in their attempt to open up a second front against the Free Ports, the Michinè had agreed to make a token gesture in the League's desperate defence of the island. General Creed had been dispatched to lead the small Khosian contingent of chartassa there. While he was gone, and with the siege of Bar-Khos entering its lowest point so far, Lord Protector Forias had withdrawn into his private mansion, claiming illness, and then had killed himself, or died in his sleep, depending on whom you believed.

Defeat had hung in the city air like a fog.

Creed, though, had changed all of that. He had returned from their unexpected victory in Coros within a week of old Forias's funeral, now hailed as a hero and seen by many as their most likely saviour. The population of the city had taken to the streets to demand he be made the new Lord Protector. In the end, the Michinè had been left with little choice but to concede to them.

And so Creed had set about defying what had seemed, until then, the natural course of the war. He launched daring counter-attacks against the imperial army; developed the network of fighting tunnels beneath the walls to stop them being undermined; roused the hopes of the soldiers and the people by the example he set for them all. Gradually the imperial advance was slowed, and the siege settled into years of resistance that no one had dared believe was even possible.

Now Bahn and the rest of them hoped for another miracle from this man.

'General!'

They turned just as they were nearing the command tent. Two Khosian cavalry scouts were approaching with a civilian rider in between them, a man with a bandana around his head and a gold ring in his ear. They drew to a halt before Creed with the nostrils of their zels snorting vanishing clouds of steam. 'A Mannian ambassador, General,' one of the riders announced. 'He wishes to speak with you. We've searched him for weapons already.'

All three of them studied the civilian who sat slouched in his saddle, something of the brigand about him.

'Greetings to you, Bearcoat,' the man declared with a rueful grin.

*

'Come on now, you have to tell us more than that!'

'Leave it alone, will you? It's embarrassing.'

Curl laughed along with the other men and women in the warm space of the medical tent. They were seated around the surgical table with their cards and coins before them, their pallid faces shining in the light of the single lantern that hung from the roof.

Andolson was playing on a jitar at the back of the room, crooning something obscene and ridiculous about the fallen king of Pathia. Kris stood next to a side-table, a collection of bottled wines and leather mugs arranged before her, carefully adding to each of the mugs drops from a medicinal bottle of sanseed. As for the rest of the medicos, they mostly chattered across each other, hands waving drunkenly over the table, parting the thick coils of hazii smoke that filled the tent.

Young Coop stumbled out once more to be sick.

'A damned waste of good wine!' Milos hollered after him.

They were a strange bunch, these medicos of Special

Operations whom Curl had fallen in with. Many had painted symbols and words onto their black leathers: the Daoist circle of unity, or quotes from all manner of sources, some even Mannian. Their hair was as often long as it was short, their faces scarred, their tempers hot, their moods unpredictable. Long inured to working in the tunnel systems beneath the walls of the Shield, they were a wild and troubled group of individuals, and they'd taken to Curl easily, and she to them.

The woman Kris was making another round of the table with her concoction of drinks. 'Some more, madame?'

'Thank you,' said Curl, and accepted the offered mug and took a welcome sip from it. The wine was strong, but still she could taste the small amount of sanseed within it; liquid dross, essentially, used as a painkiller for the wounded. 'If I'd known I could get this stuff for free I would have enlisted a whole lot sooner.'

'That's why old Jonsol enlisted,' quipped Milos. 'Isn't that right, Jonsol?'

Jonsol was leering at her from across the table. The grey-haired man leered at every female within talking distance of him, though, and Curl's scowl was a light-hearted one. Jonsol leaned back and howled at the canvas roof like a forlorn dog.

Curl had been fortunate from the outset, for the story of her outburst in the recruitment office had preceded her. The medico corps of the Specials had assumed she was a hot-tempered bitch not to be messed with, and she'd seen no reason to disabuse them of their illusions.

'I'll call,' Jonsol said loudly, and threw in a few coppers. Only he and Curl remained in this hand, and the final card lay face-up on the table between them. A High King.

Curl spread the three cards in her hand face-up on the table. More laughter sounded as they realized she had won once again. Curl acknowledged their praise and curses as she swept the small pile of coins towards her.

'You're a fool, Jonsol. You walked right into it all over again.'

'She might be a pup but she can play, I'll give her that.'

It was true, she could play a decent game of cards. Though in fact tonight, for the sheer thrill of it, Curl was cheating. Every other time it was her turn to deal, Curl used one of the many shuffling tricks her old lover had once shown her to stack the deck in her favour. She was doing so well at it, in fact, that only one of them seemed to have yet noticed, and that was Kris, who simply watched with a knowing amusement in her eyes.

They all looked up as the tent flap parted and Koolas the war chattēro stepped inside. 'Mind if I join you?' he puffed.

Exaggerated groans sounded from around the tent. 'There must be a hundred games of rash in this camp tonight,' chirped Milos. 'And yet always you come to us.'

'Well now,' replied Koolas as he found himself a free seat around the table. 'That's because you medicos have all the good drugs.'

Jeers and catcalls exploded around him. Kris gave him a bow and began to fix him a drink of wine and sanseed, while Andolson changed to a different song, making up the lyrics as he went along. He crooned about the fat war chattēro who was so in love with battle he rode along just to watch it.

'Besides,' Koolas called out, 'I'm thinking of doing a story on you all. The medicos. The unsung heroes who go out there alone amongst the killing to save who they can, or to steal the jewellery of those who they can't.'

Amidst the jeers Milos hollered, 'Unsung fools more like!'

'Aye, well, if it was truth the copy-houses wanted then I'd write of it. My thanks,' he added, as Kris brought over a drink.

They were shouting him down when Major Bolt stepped into the tent.

'Popular tonight,' muttered Milos as the tent fell silent, and Kris hid the bottle of sanseed behind her back.

'At ease,' Bolt told them all. 'I'm just here to see how you are. See if you need anything.'

'We're fine, Major, just fine,' said Andolson languidly from behind his jitar.

Bolt surveyed each of them in turn. His eyes lingered on Kris for a moment, her hands behind her back. 'Carry on, then,' he said.

As he turned to leave he gave Curl a sidelong glance and a tug of his head.

She ignored the comments around her and followed him out through the flap.

Outside in the fresh air, Curl experienced a strange moment of transition. Suddenly she stood once more in a camp of war, and the memory of what they were doing, and what still faced them, came slowly back to her. Out there somewhere was the imperial army.

She shivered, the goosebumps rising on her flesh, and held an arm across her chest.

'How are you?' Bolt asked. 'You seem to be fitting in well enough.'

'They're good people,' she replied, looking up at him only briefly. She was always nervous in the company of this man, for she could never tell what he was thinking.

'Here,' he said, and handed her something. She looked down and saw a wrap of graf leaves in his outstretched hand.

'I noticed the markings,' he said, looking at her nostrils, which were less reddened now that she had left the city, and her supply of dross had run out. 'It's just a little muscado. It'll help take the edge off a little.'

'I'm fine,' she told him. 'Really.'

'Take it,' he said, and so she did, and slipped the folded leaves into a pocket. 'You'll be glad of it once we see some action, and we start running low on those bottles of sanseed.'

She looked up into his grey eyes. 'Thank you.'

Bolt stared hard at her.

'I'd better get back inside,' she told him.

After a moment he nodded, his expression still blank. Without a word he turned and strode away.

*

They gathered in the warmth of the command tent, the space heated by the black iron stove that squatted in one corner, its chimney running up through the roof. A plain, square table stood in the middle of the tent, covered with maps and notes for the march. Bahn swept them up quickly to put them out of sight. Creed took the weight off his feet by sitting back in his wicker chair. Halahan sat on the edge of the table, his leg-brace squeaking. The Nathalese colonel was clearly fighting down his anger.

After a few moments the Mannian ambassador was allowed to enter. The guards had stripped him of his clothing before searching his cavities. The man hadn't shaven in some days, and he covered his nakedness with a borrowed red cloak wrapped about him, so that his appearance was that of some ragged beggar. It was an illusion only. The man held himself tall, and seemed hardly concerned that he stood in the heart of his enemy's encampment.

'Our spies were correct, it seems,' he said in an accent clearly Q'osian. 'Though I can hardly believe it. You must have fewer than ten thousand men here, if even that.'

Creed brought his hand to his chin. His eyes flickered to Halahan.

'State your business here, ambassador,' Halahan instructed as he removed the hat from his head, laid it down on the table. His tone was openly hostile.

'Please. Call me Alarum. May I sit?' This last addressed to Creed.

The general raised a hand in consent, and the

Mannian settled down in a chair with a long and weary sigh. 'It's been a hard ride,' he said. 'Perhaps we could share some wine and food while we talk?'

Creed's chair creaked sharply as he leaned forwards. 'Why are you here, fanatic?'

Alarum inclined his head and studied the general with his dark eyes. 'I've been sent by the Holy Matriarch to offer you terms.'

'She wishes to surrender?'

The man gave a quick, pinched smile. 'It's not too late, you know. Even now, after all these years, we can settle our differences another way.'

'Aye,' snapped Halahan. 'You can pack up your armies and go home.'

'Come, now,' responded the man. 'You know as well as I what reputations are riding on this. We can hardly simply withdraw. But what we can do is this: we can offer you the lives of your people, if only you will surrender Khos to us now, and agree to become a client state of Mann.'

'What, open our gates to you like Serat, so you can decimate the population with your purges and enslave the rest?' Halahan was incensed. Bahn could see the blood rushing to his face. 'You came all this way for this?'

'If you don't, we'll slaughter every man, woman and child of Bar-Khos. That is a promise not made lightly.'

Halahan stood up with his hands clenching. Creed held a hand up to restrain him, staring hard at the ambassador. 'You still have to defeat us first,' he reminded the man softly.

'I have forty thousand fighting men at my back, General.'

'Aye. That you do. And those men are far from home. Their fleet has departed. Their supplies are limited to what they already have and what they can pillage from the land. If they're not fast, winter will set in and trap them here without adequate sources of food or shelter.

You are hardly in any position of certainty, ambassador. Else you would not be here.'

Alarum's response was to rise slowly from the chair with the cloak held loosely about him. He glanced at Halahan as the colonel took a step towards him. Bahn felt the sudden rise of tension in the air. He gripped the pommel of his sword without thinking.

'If I may,' said Alarum, with a soft, cautious smile. 'The Holy Matriarch has sent a gift for you, should you fail to see sense in this matter.'

Creed nodded, and one of the guards at the entrance stepped forward with something in his hand. He handed it to Bahn, the closest person to him.

Bahn looked down at the sheathed dagger in his hand. It was a curved blade no larger than his thumb, and the scabbard was ornately decorated with gold and diamonds, and fitted with a cord to hang about a person's neck.

'What is it?' he asked.

He looked up even as Halahan struck the ambassador hard across the face, sending the man toppling back across the chair.

Halahan kicked him in the side of the head as he tried to get up.

'What gives you the right to this? *What gives you the right to demand that others bow down to you or they must die?*'

'Colonel,' Creed snapped. '*Halahan!*'

At last the colonel backed away, panting hard now. Nothing in the world could tear his gaze from Alarum as the man climbed unsteadily to his feet. The ambassador's lip was bloody, and he hitched the robe over his body to cover his sudden nakedness.

He glowered at Halahan as he dabbed a corner of the robe against his mouth. 'What right? By right of natural law, what other? Do I need to explain this as though to children? What is man's nature if not to take power wherever he can? The strong do what they like. The weak must endure what they must always endure. Do not blame we followers of Mann because life is this way. Blame your World Mother. Blame your Dao.'

Creed placed his hands on either side of his chair and rose slowly to confront him.

'We have a belief, amongst the Free Ports, ambassador. A belief that imbalances of power can only corrupt, so power must always flow outwards, especially to those most affected by it. The idea comes from Zeziké. I suppose you Mannians don't read much of our famed philosopher, no?'

Alarum tilted his head, saying nothing.

'I'll be honest with you, I don't always agree with him myself. But at times he made some fine points, especially about such notions as yours. If I recall his words correctly, he said that human nature is as much a result of our environment as it is the blood in our veins. And that our environment is as much a result of how we choose it to be as it is the turning of the earth and the sky.'

He leaned forwards, looking carefully at the ambassador's expression.

'You do not like that idea, perhaps? Yet you of Mann wish to shape the entire world in your image. Why is this, then? I will tell you why. Because you know this truth as well as Zeziké ever did. You know that to maintain absolute power, you must control those choices in people's lives which allow them to shape their environment. Is that not so?'

Alarum's breathing had calmed now. He dabbed his lip again, looked at the blood that stained the material of his robe. 'You talk of ideals, General,' he answered. 'Empty words of this and that. I talk of something much closer to reality. I talk of power, which in the end needs no defence. Power will always speak for itself. It will always subdue what is weaker, no matter what you believe.'

'Aye, it's an old story certainly, subjugation. Yet so is murder. And rape. And theft. Things that decent people despise and outlaw from their lives when they have the choice to do so. Because they choose to believe in man's capacity to be better than that.'

They blinked at each other as though from across an abyss. Bahn could barely see the seething anger beneath the general's impassive features, so well did he hide it.

'Now, ambassador, if you'd kindly get out of my sight,' Creed growled.

Alarum accepted his dismissal with a cavalier bow. He looked faintly amused as the guards pulled him roughly from the tent.

'I don't understand,' said Bahn at last. He was studying the dagger in his hand again.

Creed ignored him. He remained standing with his eyes locked on the flapping entrance of the tent, his jaw muscles clenching.

'The dagger,' said Halahan with a wipe of his mouth, 'is a ceremonial blade of Mann.'

'For what purpose?'

'For taking your own life.'

—CHAPTER TWENTY-ONE—

The Burning of Spire

On the fifth day of their march, the Imperial Expeditionary Force descended into the country known as the Tumbledowns, where they found themselves looking down upon the snowmelt rapids of the Cinnamon river.

To the north, high mountains stood black and ice-capped against the pale sky. To the west, the Tumbledowns ran on to the horizon. Beyond them lay fertile lands of rice paddies and orchards and vineyards, which rolled onwards past the Windrush into the flat western half of the island where most of its population could be found, and where fields of wheat rippled all the way to the Sargassi Sea.

The army turned south-west on a course that followed the Cinnamon, and which would take them into the Silent Valley and the lands of the Reach, and from there to the ancient city of Tume. The floating city was most probably heavily garrisoned by now. All knew it would need to be dealt with before they pushed on to Bar-Khos in the south.

It was here, along the Cinnamon, where the eager fighting force came across their first Khosian town. The guides told them it was called Spire, and the Imperials did not have to ask them why. It was a hilltown, situated on a high abutment of rock that protruded into the flatlands of the Cinnamon valley. A snaking wall surrounded it, rising and falling over the elevated crown on which its whitewashed buildings stood; the multiple spires of pale granite that stabbed upwards like petrified spears.

By evening, the gates of the town lay breached by cannon shots, and imperial infantry flooded through them into the winding streets within. The overwhelmed defenders fought on, soldiers of the town's Principari in the main, though with a scattering of civilians amongst them, throwing rocks from rooftops or holding out behind barricades blocking the streets. The majority of the populace had already fled westwards, harried by imperial skirmishers.

For a while a Khosian skyship ventured above the violence of the sack. It even tried to land amongst the turrets of the citadel to evacuate the defenders, but the three heavy imperial skyships were quick to chase it from the scene.

In the pale twilight, Ché dismounted from his zel outside Sasheen's command tent, where she sat slouched on a field chair next to Archgeneral Sparus. Around them lounged members of her entourage, eating fruit pillaged from the orchards that covered the valley to the south-east of the town. Their faces glowed as the flames of the town shot high into the darkening skies.

An empty field chair sat next to Sasheen. As Ché approached, he saw that the head of Lucian rested upon it; a grotesque, almost comical sight in the present setting.

Sasheen smiled as she saw him approach. 'See anything of interest on your ride?'

Ché had gone riding around the foot of the rock that Spire burned upon, to free himself for a little while of their company. He'd ridden all the way up the winding route that led to the town's gates, and to the imperial infantry loitering around them, but had stopped at the heaps of bodies stacked just inside the broken gates, and the stink of death in the air, and the still audible shouts and screams from within.

He'd decided to turn back, and had passed Romano on his way down. The young general and his coterie had been on their way to enjoy the town themselves.

'They've rescued a few granaries, I think,' he told the Matriarch. 'The wagons are coming out now.'

Beside her, Sparus gave a satisfied nod of his head. Extra grain could only be a boon to a general leading an army of this size.

'Have a seat,' Sasheen told him. 'You look weary.' She turned to one of her aides, and the man hurried to vacate his chair.

Reluctantly, Ché settled himself into it, wanting only to return to his tent and his books. The heat of the burning town was palpable even from here. Sool and the three Monbarri inquisitors were amongst the entourage, as were the twins, Guan and Swan, though neither looked at him. Guan stood staring at Spire with his mouth working a silent wordbinding. He held a devotional grip in his fist, a ball of spikes which he squeezed as hard as he could. Behind him sat his sister Swan, stroking a brown-haired puppy in her lap.

No wine this evening, he noticed. The mood was a sombre one for once, as though the sight of the torched town had suddenly entranced them all.

A croak suddenly sounded from a nearby chair. It was Lucian, his forehead pinched from the pain he was in, or the anguish.

'*Where. Are. We?*' he belched slowly, his glassy eyes bright with the reflection of the fires.

'I told you,' Sasheen snapped as though to a child. 'We're in Khos. And over there, on the hill, that is Spire.'

'*Not. Lagos. Then.*'

Sasheen chuckled, and it was an ugly sound in Ché's ears just then. 'Lagos is *gone*, Lucian. You made certain of that, you recall?'

The man rasped something unintelligible, and Ché looked away.

A rider was approaching, leading a second zel behind him bearing something long and wrapped in canvas. As he grew nearer, Ché saw that it was Alarum, his lean face shadowed by the beginnings of a beard. The spymaster greeted them with an upraised hand as he drew to a halt.

'You've been busy,' he said with a glance at the town. His face was bruised on one side, and his lip scabbed over where it had been split.

'And you, by the looks of it,' Sparus observed. 'You delivered the terms, then?'

Alarum nodded, then gently eased himself from the saddle. He steadied himself as his legs took his weight.

'To Creed himself?'

'Of course. And, yes. His answer was hardly a surprising one.'

Sasheen remained slouched in her chair. 'He did that to you?'

'No. That was Halahan of the Greyjackets. I baited them as much as I dared. Their moods became . . .' he waved a hand for the right word '. . . transparent.'

'And?' demanded Sparus.

'A drink first. It's been a long and tiring ride and I haven't stopped in hours.'

'Later. Tell me now.'

Alarum raised his eyebrows, then leaned an arm wearily across the saddle. 'Creed is confident. Don't ask me why, for his army is as small as we've been hearing it to be. I'd say he's actually looking forward to meeting us in the field.'

Sparus was listening to every word with fierce attention. 'His health?'

'He looked trim. Fighting fit.'

'What about my gift,' interjected Sasheen. 'How did he take it?'

The spymaster smiled, though it was more of a flinch. 'Oh they took it well. First they beat me a little, then they lectured me on all our wrongs. Creed gave me this as his response.' Alarum stepped to the pack zel as though his legs were sticks, and unhitched the long burden tied to its flanks.

He unrolled the object on the grass before them, and Ché peered at the thing as everyone else did.

It was a charta, the famed spear of the Mercian chartassa.

For a moment no one said a thing. Sasheen and Sparus simply blinked down at it.

A dry cough sounded next to them. It was Lucian, and he continued to make the sound until it resembled something like laughter.

Sparus paid him no heed. He looked away from the charta, as though it was distasteful to him. Lucian continued his strange laughter until Sasheen rounded on her ex-lover, her face flushing red, and kicked the chair he rested upon so that the head rolled a few feet across the grass. It came to a stop with the eyes blinking up at the sky, a single brown leaf stuck to his cheek.

'Put him back where he belongs,' she commanded to no one in particular.

Ché took the opportunity to climb to his feet. He stepped over the charta and stopped next to the head, where he grabbed a handful of hair and picked it up. It was heavier than he had been expecting. He carried it into the tent, through the hangings over the entrance and into the shadowy interior.

He made his way to the back of the space where the jar of Royal Milk stood in its alcove. Gently, he rested the head on the pedestal as he unscrewed the lid of the jar.

Ché raised the head so their eyes could meet. Lucian's eyes looked faintly yellow.

'How are you?' Ché asked him.

The man focused on his face. '*Tired*,' he said. '*Can't. Sleep.*'

'Perhaps you are asleep. Perhaps this all just a nightmare.'

The man blinked as though coming halfway to his senses. '*End. My. Shame.*'

Ché sighed, and frowned, but didn't move.

'*Beg. You*,' croaked Lucian.

Ché reached a hand out and plucked the leaf from the man's cheek. The flesh was cold to the touch. With care he settled the head into the jar of Royal Milk. The man's eyes watched him as they slipped beneath the surface.

He stood there for a moment, observing a few bubbles rising to the surface. Slowly, with great relish, he licked the ends of his fingers, and stood humming with the sudden rush of it, the vitality suddenly burning through him.

Ché turned and left the jar sitting there, deep in shadow.

*

Ash sat alone in the night, gazing out over the tents of the baggage train and the encampment of the imperial army at the ruins of Spire still burning.

The men of the army were loud tonight, intoxicated

by the action of the day and the plunder they had gained from the sack. Already, they were trading their goods with the prostitutes and merchants of the baggage train; slaves too, which were being led in silent lines to the slave traders and their caged wagons.

Ash pondered at the defiance of the town. It had seemed senseless to him, for they'd clearly stood no chance at all against the cannon of the imperial army. Yet still, the small contingent of soldiers in the town had manned the walls and fought on as long as they had stood.

Perhaps they'd simply hoped to slow the advance of the invaders for a day or two. Perhaps with their deaths they bought time for others: for the townsfolk fleeing to the west; for the Khosian army already rumoured to be marching hard to meet them.

The towns of the People's Revolution had done the same once, some of them at least. They had tried to hold off the advancing overlord forces while the Revolutionary Army mustered for the final battle in the Sea of Wind and Grasses. In the end, though, their sacrifices, their long war of resistance, had been in vain.

'*In vain*,' Ash grumbled aloud, shaking his gourd at the gutted settlement.

He gnashed his teeth drunkenly and sat back, trembling. Close by, the black night waters of a stream rushed along their rocky course. The Sisters of Loss and Longing were full tonight. They hung fat with blood above the burning town. A bad omen, he thought.

Ash held a deep admiration for what they had achieved here in the Free Ports. They had far surpassed anything that the people of Honshu had even dreamed of attaining. Yet part of him had always known that sooner or later this day would come to them. He was too aware of how fragile freedom truly was; a lonely flame cupped in the hands of a child, in a world where darkness preyed upon the light.

A throb filled his head, and he gripped it with a snarl.

The pains had returned to him today with the sacking of the town, and with them the tremors in his hand. Before he'd retired to this grassy bank next to the stream, Ash had paid a small fortune in coin to buy a flask of Cheem Fire, intent on keeping himself warm and dulling his aches.

He took another long drink of it, and watched the stars above the lesser constellations of campfires in the valley. The Eye of Ninshi shone hard and red within its hood, unblinking.

He thought of Nico, on a night like this one, high in the foothills of Cheem. He thought of them getting drunk together around a fire.

Ash drank some more.

—CHAPTER TWENTY-TWO—

Silent Valley

Ché had risen early that morning, and he huddled in his tent while he lathered some of his mother's chamomile ointment over the rashes on his arms. He hadn't slept well – too many things on his mind – and with a stiff neck he gazed out through the open tent flap, desiring the meagre daylight of dawn and the view over the valley, which was dusted white with snow that had fallen some time in the night.

In this weather, it would take the army and camp followers an eternity to ready themselves for the march. Outside, the bitter wind tore at the canvas tents of the encampment. Leaves and debris tumbled through the air. The zels were jittery, jostling together in their corrals as they tried to find a place in the warm and sheltered hearts of their small herds. A few people padded through the snow to the latrines, holding hats or hoods over their heads.

Through the open flap, he saw Swan and Guan stamp past. Guan glanced at him without expression, cool now. Swan, though, looked in and offered a brief smile.

Ché placed the jar of ointment on his bed and rolled down his sleeves. He sat there pondering for a few moments.

He checked the knife in its scabbard around his ankle then rose and stepped outside. He spotted the twins entering one of the corrals. Their tent wasn't far from his own. When he reached it, he ducked inside.

He looked about the orderly space, then pounced on the backpacks perched against the two cots. In the first pack, he found civilian clothing tightly bound in twine, a copy of the Scripture of Lies heavily annotated, and a journal with drawings and observations of Khos. He drew back when he found the small wooden poisoner's kit at the bottom of it, a kit identical to his own.

Ché glanced back to make sure he was still alone. Quickly, he rifled through the other pack. His hands drew out a canvas bag and within it a small vial. He took it out and held it up to the daylight. A thick, golden liquid was within. He pulled out the stopper, took a tentative sniff.

Ché clasped the vial in his fist and hurried outside.

*

They were still at the corral when he went to confront them, rubbing down the backs of their zels with handfuls of grass. Guan muttered something to his sister when he saw Ché approaching. She smirked, then made herself serious again.

'I know what you are,' Ché snapped, tossing the vial into Guan's hand. The man glanced down at it, then looked across at his sister.

With a laugh she grabbed a fistful of her zel's mane and leapt onto its bare back. A moment later, Guan was doing the same.

'Come for a ride with us,' she said down to Ché, and

before he could reply she kicked the animal's flanks and took off, clearing the fence of the corral in a leap, her brother just behind her.

Ché growled deep in his throat. He grabbed the mane of the nearest zel and jumped onto its back, then spurred it forwards so that it jumped the corral fence with a double clip of its hooves. He gave chase as the twins raced out through the palisade and the Acolyte camp around it, clods of snow flying from their mounts' hooves like birds scattering in their wake.

The land was good for riding beyond the camp, though the wind was strong enough to smear tears across his cheeks. Half blinded and head low, he kicked for greater speed, surging after them as they entered a small wood. His hood fell back to expose his head. He ducked down further as he wove between the gnarled trunks of trees and felt the scratch of leaves and twigs against his face. Ahead, the twins leapt a spring and turned and followed its bank. Ché veered left to cut them off. He forced his zel over the water too and tucked in close behind them, racing at full gallop.

His thighs were burning by the time he came along-side Swan. She lashed at him with a broken branch, laughing again as he fended her off with his hand.

And then from his left came Guan, veering towards him with a branch in his hand ready to strike at his head. Ché ducked and felt the breath of it cross the stubble on his scalp.

He pulled hard on the zel's mane until it reared to a halt. It skittered a few steps and then settled, the steam shooting from its nostrils. There he sat unmoving, while slowly the twins circled back towards his position, moving in separate orbits so as to remain on either side of him.

Ché simply looked from one to the other, and waited.

At last they came together and stopped before him. In the uneasy silence, the zels dropped their muzzles to the ground and began to pull at the long grasses that poked through the snow.

'Wildwood juice,' he said with a nod to Guan. 'For subduing the reflexes of a pulsegland.'

His words brought only amusement to their expressions. 'Come, now,' replied Swan on behalf of her brother. 'You thought you were the only Diplomat on this whole campaign?'

'That's what I was led to believe,' he told her sourly. 'Does the Matriarch know of this?'

'Of course she knows,' drawled Guan.

'And what are your orders?'

Silence; the wind buffeting his ears.

'We're here as backup, nothing more,' offered Guan, and Swan shot her brother a dark look.

Ché leaned back on the zel, looking at each of them in turn. He tried to breath calmly, to clear his mind.

They don't ask me my own orders.

'You know what I have been tasked to do,' he realized aloud.

Guan opened his mouth to speak, but Swan kicked her zel forwards so that it butted her brother's to one side.

'You sound troubled by your work, Ché,' Swan said. 'Does it keep you up at night, tossing and fretting?'

He studied the woman, saw how her usually pretty features were gone now in this windy place, replaced by a bitter scowl of contempt.

'We follow our orders,' she pressed. 'It would be to your advantage if you did the same.'

'What? You doubt I'll go through with it if it's required of me, is that it?'

'You hardly sound certain of yourself. What do you think, Guan?'

The brother, chewing on something, said, 'Perhaps it's his devotion that is lacking. Perhaps his heart is no longer in it.'

'I've proved my loyalty,' Ché responded hotly, regretting the words even as he spoke them.

'Oh, please,' said Swan. 'As though the Section ever relied upon loyalty. You should know as well as anyone what happens when a Diplomat strays from their mission. Your mother is a Sentiate, is she not? Well, a whore is the easiest person of all to make disappear.'

Ché blinked, the only outward sign of a sudden rage clamouring to be released from him. The heat of his anger revived him, focused him.

He leaned towards her, his eyes thinned to slits.

'If you come for me,' he said plainly, 'I will mark you out first for the carving.'

And he turned his zel away and kicked it into a trot, eager to be away from them.

*

That morning, the dawn sun rose over a plain of bleached emptiness, across which others were emerging from beneath their snow-mounded shelters, like an army of the dead rising from the frozen ground.

Ash could see his own breath in the air before it was whipped away in the wind. He huddled against the cold bite of the gusts and thought, *damned early for snow.*

The head pains had subsided to a dull throb at last, but he still carried a lingering hangover from the night before. He wandered slowly back to the camp to discover cries of sorrow mingling with the ordinary business of the day. There had been deaths in the night – mostly older camp followers or those already ill. People struggled to cut graves in the hardened earth.

Ash bought himself a breakfast of liver paste and tackbread, and a mug of hot chee from a canteen run by a husband and wife team, their supplies heaped on the back of a wagon supporting an awning under which they cooked. The Cinnamon had partly frozen over during the night, and people around him muttered about the sudden change in the weather. They worried that it was more than just a cold spell; that perhaps winter was approaching early.

It took even longer than usual for the army to set forth on the march.

First to leave were the skirmishers and light cavalry, who headed off while the rest of the army pulled itself together. One by one the steaming companies of infantry took to the road that ran along the Cinnamon valley, their passage marked by snow tramped down to mush. The Holy Matriarch and her Acolytes followed after them, protected by more screens of light cavalry. By the time the baggage train finally began to move out, the column was stretched thin and long beneath clouds dark enough to threaten more snow. The price of clothing tripled in the space of an hour.

Following the road, they came down at last into the Silent Valley, which turned them west towards Tume and the floodland of the Reach. The valley was five laqs across at its widest points, and the hills and mountains to the south of it were barely visible beyond the flat plain of tilled fields and deserted homesteads, with the Cinnamon widening and meandering down its middle. It was as quiet as its name suggested, save for the rush of air that ran through it, giving the place a lonely feeling, something oversized about it.

By late afternoon, the procession began to bunch up as those behind came up against those ahead. The van of the army had stopped for some reason. Soon, rumours were filtering back down the line that the Khosian army had been sighted ahead.

The First Expeditionary Force prepared itself for battle.

A group of rancheros were given permission to break off from their herd. They galloped forwards to see what was happening at the front, their hands clamped to their wide-brimmed hats as they whooped for effect and slapped their zels for speed. The rest of the baggage train drew up in a vast circle with the wagons dotted around the perimeter. People armed themselves as best they could. Within half an hour the price of weaponry had risen by a factor of five. The mood grew tense.

The rancheros returned after a short time and came to a stop in the press of bodies seeking news. It was an army, all right, but hardly of a size to concern them.

The gabble of the camp followers rose with excitement.

'When will the army engage?' someone wanted to know.

'Tomorrow morning,' one of the rancheros replied. They would rest and ready themselves tonight, then attack at first light.

'What if they attack us first?' came Ash's cool voice from the back of the crowd.

They laughed at that, for they thought it was a joke.

The mood lightened after this appraisal of their position. Profit, most people were talking of. A battlefield after the fighting was done could be a place for rich pickings. With hungry eyes, they settled down around their fires to wait.

—CHAPTER TWENTY-THREE—

Bearcoat

'Rather a lot of them,' Halahan casually remarked, puffing on his pipe beneath the brim of his straw hat.

General Creed showed no sign that he was listening. He stood in the cold twilight on their vantage point above the valley, his long hair hanging in stillness about the shoulders of his fur coat, his eyes fixed on the imperial encampment in the far distance, the campfires already glittering in their hundreds.

Bahn and the rest of the officers waited in silence as

the colours of the day slowly faded. Early stars were already pricking through breaks in the clouds, which had thinned in the last hour without dumping further snow.

The imperial army had settled in for the night on a stretch of the road around a hamlet known as Chey-Wes. As far as the eye could see they occupied the road and the valley plain that it followed, bordered on the north by the flow of the Cinnamon and Hermetes Lake, and on the south by a thin ribbon of elevated land, one of several that ran along the spine of the valley like the ridged back of a whale.

'No earthworks around the main force,' commented Halahan, hoisting the fallen branch he had been leaning on to jab at the distant camp. Trickles of snow fell from its tip. 'They reckon themselves safe in their numbers.'

Bahn listened to these remarks in silence. He was trembling, and he didn't mind admitting to himself that it was more than the mere chill of his armour. He looked away from the awful sight of the invasion force and turned his head to look back at the setting sun, savouring it for long moments as though it was his last. In its diminishing glow the Khosian army was preparing its own camp for the night, small enough to remain hidden behind the rise of ground the officers stood upon. Far beyond it, he could just about discern the sparkles of Tume reflecting off Simmer Lake.

The officers waited for Creed to say something, to lead them, but he was still deep in thought, his jaw muscles working as he ground his teeth in concentration.

Bahn knew all these men in his capacity as Creed's aide. From the corner of his eye, he studied each of them in turn. General Nidemes of the Hoo, and his old rival General Reveres of the Red Guards, two grey-haired veterans who could have been brothers for all their similarities in features. Colonel Choi of the Free Volunteers, Coraxian by birth. Major Bolt, commander of Special Operations for the field army. Colonel Mandalay of the

Lancers, their contingent of cavalry. And Halahan, positioned closer to Creed than the rest of them.

Each wore a pair of Owl goggles about their necks, priceless items of equipment made with lenses cast in the Isles of Sky. Each stood with his cloak wrapped tight about his armour, travel-stained with all the days of forced marching. None looked remotely happy to be there, save for Halahan.

'There are six thousand of us, brothers,' Creed declared as he turned his back on the imperial army. 'In all, we face over six times our number. I can tell you now, from what information we have gained from captured scouts, that many are veterans of Lagos and the High Pash campaigns. Two thousand more are Mannian Acolytes. For cavalry, the numbers are unclear; we believe they lost a large number of zels during their voyage. They have a sizeable contingent of archers and riflemen. Added to that, of course, is their artillery. They have ten heavy pieces for every one of ours.

'Options, if you please.'

General Reveres of the Red Guards cleared his throat and spoke first. 'We dig in here and fight a holding action. We can hardly defeat them in open battle with so many cannon facing us.'

'May as well have stayed in Bar-Khos then,' quipped General Nidemes.

'You disagree?' asked Creed.

Nidemes's gaze was hard and unflinching. 'Absolutely. We should attack them at first light. It will be the last thing they expect of us. If we're lucky, we might catch their batteries unprepared.'

'That still leaves forty thousand fighting men to contend with,' argued Reveres.

Nidemes was unimpressed. 'So? We were outnumbered in Coros too.'

General Creed wore his heavy bearskin coat over his armour. He tugged it tighter around himself, then crossed his arms in silence.

'I agree with Reveres,' said Choi, the bearded, blond-haired colonel of the Volunteers. 'We should dig in here and hold them off as long as we can. You said yourself our intention was to buy time.'

'Colonel Halahan?' Creed enquired of his old friend.

The colonel replied with a wolfish grin. 'You know what I would have us do, General.'

Creed fell quiet again, musing.

Bahn watched the general and waited. Even now, he believed the man could save them.

'You know how I killed this bear?' Creed asked suddenly to no one in particular, and held his fur coat open for show.

'It chased me off when I was checking some fish traps my father had placed in a stream. I was a boy, and I had a gutting knife with me, a tiny thing, about twice the size of this one,' and he looked down at the curved dagger that hung against his chest, the Mannian ceremonial blade, which he had placed there for some reason known only to himself.

'I needn't tell you I was scared out of my wits. Couldn't move for the life of me, in fact. But when my heart started beating again, and I saw how the bear was breaking into the traps, I knew I was even more terrified of what my father would do if I stood there and did nothing. So I charged at it, tried to frighten it away, if you can imagine that. The most foolish thing I've probably ever done in my whole life. And that's when it grabbed my arm in its jaws and tried to rip it off me. Still, I had the knife in my hand. I fought back with it. Next thing I knew, I was lying on the ground with the blood pumping out of me, and the bear was gone.

'I crawled back to the homestead, where they saved my arm. And the next day, my father tracked the bear through the hills, and found it dead a few laqs from the broken traps. It had bled to death from the stab wounds in its throat. I was sorry to hear that. But proud too.'

Creed tilted his head back and looked at them all.

'And that's what we shall do here, with these invaders,' he declared. 'We will get in close, and we'll go for their throats while they try to crush the life from our body.'

'Sir?' said Bolt, taken aback.

'We attack. We attack tonight while they sit huddled in their tents waiting for the sun.'

Around Bahn the officers shifted in their stances. Bahn felt his stomach fall away.

'Colonel Mandalay!'

The cavalry officer stood to attention. 'Sir.'

'Your men are to advance on the enemy position. As soon as they spot you, charge the camp, understood?'

'General,' acknowledged Mandalay after a pause.

'Don't linger. Head straight through the camp until you're into the baggage train. Destroy as much as possible while you're there. Look for powder wagons in particular. The quartermaster will furnish you with some firebombs for the task. And if you can, disperse the remainder of their zels too.'

It was a tall order, thought Bahn. The skin of Mandalay's face had grown tight.

'Major Bolt. The Specials will follow closely behind the cavalry charge. The enemy will be alerted by the time you reach the camp. We must hope they will still be in some confusion. Your task is to maintain that confusion, and to stop them from easily forming ranks until the main body of infantry can strike.'

Bolt nodded his head, his face impassive. *Cool*, thought Bahn, *for a man just handed a suicide mission*.

'I'd like to leave my medicos with the main force, general,' Bolt requested. He did not need to explain why.

Creed consented.

'Nidemes. Reveres.'

The two generals waited at attention.

'The main body will move in behind these actions in a warhead formation. General Nidemes – if you would, I'd like the Hoo to take the centre. General Reveres – the Red Guard chartassa will take positions on our flanks.

We will break through their lines and proceed directly to the imperial standard, wherever it may be flying. That is the throat we must work upon. We'll be going for the Matriarch herself.

'Colonel Halahan – we have reports of a mortar position on the ridge along their southern flank. You and a company of your Greyjackets will be dropped behind the imperial lines. Overrun that ridge and hold it at all cost. I repeat, at *all* cost. We must have the high ground for ourselves.'

General Creed, Lord Protector of Khos, faced his officers with a sombre intensity. The story he had offered was as close to a rousing battle speech as he would ever make. He wasn't a man to spoil it now with some glib words of victory and duty, not when asking men to lay down their lives at his command.

'Questions?'

Bahn waited to see if anyone else would speak. 'Our cannon,' he said at last, his tongue a dry slab in his mouth. 'What of our cannon?'

'They'll be of little use to us once battle is joined. And vulnerable too. Better if we send them to Tume along with the rest of our baggage. Anything else?'

Still no one spoke up. By the general's side, Halahan observed their uneasy silence with a quiet amusement. He hunched slightly over the stick of wood he leaned upon, using his weight to screw the tip of it deep into the snow, then cocked his head a little to one side. 'Aye, General,' he said; and he exhaled a puff of smoke from around his pipe, simple tarweed for once. 'I was just wondering why you were carrying that damned Mannian knife around your neck, is all.'

'Why?' responded Creed with a flash of his eyes. 'Because, Colonel, if we reach the Matriarch herself, I intend to cut her bloody throat out with it.'

CHAPTER TWENTY-FOUR

Clash of Arms

Ash awoke to the ground pounding against his ear, and recognized the sound in an instant.

The old Rōshun leapt up with his sheathed sword in hand and scanned the perimeter of wagons. Riders, tearing in through the night. Shouts of alarm rising in their wake.

A zel vaulted the yoke of a drawn wagon, threw up clods of snow from its hooves as it landed and regained its footing. Its rider yanked hard on the reins and Ash saw something in his hand with a smoking fuse trailing from it. The man tossed the jar into the wagon, which instantly burst into flames.

Someone screamed through the night. More riders were charging into the baggage camp, throwing firebombs at every wagon they could see. People yelled and ran for cover. The riders cut them down as they ran.

This is my chance.

Ash glanced to the north, where the tents of the Matriarch's encampment stood glowing with inner light.

He started to jog.

*

It was a damned foolish time to be flying. The air up here was frigid enough to cover everything on the little skyboat with ice. The silk envelope overhead, the sweeping control vanes along its flanks, all shone with a stark whiteness, while frozen diamonds of moisture covered the frozen tiq spars and rigging that fixed the wooden hull to the gas bag. Even worse, the light could not be relied upon, for the snow-covered valley floor below them kept fading into blackness each time a cloud obscured the waning moons, reducing their visibility to

almost nothing. For Halahan, it only made the experience more thrilling.

'A cold night for it!' he said to his staff sergeant over
the sound of the thrusters.

The man was huddling amongst the men at the very
centre of the narrow deck, as far from the rails as he
could be. Staff Sergeant Jay, a fellow Nathalese veteran,
only smiled miserably and closed his eyes again, and continued to chant a prayer beneath his breath.

Halahan casually chewed on his unlit pipe and surveyed his fellow Greyjackets. They held their longrifles
upright in their arms and shivered beneath their coats,
eyes flashing white in the gloom. A few passed around
flasks of spirits, though none of them spoke beyond the
odd whisper. Good fighters, all of them, he knew. Men
he could rely upon, each one an exile from a conquered
land.

Past their heads he spied the distant lights of the imperial army, and he chewed his pipe a little harder.

His own homeland of Nathal had fallen years ago,
after he'd spent half his life as a preacher of Erēs teaching the oneness of all. Now, Nathal was nothing more
than another colony of Mann, the people exploited and
oppressed worse than they ever had been by their own
Nathalese nobility.

Halahan massaged his bad leg where it was throbbing
from the chill – or perhaps it was from nothing more
than old memories. He had gained the wound after the
Imperial Fourth Army had invaded his homeland, a ca-
lamity that had caused him to set aside his preaching,
and in the greatest of ironies to fight alongside Queen
Hano and her forces. In the penultimate battle of the
war along the banks of the Toin, his leg had been crushed
by a skipping cannon shot, and he'd been left for dead
when the army had been routed. Dragging himself away
in the darkness, only the kindness of a local forest
woman had saved him.

In the aftermath, with the country set upon by the full force of the Mannian occupation, his faith had been the very last thing he had lost.

Halahan shifted his leg, blinking from the pain of it.

He looked to the pilot behind the wheel, wrapped in leathers and a scarf and ordinary flight goggles. The man pulled on levers next to the wheel to fire short bursts of the thrusters along the sides of the hull, while another crewman clambered through the icy rigging overhead, and struggled to open a frozen valve cap on the envelope itself, needing to release air from one of the ballast bladders to keep their nose low. Two more crewmen worked on this little skyboat commonly known as a skud. One sat behind the swivel-cannon as immobile as stone. Next to him perched the lookout, a woman wearing a pair of Owls, guiding the pilot on his course with silent gestures of loosehand.

The colonel watched her glove glow a ghostly blue in the dimness, impregnated as it was with a dye derived from the lakeweed of Simmer Lake. Each fresh signal was answered with another short puff of the thrusters, or a creak of ropes as one of the manoeuvring sculls was adjusted.

He patted Sergeant Jay on the shoulder and made his way forwards through the press of men. Neither of the two crewmen at the prow acknowledged his presence; both peered over the forward rail with utter attention. They stank of sweat, but then everyone on board did, including Halahan. Worse was the wind from all their loosening bowels.

They'll smell us before they see us, he thought wryly.

Ahead of the skyboat, the lights of the imperial encampment grew ever closer. Shouts came to his ears, men bawling in surprise or panic. A low rumble announced the Khosian cavalry charging through their camp.

The skud was shedding height fast as it approached the enemy positions, picking up speed in its descent.

Halahan shifted around in his crouch to look back along the deck over the heads of his men. Following the skyboat, he could see the odd flash of light against the night sky as one of the other skuds fired a brief burst, manoeuvring itself to stay on course in their wake. Seven squads of men in all, ten Greyjackets in each one. He hoped it would be enough to take the ridge and hold it.

The pilot burned the thrusters for another second, but then the lookout raised her hand and made a fist.

The pilot cut the thrusters and they drifted downwards in silence.

They were sailing over a fringe of the camp now. To the left, Halahan could see the road exposed beneath churned snow, and the distant travellers' lodge and cottages around it, their windows all lit, and the countless glimmers of the camp covering the surrounding plain. Shadows were flitting across the open ground. Specials, running towards the enemy lines in their four-man squads.

A cloud was moving clear of the moons, lighting up the scene below once more. The struts creaked as the gunner scanned the skies ahead, searching for Mannian birds-of-war. Ice cracked on tensing ropes. The high breeze was pushing them slightly sideways as they went, and the pilot peered through the gloom at the luminous glove of the lookout, but she held it there, still clenched in a fist, not moving.

There it was. A ridge of high ground running along the southern flank of the imperial camp, its slopes dotted with sparse, scrawny trees. The skud was approaching on a diagonal course that would take them past the westernmost point of the ridge, where it rose in a steep and treeless bluff. Soldiers were moving on the ground directly beneath them, rousing themselves and gathering arms, though it looked as if their attentions were fixed on the attacks in the main camp.

The skud was coming in low now. A treetop brushed

against the bottom of the hull. Halahan peered over the side with anticipation surging in his veins.

One minute, the lookout signalled.

Halahan's Greyjackets gathered by the rails next to the furled rope-ladders. The nose levelled off and the skud began to slow. Still the breeze carried them sideways. Halahan spotted a few faces looking up at him, but their shouts of alarm were lost in all the confusion. The skyboat passed over a frozen stream, and then the snow on the ground became broken and uneven, and white pools of ice stood amongst fronds of marshgrass that ran all the way to the base of the bluff. The area here was clear of men.

Something flashed on top of the bluff. A shot skittered against the hull, then another.

The lookout turned back to the men on the deck, her eyes hidden by the Owls. She jabbed downwards with her thumb.

At once the Greyjackets cast the rope-ladders over the sides and began to clamber down them. Sergeant Jay was first off the boat. Halahan adjusted his hat and climbed down after him, the ladder swaying beneath his boots.

He landed ankle-deep in water as his feet broke through a thin crust of ice.

Wonderful, he thought. *Now I'll have wet feet all night*.

It was darker here with the moons hidden by the rise of ground. Shots were slapping into the water all around them. Halahan crouched down amongst the marshgrasses as his men spread out into a skirmishing line and began to return fire.

The skud rose sharply as it shed the weight of its load. A few Greyjackets had to jump from the ends of the ladders. A second boat was coming in now, more Greyjackets climbing down from the ladders. Halahan saw the third skyboat crossing the stream. Shots were racing towards the drifting skuds from the top of the bluff, the odd one leaving a brief fiery trail like an after-image in the eye.

'Riflemen!' Sergeant Jay shouted with a hand on his helm. 'I was hoping they'd all be archers!'

The first skuds had ignited their thrusters on full and were climbing away to the right, their swivel-cannons spitting flames and grapeshot through the defenders on the ridge. Halahan saw pieces of wood flying; a scraggly yellowpine on the slope topple in half. He waited until the third skyboat had unloaded, knowing there was no time to wait for the others, and signalled for the second and third squad to advance on the bluff, while the first maintained fire to cover their approach.

He glanced back across the stream. Imperials were gathering and moving on their position. The remaining skyboats were coming in hot, with their thrusters trailing fire, the Greyjackets on board shooting down from the rails at the approaching men.

Sergeant Jay looked to Halahan as the assault squads jingled past them, their rifles on their backs and their shortswords naked in their hands, a few armed with pistols or miniature crossbows. Under gunfire they splashed forwards towards the slope.

Jay nodded to him. 'I'll see you at the top,' he said, and the man drew his sword and set off after them.

Halahan wished him luck.

*

'Hurry up, man,' snarled Sparus as his aide rushed from the archgeneral's tent with two slaves dashing after him, each one bearing pieces of his armour.

Sparus stood in his underclothing, barely noticing the cold as he studied the chaos unfolding in the camp below.

The Khosian cavalry was rampaging through the baggage train now. Moments earlier they had rolled in out of the night like a ghostly host, while most of the men of the Expeditionary Force slept in their pup tents or climbed to their feet too stunned to act. If they'd stopped there it would have been bad enough. But instead they raised hell as they carried on through the camp that stretched long and thin between the lake and the far ridgeline, so that now, in the exposed circle of the baggage train, flames were rising from blazing wagons.

Khosian skirmishers had followed in the wake of the cavalry, fighting within the camp itself. They were good, whoever they were, and Sparus watched groups of figures fighting amongst his surprised troops, avoiding those islands of order where his officers bellowed at their men and roused them into some kind of formation.

'Is it a raid?' asked the young priest who stopped by his side, his eyes bleary with sleep. It was Ché, Sasheen's personal Diplomat.

'No,' Sparus told him, and looked to the west along the valley floor, where a bristle of spear-points glistened in the moonlight. The Diplomat followed his gaze, and stared at the sight without comment.

'The Matriarch, is she up yet?' Sparus asked of one of his aides as they helped fit his armour.

'Barely,' the harried aide replied. 'She took a draught to help her sleep. A heavy one, they say.'

'Romano?'

The aide was about to reply when a roar sounded from Romano's tent, and they all turned in time to see an Acolyte being flung out into the snow with Romano emerging after him, naked and wild-eyed and gripping a shortsword in his hand. The young general staggered in the snow and righted himself. He saw Sparus strapping on his cuirass.

'Tonight?' he shouted across at him. 'Tell me I'm dreaming, for pity's sake!'

'You are,' drawled Sparus. 'We all are.'

Romano rubbed at one of his eyes and swore.

'Where is my armour?' he hollered, stumbling back inside his tent.

Archgeneral Sparus pulled tight on the last strap of his cuirass and grabbed one of his greaves from the hand of a slave. He checked the camp again, the flames bright in his eye.

They attack us, and at night, he mused silently.

Beside him, the Diplomat spoke without looking from the approaching chartassa.

'These Khosians have balls,' he declared, as though reading the general's mind.

*

It was a desperate sight that faced Colonel Halahan as he made it to the top of the bluff. Imperial infantry and riflemen had been posted there to guard the mortar crews, and they were making a fight of it.

Out of the darkness an imperial soldier ran at him, hollering with spirit. Halahan tugged a pistol from his bandolier, pulled back the primer that would pierce the cartridge of water and blackpowder, and aimed it between the man's eyes. He pulled the trigger and watched through a blossom of smoke as the man fell back to the ground, half his skull missing.

Absently he reloaded the pistol, breaking it open to pull out the spent cartridge, replacing it with another, closing the piece again.

He spotted another soldier running in from his left where the Greyjackets were locked in hand-to-hand melee. Halahan fired again, and didn't miss.

The colonel took in the progress of the fight, and decided it was still too close to call. Behind him, down at the base of the slope, the rearguard squads fired at the Imperials rushing across the stream at them. Unconcerned, he gazed out over the snowy plain to the west. He could see glints of steel massed around a thin core of flickering torches, the Khosian chartassa, moving to engage the Imperials.

Again he reloaded the same pistol, though four other pieces lay snug in his bandolier. He stood there and waited, and had time enough to feel pride for these men under his command even amongst the ugliness of the fighting. Their anger could be seen in the way that they fought. This was personal to them. They had scores to settle, families to be avenged, memories to be released through the sharp end of a blade.

The tide was beginning to turn in their favour now. He saw the moment in which it happened, and it was neither relief nor surprise that occupied him while he waited for it to be over. Instead it was simple impatience.

As the remaining few Imperials were dispensed with, he strode out amongst his Greyjackets, watching the medicos move in to do their work on the wounded. A man swore and scrabbled at his blinded eyes while his comrades tried to hold him down. Another had lost a hand; he stared balefully at the severed appendage lying in the trampled snow as though it was a wife who'd left him for another.

In one spot, two Pathian brothers worked with their knives on a wounded imperial soldier. They were making sport of him, drawing sobs from his lips. Halahan didn't stop them.

Instead he took out a match and fired up his pipe.

The ridge was theirs.

Now, all they had to do was hold it.

*

Soaring flames roared into the darkness of the sky. A rider bore down on Ash with a lowered lance. Without thinking, he slashed his sword up and cut the lance in two. The rider veered away, heading deeper into the circled baggage train.

Ash ran on towards the burning wagons at the perimeter, but he found his way suddenly blocked by groups of camp followers, those who had been near enough to witness his quick work with the sword. They gathered around him with their own knives and makeshift clubs, clearly decided upon staying as close to him as they could. Ash struggled to free himself from the press. He growled and swept the flat of his blade to force a way through.

'Get back!' he shouted at them all, for he could feel his chances of reaching Sasheen in time slipping away by the moment.

It was no good. Still they pressed tight around him.

Ash smashed a man's nose flat across his face with a single punch, spilling him to the ground. He kicked another in the kneecap, heard the crack of it even amidst all the noise. The crowd pulled back in shock.

He panted down at the two prone men, saw the darkness of blood upon the slush of the ground. They were holding their hands up, trying to ward off any further attacks.

His anger dimmed, turning to shame.

I haven't the time for this.

The crowd parted before him as he sprinted onwards. Ash didn't look back.

—CHAPTER TWENTY-FIVE—

In the Soup

The line of chartassa appeared out of the night with spear-tips raised and shields interlocked, their eyes and teeth gleaming within the curves of their plumed helms, each man shouting in time to the drumbeats that were helping time their steps.

The purple-cloaked Hoo marched at the fore of the advancing Khosian army, forming the chartassa at the very tip of its warhead formation, while the Red Guards formed the flanks and the rear. In the first two ranks of each chartassa, the men bore short stabbing swords with leaf-shaped blades, designed for the intimate butcher's work of the front line; in the ranks behind the swords were sheathed, and the men carried their massively long chartas raised in the air, ready to lower them once the enemy was close enough to engage.

Behind the line of phalanxes, and in the spaces in between them known as the gutters, step sergeants jogged to and fro with staves in their hands, bawling at those who were stepping out of time, lashing with their sticks at sections of men bulging outwards, maintaining the mobile coherence of their chartassa. Command flags appeared above the heads of the men. Shrill whistles blew.

The bristling forest of spears descended as one with a unified *hoo*.

Panic sounded from the enemy soldiers scattering before them. With the steady, unstoppable momentum of a ship cutting through water, the Khosian formation carved its way into the imperial camp.

Time was crucial here, and all knew it. With each collective step they took they thrust deeper into the disorganized encampment, leaving a swathe of dead and wounded in their wake. Given long enough the Mannians would rally, and the imperial predoré would crush against the flanks of the many chartassa like a vice. Already, action was occurring at the front, while imperial battle colours were being raised all around them, men massing in ranks and files.

Bahn trod behind the centremost reserve chartassa, keeping in close step with its captain and General Creed. He wiped sweat from his eyes and watched their three skyships flying overhead, scattering grenades onto the imperials below. Beneath his armour, his whole body shook from head to toe in its usual physical response to violence. His movements were awkward, clumsy even. It felt like a dream, walking ever deeper into the imperial encampment, like stepping into the sea until your feet lost the bottom and the riptide caught hold; too late to turn back.

At least General Creed was in his element here. The Lord Protector was surrounded by his personal body-guards, their shields held high to protect him from the occasional incoming arrow. Creed was hardly making it easy for them. He wore a pair of Owls over his eyes like the other high officers of the army, and he strode from one side of the chartassa to the other, spotting along the gutters between it and the next one, spying out the lie of the land ahead.

'What of the Specials?' Bahn heard himself ask as the general returned to his position.

Creed's eyes left the growing intensity of the fighting ahead and settled on his lieutenant. 'What?' he shouted through the noise.

'The Specials, sir,' repeated Bahn, and almost tripped on something – the body of an imperial soldier. 'They should be heading back by now.'

'No sign of them,' replied the general, distracted. He was looking for something amongst the imperial masses.

'Nidemes!' he hollered to the commander of the Hoo. The old general was ranging behind the line of chartassa in much the same way as Bahn and Creed. He turned at the sound of his name.

General Creed chopped his hand sideways, telling him to veer his men left. Nidemes acknowledged and shouted the commands. Flag bearers waved the change in direction for the benefit of the captains. Within mo-ments, whistles were blowing to inform the men. The entire line began to shift about.

Bahn caught a glimpse ahead and saw what they were turning towards. A small mound of ground in the dis-tance backlit with stars; tiny glimmers of tents with the Matriarch's personal banner flying high above them, a black raven on white.

The general was aiming the army straight for Matri-arch Sasheen herself.

*

On the plain of Chey-Wes, Ché saw how the Expeditionary Force was rallying at last, thanks to the arrival of Archgeneral Sparus. While the Khosian formation thrust its way deeper through the camp like a glistening warhead, imperial squares of predoré engaged them now on all flanks, stretching and pushing them out of shape. Even though surrounded, the Khosians continued to push closer towards the Matriarch's position – for it was clear now that *here* was their intended destination, and it was Sasheen herself whom they wished to confront.

'Leave me be,' came Sasheen's sleepy voice amidst the splash of water, her aides dragging her from the wooden bathtub filled with snowmelt.

'Matriarch,' Sool tried again. '*We are under attack.*'

'Yes, I heard you the first time,' mumbled the Matriarch.

Sasheen stood naked on a rug with the wet cast of plaster on her arm. She swayed in her half sleep as they dried her roughly with towels, trying to revive her as best they could.

'Some rush oil,' she said to Heelas, her caretaker. 'Fetch me some.' Heelas already had a pot of the stuff in his hand, and he opened it and handed it to her. With a grimace, Sasheen rubbed the white cream onto her lips.

Ché stood at the entrance of her great tent. His large knife was belted around his waist, as was a pistol that he had already loaded with a single, poisoned shot.

Outside, Acolytes and priests were hurrying back and forth through the Matriarch's encampment. Her personal honour guard, fitted out for battle, had already gathered with their mounts. One of them held the reins of her white war-zel. The creature was twitching with impatience.

'For my son,' he heard Sasheen say from within, and her voice already sounded a little firmer. 'I will dedicate this victory to my son.'

Alarum came marching into the tent, wrapped in a

heavy wool cloak. He clapped Ché on the arm as though glad to see him. 'They had to choose tonight, didn't they?' he said as he stomped the snow from his boots.

Ché watched him as he went inside to speak to the Matriarch, then turned back to the night plain beyond. He was intent on the distant action, though in a detached way, removed from it by distance and lack of sentiment, so that he felt like a spectator at the Shay Madi, watching two gladiators competing to win and live. What held him so rapt was the obvious skill and discipline of the Khosians. He possessed some vague understanding of what it must take to move so many men in unison and fight at the same time, even more so to change their direction during a battle.

Watching them roar and shift their heading earlier had caused his lips to part and his pulse to beat faster. He hadn't thought such things were possible.

I don't care who wins this fight, Ché realized with a start. And then it struck him how that was a lie: he did have a preference in that moment.

It was only that it was the wrong side.

*

Something rattled off Bull's helm, and he looked up from behind his shield and saw the man in the file to his left go down in the darkness and the jostling scrum that was the belly of the chartassa.

Bull shook his head to clear his eyes of sweat. Another man stepped forward to take the space of his fallen comrade. The soldier stumbled over the fellow on the ground as he set his shield against the Red Guard in front of him, and leaned into his back and began to shove. He was partially covered by Bull's broad shield, and he looked up at him, and widened his eyes in recognition. The man bared his teeth in a crazy grin.

Bull nodded his head by way of a greeting.

With ease Bull was shoving too, pushing his shield

against the back of young Wicks as his feet slipped in the thick mud. Missiles were clattering all around them, and the lad was hunching down as though naked in a hailstorm, offering little protection for Bull, who stood a good foot and a half above him.

His height had always been a disadvantage in the inner ranks; he had to bend low to get properly behind the shield of the man next to him, so that already his back was screaming from the pain of it. Not like the old days, he reflected bitterly. Back then he'd been trusted enough to be a point man, the soldier at the very front who could be relied upon to stand and fight; even eventually a file closer, the leader of the file who stood at the very back, maintaining order.

At least his present vantage gave him a view of what was happening near the front, though a passing bank of clouds was now scudding across the Sisters of Loss and Longing, diminishing what he could see. In the last few minutes the fighting had grown fiercer.

Over the bronze rim of his shield he could just make out the three men before him in the file. Wicks, close enough to the front now to jab wild and blind with his charta over the shoulders of those ahead of him, as much a danger to his own comrades as to the enemy infantry; the man before Wicks, thrusting with more composure as though he had done this before; and the man at the very front, only a vague shape in the darkness, standing over the Red Guard who had just been there, distant flames glinting off his helm and his sword as he swerved and thrust with his life depending on it.

Bull could barely see beyond to the mass of enemy infantry they were fighting, save for how their spearheads poked and probed amongst the men to either side of him. Even so, over the chorus of the battle he could hear the shouts and grunts of collision up there. The enemy were doing damage, whoever they were. In quick succession he'd stepped forwards over three men, all of whom were dead, their helms and shields caved in, their faces pulped, their arms snapped like branches. It was the same in the file on either side of him too. They were moving up the ranks faster than the chartassa itself was moving.

For a moment, moonlight shone down from a break in the clouds. *Sweet Mercy*, Bull thought, as he caught a glimpse of something, a figure too tall to be believed, visible for an instant before it was smothered in darkness.

And then the file moved forward again against Bull's pressure, and he was stumbling once more over another body on the ground, a Red Guard with a dent in his helm the size of his skull.

Young Wicks glanced over his shoulder, his mouth open in a wide O. Only a single Red Guard stood between the lad and the enemy. Bull lowered his own charta over the young man's shoulder and waited a moment for the balance of the point to settle, counterweighted by the spike on its base known as the toe-clipper. The Red Guard behind Bull did the same.

He could see them now. Three giants – there was no other word for them – three men standing side by side and at least eight feet tall, their heights increased yet further by crests of wild blond hair. Northern tribesmen, he realized, seeing the warpaint on their faces. Some were said to grow this tall.

For an instant, Bull did something that he'd not done since he was a young man in the ranks. He froze in shock at what he was facing. With a dry mouth he watched the swing of a great warhammer come down like the falling of a tree, and the point man disappear beneath it.

The warhead of the man's charta behind him tore open Wicks's cheek as the lad tried to push back against Bull. The lad had dropped his own charta. He was cowering beneath his shield as the giant raised his hammer above his head.

In desperation, Bull thrust his charta against the giant. The warhead struck off his great rectangular shield and Bull pulled it back for another lunge.

More chartas licked out at the giant. *Come on then, someone bloody poke him one.*

He tried to find a target beyond the great shield, but his aim was blown when a man to his right jostled him.

Wicks went down with a muffled shout and a crump of metal.

Bull stepped forwards with his legs on either side of the lad, stabbing as he moved. He was taller than any that stood in the whole chartassa, yet still he was dwarfed by the three mammoth tribesmen, brothers for all he knew. In the moment he took to draw a breath, he saw the black silhouette that faced him flash its teeth in a grin.

A man fell against his left side, struggled to keep his feet. Bull lifted his shield and thrust blindly from behind it. His warhead punched through the giant's own shield and scraped along armour. The giant swung his warhammer down on Bull's charta, snapping it in two and knocking the broken shaft from his grasp. Movement between his legs. Wicks, still alive down there.

Bull swept the shortsword from its scabbard and dug his feet firmer into the mud. 'Go, lad!' he hollered down at Wicks with his spit flying. 'Go!'

*

The medico bag slapped against Curl's hip as she followed Kris across the frozen ground. They were jogging through the screen of Volunteers and Red Guard light infantry that protected the flanks and rear of the formation as it ground its slow way onwards. The soldiers were exposed out here in their looser formations beyond the protection of the main body, and their casualties were mounting fast.

Kris gestured to a fallen man and kept running, not looking back to see if Curl acknowledged her or not.

A flare shrieked into the night air as Curl squatted down next to the wounded Volunteer, lighting the scene for a few lingering moments in shades of harsh green. The man's eyes were rolling in their sockets. Blood flowed from his hip just beneath the edge of his cuirass. She couldn't tell what had caused the wound. There could be a bullet lodged in there for all she knew.

'Kris!' she yelled, but the woman was already out of sight, lost amongst the fighting groups of men.

This is insane, she thought as she stared down at the wound. *I'm not trained for this. I'm not ready for it.*

She squatted there, frozen amidst the madness of the night with the cries of dying men filling her ears and the violence all about her, hating it with every fibre of her being, hating this need in men to fight and conquer, to tear the world asunder to sate their childish desires.

The wounded soldier groaned in pain and muttered something from his dry lips. She looked down at him. He was bearded, middle-aged. Someone's father. Someone's husband. Curl remembered what she was supposed to be doing here.

She checked his pulse, found it was still beating strongly. With haste she fumbled through her medico bag for the glass dropper of sanseed. She squeezed his mouth open and shook a few drops against his tongue. He groaned again, and she poured a dribble of water into his mouth from her flask. 'Thank you,' he gasped, and tried to roll onto his side.

'Don't move,' she said to him, and took out a compress bandage and held it against his wound.

Around them the light infantry were being pressed back by an approaching formation of Imperials. Men fired darts at the enemy, grenades, arrows. Squads rushed past her, trying to outflank the approaching mass. An explosion ripped through the night. A man fell face down in the snow not ten paces away.

'Press hard!' she shouted into the Volunteer's face, and she took his clammy, hairy hand in her own and pressed it against the bandage. His eyes rolled again and then refocused on her. 'Press!' she told him. He blinked to show he understood.

Curl yanked one of the thin poles from the quiver on her back. It was fitted with an arrowhead on one end, and she cleared away some snow and stabbed it into the ground until it held firm. She unfurled the little white flag on the top of the pole, so that the stretcher-bearers would see the wounded man more easily. She glanced across at the other wounded man lying nearby.

Hand over her head, she ran towards him.

*

'General!' Bahn shouted as they walked step by step with the front line of chartassa. 'General Reveres requests re-inforcements on the left. He says the Seventh Chartassa has been lost and the Sixth is being pushed back.'

'Lost?'

'They were detached from the main force somehow. He's not sure where they are.'

The general stormed towards Bahn with his body-guards in tow, his long hair hanging wet about the shoulders of his bearskin coat. In anger, the man seemed to loom larger than life.

'The bloody fools, what are they playing at over there?'

Bahn had no answer for him.

Creed straightened with a snort and clasped his hands behind his back. He looked behind to the archers and the boy slingers loosely positioned in the long corridor of space within the tight formation of the army. They had no shields to protect themselves from incoming fire, and were taking losses as a consequence. Behind them, beyond the medicos and stretcher-bearers running back and forth, it was too dark and distant to see the light infantry who held the rear of the formation, marching backwards in step to the army's drums. The general scanned ahead again to the front lines.

A dart struck one of the outstretched shields that protected him. The bodyguard looked sceptically at the barbed tip protruding through his shield, the third one so far. They were coming down like a hard rain now.

Not more than six paces from Bahn a flying spear skewered a medico to the ground. The young man floundered, screaming, a pink froth bubbling from his wound.

Bahn panted, numbed to all that was occurring around him. The advance had slowed badly. They were still pushing forwards, though only marginally, and now it seemed the Imperials were forcing them back on the left. Worse, the entire army was surrounded now, with no hope of escape.

Captains and step sergeants swore at their chartassa and shouted to push harder. Close to his left, a captain was physically shoving at the backs of his men as he screamed obscenities over their heads.

'Send a runner to Ocien in the Ninth,' Creed shouted into his ear, and nodded to the few remaining reserve chartassa barely visible on the right. 'Have him send a chartassa over to bolster the left.'

Bahn marvelled again at the general's ability to store the names of every officer under his command.

'And, Lieutenant,' Creed hollered as Bahn turned to find a nearby runner. 'Inform General Reveres that if he gives away any more ground, I will go over there personally and sort out his affairs.'

'Sir.'

As he dispatched a runner to Ocien, Bahn wiped his face with a trembling hand. An explosion nearby made him jolt.

Nothing could prepare a man for the sheer noise of a pitched battle. He recalled the first time he'd ever heard such a thing, the first day the Mannians had assaulted the Shield; how his bowels had turned to water and his mind to mud. It was like being in the midst of a thunderstorm: your bones shivering, your ears hurting even more than your throat that was screaming itself raw just to be heard.

The sounds from the front ranks were unimaginable now. It was bloody murder out there on the fringes, and he witnessed the action only as its consequences emerged in the form of bodies beneath the rear boots of the advancing lines. The stench too was hard to cope with. Blood soaked the muddy ground, mixing with everything else that bodies released at such times as these; a reeking, slippery mess that he'd fallen into more than once so far.

In the middle of the army's formation, the open space was piling up with the dead and wounded. Stretcher-bearers ran back and forth over-burdened by the rate of casualties, struggling to move them all in pace with the army's momentum. Monks helped where they could. The medicos fought their own battles trying to hold men together. The injuries were hard on the eyes; even to Bahn, who had witnessed his own share of gore on the walls. Open wounds bled with profusion, the exposed flesh shockingly vivid. Feet slipped on grey intestines lying unravelled across the mud. Skin flapped. Eye sockets gaped empty. Bodies shorn of limbs jetted blood.

On the ground some of the men seemed entirely unhurt, and simply sat sobbing or staring dazed into space. One man was trying to pull his armour off. He'd been at it for several minutes, and still he couldn't manage the simple task of removing his breastplate. Worst of all were those unable to walk. Some were being left behind as the entire warhead-shaped formation advanced in step, trampled where they lay by the rearguard.

Bahn turned away from it all. He sought out the reassuring bulk of General Creed, saw that Koolas, the war chattēro, was bending his ear.

'We seem to be grinding to a halt!' the man was saying.

'What?'

'I said we seem to be grinding to a halt! Is there any-thing we can do?'

'Do?' replied the general. 'If there was something we could do, man, we'd be doing it.'

Koolas looked as though he'd been hoping for some-thing more inspiring than this. He glanced at Bahn, and Bahn could see that he was visibly shaking.

'We still have one advantage,' declared the general, and both Koolas and Bahn leaned closer to hear him. 'Since we're entirely surrounded, our men have nowhere to run. We will not be routed, in any case.'

Bahn blinked rapidly. Creed slapped his arm, almost bowling him over with the force of it.

'We grabbed hold of the bear! Now we must suffer its grip while we work our way to its throat.'

Even now, Koolas had his mind on his story. 'And what if she runs for it, General? The Matriarch. What then?'

'Then her own people might finish her for us. These Mannians hold great store in their leader's courage.'

'And you think – if we kill her – they will break?'

'Perhaps. Or perhaps Sparus will succeed in holding them together. Who knows?' General Creed flashed his teeth, a rare display. Perhaps it was only for the benefit of this man and his writings. He turned away and started to holler more orders.

Despite what the general had just claimed, men were starting to break from the front ranks to the left. Offi-cers struck the fleeing soldiers down or screamed in their faces, shoving them back into the lines.

'*Where are you running to?*' Bahn imagined the offi-cers shouting. '*Where is there to run, you fools?*'

Koolas was feigning his composure well, for all the trembling of his body. Bahn warmed to him a little in that moment, and he offered a nod of the head as the chattéro fixed his cloak tighter about his belly then strode off towards the troubled ranks.

Another runner approached Bahn from the forward

chartassa. He stood to attention, his reddened cheeks blowing in and out as he gasped for air. 'Chartassa Three – they've been stopped – by a fresh assault. Acolytes, they're saying.'

Chartassa Three, thought Bahn with a twist of fear in his belly. That was a square of Hoo, in the vanguard of the formation just to the right of centre. Their very best.

Sweet Dao, they were no longer even advancing.

He took a deep breath before he approached the general with the news.

'Acolytes,' Creed spat. And he put his hands to his hips, feet wide apart, and looked for inspiration somewhere high up in the night sky.

—CHAPTER TWENTY-SIX—

The Ridge

They came along the top of the ridge, a squad of imperial infantry with their shields interlocked and shortswords at the ready. Ghazni regulars, by the look of the feathers sprouting from their helms.

'Stand firm,' Halahan shouted to the two lines of Greyjackets standing along the waist of the ridge, the foremost covering the rear with borrowed shields. He didn't doubt that they would. He simply wished to remind them that he was there, that they weren't alone.

It was the first organized counter-attack since his Greyjackets had taken this high position overlooking the imperial camp. On the slopes of scraggly yellowpine, the bodies of imperial troops lay contorted where they had fallen, after their initial ragged attempts to retake it. Since then, the Imperials had contented themselves with firing missiles onto the position, rifle shots, arrows and bolts mixed with the occasional grenade. His own men lay around the westernmost spur of the ridge in a thin perimeter of defence. They were firing down on the enemy while they used bodies and propped shields for cover.

In the very centre of their position, other Greyjackets had taken over the imperial mortars they had captured there. The men handled the shells with the utmost care and attention, removing them from their waterproof wrappings like newborn babes. Each shell resembled an oversized rifle cartridge, though with a short fuse poking out from the open top of cartridge paper. After a crew soaked the fuse from their water flasks, they would quickly drop the thing down the stubby mortar while they flung themselves behind the cover of the wicker screens already in place there. An instant later, with the charge punctured by a firing pin at the bottom of the tube, the blackpowder ignited at the sudden exposure to moist air and the live shell – nothing more than a large grenade – shot out of it too fast to see with a solid *whump*.

Halahan watched them for a lingering moment then looked away. He had more pressing matters at hand – the enemy assault along the ridge, for one.

'Fire away!' Staff Sergeant Jay shouted at the Greyjackets along the waist, and they unleashed a volley that struck into the front rank of the advancing infantry. Half of the Ghazni regulars went down. Others stumbled over them.

Their vacant positions were quickly occupied. Imperial officers shouted orders to keep the line and press on. Another volley of rifle shots, another bloody tumble of men. Still they advanced closer.

With ten feet to go, the advancing infantry gave a roar and charged. The two lines met with a crash of men and shields. Halahan watched through a puff of drifting pipe smoke.

The shock of such a clash could be enough to stun some men, so that they froze with open mouths while they pissed their breeches or worse. Sometimes, if they were truly green, they could even drop their weapons and hold their hands out against the press, calling out to their assailants to stop, pleading for sanity, for respite.

Two of the inexperienced Greyjackets went down quickly like that, stunned into inaction or breaking entirely. Then three. Then four.

Halahan wasn't overly concerned as he watched the medicos rush to give them aid. It always went this way at first. As for the fallen men themselves, those who would not recover, who would leave loved ones grieving behind – Halahan had no time for such sentiments. Leave them be until later. Leave them for the bottle.

A fifth man fell, a stump of an arm shooting blood. The line bulged inwards.

'Staff Sergeant Jay – half the men in the first platoon to reinforce the second!'

Sergeant Jay ran along the crouched Greyjackets on the southern edge of the ridge, tapping every other man on the shoulder. They stood in turn, drawing their swords and, grabbing what shields they could find, rushed to join the fighting. The line almost broke, but it steadied itself with the timely arrival of the reinforcements. Slowly, they pushed themselves back into shape.

Halahan strode towards the northern edge and the Greyjackets firing down from their prone positions there. Missiles hummed through the night air or struck the slope with dull slaps. Halahan ignored them.

A flare shot into the sky. It screamed like a firework as it rose on its smoky trail, lighting the boiling scene beneath it in hues of green. It illuminated a bird-of-war far over the east of the camp. Another skyship was pursuing it, firing its prow gun at its envelope.

The ridge ran from west to east along the edge of the imperial camp, and afforded a full vantage over the field. It was going badly down there, he could tell. The Khosian formation stretched before him long and thin, a great dark mass of glinting squares surrounded by hundreds of torches and thousands of the enemy. In parts it was bulging inwards, or breaking apart. Far off to his right, he could see how the front of the formation had been stopped in its tracks. At this rate, the army wouldn't last another half-hour.

Halahan doubted he could hold on to the ridge for half that time.

He squinted, judging the distance between their position and the Khosian formation. He called for the corporal of the platoon that was manning the mortars.

'Curtz,' he said as the rangy man towered above him. 'The front enemy lines there, facing our chartassa,' and he pointed to the forward clash of Khosians and Mannians. 'Could those mortars make it from here?'

The man studied the distance, then held his nose in the air to catch the breeze. Curtz had been an artillery sergeant in the Pathian army and knew his business well. 'Aye, Colonel, I think so. We'd have to be right careful though.'

'Pass the command, then. Target the lines directly in front of our own chartassa.'

The order was passed on. Curtz handled the first shot himself, adjusting the elevation of the mortar and noting its setting. He soaked the fuses and slotted the cartridge into the tube then squatted there while his men retreated behind the nearest screen.

Whump went the shell. Curtz gazed down on the plain, waiting. Long moments later, a brightness of flames erupted amongst a dark mass of predoré not far from the Khosian front. A remarkable shot.

He turned his face to Halahan. 'I can't do any better than that.'

Halahan chewed the stem of his pipe.

'Continuous fire!' he barked.

*

Beyond the Matriarch's encampment, almost deserted when Ash came to it at last, he followed a column of white-robes as they marched at the head of the imperial standard towards the scene of fighting. At their fore hung Sasheen's raven standard.

He paused as he came upon a medical station blazing with light within the main camp. Stretcher-bearers were moving in a steady flow towards it, and corpses had been arrayed in the snow behind the main tent. No sentries were in sight.

Boldly, Ash walked up to the corpse of an Acolyte and pulled free the white cloak and then the mask. He glimpsed a surgeon at work within the brightly lit tent, the man sawing through a limb as his patient gabbled in delirium.

Ash moved on, shadowing the Matriarch as she headed towards the clash of arms.

*

They were taking heavy losses now. Bahn himself had been wounded by an arrow that had gone through the flesh of his lower arm, nicking his tendons, he thought, for he could no longer clench his left hand fully. It hurt like fire, and as he kept pace with General Creed he gritted his teeth and bore it silently while a medico hastily treated the injury.

All was not lost, for they were moving again. Halahan's Greyjackets on the ridge seemed to be lobbing mortar shells onto the imperial lines directly before their formation, thinning them enough to allow the forward chartassa to push through. Creed's mood had lifted at this development, as though his prayers to the sky had been answered. The general eyed the fighting chartassa before him, willing them onwards.

'Keep your arm still!' the medico hollered at Bahn as she cleaned out his wound with a flask of alcohol.

Through the pain of it, he looked down at the young woman in the black leathers of the Specials, noticing her properly for the time. She was no more than a girl, he saw, and pretty too, in a thin, fragile sort of way. Her tongue poked out from the corner of her mouth as she worked. Her honey-coloured hair was smeared over her head in a flattened mess.

For a moment he didn't recognize her. Not here. Not in this place.

'Curl?' he croaked in surprise. 'Is that you, girl?'

Her eyes met his for a moment before they returned to her task. 'I wondered if you'd recognize me,' she panted.

'What are you doing here, for Fool's sake?'

'Fixing your arm, so you don't bleed to death.'

'Are you all right?'

She paused to look up at him. 'No,' she said with a shake of her head, and tugged a bandage from her bag. 'Are you?'

She was white with fear, he saw, and her eyes held a haunted look to them, as though she had witnessed things she'd vowed never to see again.

He recalled that she was a Lagosian, and that she'd survived all the crimes the Mannians had perpetrated against her people. In that moment, and with the greatest of intensity, Bahn thought: *These bastard Mannians . . . if there is any justice in this world at all, we will somehow win this fight, and crush this army, and hang their Holy Matriarch by her stiff neck.*

A body in the way, clearly dead. They both stepped over it as they walked onwards. Curl pressed a wad of bandage against his wound. 'Hold that a moment,' she told him, and searched through her bag again. She pulled out another bandage, began to wrap it around his arm. 'You can let go of it now.'

Bahn reached for his flask of water. He pulled the cork out with his teeth and held it in the same hand as the flask and took a quick drink of the cool water. He was losing track of time here. How long had they been fighting now?

'Drink?' he asked Curl.

She opened her mouth and let him pour a little into it. When she finished tying the knot in his bandage, she took the cork from his hand and closed the flask and hung it across her shoulder from its strap. 'I need it more than you,' she told him. 'For the wounded.'

He missed his chance to reply. Creed had spotted something up ahead, and was striding forwards to peer through the bristling spikes of the forward chartassa.

Bahn followed his gaze, barely believing what he saw. The Matriarch's standard was flying directly ahead of them. Sasheen had joined the battle.

Sweet Dao, we might still reach her yet.

With the mortar shells continuing to fall down before them, shattering the enemy lines in confusion, Bahn experienced a momentary spike of hope.

If only Halahan can hold on to that ridge.

*

'Colonel Halahan!'

'I see it, Staff Sergeant.'

The Mannians were trying to attack from the other side of the ridge, the southern side away from the battle. He'd been expecting that for some time. A dozen Greyjackets were positioned there, crouched behind a low wall of snow and whatever dirt they'd been able to scrape up from the ground. They aimed their rifles and fired down on the enemy troops that scrabbled up the slope towards them.

A hail of rifle shots crackled back in reply. A Greyjacket tumbled backwards. The defenders managed another volley, and then they were drawing their shortswords to meet the attack.

The rest of the ridge was a similar scene of dispute, every flank hard pressed.

On the east flank, across the waist of the ridge, the surviving Greyjackets stood in two ranks and chopped and shoved against seemingly endless numbers of Ghazni regulars. They were exhausted, and being forced back step by step.

On the northern side, the majority of Greyjackets

fought hand-to-hand against more infantry climbing
the slope. Behind them, in the centre, the mortar crews
maintained their fire as fast as they could, though their
supply of shells was starting to run low.

Watch it.

A Mannian broke through from the southern side
where the newest attack had been launched. Colonel
Halahan took the man in the chest with a shot from his
pistol. He reloaded the piece as he studied the buckling
lines, looking for areas of stress and weakness, judging
tensions, breaking points, knots of strength, as an arti-
san might inspect the materials of his craft.

The lines were too damned thin. Two more Imperials
broke through from the south. The colonel fired his
pistol, yanked out another with his other hand, cocked
it and fired that too. They were going to break at any
moment, and after that the men across the waist would
fold, and the rest of them would be finished.

'Staff Sergeant Jay! Five men from the mortars to
support the waist. Another five to the south.'

It was all he could do; if he relieved the mortar crews
of any more men, their effect on the Mannian lines
would be minimal.

Halahan leaned on his good leg as he drew life back
into his pipe. He wondered if it was the last time he
would experience the simple pleasure of a smoke. He
hoped not, for the taste of it was bitter in his mouth just
then.

Strange how his own mood could do that.

Halahan grunted. It seemed he was fated never to
defeat these people.

Sergeant Jay was shouting something from the northern side. Halahan turned and saw Imperials breaking
through all along the line. The staff sergeant was laying
into them left and right with his curved Nathalese tulwar
as he yelled back over his shoulder. Halahan took
aim and fired, sending an Imperial beside the sergeant
spinning away. He swung around in instinct, drawing

another pistol and cocking it as he twisted, pointed it over his shoulder at a soldier rushing at him with a raised sword. Halahan pulled the trigger.

The firing arm snapped down, but nothing happened.

Halahan was too old to gape at such a surprise. He swerved a wild slash of the sword and punched the barrel of the gun into the man's throat. His eyes saw him go down, but his mind was already taking in the line to the south.

It was collapsing too.

'Hold tight!' he roared around the stem of his pipe, fighting an urge to rush to the aid of his men. He discharged his fifth pistol into a soldier attacking the remaining mortar crews in the centre. He tossed it aside and drew out his last gun.

This is it, then, he thought grimly to himself. *At least we took the fight to the bastards for once.*

'Colonel!'

Staff Sergeant Jay stood panting in exhaustion on the northern flank. All of the Greyjackets there were panting hard, steam rising off their bodies, swords dripping, looking down the slope. Somehow they'd fought off the attack.

Halahan left the desperate melee behind to step over and join them.

On the slope amongst the trees, black-garbed figures struggled upwards stabbing through the remaining Imperials as they climbed; Specials, all of them.

For an instant, Halahan was indeed surprised.

Hands reached down to aid the new arrivals. Faces appeared out of the night's gloom, filthy, grim, wide-eyed. Perhaps forty in all, many of them wounded.

'Glad you could make it,' said Halahan as he pulled a woman to the top.

'Glad to be here,' she replied without breath.

'Any officers?'

'Dead,' she told him.

Typical that, of the Specials, for their officers always

led from the front. Halahan faced the newcomers. 'Quickly, now. Those who can fight, spread out to support the lines. We are required to hold this ridge for as long as we can.'

Every one of them moved into a position of defence. In moments the lines stabilized and the remaining attacks were repulsed, save for the continuing thrust along the waist. At least they were holding their ground now.

Along all sides of the ridge, bodies were rolled against the makeshift walls to strengthen the defences.

'Well done, Staff Sergeant.'

'Thank you,' said the old smith, dabbing at a cut on his brow.

'Pull back those who need a few minutes to rest. See to the wounded, and pass out some water.'

The sergeant nodded, eyeing the Specials spread out amongst them. He leaned towards Halahan.

Quietly, he said, 'You know that if they attack again, it still won't be enough?'

'I know it. But let's keep that to ourselves for now, shall we?'

*

Now that Curl was within the relative protection of the main Khosian force, and had time to look about her, to think and feel, she found that terror was beginning to swamp her.

It was no longer even the madness of the violence, nor the risk to her own life. No, it was her proximity to these soldiers of Mann, just on the other side of the chartassa – some even running amok within the formation itself. They were the same men who had gutted her people and laid her homeland to ash and waste.

Curl was ashamed of the fear they instilled in her; it was beyond reason, something primal in it like fear of darkness. It was appalling, this power they still held over her.

With haste she finished fitting Bahn's wounded arm

into a sling. It was good to stand next to him, a familiar face in the storm. The man was frightened too, she could see.

'Thank you,' he told her as he inspected the sling.

'Have it seen to properly when you can,' she told him.

They looked at each other for a moment, something unspoken passing between them. Bahn opened his mouth to speak, but then his eyes flicked to the side, and she saw it too – a squad of imperial soldiers behind their lines, one of them tossing a grenade in their direction. Someone shouted a warning. Bahn launched himself at Curl. His arm wrapped around her, and then a bang knocked the senses out of her and she was engulfed in a wash of cold air, and then a hot blast.

She was lying on her back with the wind knocked out of her, and Bahn pressing against her body.

'I'm fine,' she said. 'I'm all right.'

But his eyes were closed. She couldn't feel him breathing.

With a shove she pushed him off her and onto his back. His left cheek was torn open. Blood leaked from the ear on that side. Another man lay close by them, his eyes staring blankly at the night sky.

'Bahn!' she shouted as she checked his pulse. It was hard to find, but it was there, faintly beating.

She was fumbling for her bag when General Creed himself came stamping towards her with his bodyguards trying to keep up. 'Is he alive?'

'Barely!' she shouted back.

The general glanced across to where an officer was calling out to him. He returned his attention to Bahn sprawled on the ground.

'Look after this one, you hear me!'

She nodded her head. Creed took one last look at Bahn then strode off towards the officer. 'Look after him, you hear?'

*

'Matriarch,' said the captain of her honour guard. 'We should withdraw to a safer position. You are exposed here.'

The captain was right. Sasheen was deep within the imperial lines, a position she'd sought for good reason.

'Captain. When we win this battle I do not wish it to be said that I sat and watched it from the rear. You are my bodyguards. Protect me.'

Ché listened to the exchange with interest. They stood in a clear space of field between the multitude of formations still to be employed in the fighting, and those in front already embroiled in the action.

The Khosians were edging ever closer.

Archgeneral Sparus had been beckoned to her side some moments earlier. He came now on foot, trailed by his own retinue of officers.

'Can't you stop them, Archgeneral?' Sasheen demanded, sitting astride her zel as she considered the scene ahead. 'I thought they were nearly finished?'

Sparus looked up at her with his bloodshot eye, like a man long ready for his bed. 'They are, Matriarch. But they have mortar crews holding a superior firing position on the ridge to the south.' He pointed for her benefit. 'They fire down upon our forward lines. It allows them progress.'

'Then *retake* the ridge and have us finish this.'

He hid his annoyance well. 'We're trying to, Matriarch. It will be ours again presently.'

She waved a hand to dismiss him, and Sparus gave a curt nod of his head.

Ché turned his back on it all. Behind them the fresh infantry was standing impatiently, waiting for their turn to join the fight. They seemed eager to get this business finished too. It was cold in that armour of theirs on this frozen valley floor. Many were likely hung over, or at least still tired from being awakened so rudely from their sleep.

As a Rōshun, and then as a Diplomat, Ché had been trained to spot the important details first. Something drew his attention now, and he squinted between the formations of men at a lone Acolyte moving towards the Matriarch's position.

It took Ché a moment to become conscious of what was wrong with the image. The man wore leather leggings beneath his robe.

Ché's hand fell to the hilt of his knife.

*

Ash was close.

He could see the Matriarch astride her white zel, a golden mask over her face, surrounded by white-robes and mounted bodyguards and her standard hanging above them. His eyes narrowed.

He marched along the edge of a waiting square of men. Deserted camp equipment and trampled pup tents lay scattered across ground that had been churned into a filthy mush. He strode through the remnants of a campfire, scattering ashes and still-glowing embers. His hand closed around the hilt of his sword as he neared the outer ring of Acolytes gathered about the Matriarch.

Behind Sasheen, off to one side of the white-robes, a young Acolyte stood watching Ash.

Ash stopped.

The man drew his blade and stepped out to meet him.

*

As the Khosians pushed closer towards the Matriarch's position, the imperial light infantry of the Eighty-First Predasa – less hardened auxiliaries in the main, freshly returned from garrison duty in the northern hinterlands, all of them now sober, tired, and positioned in the thick of the action next to a hardcore of Acolytes – decided that losing over half of their numbers to mortar fire and grenades, including most of their officers, was too much to tolerate for a single night, and decided to beat a retreat to safer ground.

They broke, in fact, when the largest and fiercest of their number, Cunnse of the northern tribes, there for the money and little else, threw aside his shield and sword and shoved his way back through the loosening ranks, shouting that enough was enough, it was time for someone else to meet the slaughter. It took only a moment for the rest to follow his lead.

In no time they were rushing back towards the lines behind them, back towards where the Matriarch was positioned. Others in the fore joined them, retreating from the concussions of mortars raining down from the overlooking ridge.

Ché was shoved from behind by this sudden surge of men as he tried to stride forwards.

He fell, rolling through the muck as he held fast to his sword. When he regained his feet he saw men flooding past Sasheen's position. Her Acolytes and mounted bodyguards struggled to shove them aside or back into the fray. Swords swung, felling some of them – dead men being better than routing ones.

Ché looked back. He could no longer see the impostor in the sudden milling press of bodies.

What am I doing? he demanded of himself.

He had more urgent matters at hand. The Khosians were fast approaching the Matriarch's position, who sat shocked on her jittery white zel with its tail dyed a pretty black.

Ché shoved a fleeing soldier out of his way. He took out the pistol loaded with its poison shot.

Waited to see what Sasheen would do next.

*

Bahn came to a with a gasp, and found that he was being dragged along the ground by a bearded soldier.

A woman was fussing over him.

'Marlee?' he croaked.

It was Curl, though, not his wife, and she was bent over him with a vial of smelling salts in her hand. She looked surprised at his recovery, even managed a nervous twitch of her lips.

'Don't move,' she said. 'You may be concussed.'

He looked up into the bruised and bloodied face of the soldier. The man nodded to him, kept dragging him along.

He had no recollection of how he'd come to be here. One instant, Curl had been treating his wounded arm . . . then blackness. 'What happened?' he rasped.

'You're all right,' she told him. 'You're going to be fine.'

'Was I hit?'

'You were caught in a blast. You're lucky to be in one piece.'

He looked at his body, saw that everything was still there.

Around them the battle was still raging. The entire formation continued to push forwards. 'Get me to my feet,' he said, and held his hand out weakly.

Curl frowned, then grasped his hand, and she and the soldier hauled until Bahn stood on his own two feet. He felt faint, nauseous.

'We're still here, then,' he said.

'Aye,' said the soldier in his roughened voice. 'Afraid so.'

—CHAPTER TWENTY-SEVEN—

Contact

It was unlike him, to be thinking so fluently in the midst of action. Ash was wholly unable to find his stillness here on this icy field.

The Acolyte who'd been about to challenge him had vanished in the confusion of the rout. As Ash approached Sasheen's position, cold anger was all that he felt now.

Within it, memories were surfacing like corpses, bloated and awful.

He recalled Nico, standing behind the bars of the Bar-Khos jail where they'd first been introduced, the boy scared and red-eyed from crying with his mother, Reese, a woman determined to save her son that day. He had made a pledge to her, a promise to protect the boy, even if it meant giving his own life first.

He saw Nico on the burning pyre again in the Q'os arena, his apprentice breathing his last breath, dropping his head as fiery tendrils took hold of his body.

Ash's anger was complete. He pushed his way through the routing troops, shoving them aside as he strode forwards. Without pausing he slipped through the ring of Acolytes that surrounded the Matriarch and her mounted bodyguards.

The guards' war-zels stood firm against the flow, redirecting it around the animals' steaming flanks. Ash stopped as a guard turned his zel to block his way.

A flare was peaking in the sky above the man, illuminating a passing cloud. Half blinded, Ash ducked as the man swung his blade downwards, bending from his saddle to reach him.

Ash blinked with the light still cloying in his eyes. He reached up and grabbed the man and jerked him from the saddle. Brought his boot down upon his neck, then stepped over him. In the midst of her guards Sasheen was trying to turn her zel around, to get clear of the position.

A space opened in their rear and Ash sprang forward.

*

The Khosians were chanting as they pushed forwards. Arrows had begun to pepper down around the Matriarch's standard. Archgeneral Sparus, not far from her, was exhorting his officers to maintain the line, trying to restore solidarity to an army tottering on the dangerous edge of individualism and full rout.

Ché looked towards the Matriarch's position, where she was desperately close to the advancing Khosians and the explosions of mortars that seemed to be walking towards her. She was attempting to withdraw, despite Sparus calling out to stand firm.

So it had come to this, then.

Some part of Ché was suddenly awed by the possibility now facing him. The pistol hung loose in his hand. To kill a Holy Matriarch; to topple her from her empire with a single shot to the head . . . His mouth went dry at the thought of it. His features set into a hardened mask.

It's hardly different from all the people you've murdered at her whim, he tried to tell himself.

Ché licked his lips and glanced around in search of Swan and Guan. He was fairly certain they had orders to kill him once this campaign had reached its end. The note left in the Scripture had been right. He knew too much.

Don't stay, then. Leave now and hope they consider you to be amongst the dead. What is there for you here but more pain and anguish?

Only his mother, he knew. But she'd already been lost to him, and he from her, all those years ago when he'd first been sent to Cheem to be turned as a Rōshun. Nothing had been left to him by the order of Mann, nothing but this hollow complexity of a life that he'd never wished for, had never chosen.

Ché chose now to raise the pistol firmly in his hand.

He steadied it with his other hand, tried to draw an aim on the Matriarch as he waited for an opening in the ring of mounted guards surrounding her. A flare went up. Men illuminated in shaking light jostled past him, interrupting his aim.

Ché fought to hold steady. He caught a brief glimpse of Sasheen as she tugged her zel around, and then she was blocked again by the tightening shields of her bodyguards. She would be away within moments.

Damn it, he swore silently.

He couldn't get a clear shot.

Suddenly, one of the bodyguards swung around with his zel. The man's sword rose high in the air then drove down onto someone on foot. As he carried through with the swing, the bodyguard bent low in his saddle.

Sasheen's head came into view.

Ché's pistol flared and fired.

*

Ash saw Sasheen lurch backwards in her saddle as he closed with her. The Matriarch's white zel cried out as it reared up on its hind legs, backing a few steps towards him. Riders jostled and hollered all around them.

He saw the Matriarch lying next to her white zel, sprawled in the muck with her life-blood pumping from her neck. Her bodyguards were gathering where she lay, holding their shields aloft to protect her, their movements as jerky as frightened boys'.

He cried out as though robbed of a prize rightly his, struggling to his feet with his sword hanging like a thing forgotten.

Ash barely noticed the mounted bodyguard circling around him. From the corner of his eye, he spotted the guard raising his sword. His gaze remained fixed on the motionless bundle that was the Holy Matriarch of Mann.

She was dead or dying. That was all that mattered

Ash was stillness.

The sword came down.

CHAPTER TWENTY-EIGHT

A Fighting Retreat

Ché stuffed the pistol into his belt and fought his way through the jostling infantry towards Sasheen. He caught a glimpse of her body lying unmoving in the mud. Someone had removed her mask. A wound in her neck pumped profusely.

Not far from the scene, a lone Acolyte lay sprawled on the ground. His cloak was splayed open to reveal a pair of leather leggings. Ché tore the mask from the man's face. He gasped and stood back in surprise.

Ash! he thought as he took in the black skin of the old farlander. One of the Rōshun, here, of all places.

Ché reeled with his thoughts asunder. Blood was coursing from a swollen lump in the man's head. He was still alive, then.

Ché looked about him for a moment, at the masks and the stark faces of strangers.

He knelt and slapped the farlander's face. Ash's eyes fluttered open, then closed again. He seemed to weigh nothing but skin and bones as Ché lifted him and threw him over his shoulder. He grabbed the reins of a loose zel, threw the old man over the saddle. The animal tried to skitter away as he bent to reach for the fallen sword. He pulled it back towards him, then mounted behind Ash.

He kicked the animal into a trot.

*

For a moment the battle hung in the balance.

Perhaps if the imperial army had learned nothing from the previous fifty years of land war – or if Sparus's own five hundred Acolytes hadn't positioned themselves in the direct path of the Khosian advance and stood firm –

or if one more man in the ordinary ranks had yelled in fear for his life – then the First Expeditionary Force might have broken.

But it didn't. Instead it rallied gamely and began to fight back. And in the way of these things, the collective shame of its near-defeat lent an impetus to the army's efforts, and they fell upon the Khosian flanks like a flood.

The Khosians reeled.

*

'She fell, sir, I saw it with my own eyes.'

The Red Guard captain stood with a slight stoop as he spoke. He held a bloody hand across his stomach.

'Very well,' said General Creed. 'Now go and find yourself a medico.'

The officer gritted his teeth – perhaps it was an attempt at a smile – and hoisted his charta before returning to the lines of the right flank. They were disintegrating now, much like the rest of the formation.

Bahn paid little attention to the news of the Matriarch's possible death, or even to the destruction of the army taking place all about him. He was in something of a daze as he stood fighting down his nausea, the blood leaking from an ear he could no longer hear from.

'That's four sightings, Bahn!' barked General Creed by his side, pulling him from his scattered thoughts.

Bahn blinked dumbly in reply.

The general stood with hands behind his back, taking in the imperial onslaught on all sides. 'They rallied well, don't you think?'

'Like Khosians, sir,' Bahn finally replied, feeling giddy.

Creed examined his lieutenant. The flesh around the general's eyes was swollen from exhaustion. 'We've accomplished all we can here. I think it's time that we left, don't you?'

'General?'

'You'd rather we stay here a while longer?'

He tried to shake his head, but it only caused more sickness to wash through him.

'Not – for a single moment,' he said.

Creed turned to one of his bodyguards. 'Have a runner sent to fetch General Reveres.'

'Reveres is dead, sir,' replied the bodyguard.

'What? When?'

'I'm not certain, sir.'

'Nidemes, then!'

It was some minutes before General Nidemes limped towards them through the darkness. His helm was missing and his greying hair was matted to his head in the semblance of a bird's nest.

'Nidemes, we're leaving as of now. We'll perform a heel turn and proceed to the lake as fast as we can.'

With obvious relief the general hurried away off to pass on the order.

'The lake?' asked Bahn.

General Creed's breath formed a rising cloud in the air. 'I'm sure that by the time that we get there, you'll have worked it out, Bahn.'

*

'They're heading for the lake,' observed Sergeant Jay.

Halahan saw it. What was left of the army had turned about and tightened its flanks, and now was forging a path through to the lake on the northern side of the battlefield.

'About bloody time,' breathed the colonel to himself.

He turned to face the remnants of his own small force. The imperial mortars had been abandoned – three of the pieces had seized up finally, too hot to fire any longer; a fourth had blown up, though only the charge had exploded, miraculously, not the explosive shot itself. Their crews were gulping from small flasks of spirits, looking as though they'd just survived a deadly game of blind-man's duel.

The riflemen defending the perimeter had run out of ammunition too. They were exhausted to the man, and they were nervously watching as the Imperials regrouped again along the waist of the ridge and around the base of its slopes. All knew that the next assault would finish them.

Colonel Halahan drew in a breath and bellowed: 'Someone send up a signal flare – we're leaving!'

The men roused themselves, brief burns of energy returning to their spent frames. 'And let's destroy the rest of these mortars, shall we?'

Halahan scanned the bloody carnage of the ridge. The dead would have to be left where they'd fallen. He struck a match to relight his pipe. Exhaling smoke, he gathered all the precious pistols he'd tossed aside so far. As he stood next to the sergeant the signal flare shot upwards into the air, burning yellow as it stalled and fell back to earth.

Beyond it, skyships were blasting each other with spurts of cannon fire.

'Let's pray our skuds are still up there somewhere,' said Sergeant Jay, and they both stood together, scanning the dark skies in silent hope.

*

Ché drew the zel to a halt in front of the twins' tent. He leapt off it, leaving Ash across the saddle; ducked quickly inside without waiting to see if anyone spotted him.

Guan and Swan's packs were lying on the ground next to their cots. Ché rummaged through them until he found the vial of wildwood juice, then ran back outside with it. He led the zel to his own tent and went in to grab his pack. He threw his books into it, shoving them in next to the bundle of civilian clothing he had brought with him. He left his Scripture of Lies face down on the bunk.

'How's it going down there?'

A silhouette filled the entrance to the tent. A priest.

Ché rose slowly as he tightened his grip on the straps of his backpack.

The silhouette raised its hand to its mouth, took a bite from something. Ché scented the sweet narcotic scent of the parmadio fruit.

'Hard to say,' he told the spymaster Alarum. 'I'm no expert on war.'

The spymaster stood there with a blanket wrapped across his shoulders. Ché glanced at Alarum's other hand, saw it hanging limp by his side next to a sheathed dagger in his belt. Ché knew this man was dangerous.

'For a moment I thought we were being overrun, the way you came charging into camp like that.' He gestured to the pack in Ché's hand. 'Going somewhere?'

Without warning, Ché swung the backpack and threw it at Alarum's face.

He was a step behind it. He punched the man in the stomach to knock the wind from him, doubling Alarum over with a whoosh of air. Ché locked an arm around his neck, snatched the knife from the man's scabbard, drew him back away from the entrance with the edge of the blade pressing against his throat.

'*Wait!*' Alarum hissed through his teeth.

He struggled, strong for his thin build, gripping Ché's wrist as he tried to stop him from cutting his throat. One of the bunks toppled over as he kicked it with a foot. '*Wait a moment!*' he hissed in a strangled whisper, white spittle flying from his lips.

The man forced his sleeve back from his arm, held the skin up for Ché to see. Ché stared at it, saw the scaly patch of skin along the spymaster's arm. His grip loosened a fraction.

'We may share the same afflicted blood, Ché,' came his strangled voice. 'I just might be your father!'

He released the spymaster. Alarum gasped for air with a hand to his throat.

'My mother slept with many men,' he said. 'That proves nothing.'

'No, it doesn't, not for certain. But still, don't you wonder?'

Ché tossed the knife quivering into the ground. 'You left the note for me in the Scripture,' he said as the realization came to him. 'That was you.'

'I see you're paying it some heed, too. Good. If you stay they'll kill you. I'll do what I can for your mother, what little that may be.'

'You can help her?'

'Perhaps. If I'm quick enough about it.'

Ché hesitated, caught between sudden emotions. He looked at the man, his gaunt face and dark, intense eyes, wondering if it might be true.

A few priests rushed past the entrance of the tent. Someone was shouting in the distance.

'Wait!' shouted Alarum as Ché swirled away, leaving him standing there in the middle of the tent next to the overturned cot.

Ché's mind raced with uncertainties as he stepped outside.

'Come on, old man,' Ché said to the unconscious Ash, climbing back into the saddle with his pack. He nodded to Alarum as the spymaster emerged from the tent. The man seemed to be struggling for words.

With a kick and a whip of the reins Ché galloped out of the encampment, Alarum and the Acolyte guards at the entrance watching him go.

*

A bodyguard ducked behind his shield as something whistled past close by. For once, Bahn stood cool and unflinching.

'Our scouts tried it before we attacked,' Creed was telling Koolas the war chattéro. 'It should hold, so long as we're careful.'

The surface of the lake had frozen solid. It was strange,

to face such a silent, open expanse of ice with the intensity of the battle still raging behind them.

'With luck, Mandalay's cavalry have scattered their zels. It should take them time to organize a pursuit.'

Creed and the others stood on a spur of land that projected into the lake for a hundred feet or more. The remnants of the army were filtering onto this projection, heavy and light infantry alike. Already, at the instructions of their officers, men cast aside shields and helms, shrugged out of their heavy armour, before they headed out onto the lake. They spread out so as to distribute their weight more evenly. Stretcher-bearers carried off what casualties they could. The ice, still reasonably thin, creaked beneath their feet, but held.

The army was subliming away.

Past the heavy press of men still heading towards the ice, Bahn could barely see the rearguard that stretched across the mouth of this projection of land. They had formed into a single chartassa, and they fought alone to hold off the imperial attackers; a mixture of Hoo and Red Guards, many badly wounded themselves, each a volunteer for this role.

Bahn found it hard to look at them.

More than anything else now, he wished to get back to Bar-Khos so that he could be in the sanctuary of his own home with Marlee and the children. He could see it in his mind's eye. It was raining outside the house. The fire was lit. Marlee toasted sweetcakes on the flames while Juno his son played with his model ships and little Ariale gazed at him; Bahn, sitting deep in his armchair in a glow of contented peace.

General Nidemes approached, flanked by Colonel Barklee, one of his Red Guard officers, the man holding a shield aloft to protect them from the missiles that still thudded down. 'Time to go,' Nidemes told Creed. General Creed's eyes glimmered in the dimness. 'Have you taken all the neck chains from the rearguard?'

'We have,' Barklee replied, hoisting a bundled cloak that chinked with the many identity chains within it.

'We must find some way to repay them for this,' announced Creed.

Koolas the war chattēro listened from behind.

Bahn turned to the rearguard again. They were being pushed back step by step.

Once more, Bahn stood on the sidelines, watching from afar the bravery of men as they laid down their lives for the sake of others. For some reason, since regaining his feet, Bahn had found that he no longer felt any fear at all, as though he'd shed a heavy cloak he had forgotten he was even wearing. More than ever before, he understood why he was here, and why the men of the rearguard were here, giving up their lives for the sake of their people.

'I'm staying,' he told Creed as the general turned to leave.

Creed cast him a look of surprise. 'What's that?'

'I'm staying,' he said as he took the chain from his neck. 'With the rest of those men.' And he tossed the chain across to Barklee.

Creed frowned and quizzed him with his eyes. 'You're in shock, Bahn,' he decided. 'You don't know what you're saying. We've won here, damn it! Even if it doesn't seem so just now, we've scored a victory here!'

'Hold Bar-Khos, no matter what, General,' Bahn told him. 'That's the only way you can repay these men now.'

Before Creed could answer, Bahn turned and walked away.

'Bahn!' Creed shouted after him. 'Bahn!' he commanded.

But within half a dozen footsteps, Bahn was lost amongst the confusion of men.

CHAPTER TWENTY-NINE

Tume

It was quiet in these hills to the south of the Silent Valley, and the pale morning daylight brightened only slowly beneath a layer of clouds. Snow still lingered in clumps within the shadows of yellowing grasses, which swayed and sighed in the breezes coursing through the small side valley where they had camped.

So this is Khos, Ché thought to himself, as though only now, in his relative solitude away from the demands and company of Mann, he could truly appreciate the landscape of this island.

Ché sat on the wet ground with his back resting against a saddlebag. He had removed the piercing in his eyebrow, and he was dressed comfortably in plain woollen trousers and a thick cotton shirt that had cowry shells sewn along its sleeves. Over it all, his cloak was keeping out the worst of the wind. During the remains of the night he'd left his ammunition belt strapped around his waist, where the pistol hung in its holster, and his knife too. He'd watched and listened for signs of pursuit, not sleeping at all.

Now, in the early light, Ché was watching a hawk as it balanced with delicate twitches of its wingtips above the opposite slope of the little valley, silently hovering as it watched for prey. Before his outstretched legs, a small campfire of twigs smoked and crackled in a circle of stones. The meagre flames offered little warmth save for the mind.

The hawk suddenly dived with wings folded tight. It vanished behind a line of grasses, appeared once more with talons empty. It must be young, thought Ché. Still learning to kill.

Try again.

The fire spat, and he stared at it, watching the two

fresh branches he'd recently laid across the embers. Their bellies glowed red, the occasional flame struggling upwards, flickering, dying again. Ché's eyes narrowed, heavy with tiredness.

The old Rōshun snored on the other side of the fire. The farlander was suffering from a bad chest, his breathing laboured and shallow. Indeed, he coughed just then, and stirred beneath the cloak Ché had placed over him for a blanket.

Ash's head came up, and the man opened his bleary grey eyes.

He took a long look at the young man before him. Blinked in recognition.

'Ché,' he rasped.

'Easy,' replied Ché, as the old man clutched his head and struggled to rise. 'I think you're concussed. I've been trying to keep you awake all night.'

Ash sat up with some care. His fingers inspected the lump on his skull and the fresh stitching there.

'That would explain why I feel like death,' croaked the farlander, as he gently placed a palm against his skull.

Ché tossed the flask of water across to him. The old Rōshun drank from it long and deep. He gasped, and his neck craned as he took in the sky and twisted as he looked at the valley slopes beneath their campsite. He took another sip of water. Smacked his lips and stared at the flask between his legs for some moments.

At last he lifted his head with some clarity in his eyes. 'The battle,' he said. 'What happened?'

Ché offered a weak shrug. 'The Expeditionary Force rallied. The last I saw of the Khosians they were fleeing across a frozen lake.'

'Sasheen. Is she dead?'

'I hope so. She was shot through the neck. I'm curious, though, why you were there trying to kill her?'

Ash was fumbling for something in his tunic. He drew out a leather pouch, dug his fingers into it to find that nothing was there. In disgust he tossed the empty pouch into the fire. He coughed long and hard, his eyes screwed in pain. At last he coughed a gob of phlegm into the flames, where it sizzled for a moment while he hung his head between his knees.

'The boy was yours, wasn't he? The apprentice she burned to death in Q'os?'

'Aye, he was mine,' came his voice, husky.

'But he wasn't wearing a seal.'

'No.'

So the old farlander was human after all, Ché mused.

He studied the man in the pale daylight. Ash had aged since Ché had last seen him all those years ago in Cheem. He was thinner than he recalled. The bones of his face were sharp and pronounced beneath his dark skin, which was creased with wrinkles, and papery thin. His wedge of grey beard had overgrown. His eyes were sunken in their sockets and faintly yellow.

He looked like a man nearer death than not.

'What am I doing here?' Ash asked him. 'This makes no sense to me.'

'I've been sitting wondering the same thing myself.'

The farlander lifted his head and studied Ché for a long moment. His eyes settled on the stubs of the young man's little fingers. He winced. 'What are you doing here, Ché?' he said. 'Are you one of them?'

Ché turned away.

'Ché?'

As the moments dragged on, he could sense the old man's suspicions growing.

'You left Sato without telling us,' ventured Ash.

Ché looked to the bird once more, saw it hovering again. Part of him wished to confess it all to the old man just then, to tell him what part he had played in the destruction of the Rōshun order. But he found himself unable to say it.

Still, realization gradually dawned on the old farlander. 'You were with them all along. With the Empire. But how? The Seer would have seen it in you.' Ash sat up straighter, though it brought him pain. 'Ché – what are you? What have you done?'

'I'm a Diplomat,' snapped Ché, 'who lacked any other choice but to live. And what I did, old man, was save your life.'

Ché tried to calm himself as the farlander peered at him in disbelief. Emotions swelled in his body.

It is over, then, the ancient Seer had said to Ché sadly as they'd sat watching the Rōshun monastery burning in the Cheem night. All the people he had known over his years of living there, the ones who had befriended him, who had been a family to him, all dead or dying in the flames.

Better finish me, Ché, the old Seer had told him. *Do it now, for I would prefer that it was you and not some stranger.*

Ché swallowed. He looked at Ash across the pitiful fire, knowing that the old Rōshun was one of the last of his kind now, and that he did not even know it.

The knowledge felt like a dirty secret in his mind.

'They know the Rōshun are in Cheem,' Ash finally said, and his eyes swept up to accuse him with sudden anger.

Ché would not speak of it.

The old man threw aside his cloak and made a lunge at Ché, though he collapsed to the ground before he could reach him. Ché remained still. He watched as the farlander tried to push himself up, but it was beyond him.

He stood and dragged Ash back to where he'd been lying. Threw the cloak over his shivering body again. Ash looked up at the clouds with his chest rising and falling fast. Ché was moved enough to speak, to share with him something of his own loss, but then he paused, his mouth gaping.

The old Rōshun was chuckling; a broken sound filled with bitterness.

'All is lost,' Ash cackled to himself.

Ché tilted his head to one side, curious. He watched the smile fade from the farlander's face, Ash growing sober once more.

Ché said, 'You wish to kill me, I suppose.'

The old farlander stared at him hard. 'When I have the strength for it.'

He looked away, saw the young hawk lift from the far side of the valley, its great wings flapping. It clutched something in its talons, a shape struggling to be free.

He lay back and closed his eyes.

*

In the early glow of dawn, Bull watched imperial soldiers searching the battlefield for survivors. They were moving in pairs, and when they found one of their own still breathing they called out for a stretcher-bearer, and when they found a wounded Khosian instead they checked first that the man wasn't an officer, then stabbed him dead with their spears.

A pair of these clean-up men had stopped not far from where Bull was lying. They looked down upon a wounded Red Guard as the soldier lifted a hand above the surface of corpses around him. One of the Imperials kicked the hand aside and stood on his arm to keep it down. His partner stabbed him twice, his eyes as blank as the grey sky over their heads.

Bull looked away, tired and beyond hope now.

All night he had lain trapped under the mountainous weight of the northern tribesman. The flow of the giant man's blood had steamed in the freezing air, warming Bull's torso even as his great body died, so that he wasn't cold, only near suffocated by the pressure on his broken cuirass, which was enough to tighten it against him and make breathing a laborious command of will.

It had taken Bull the finest bladework of his life to bring this giant down in the heat of the battle. They'd fought like two pit-fighters up close and physical. Bull had taken the worst of the battering. He'd known there was only a slim chance of winning the fight – and he'd taken it, boldly, even as his own legs were giving out on him. A perfectly timed jab caught the northerner in the lower thigh, hamstringing him, and Bull had experienced the brief thrill of victory before the giant had lunged out and grappled him, and his weight had borne Bull to the ground, trapping him where they fell.

Blood caked his face where his right cheekbone seemed to be fractured. He was unable to open his right eye, nor move his left hand. With all his strength he'd been unable to move the man off him.

A fine mess, Bull had thought to himself, and had stared at the night sky overhead, listening to the ever-fading clash of arms, knowing that he had been left behind.

Around them, the dead and wounded had lain scattered and draining of heat. A man wept, broken; others sobbed from the pain and shock of missing limbs. A youth cried out for his mother, long past shame for such a thing, then howled that he was not ready to die. Voices gasped, whispered prayers; not only Khosians, but the Imperials amongst them too. Someone in a northern accent talked to their wife, telling her he would be back soon, that he loved her, that he was sorry for betraying her. Another called to comrades now gone from the field, or lying dead nearby, for no one answered him.

At one point, the great tribesman had awakened with a shudder. He spat blood and looked about as best he could, his lips trembling. He tried to move his great body without success. He sensed Bull lying breathing beneath him, still alive.

In guttural Trade, the man asked how long it might be before dawn.

For a time they had chatted.

Ersha, he offered for his name. A mercenary from a tribe called the Sengetti, all the way from the cold northern steppe.

The man had slipped once more into unconsciousness

as snow had fallen again in the middle of the long night, settling over their twisted shapes like a blanket thrown upon them by the great Mother of the World.

Now, in the gathering daylight, a groan sounded from Ersha; a gasp of air escaping his lips as though he'd been holding his breath for an endless time. They had fused during the night into one single mess of drying blood and numb muscles. Once more the tribesman shoved hard with his arms in an effort to pull free from Bull, but he failed, nearly crushing Bull as he settled back down with a sigh.

'You Khosians make for poor beds,' the tribesman commented in his rough Trade.

Bull grunted. 'And you northerners make for poor quilts.'

A wheezing sound. Something like laughter.

Bull grimaced as the tremor of it ran through the weight that pressed down against his broken armour. The two men said nothing more for a while. The tribesman seemed to be having his own difficulties with breathing.

It was the discomfort in the end that caused Bull to speak again, if only to take his mind away from it. 'Tell me,' he asked. 'Is it true your women pierce their parts with jewellery?'

Ersha lifted his head, and his bearded face turned to look down at him. His teeth were sharpened into points. 'Aye. It's true. It was our way long before the Q'osians began doing the same.'

'Your women must make for interesting bedmates.'

'Don't,' wheezed the man. 'You'll have me thinking of my wives. I doubt you'd want me to have a hard-on just now.'

Bull tried hard not to laugh blackly.

'Let me tell you. You already have one.'

'You jest.'

'I wish that I was.'

A moment of silence followed. 'You would think,' came the tribesman's hushed voice, 'that bleeding out all night would diminish such a thing.'

'You would.'

'That was a nice cut to my leg, by the way.' It was the second time the man had offered him the compliment. Bull replied with the same words as before.

'You left it open. Your lower defence is wanting.'

'It's the height. You must have the same problem.'

'Aye.'

The clouds were brightening above their heads. They moved almost imperceptibly, though the longer Bull stared at them, the more he felt that it was he that was moving, and the rest of the world beneath him.

In the distance, another voice was cut off in mid-shout.

'You should be glad, Bull. What is better? To die like this next to your broken charta, or to rot away in a cell for the rest of your life?'

'This is hardly a glorious end here, pinned to the ground by an erection.'

'Don't,' chuckled the man again. 'It hurts, very badly, when I laugh.'

Bull winced at the shaking weight of him.

'You did not tell me what you did – to deserve such a punishment as that.'

Bull smacked his dry mouth. His throat was burning from thirst. 'I killed a man,' he said. 'A hero of Bar-Khos.'

'A hero? And what had he done to you, this hero?'

'He took advantage of my younger brother. And then he broke his heart.'

'Ah, now I see.'

For a while he listened to Ersha's breathing as it grew ever-more shallow. The man was struggling to remain conscious.

Bull had met Adrianos once, hero of the Nomarl raid. Two years ago, when the crowds had come to watch

Bull take on the champion from Al-Khos. He had liked the man and his quick wit, had even felt a measure of admiration for what he'd accomplished against the Imperials.

Bull's younger brother had admired Adrianos too, when he'd first become a Special under his command. Last year, only twenty-four years of age, he had died in a fight in a taverna, a fight he'd started when a group of Adrianos's friends had walked in proclaiming the man's virtues. Bull had been shocked out of his mind by his younger brother's death; even more so when he'd discovered the reason for the fight and for his sudden hostility towards Adrianos.

He felt his anger start to rise just in recalling it.

Bull turned his head to one side and breathed the memory out of him. Through his tears he could see nothing but bodies, a carpet of them in every direction he cared to look. He hoped that Wicks was all right. He hoped the lad wasn't lying here somewhere amongst the fallen.

A pair of boots stepped into view. Bull blinked his eyes clear, looked up to see two soldiers leaning on their spears and gazing down at him.

'Here's one,' said the shorter of the two men, and hefted his spear and aimed the bloody warhead at Bull's neck.

Bull refused to flinch. He waited with open eyes, only wishing for it to be swift.

'No,' croaked Ersha, and the great man twisted his neck to look at them. 'This one – this one is mine.'

The soldiers squinted, taking in the giant man's condition.

'They gave the order,' said the shorter of the two. 'No slaves to be taken. Kill all save for officers.'

'I don't give a shit for their orders,' growled the tribesman. 'This one is mine, do you hear me?'

'Yours? You'll be lucky to see the end of the day.'

The tribesman tried to reach his side. He swore, then jerked something free. A black string hung from his grip.

Ersha wheezed as he placed the necklace about Bull's head, pulled it down onto his neck. The necklace carried a stone marker.

'*Mine*,' he said through gritted teeth.

*

Ché and Ash spoke little as they travelled through the lowland hills bordering the Silent Valley, trying to distance themselves from the scene of battle by skirting west along the valley's course. Even higher ground rose to the south of them, and beyond it mountains with spindly peaks covered with ice, glimpsed through the boughs of trees as the pair traversed ravines and sage-choked valleys.

Both of them had reversed their white cloaks so the grey inconspicuous lining faced outwards. Ché led the zel while Ash rode in the saddle. The farlander was still weak. Often he called for a halt so that he could be sick amidst plumes of his own breath.

They had nothing to eat between them. Ché plucked berries as they went, though Ash refused them, claiming he would not hold them down. It was a concussion all right, and Ché knew that the last thing he should be doing was moving the old man like this. But another night in the freezing cold might be even worse for him. Ash didn't have the look of a man who would survive that.

By late afternoon they halted on a high ridge with their eyes narrowed against the biting wind, and looked down onto the broad floodplain known as the Reach. The fertile land was dusted white with frost and snow. Farms and villages dotted the open fields, and stands of birch and yellowpine and tiq. Amongst them, pillars of smoke rose from burning fields where immature crops still grew. Along the dirty scratches of roads, families were pulling carts and driving cattle as they left their homes behind them.

The air was startling in its clarity today. He could just make out Simmer Lake ten or so laqs to the north-west, where the city of Tume floated as a pale smudge, a sliver of black rising from the heart of it; the ancient citadel, he presumed. Directly to the north, the frozen Cinnamon snaked its way towards the lake, accompanied by the straighter line of the main road. The road itself was clogged with trudging men: the Khosian army in retreat.

'They head for Tume,' Ché declared.

He squinted, taking in the great lake again and the island city. A black dot was moving in the air above the citadel. A skyship.

He looked up at the clouds growing ever darker, suspecting it would snow soon. Ché glanced back at Ash in hope that the old Rōshun might offer a suggestion. The farlander's head, though, was nodding in exhaustion.

'Sparus and the army will be coming through here soon enough,' Ché muttered, almost to himself. Then, louder, so that Ash might hear him: 'No choice for it,' and he tugged the zel along as they set off towards the city.

*

'Sweet Mercy,' declared Kris, hitching her medico pack higher on her back. 'I think my feet are about to drop off.'

Curl looked at the older woman and found she hadn't the energy to think of a response. Her own feet ached terribly, made only worse now that they were crossing the hard planking of the floating bridge that led into Tume.

They were surrounded by the walking wounded, battered soldiers who limped and shuffled and helped each other along as best they could. Like Curl, the men were too far gone for talk now. Their dull expressions were filthy with grime and blood save for where their helms had covered their faces. Their eyes looked blasted, as though they'd been staring hard into a furnace all night. Curl felt a fierce camaraderie with these fighting men now. Together they had come through the worst of it. Today, she found that she no longer carried herself like a civilian, but as one of them.

Against the flow of the army, a much more presentable stream of Tume citizenry were pushing and pulling their belongings along as they attempted to flee the city. They glanced nervously at the soldiers in passing, seemed to see them not as saviours but as harbingers of defeat. Curl wasn't certain that they were wrong.

She tugged her cloak tighter about herself against the falling sleet. Her hair was pasted wet across her skull and her ears burned from the cold, making her wish dearly that she had a hood with which to cover her head. She swiped her face clear and kept her narrowed eyes focused on the back of the soldier before her. The man was shivering, his own cloak gone and his arms clutched tight around his sides. His breath rose over a bloody bandage wrapped about his skull.

Past him, along the far-reaching lines of trudging men, a fortified gatehouse stood at the end of the bridge with its gates cast open. Tume sprawled beyond it and ranged far to either side.

Only the citadel stood on firm ground, the walls and turrets built on a prominence of rock that rose high above the rooftops. The rest of the buildings of the city, all of them constructed of wood like the bridge itself, floated on great rafts of what Kris had simply called lakeweed; some form of vegetation natural to the lake, which filtered the water for minerals and nutrients and kept it clear as a mountain pool. Curl could see all the way to the muddy bottom, the algae-covered rocks and plantlife down there. Near the surface, she glimpsed shoals of fish nibbling on the loose tendrils at the edges of the floating weeds.

It was clear to her now why the lake had been given its name. It bubbled in parts, particularly along the southern shoreline, where the surface churned and boiled and released wafts of mist into the cooler air.

'If you go down to the shoreline there,' Kris said, noticing her interest, 'you can dig a hole, and wait for the water to seep into it, and then cook your breakfast.'

Curl managed a nod. She wondered how anyone could even think about eating in such circumstances, when the air smelled so badly of rotten eggs.

Ahead, she noticed that some of the men were looking off to the east and the far shore there. Curl could not see what they were looking at for all the citizens passing by.

'Listen,' said Kris, and she did. The breeze across the water shifted, and the sounds of it came to her, dull cracks of gunfire.

'They're coming,' said Kris.

The people of Tume could hear it too. A murmur passed along their column, then shouts of alarm. Some began to turn around, to return to the safety of the city. Others began to push harder, wanting to be clear of there.

The army marched onwards, thinking only of shelter and a hot meal.

—CHAPTER THIRTY—

Burning Bridges

It was said that the tortoise was three hundred years old, as old as the citadel it had known all that time as home. In its long and ponderous life, the creature had lived through times of famine and prosperity, of peace and war, even of revolution. Its eyes had witnessed the ruling family of Tume grow old and die within these damp walls of stone, one generation after the other. It had seen the bloody births of children, the grand balls and banquets, the bitter arguments, the feuds, the affairs, the mortal illnesses, until it had become a part of living history itself, a connection to ancestors gone and descendants still to come.

The tortoise seemed hardly concerned with its prestigious heritage, balanced as it was against a low table on its hind legs, its neck stretched long and leathery as it reached for a green apple in a bowl of fruit, fastidiously ignoring the many soldiers seeking spaces for themselves around the walls of the great hall.

So calm was its temperament that it even ignored the pair of gauntlets that crashed onto the table next to the bowl, and the man marching past the table without breaking his stride. The tortoise dragged the apple to the floor, began to munch away on it as the figure marched towards the people gathered around the fire in the central hearth.

The man looked huge in his anger and his great bearskin coat.

'Where are my damned reinforcements?' General Creed hollered to the Principari of Tume, his voice ringing beneath the domed ceiling of the hall. 'The Al-Khos reserves?' he shouted, as he saw the man turn from the flames to confront him.

Vanichios opened his eyes a fraction wider beneath the brim of his blue velvet cap, his face bare of the paint usually worn by the Michinè.

The Principari gave a nod of his head to dismiss the men gathered around him, all clad in the grey garments of advisers. He clasped his hands behind his back and waited as Creed approached him, his diamond jewellery glittering within the sheen of his silk robes.

Creed stopped before him out of breath. He was surprised when Vanichios held out his hands, and offered a kiss on each cheek as though they were still friends. The Principari smelled faintly of elderberries and soap.

'General,' Vanichios said in his smooth voice, appraising Creed's condition with concern. 'Come, we must speak.'

Without waiting for a response, he led the way to an alcove free of soldiers, where his wife, Carine, oversaw a group of servants removing paintings and precious books from the shelves that were nestled there.

'Carine,' said Vanichios softly to his wife. 'Please, leave it all. You and the children must make yourselves ready.'

Carine brushed the grey hair from her face, and stared at Creed as her husband introduced them.

'Welcome, General,' she said with a nod. 'Please, make yourself at home, you must be exhausted.'

There was no rancour in her voice, only civility. At once, Creed felt abashed at his loud words, standing there in his reeking armour with his men making themselves at home all about her. He bowed his head in reply, not knowing what to say.

In truth, he'd expected a cooler welcome in this hall of the Principari, this man who had once been his friend, when both had been bachelor officers in the ranks of the Red Guards. They hadn't spoken in fifteen years. Not since the day of the duel, and Creed's subsequent marriage to the woman they had fought it over.

As Vanichios bade his own wife to depart – and with the duelling scar still clearly visible on his right cheek, his face drawn tight and haggard by sleeplessness and worry – Creed realized that of course all that was so much water under the bridge; that he'd stomped angrily into the home of a man who bore him no ill any longer, the home of a family suddenly beset by the arrival of war. He watched the looks exchanged between the two of them, the bond they shared, as Carine turned to leave.

Marsalas felt a pang of longing, though not for this woman. For his own.

'The reserves,' prompted Creed, quietly now, as Vanichios gestured to a chair then sank himself into the one opposite. 'Why are they not here?'

'Because they are as yet four days' forced march away,' announced the Principari as he gently settled himself, and tossed a corner of his robe about his lap. 'They left Al-Khos only yesterday.'

'What?' exclaimed Creed.

'It would seem that Kincheko has been quibbling over the matter of releasing his reserves to us.'

Creed grasped for his forehead as though in pain. For some moments he composed himself, letting the import of the news sink in.

'I'll have his damned head for this.'

'Not if I have it first,' Vanichios replied, and Creed saw how incensed he truly was behind the cool facade of his manners.

The general straightened in his chair, his armour and the ancient stuffed leather both creaking. He fixed Vanichios with a stare. 'We can't hold this city. Not without the heavy cannon they're meant to be bringing.'

Vanichios's gaze was just as firm. He gave an almost imperceptible nod of his head.

'We have the guns you sent us,' he said.

'Those field guns won't be much use in the siege that's coming. I was only hoping to keep them out of Mannian hands.'

He could see that Vanichios already knew this.

Creed blew out a breath of frustration and looked about the hall. He followed the smoke from the fire pouring up to the domed ceiling, filtering out through its circle of blackened chimney slots or recoiling from sleety gusts. Trees were growing up there, purple-leaved nightshades sprouting from the walls themselves and hanging out over the hall. Below their high canopy, his men sat or lay resting across the littered floor. Others were still coming in, collapsing wherever they could find a clear space on which to sleep.

'Four days late,' he mused, without looking at Vanichios. 'What prompted him in the end?'

'I threatened Kincheko to a duel if he did not send them.'

'Hah!' exclaimed Creed. 'He must be a worse blade than you, then.'

Together they smiled in the midst of their troubles. Vanichios even flicked the scar on his cheek, mock indignation on his face. They laughed aloud, drawing the attention of the men around the chamber.

'It's good to see you are well and still in one piece,' said Vanichios, with warmth. 'Truly, I mean that. We have left this reunion much too long, and now . . .' He waved a hand in the air. 'Now we are neck-deep in trouble, with no time to catch up at all.'

Creed wiped a tear of laughter from his eye. Yes, it was good to be here, he realized. Good to be speaking again.

War could be many loathsome things, yet it cut through the ordinary nonsense of life like nothing else. Creed was reminded of the decency of this man before him, his humanity towards those less fortunate than himself when even Creed would see nothing but wretchedness. A result, he always supposed, of the fact that Vanichios had grown up as the youngest of four brothers, the lowest position within the traditional pecking order of a Michinè family.

Vanichios had outlived his father and his brothers, and he'd found himself the lord of Tume after all; the last thing he'd ever wanted to be, Creed knew. Yet he wore the role well, Creed thought now. It fitted him.

Vanichios leaned forwards to narrow the distance between them. His voice was gentle as he said, 'I sent my condolences. I hope you received them in time.'

'Yes,' said Creed, blinking. 'I appreciated your words.' He remembered that now. A letter had arrived after his wife's funeral. In his black grief he had ignored it, and somehow over time it had become lost.

'I wept, when I heard the news of her passing,' Vanichios said bravely, then looked away quickly, as though to stop himself from saying more. He had loved Rose deeply himself.

Creed patted the arm of his chair, not knowing what to say in return. How poor he was at these things.

A puddle was gathering on the floor beneath him, his greatcoat shedding its melted sleet. Droplets plopped into it loudly. 'They're right on our heels, old friend,' he declared. 'We need to burn the bridge now, before they can storm it.'

Vanichios drew his hands together beneath his chin. Again that tiny nod of the head, his lips pursed.

'That should hold them off for a few days at most until they string a new one across. After that . . .' Creed shook his head, thinking on his feet. It was the talent he most relied upon. 'We must begin a full evacuation of the city,' he decided. 'And we must begin it now.'

The Principari's left eye twitched. 'You really think our situation is as bad as that? I heard rumours that the Matriarch was dead.'

'Rumours, aye. We don't yet know for certain. Either way, they'll want Tume before they push on for Bar-Khos. It's too risky for them to leave us here at their backs.'

Vanichios inhaled, filling himself up with it. 'This citadel has stood for three hundred years, Marsalas. I have five hundred men in my Home Guard. Sound men, men who will fight hard.'

'This citadel was built for different times. For armies with ballistae and tub-thumpers. With the Empire's cannon, they'll have the gates down in a matter of hours. You know this, old friend.'

'That is hardly the point,' said the Principari. 'Tume has been my family's home for nine generations, Marsalas. I cannot simply desert it.'

'If you don't, you'll die here.'

A lively silence fell between them.

'I should never have allowed them to take away the city's guns all those years ago,' Vanichios mused. 'We would not be in this fix now, if only I had stopped them.'

'Then the Shield might have fallen. This is hardly the time for ifs and buts.'

'The Shield may yet fall. It's under heavy attack even as we speak. General Tanserine is hard pushed to hold Kharnost's Wall.'

It was Creed's turn to wince. Tanserine was the soundest defensive general that they had. If he was struggling to hold, the attack must be as bad as they'd ever seen.

The doors of the hall swung open, allowing a gust of sleet to enter. A breeze blew across the nape of his neck.

Men cursed and shouted to close the door. For a moment, as the new arrivals struggled to close them, the sound of cannon could be heard in the distance, the army's pitifully few guns firing onto the shore.

'We must hurry,' commented Creed, though he found that he was unable to rouse himself.

'Yes,' agreed Vanichios, not stirring either.

In exhaustion, Creed looked around him, seeking to call out for Bahn. But then he recalled that Bahn was not with him this time. That Bahn was most likely dead.

He rubbed his face and eyes as though shutting out the world for a welcome moment. Grief for the men he had lost lay waiting at the back of his mind; but there was relief too, that his plan had worked, miraculously, that somehow he'd led them into battle and led them out again without losing them all.

The sensation of it was so powerful it made Creed's fingers tremble, his eyes smart with emotion.

'Are you all right, Marsalas?'

'I'm just tired,' said Creed, feeling lost for a moment. Old.

'War is for young men,' Vanichios offered, 'and fanatics of self-worship bent on conquering the world.'

'That it is.'

'Well, piss on all of them,' the Principari declared, and his eyes gleamed with a sudden proud fierceness.

It was a look that took Creed back fifteen years and more, and it brought a lump to his throat, and sharp affection in his heart.

He realized that his old friend was preparing himself to die.

*

Ash pulled his cloak over his head, though it irritated the stitched swelling of his wound. He was trying hard not to cough for the pain that it caused him. The zel plodded wearily along the wooden boardwalks of Tume, and he lolled with the rhythm of it, half asleep, half awake, aware of all that was happening in a dreamlike, disjointed way.

The Diplomat walked ahead with the reins held in his gloved hand. Around the young man, thousands of people were thronging the boardwalks, carrying what they could as they headed towards the canal that ran parallel to the main thoroughfare. Boats of all sizes were setting off into the lake, or rocking deeper in the water as they filled with people and belongings. A horn was blaring incessantly from the nearby citadel, and bells tolled from the temples, only adding to the sense of urgency.

Ash had never felt so tired in all his life. Through his swimming vision he watched a lone boy, only four or five, standing in the street with tears running down his reddened cheeks, shuddering with the fear of being left alone. Ash tried to speak to the child as he plodded past him. His mouth was a dry numbness, though, and he only coughed a few times, looking back even as the small figure was lost amongst a squad of soldiers trying to maintain some semblance of order.

'They're leaving,' Ché was shouting up at him. 'They're all leaving!'

Ash merely squinted at the man. He heaved a dry

breath of air and coughed again into his hand, a harsh and rattling sound.

'All right,' said Ché. 'I hear you.'

They turned into a side street and wound their way through a district of dark-timbered tenement buildings. The zel trod along a narrow boardwalk with the bare, brown lakeweed visible on either side. Up close, the vegetation looked like seaweed, flat fronds tangled together with boils of air bulging along them. People were taking shortcuts across the slippery surfaces with arms held out for balance.

They crossed smaller canals and further streets until they neared the western shore of the island, and entered an area of finer housing, three-storey mansions walled within their own grounds, their gates locked, their windows firmly shuttered, no lights within. The street was deserted here, but at the end of it a wide thoroughfare ran from north to south. Beyond the road, through a fall of sleet, tangles of lakeweed ran down like oily beaches into Simmer Lake, the surface dull in the twilight, stretching away to a hazy shoreline of dark trees.

Ché fussed at a locked gate while Ash gazed at the boats already heading across the water away from the island, not thinking much of what that meant.

The Diplomat cursed and shook his hands to warm them. He glanced back once at Ash as though daring him to comment. Ash looked up at the house that stood before them, wondering if he was dreaming. It was a fancy Khosian country house, with quality glass in its windows and a roof the shape of a bell, the eaves reaching far out from the structure and curling wildly at the edges to form elaborate gutters; cisterns stood beneath them at every corner to catch rainfall.

The gates creaked open and Ché led them into the grounds of the place. He stopped the zel and approached the front door. A gust of wind blew hard against Ash's face, stirring some life back into him. He saw Ché open the front door to a dim interior within.

Ash tried to climb down from the saddle, but his body wasn't working right. He fell heavily to the ground and simply lay there, gasping, as Ché muttered something about sorry old farlanders and grabbed him beneath his arms. He dragged him into the house.

*

'There,' said Halahan, looking through his eyeglass. 'On the right. A shoulder.'

Hoon squinted through the scope on his longrifle. It was trained on the end of the bridge through wind-blown sleet and twilight. A line of log siege-shields was slowly creeping along the planking, pushed by imperial Commandos, the distant figures staying in cover behind them. Hoon shifted his aim by the slightest of degrees. 'I see it,' he said, then exhaled and pulled the trigger.

The gun went off with a sharp report that once would have left Halahan's ears ringing for days, but which now he barely registered, for his hearing was 'shot', as they said. He watched the magnified image through his eyeglass, which trembled only slightly from the cold shiver of his hands, and saw a dark spume appear on the shoulder of the Commando behind the rightmost shield, before the man vanished from sight.

'Confirmed,' he commented in the lingering reek of the blackpowder. Hoon broke open the longrifle, took out the spent cartridge and placed it in his bag of cast-offs. He blew into the breach for luck and reached into his ammunition belt for another one.

They knelt on a balcony on the right turret of the gatehouse that spanned the entrance to Tume. His men were tired, though those who had been with him on the ridge had been able to snatch a few hours' sleep after the skuds had dropped them off in the city. Halahan had ordered rush oil to be passed around to keep them alert, and made sure they were well fed.

Above them, on the very top of the gatehouse, one of the army's field cannons fired a blast of grapeshot towards the far end of the bridge. The chains lashed and skittered across the planking, taking the side rail with them before they splashed impotently into the water.

Halahan stayed fixed to his eyeglass, focused on those few siege-shields that had paused in their movements on the bridge. They were being used as sniper positions; puffs of smoke blossomed and then the claps came a moment later, a sense of detachment to it all as he looked on, even when the odd shot spat into the stone-clad crenellations protecting him and his men. Already, young Cyril lay dead with a hole in his forehead the size of a coin. The other Greyjackets who kneeled around the parapet ignored the dead boy, and fired grimly at the enemy advancing over the bridge, keeping their heads low, remaining calm.

'Get a move on,' Halahan muttered as he adjusted his focus to take in a scene much closer to them: the Tume Home Guards in their tan cloaks, pushing their own siege-shields across the bridge in a ragged line. They were almost halfway across now, and coming under sustained fire from the opposite wall of shields and from the secondary snipers positioned on the far bank. Behind the Home Guards lay a trail of dead and wounded. More were rolling great clay jars of oil along the planking, dragging bodies out of the way as they went.

Their shield wall had stopped moving, Halahan observed. The men who had been pushing them were drawing their blades and fitting arrows to bows.

He swept the eyeglass towards the enemy siege-shields, readjusting the focus.

Movement there. Commandos pouring out from behind their cover, rushing the long expanse of bridge between them and the Home Guards. Four squads, Halahan counted, as the Commandos clustered into loose groupings, seeking what little cover they could along the side rails.

One fell as the snipers on the left turret of the gatehouse opened fire on them. The men on his own balcony did the same, their guns popping. Overhead the cannons bucked and fired, and wood burst asunder on the bridge. The Commandos moved through the incoming fire with grim determination.

He swept the glass back to the Home Guards. One of their sergeants had turned to wave back at the men who were rolling the clay jars. The nearest was still half a throw away from him; the soldier stopped and looked back at the others strung out behind him. The sergeant shouted something. The soldier drew his sword and chopped off the mouth of the jar. Oil splashed out.

'Not yet, you fools,' muttered Halahan, and then he saw the rest of the soldiers drawing their blades and hacking at the jars too. Halahan chewed on the end of his unlit pipe as his worst fears played out before his eyes.

A grenade went off in front of their siege-shields. Men hunkered down as a cloud of smoke enveloped them.

The sergeant stumbled out of it, waving again, shouting again. One of their archers tried a shot at the closing Commandos; Home Guards jostled for position behind the shields.

Another explosion; this one behind the shield wall. Men fell to left and right. A burning shard went spinning towards the nearest soldier emptying one of the clay jars. The man simply stood there gaping as the shard bounced through the spreading pool of oil and ignited it. Flames combusted across the planking; blue flickers rising into fiercer reds and yellows. The soldier turned to run as fire washed over him. He ran like a burning wick to the rail, where he pitched over the side with his arms waving and plummeted into the crystal-clear waters.

Halahan chewed his pipe, watching a sandal burn on the surface as its owner sank into the depths.

'Sweet Mercy,' intoned Hoon as he straightened from his gun.

Halahan lowered the precious eyeglass and scanned

the bridge with his own eyes. It was all going up in
flames, this side of it, anyway. Burning men shrieked and
dived from the edges. The Home Guards at their shields
fought a holding action now against the Commandos,
pressed hard by their assault and by the fires roaring behind them.

'Half a bridge,' Halahan cursed as he stood to feel the
heat of the flames against his face, smelled the reek of
burning oil and lakeweed on the wind. His men watched
him as he turned from the scene and strode fast for the
steps.

'Half a bloody bridge!'

*

It was for her own good, Klint, her personal physician,
had explained in his soothing tones. If she moved a
single muscle in her neck she might die. So Sasheen lay
there on the bed with a wooden brace strapped to her
head and shoulders, immobilized by it, feeling weak
and feverish, a little ridiculous.

She'd been shot, Klint had informed her. The lead ball
had partially fractured going through the armour that
protected her neck, and while most of it had passed
cleanly through her, he'd removed a small fragment
lodged in her flesh. Beyond the coagulants and the remedies to ward off blood-poisoning, there was nothing
more he could do with what he had.

Will I live, Sasheen had asked in a whisper, upon first
hearing what he had to say.

Klint had placed a clammy hand on her arm, though
she could barely feel it. *Perhaps, with a miracle,* he told
her grimly. And then he had smiled, and asked for her
permission to perform one, explaining how.

Moments later, the physician had returned with a vial
of Royal Milk held aloft in his hands. With care he'd
peeled off the bandages on her neck, and as her aides
held her down had poured some stinging drops into the
wound.

Now, in the draughty heart of her tent, with the canvas flapping and tugging all about her and the priests and generals arguing at the top of their voices, Sasheen felt calm, and strong, as the Royal Milk still coursed through her blood. They were arguing over what to do with her; what to do with the army's advance. Sasheen barely listened to their words. For a while she studied the flames of one of the braziers as a draught coaxed and flattened them, the smoke lingering beneath the roof before it trickled out through one of the vents. She thought of Q'os and home and the son she had so recently lost. But their voices grew more insistent, became a cacophony in her head.

'*Enough*,' she commanded in a croak, not at all what she'd been expecting.

Still, it silenced them.

'Matriarch,' said her old friend Sool as she hurried to her bedside. 'Please, you mustn't talk.'

'Hush yourself, woman,' Sasheen responded. 'Talk is all I'm good for now.'

Sool hesitated, then bowed and took a few steps backwards. Sasheen asked for water, and caretaker Heelas dribbled some past her dry lips. 'Did we win?' she asked him quietly.

The old priest nodded his head, concern in his eyes.

She spoke up as best she could. 'Archgeneral,' she said to Sparus, who was standing with his helm under his arm, facing young Romano, both their faces flushed. The two generals turned to regard her. 'What is our situation?'

'Matriarch,' Sparus began with a bow of the head. 'Creed has taken refuge in Tume. He evacuates the citizens and has torched the bridge, though we hold one half intact. We will begin rebuilding it at first light. Our light cavalry and skirmishers surround Simmer Lake as we speak. Our artillery is moving into position. It's only a matter of time before the city falls.'

'So what is at issue here?'

Sparus looked to the ground with his lips pressed tight. 'General Romano?'

The young man stiffened. He looked at her as a wolf looks at its wounded prey. She noted how he did not bow, and in an instant all her loathing for him came flooding back. 'Matriarch.'

'Speak your mind.'

'We have no idea how long it will take for Tume to fall. According to our local guides, winter may be coming early to the islands. It will hamper us badly, should we fail to take Bar-Khos before it fully arrives.'

'And?'

'We can take half the army and push hard for Bar-Khos. Nothing stands in our way now.'

'Archgeneral?'

Still Sparus would not meet her eye. It was her physician, Klint, who spoke out. 'We can't move you far in your condition. A jolt on the road might still kill you.'

She blinked at the ruddy-faced man, then at Romano. 'I see,' Sasheen said, seeing the bind that she was in.

Romano wished to push on for Bar-Khos to gain the glory for himself, knowing it would strengthen his claim for the throne. And if she sent Sparus instead, that would only leave her in the hands of Romano, surrounded by men loyal to his purse.

I'm holding up our plans, she realized, and her gaze flicked around the tent, seeing the downcast faces, how they refused to meet her eye. She saw how pitiful she must appear to them, the divine leader of the Holy Empire, immobilized in her bed with her doctor fussing around her.

Her hands clawed at the sheets. Sasheen found herself trying to rise from the mattress.

Sool rushed over and pushed her down hard. '*Enough now!*' the woman hissed. Sasheen tried to fight against her for a moment, but it took what little strength remained in her. She ceased her efforts and collapsed back against the mattress, her nostrils flaring. A sense of help-lessness washed over her, filling her belly with nausea.

Sasheen's sigh filled the awkward silence of the tent. There was never any respite from it, she reflected. Even here, on campaign, she must fight always to maintain her position. And as she thought of that, she felt her body grow suddenly heavy, as though all the burdens of these few years in power were trying to crush her.

Perhaps the Royal Milk was wearing off at last.

'We must stay together,' she croaked to them. 'All of us. At least until we have taken Tume.'

Her words brought a scowl to Romano's face. Sparus bent low, though, as did the rest of them.

For a moment, Sasheen closed her eyes and drifted.

'Matriarch,' came a distant voice, and she looked about her, and sensed that some time had passed.

'Leave me,' she whispered, but then she saw that they had already gone, and only Klint remained, warming his hands by the brazier, and the twins Swan and Guan were there too now, standing over her bed.

'Matriarch,' Guan said again. His face was wet, and he rubbed a hand across his scalp to clear the water from it. 'There is something you need to know. Your Diplomat has deserted.'

'Ché?'

Some droplets fell from his chin as he nodded his head.

'You are mistaken.'

'He was seen leaving the encampment after you fell,' Swan told her.

Sasheen was too tired for this. 'You are mistaken,' she breathed. 'He is loyal. He has proven it to me.'

'Holy Matriarch. He has *gone*.'

Klint stepped into view next to the two Diplomats, though they ignored him and continued to gaze down at Sasheen.

She couldn't fathom what it meant, and she stared at

the canvas roof of the tent as it flapped violently in the wind, something forlorn and angry about it.

'Do what you must,' she said quietly, and she closed her eyes.

—CHAPTER THIRTY-ONE—

A Game of Rash

Ash awoke coughing in a darkened room. He tried to recall where he was while his hands groped against bedsheets soft and luxurious.

'Easy,' said a voice, and he turned his head towards the source of it, his breath wheezing. A figure rose from a darkened window, approached the bed with something held in its hand.

Ash pushed himself up against the deep pillows and accepted the wooden gourd passed to him. He coughed once more as he took a sip of cool soothing water, then drank more deeply.

'Thank you,' he rasped as Ché returned to a chair by the window.

With delicate care, Ash swung his feet off the bed and settled them on the cold wooden floor. His head lurched with nausea. His skull throbbed dully where the lump had formed. He felt hardly rested at all.

'Where are we?' Ash managed after a few shallow breaths.

The silhouette of Ché turned to regard him. 'Holed up in a city that everyone else seems fairly desperate to leave,' the man said, and then turned back to the view beyond the window.

Ash rose to his feet, cracked his back with loud pops while he waited for his head to stop reeling. Gunfire could be heard in the distance, and he smelled something burning in the air. With a groan he padded over to the window to look outside. The sleet had stopped at last, and the wind tore at the clouds so that occasional starlight filtered through. It was enough to light a band of smoke spreading high and thin from the city.

Ash observed the fleet of boats heading westward, the vessels leaving an eerie blue glow in their wakes. Ché said, 'With our chances of leaving diminishing with every boat that departs.'

Ash placed a palm against the windowframe and leaned against it. His chest burned with every breath he took, but the air seemed to help a little, laden as it was with its harsh whiff of sulphur.

He narrowed his eyes and took in the vague shoreline around the lake. There were pinpricks of torchlight out there, a great number of them. They could be seen all along the southern and northern edges, and fires too shooting up into the night, buildings alight. As he watched them, he saw how the torches were spreading, creeping slowly along the western shore that was the edge of the Windrush forest.

'On a lake presently being surrounded by the enemy.'

Clumsily – for his coordination was still off – Ash dragged another chair across the room, banging and catching it against a leg of the bed, the sounds seeming overly loud in the empty house. Beside the window he sat with his gourd of water, sipping occasionally as he and Ché both gazed out at the night.

'Leave if you wish to,' he told the dark form opposite him. In the dimness, he saw Ché's eyes regard him coolly.

'I wouldn't wish to rob you of your retribution.'

Ash tossed the gourd into the young man's lap and observed the flinch of his eyes. Ché righted the gourd as water dripped from his lap onto the floor.

'You think,' growled Ash, 'that because you saved me from a bad spot, you have paid for all you have done? Do not think that, Ché. And do not jest about what must be settled between us. I find no humour in it.'

Ché turned his face back to the window. 'Do what you

must, old man,' he sighed. The Diplomat scratched at his neck lazily, and Ash was reminded of this young man when he had been a Rōshun apprentice at Sato; a small intent boy with troubled eyes; a laughter that could burst from him at any moment like a rush of startled birds.

'You were one of us,' Ash accused him.

'So I believed too.'

'Yet you left us for Mann.'

Ché set his thin lips in a humourless smile. 'I was always of Mann,' he mused. 'I just didn't know it at the time.'

'Explain yourself.'

The young man scratched even harder, barely noticing he did so. Gently, Ash reached over and grasped his wrist. He felt the shock of their connection, then slowly drew Ché's hand away from his neck, the man's pulse beating fast beneath his grip. 'Ché?'

The Diplomat closed his eyes for a moment. When he opened them, he spoke as a man reciting the story of another, without any emotional attachment at all.

'The Mannian order has ways of playing with your mind, Ash. They played with mine, as a boy. They made me think I was someone else, then sent me off to be play at being Rōshun. Truly, it was no deception of mine. I thought I was nothing more than an innocent apprentice. But when I became twenty-one, my real memories came flooding back to me, as my handlers intended they should. My mission became clear.

'*Now*, remove your hand, old man, before I remove it for you.'

Ash drew his hand clear, sat back in some bewilderment.

'You have condemned the lives of everyone at Sato,' he told him.

The young man was a mere shadow on the chair, the whites of his eyes gleaming as they stared out at the lake. 'I acted as I did to protect the life of my mother. So they wouldn't harm her. There was no other way for me, you understand?'

'You had no choice.'

'No.'

'And what of your mother now, Ché? Will they harm her now that you have deserted them?'

The young man's eyes were bright.

Ash suddenly regretted his words, though before he could say anything, the moment was lost in another fit of coughing.

Ché offered the water again as Ash leaned and spat onto the floor. He took a drink to soothe his throat, and then Ché reached down and picked something up and tossed that onto Ash's lap too. It was a loaf of stale bread wrapped in paper, half of it eaten already. Ash heard his stomach growl as his eyes devoured it.

Something within Ash gave way as he ate; the anger he felt towards this young man, the sense of betrayal, crumpled into itself. He chewed the last mouthful and swallowed it down, and sat there unmoving for a while, not knowing what to say. Flocks of birds flapped through the night, calling out to each other, disturbed from their roosts by snaps of gunfire that sounded like nothing more than fireworks. A man called someone's name frantically in the streets outside.

'We could swim for the shore, if it comes to it,' Ash said.

Ché looked him up and down. 'In this weather? You look as though a cold bath would be enough to finish you off, never mind a swim.'

'Give me a day or two, you will see. Besides, the water here is not so cold.'

'What will you do then, if we make it out?'

Ash followed the torches as they spread across the western shoreline. After some moments, he released a long, pent-up breath. 'I will warn my people, Ché. That is what I will do.'

He felt the weight of the clay vial about his neck, tugging at his conscience.

'But first, I must see a mother about her son.'

*

There was a trick to falling asleep at night, and Ché had known it once. He'd been able to lay his head against a pillow and relax ever more deeply into his breathing, until after only a short time he would slip into a welcome oblivion.

But he'd been a youth then, when he had known the trick, and he had lived in the moment as all youths do, rather than in the days behind him or the ones still to come. He had not yet suffered from that fretful mindset of adulthood, where his thoughts became a chattering compulsion that only heightened in the silence of a bed, so that falling asleep became a matter of will rather than relaxation, a fight rather than a submission, in which the trying caused the simple knack of it to be lost.

And so, despite his great weariness, Ché tossed and turned throughout the long hours of that night, barely sleeping at all. He kept thinking of his mother in Q'os, and of phantoms with garrottes stealing towards her where she lay. He thought too of a boyhood spent in the heady confines of the Sentiate temple, lonely in his play without other children his age, bored with the endless schooling on Mann, hardened by the occasional Purging.

Most of all, though, he thought of how he wasn't free of them even now. He knew the order would never allow a Diplomat to turn rogue and survive.

Some time during the night, he heard Ash knocking something over in the bedroom next to his. His ears followed the creaks of his steps as the old farlander walked down the stairs; the rattle and bangs in the kitchen; the footsteps returning, the bedroom door closing once more.

The Rōshun was only another concern to occupy his mind.

In the end he gave up on any notions of sleep, and groaned and rose from the bed, rubbing his face to rouse himself.

In the next room, Ash lay wrapped in blankets, breathing heavily as he slept. There was an empty bottle of wine on the floor next to the bed, and a jar of what smelled like honey. The farlander coughed a few times, scratched himself beneath his blanket, but he did not wake.

Ché took the blanket he had been using and threw it loosely over the sleeping man. From the table in his own bedroom, he rifled through his backpack until he found the wrapped vial of wildwood juice. He tried to recall how much he was meant to take in order to suppress his pulsegland, for he'd never used the stuff before. It was easy to take too much of it, he knew that much at least; and too much could trigger the suicide response that was otherwise only summoned by will.

He placed a tiny dab of it on his tongue and returned the vial to his pack, then pushed the pack under the bed where it would be safe. The wildwood juice tasted foul and bitter in his mouth.

Ché checked that his pistol was loaded and tucked it into its holster. His cloak was still sodden through, and he glanced at the sky through the window, saw that stars were clearly visible between the scattered clouds. He opened the window and hung the plain cloak out to dry.

The juice was tingling against his tongue as he descended the stairs to the ground floor of the big empty house, and stepped out through the front door and the gate beyond. On the wet boardwalk of the street he stood for a moment, listening to the exchanges of gunfire in the east.

Ché looked in the opposite direction at the nearby

waters of the lake, a black expanse visible between the two rows of housing. Drawn to it, he walked along the street and crossed the broad thoroughfare, and scrambled down onto the slick littoral of lakeweed until he stood with the water at his feet.

Campfires twinkled now all along the far shores. Rafts still drifted across the lake. They would be heading for the mouths of the Chilos and the Suck, hoping to make it clear to safety.

I should be on one of those rafts, he thought sourly. *I should be getting as far away from here as I can.*

Reluctantly, Ché turned his back on it.

He faced the distant lights and noise of the city's heart, wondering how long he had left before they came for him.

*

The old woman crouched on the shoreline of the floating island, ankle-deep in the water with her skirts tied up around her thighs, using a knife to cut through a strand of lakeweed, which she dropped into a bucket by her side.

For a moment the guns ceased firing from the direction of the crackling bridge. The old woman heard a tiny splash not far from her, and then the sudden sluice of water running clear of something.

She stopped what she was doing to look up, her free hand settling for balance on the basket.

'Who's there?' she demanded, her voice shaking with age.

No one answered, though she could sense the presence of someone nearby, watching her.

She stood up with the knife in her hand. Another splash. More water running free. 'Who's there!' she demanded again, and took a few steps backwards until she was clear of the water.

'It's me, old mother, your child,' came a female voice, young, close. It made the old woman jerk in alarm.

'What? I have no children. Who is that?'

She felt a ripple of water spill across her toes. Smelled a spicy breath against her own.

'Stop playing with her, can't you see that she's blind.' A man's voice, a whisper. 'Swan, help me with these clothes before we freeze to death, will you?'

'Blind or not, she's still a witness.'

The woman's heart stopped as a cool edge pressed against her throat. She did not dare move. Her useless eyes moved of their own accord.

'Old blind woman with no children,' chided the woman's voice once more.

'*Swan!*'

A burning pain shot across her throat. She coughed wetly, choking, held a hand up to her neck to feel a hotness spill across her fingers. Her knees gave out, and she sagged to the surface of lakeweed, one hand lolling into the water, her mouth gasping like a landed fish.

'This one should thank me,' was the last thing she ever heard.

*

Hundreds choked the streets and milled in confusion around the great Central Canal, competing for spaces on the few boats still preparing to leave, or those ferries with crews brave enough to have returned for more.

Ché saw folk desperate enough to be loading families onto makeshift rafts, mats of lakeweed with doors thrown across them; women clutching babes in their arms, children holding baskets, pots, the leashes of barking dogs; old grandparents muttering prayers.

The Khosian army had bedded down in the citadel at the heart of the floating city, and in the streets and buildings that surrounded it. The Tume Home Guards struggled to maintain some sense of order, while soldiers of the army staggered drunk and weary, or pissed in alleyways, or splashed like children in public cisterns, or fornicated with prostitutes desperate enough for coin to linger a while. He stepped over a Red Guard snoring in the middle of the boardwalk, and beneath the awning of a shop he glimpsed a brief fight between two squads of men, one of them spilling backwards with a knife sticking from his thigh.

The aftermath of battle, Ché supposed. Men like himself, exhausted to the bone but now, having survived the fight, too spirited for simple rest. They hardly seemed the same men that had impressed him so deeply the night before as whole.

A door was flung open as he passed the mouth of an alleyway, and a couple tottered through it, shrouded in smoke. Music and laughter following them from within. Ché stopped to look at the sign above the door; Calhalee's Respite, it read above a picture of a wavy-haired woman with a fish dangling from her mouth.

He'd read of that name before, somewhere. *Calhalee*. Founding Mother of Tume, her twenty starving children the progenitors of the city's major blood clans.

Ché approached the open doorway and stepped inside. He descended a set of wooden steps and entered a long basement, barely large enough to hold the few hundred soldiers who filled it from wall to wall. The men were riotous drunk, all of them competing to see who could shout the loudest above the noise of the band playing on stage. He could taste the musty humidity of sweat in the air, amongst the smoke of hazii and tarweed that swirled thick as clouds.

Ché could hardly hear himself think here, and he was glad of that. He stepped towards the bar that ran along the left side of the long room. Officers had gathered there, lounging on stools or standing against it, a host of prostitutes amongst them. His foot slipped beneath him and he looked down at a puddle of dark liquid, and saw that he stood upon a section of floor made from glass. A large well lined with wood had been cut through the deep foundations of lakeweed beneath them. Between pairs of boots, he saw glimmers of ghost-light in the waters deep below.

It was a gambler's instinct that caused Ché to push onwards until he reached the back of the room, where he saw a large oval table and a game of rash in play. The room was quieter at this end, the men intent on their cards.

He studied the game for a moment and saw that two players remained in the pot, a man in the purple robe of the Hoo and a short-haired girl in the black leathers of the Specials. The chairs were all taken, though one of the players sat with his head lolled back and his mouth open, soundly asleep. With a finger, Ché gently pushed his shoulder until he fell sideways off the chair.

A few chuckles arose as he slid into his place like a jockey settling into the saddle. Cards were shown; the girl in leathers watched her coins being scraped away from the centre of the table.

'What's the limit?' he asked those around him.

'Our souls,' rumbled a voice from his side.

The man was dressed in civilian clothing and was large around the stomach. He had a mug of wine and a plate of meat skewers laid out before him, and he licked his greasy fingers as Ché offered him a nod.

'High stakes,' replied Ché, and took his money pouch from his pocket. He slid a handful of coins into his palm, and settled them in a column on the table. They were local currency, silvers and a few eagles; his emergency stash.

The dealer dealt out a fresh round of cards while each of the players threw a copper into the pot. Ché glanced at the girl sitting opposite him. Her eyes were closed now, but when the old soldier to her right looked at his cards and threw them away in disgust, she opened her eyes a fraction to study her own cards, her lips pouting as she did so.

A little young for a Special, thought Ché, before he noticed the white band of a medic around her arm.

Carefully, she took a silver coin and tossed it towards the pot.

The man on her left looked at her askance, threw his own cards away. The folds continued around the table. When it came to the fat man's turn he matched the bet, then scribbled something on a notebook before him.

The girl met Ché's gaze with her large, intoxicated blue eyes.

'Are you playing or staring?' she asked him.

'A little of both,' he told her, then looked down to study his own two cards; a three-armed black Monk and a white Foreigner.

Ché considered his position. He wasn't bothered about winning tonight. He was content enough to sit in the familiar environment of the gaming table and forget everything else for a while. On a whim he matched the girl's bet, then raised her by throwing in two more silvers, wanting to see her reaction.

The girl half closed her eyes again, and settled back in her chair while she waited her turn.

'Your accent. You're not from Khos, are you?' It was the fat man again, sipping wine.

'I come from all over,' Ché answered casually.

The man wiped his hand on his woollen tunic and held it out to him. 'Koolas,' he said.

'Ché.' They shook, and Ché wondered if the man was merely gaining the measure of him.

'What brings you here, friend?'

'Some business,' said Ché. 'And you?'

'Me? I dabble in war correspondence, when I'm not writing my own impressions.'

'Koolas?' Ché in surprise. 'The same Koolas who wrote *The First and the Last*?'

The war chattéro smiled proudly at that. 'The very same,' he admitted. 'You're well read, friend. They didn't make that many copies.'

Ché offered a modest tilt of his head.

The dealer spread four cards on the gaming table, face up. Ché spotted a red Foreigner before he glanced at the rest. Two of the other cards were red too.

Again the girl bet first, this time even more strongly, throwing five silvers clinking into the pot.

Ché sat back and tried to read her. *Calm*, he thought. She didn't look as though she was bluffing. There was every chance that she had something, even a flush.

They waited on Koolas, the big man studying his cards and those on the table, his left eye squinting. He glanced at the girl.

'Nope,' he said, flicking his cards away.

Ché was enjoying himself. He knew that he was probably beaten here, yet still he reached for his stack of coins, and played with them for a moment, listening to their metallic clinks. She was pretending to ignore him as he stared at her, and he used the moment to glance down at her chest, its curves compressed by leather.

You can't bluff this girl, he decided at last, and with regret slid his two cards forward. He gestured with his hand to the pot. *It's yours.*

She retrieved her winnings without expression. Just once she chanced a look at Ché, and a small smile tugged the corner of her mouth.

A damned bluff, he realized with a start. The little bitch had bluffed them all.

Ché leaned back and barked with laughter. It felt good enough just then that he kept on laughing, the sound of it lost in the din of the crowd, and when he finally stopped he felt better for it, and another hand was already in progress. He caught the eye of one of the barmaids and called for her to bring some water, and good wine.

The wine she brought him was passable, the water tasted as though it had come from the lake.

'How goes the evacuation?' enquired Koolas.

'Shouldn't you be seeing it for yourself, correspondent?'

'I've seen enough for now, thank you,' the man replied quietly.

Ché folded his next few hands, too worthless even to bluff with, wanting to see the run of play and the styles employed by the other players before he started working them.

A fight broke out near to the bar. A man was standing on top of it, his prick hanging out, waving it over the jeers of his friends. A table crashed to the floor spilling drinks. The drums of the band picked up a beat, and the music ran without pause into a different song, the singer wailing with urgency and passion now, her words a high ululation of purest old Khosian, almost Alhazii in their intonations. Ché turned around to watch her perform.

The singer was dressed in a black, skin-tight dress of satin. Her hair was bound up by sticks of lacquered wood. Her eyes were lined with kohl. She swung her hips as she sang, moving in a way that caught the eyes of the men in the room, and the women too, so that they all gazed transfixed in desire of her, or desiring to be her. The woman held their stares, her arms cradling her head as she writhed amongst the coils of smoke.

'Calhalee!'

Ché turned to the table. 'What?' he replied to the girl.

'Calhalee,' she shouted again over the noise. 'They say she owns this place.' He noted how the girl spoke with the thick burr of a Lagosian accent.

'She's good,' he said, glancing back.

The wine was heady stuff; he could feel it already. Ché leaned over the table and extended his hand. 'Ché.'

'I heard,' she replied, and she studied him for a moment, before reaching out to clasp his hand, 'Curl,' she told him, and as their skins touched he felt a quickening of his blood and saw her lips part slightly. He squeezed her hand tighter, wanting her.

CHAPTER THIRTY-TWO

Desires

'General Creed, some trouble has broken out in the western quarter.'

It was Corporal Bere, holding the reins of his sweat-lathered zel. The officer was freshly returned from relaying a message to Captain Ashtan, who was manning the western shore of the island with units of Red Guards.

'Trouble with whom?'

'Some panicked civilians. They've decided not to heed our warnings about the Suck and the Chilos. They think they can still make it through on rafts.'

Creed looked at the man in the pearly light of dawn. Bere was filthy, as they all were. His helm was gone, his hair sticking up wild and hard, and his crimson robe hung tattered over his armour. Yet he stood with his back straight and his eyes sharp – a good man, it seemed, when the pressure was on him.

Creed recalled that he was in need of a new chief field aide. But that involved accepting that Bahn was now lying dead at Chey-Wes, and that was something he was not quite ready to do yet.

'And what would you suggest, Corporal?'

Bere looked surprised to be asked his opinion. 'I don't know, General. Perhaps more men to contain them.'

Creed considered his words.

'They're still a free people,' he decided. 'If they want to chance it, let them chance it.'

The corporal nodded and climbed back onto his zel. Creed's bodyguards cleared the way as he kicked the animal into a gallop, scattering the soldiers that clogged the city boardwalks.

Creed was standing in the middle of the bridge that spanned the wide Central Canal. He placed his big hands on the rail with a slap, and looked out over the scene of chaos without expression. A skyship was lifting off from the roof of a nearby warehouse, overloaded with wounded men and civilians.

The mood of the remaining citizens was becoming desperate as a new day rose around them and they found themselves still here. They wanted out by any means now. But the two rivers that flowed out of the lake, the Chilos and the Suck, had effectively been sealed off by the Imperials, so that anyone passing into the mouth of either river ran a gauntlet of missile fire from both banks. An hour previously, Captain Trench, of the skyship *Falcon*, had reported that the Chilos was running red with corpses.

They have no faith in us to protect them, Creed reflected as he watched the pandemonium around the canal.

He could hardly blame them for that. The army had staggered into Tume shattered and harried by the enemy. They hadn't looked as though they could hold a single bridge, let alone a city, and without heavy cannon it was doubtful they could.

A cold breeze ran fingers through Creed's long hair. He tilted his head back, smelled the dank rot of the lakeweed amongst the other scents of the city. He had always liked it here in Tume, those times long ago when he'd visited with his old comrade Vanichios to wench and gamble and drink like the bachelor officers they were, and with all the luxuries afforded to the son of the Principari.

Beyond the Central Canal stood the citadel, an ancient fortress on the crown of the rocky island. A moat circled the base of the small island in the form of a canal. It was empty of boats now that Vanichios had sent away his family and civilian staff the previous night.

His friend refused to be dissuaded from his decision to stay and fight. Even now, his remaining Home Guards pulled wagons of supplies inside the citadel for the forthcoming siege, while on the parapets the canvas covers were being removed from the ballistae and bolt-throwers. Despite Vanichios's own belief, the Principari's Home Guard had been deserting in droves throughout the night, so that less than half of them now remained for its defence. Vanichios had cursed and called them cowards and dogs in their absence. With his eyes gleaming, he'd exhorted Creed not to evacuate the army from Tume, but to stand and defend the city by his side.

For a moment Creed had been swayed by his old friend's passion. It was galling to run once more from the Imperials. Yet cold, common sense had returned before he could speak.

Tume was a grave waiting to be filled. To defend the city now would cost the lives of his surviving men, for the Al-Khos reserves were still three days away with their heavy cannon, too far to make a difference now. Meanwhile, word had just arrived from the gatehouse that the Imperials were starting work on rebuilding the half-destroyed bridge, even though the defenders were keeping them under fire. By their reckoning, the enemy could have it finished within a day if they pushed hard and recklessly enough. Creed had no doubt that they would.

It would be street-to-street fighting once they were across, with no telling how long the defenders could hold on as a cohesive force before it became every man for himself, his army disintegrating around him.

No. He wasn't going to let that happen.

The general gazed down upon the Central Canal and the ferries moored there, those that had made it back from their last runs.

The tall boats were covered with gangs of work crews hammering and sawing wood as they fixed sections of roughshod armour into place, protection for the rails and boathouse on each hull. Colonel Barklee of the Red Guards strode amongst them, jumping on and off the boats to inspect the firing holes they were cutting into the wood, the only experienced marine officer that they had.

The boats would need all the protection they could get. Once the remaining civilians and wounded were lifted out, there was still the matter of evacuating the rest of the army. Some could be taken out by the skuds and skyships. The rest would have to cram onto the ferries and run the gauntlet of the Chilos river mouth, hoping to break through so they could drift south with the current to Juno's Ferry, where Creed had decided to rally and draw a defensive line.

They were fortunate, in one respect, for they still controlled the skies, the imperial birds-of-war having withdrawn after a few initial engagements. How long that would continue, though, no one could know.

Creed was intent on getting everyone out by tomorrow morning, before the Imperials finished repairing the bridge.

Anyone still here after that would be on their own.

*

Curl liked this one. There was something lonely about him, and rootless, and wounded, though he carried himself well, with a kind of last-stand defiance in his eyes, and his honest laugher was infectious.

Who are you? she wondered as she watched Ché play. He didn't have the look of a Khosian. She noted the blond stubble on his scalp, shorn close like a military man. The eyes that were dark and quick beneath thin brows. The square handsome face. His fine hands.

For once, Curl felt the need for some male companionship. Or at least she had, during the night when she'd wakened on the cold floor of the warehouse they had been quartered in with the wounded, chased from sleep by the ghosts of nightmares, the faces of young men crying out at her to save them. While some volunteers and monks from the city tended to the needs of the wounded,

Kris had lain soundly asleep, the woman snoring, and Andolson too, with his jitar, whom they'd spotted when they entered Tume. He had informed them that Milos and young Coop were dead, and the rest of the medicos they had known likely scattered throughout the army.

Elsewhere in the cold space of the warehouse, she had heard a young man calling out from his own nightmares of the battle.

Curl had risen quietly, and had ventured out alone in search of some distraction. From a busy street vendor she had purchased a wrap of dross folded in graf leaf, and had taken it all before wandering towards the sound of drifting music.

Finding herself in the Calhalee's Respite, she'd sat down at the game of rash with the grey dust blowing through her blood, and had played with half her mind on the game and the other half on the men around her, the young and pretty ones, and the spirited veterans.

She'd placed Ché in the former category when first he had sat at the table opposite her and flashed his winning smile, and there and then she had thought, *This one*. The man played good cards, won more money than he lost, though in a loose uncaring way. And gradually she'd got into the game too. Played with him and the others with their cards and their coins, losing herself in the same way that she might have done with a man in bed, getting more drunk with every mouthful of the bitter Keratch she bought from the bar.

By morning the rash game had settled into an endurance event, the basement taverna calmer now that the soldiers' needs had turned to food and sleep. Hot meals were doled up by the few remaining members of staff, with Calhalee the owner amongst them, the woman refusing all payment now. Lanterns were refilled around the room, though the natural light brightened from the glass floor so that it reflected in blue flickers along the ceiling and walls.

Men left the table and were replaced by others, but a core remained, the fat war correspondent Koolas amongst them, and the man Ché, who appeared to be on a similar mission of drunkenness and distraction to her own, for he drank heavily.

Her thoughts spun slow and languid like the passing hours, her mind blown. She talked with Ché and the other players at the table, making jokes and laughing in return; but all the while, some frightened stunned part of her was still standing on the night field of Chey-Wes, while around her men stabbed and hacked each other to death.

'Tell me,' she said to Koolas. 'What can those of Mann lack that makes them wish to conquer the whole world?'

The man was scribbling something in his notebook while he played. He looked up with a start. 'Hair?' he suggested simply, before returning to his notes.

'We have a story in Lagos,' she went on. 'The story of the Canosos. Of the end of the age. It tells of how a time will come when lies are seen as truth and truth is openly despised. A time when a host of dead souls rule the world in their own image. When only a few men and women remain to resist them.'

Koolas nodded absently. 'I believe I've heard of it. Lagos ends up drowning in its own tears, am I right?'

Curl recalled that part of the tale too. Her face flushed, even as Koolas looked up quickly, and said, 'I'm sorry. I didn't mean to—' His words trailed away, the man suddenly awkward.

'There's a similar story told in the High Pash,' Ché interrupted in his slurred, drunken voice. He was still cradling her skin of Keratch, which she'd allowed him to try. 'About a Great Hunger that turns man against the world itself. Erēs swallows them up in the end. All but those who resisted.'

'I hope it's true,' she said, and she could hear the shaking hatred in her own voice, surprising her with its venom. 'I hope that every last one of them is wiped from the face of this world.'

The man Ché was watching her oddly, one eye partly closed.

'I might have known I'd find you here.'

Curl looked up to see Kris standing there, the woman holding a cup of something in her hand.

'Kris. Come and join us.'

The woman shook her head. 'Not my thing. I'm just doing the rounds to see where everyone is.'

Curl reached over and retrieved the skin of Keratch from Ché's grasp. 'Any word on when we're pulling out yet?'

'Tomorrow morning, Bolt just told me. He needs some medicos to stay until the last boats are leaving.' She watched as Curl took a deep drink. 'Better take it easy with that stuff. It's getting crazy out there.'

'Kris, it's either this or scream at the top of my lungs for an hour.'

'Still, watch yourself. Don't go wandering around on your own.'

'I won't,' Curl replied, as though she meant it.

Kris glanced to the man Ché then back at her.

'Catch you later.'

*

'Hoon – get your bloody head down, man!'

Halahan hollered the words even as another cannon shot crashed into the crenellations in an explosion of dust and masonry. Hoon was unharmed, miraculously, as he rolled choking from the dust with a fellow Grey-jacket, Halahan patting them down as though they were on fire.

Another shot smashed against the thick facade of the gatehouse, even as their own cannons replied in kind, tossing balls over the partly destroyed bridge to land before the enemy artillery on the far bank. The imperial snipers were firing rapidly now. It was hard to breathe with all the rock dust scattering and falling over the balcony. Halahan's ears rang so loudly they hurt.

The fire-position looked like a scene from the Shield in the earlier days of the war. The men hunkered down as low as they could on the debris that covered the flagging, cleaning out their barrels or struggling to reload. A medico was applying pressure to a Greyjacket's bloody side; three others lay dead at the back of the space, their eyes still open. Halahan stayed low as he crossed over to Staff Sergeant Jay, who was crouched against the parapet, watching the bridge and the far bank through Halahan's eyeglass.

The sergeant seemed to sense Halahan's approach. He turned just as Halahan bent beside him, and shouted into his ear without preamble, 'We're getting the thick of it now!'

Halahan accepted the eyeglass and adjusted its focus until he saw the heavy cannon belching smoke some way back on the opposite shore. The Imperials had three batteries positioned against them now, heavy guns with longer ranges than their own smaller field cannon.

He handed the glasses back to the sergeant, looked down at the bridge. The burned half, the half closest to them, lay low in the water, the wood a long ribbon of charcoal black. Much of the lakeweed it sat upon had sunk just beneath the surface, and where it rose again intact, a line of Mannian siege-shields stood protecting the snipers there and the work crews behind them. Around the shield wall, groups of figures darted forwards burdened with bundles of lakeweed and logs of wood, tossing them onto the remnants of the collapsed bridge before running back for cover.

They were slaves – Khosians by the look of them. At first the Greyjackets had refused to shoot at the running figures, but then Halahan had gritted his teeth and given the command, and his multinationals had bent down to the grim task of picking them off one by one, while the

Khosian soldiers watched on in stunned silence. The slaves fell like ragdolls, but there seemed to be endless numbers of them. Gradually, the ruined portion of the bridge was being rebuilt.

A tremor ran through Halahan's feet. Another cannon strike. A portion of the parapet slid away to their left, and part of the stone floor too, so that Hoon and his fellow sharpshooter had to jump backwards to safety.

Through the gap, Halahan looked across the gatehouse to the balcony on the left, where Captain Hull, his Lagosian second-in-command, was likewise stationed with a platoon of men, all of them cowering down against the sudden volley of cannon fire.

'*Oh no*,' someone said as they watched the balcony slowly crumble apart beneath their comrades' feet.

'Get out!' someone else yelled with their hands cupping their mouth, but it was too late. An outer section of the curving parapet went first, men toppling out over the crumbling crenellations. He saw Captain Hull in his white scarf, waving the rest of his men back towards the stairwell – and then the whole balcony fell away in a crashing spilling roar, with Hull and the others tumbling amongst it.

A cry rose from the far shore. The Imperials baying in victory.

Halahan closed his eyes for a moment. Slowly he wiped his stubbled face with hands grown numb from the cold. He hadn't slept in two nights now. With a growl he turned his back on the scene and tried to think through his fugue of fatigue and anger. The rest of the men were watching him, ready to run at the first command.

He gave a single nod of his head.

The Greyjackets began to grab up their gear and dart for the stairwell.

In the street below, rifle shots were whining overhead or skipping off the walls of the gatehouse. His men scattered to their secondary fire-positions in the surrounding buildings. Red Guards were still manning the streets behind the cover of makeshift barriers.

Halahan ran across Sergeant Jay as he jogged over the smashed gates.

'We're falling back to our secondary positions,' he called out to the sergeant.

'Any word yet on when we're being relieved?'

They both jumped over a line of rubble, Halahan holding on to his straw hat.

'Our orders remain the same, Staff Sergeant. We hold this position until the morning.'

The sergeant glanced at him sidelong.

'I know, old timer,' said Halahan. 'I know.'

—CHAPTER THIRTY-THREE—

A Meeting of Diplomats

Ché had forgotten he was playing a game of rash, so drunk was he by then.

It was the girl's fault, Curl with the pretty face who conversed with him occasionally as she played or laughed at one of his jokes, but who mostly just shared her large wineskin of Keratch while pretending not to be interested in him. Ché drank until the noise of the taverna became something muted, distant, unreal, and he fell ever deeper into himself.

At some point, Koolas and the rest of the players gave up trying to jeer him back to life. Instead, they lifted him – chair and all – away from the table so that another could take his place. 'Get away,' he drawled at them, but they paid him no heed.

Ché's head was pounding. He couldn't recall a time he had drunk as much as this. For a while he simply sat in his chair while something tried to push its way out of his neck. He swiped at it, but the throbbing sensation refused to go away.

They had seated him at an empty table, it seemed. He saw a mug in front of him, filled with water, and he drank it down gratefully.

He found himself leaning to one side as though his balance was adjusting to a tilted world. The motion was checked by someone's shoulder. It was the girl, sitting next to him.

'Come back with me,' he heard himself say into her ear.

'And why would I want to do that?' she teased.

He tried to focus on the words he needed to say. 'Because,' he began, 'I'd like you to.'

A press of a knee against his own.

'We can get a room here,' the girl suggested. 'Have some food sent up. You look as though you could do with some.'

The girl helped him to his feet, and then he stood there swaying as she wandered off for a moment. When she returned she was smiling. 'This way,' she said, and led him towards a set of stairs lit by a single flickering lamp.

Someone whistled behind them and shouted words of encouragement. He glanced back but couldn't see who it was.

He failed to notice the two figures stepping into the taverna, a man and a woman dressed in civilian clothing, their shaven heads covered by felt hats, their hard stares fixed upon him.

*

Through the eyeglass, Archgeneral Sparus watched a pair of skyships taking off from the heart of Tume, Red Guards standing along the rails, their cloaks blowing in the breeze as the vessels lifted ponderously into the air. He snapped the eyeglass together and handed it to the officer closest to him, Captain Skayid. So it was true: Creed was evacuating the fighting men from Tume now.

Sparus knew that the Lord Protector would be one of the last to leave the floating city, and, knowing that, he was pushing the bridge rebuilding effort hard.

He was loath to allow the man to escape once again. He wanted Creed alive; he wanted very dearly to set his best people to work on him. They would break him, as they broke everyone, with narcotics and mind games and carefully applied measures of pain, until Creed was nothing more than a wreck of a man, malleable to all that they demanded of him . . .

It had become his favoured fantasy, ever since the aftermath of the battle and the Khosians' close escape. The Lord Protector, chained and naked in a cage and renouncing aloud all he had ever stood for, while Sparus paraded him in front of the walls of Bar-Khos for the Khosians to witness what had befallen their great war leader.

Perhaps Creed could even join the severed head of Lucian as another living trophy. That would be only fitting, Sparus mused. In defeat, the Lagosian insurgency had shown itself to be nothing more than another reckless folly. Soon now, the defiance of Khos and the Free Ports would become a fallacy too; the battles of Coros, Chey-Wes and the Shield would be remembered as the last bright moments of a people stuck stubbornly in the past, futile attempts at denying the new world order.

Sparus didn't doubt this, for he had seen it time and time again. While the scholars liked to quip about victors writing the books of history, Sparus knew that it went much deeper than that. It was victory itself which shaped the history in people's minds, which showed the righteousness of a cause and the mistaken beliefs of those who had been defeated. Victory had power in it, while defeat . . . defeat was nothing but a husk, quickly discarded save for what seeds lay within it, those hopes of future triumphs.

When Mann finally conquered the Free Ports, and

then the lands of the Alhazii, it would be the end of the contest of the ages, the contest of beliefs. And the victory itself would be the proof of Mann's righteousness.

Still, he had a personal score to settle with this man first, this Lord Protector who had made him look the fool twice now, first with his night attack, and then with his unexpected escape from the field. And Sparus knew precisely how he was going to achieve it.

'Colonel Kunse,' he said, and the colonel snapped to attention, along with the other officers around him. 'Prepare our Commandos for a night attack. Have them build some rafts so they can get across. When it starts nearing dark, redouble the efforts on the bridge. Offer gold to attract volunteers if you have to. I want it completed tonight, not tomorrow, do you hear?'

He looked to the west with his single eye, over the imperial heavy guns that pounded away along the southern shore. Another Khosian skyship was returning just then across the lake.

'And do something about those skyships, will you? We should be contesting the skies, not leaving them open for the Khosians to escape in good order.'

'But our birds are still under repairs, Archgeneral.'

'I don't care, Colonel. If they can fly, get them in the air.'

Sparus was demanding the impossible, but he didn't care. It was what a general did.

'We'll take the city tonight, and Creed himself, while he's still evacuating his men.'

A few of them smiled now, seeing the irony of it.

Aye, Sparus thought. *Let us see how these Khosians like a taste of their own medicine.*

*

A clatter of wooden plates jolted Ché from his drunken stupor.

He saw that food had been laid out on a small dining

table, and that he and Curl sat in a room of their own. A neatly made bed stood along one wall. A pair of velvet curtains covered a window at their backs. A plush rug lay on the floor. Despite the clean condition of the room, it still smelled of dampness and mould.

A murmur of laughter sounded through the closed door from the hallway and the taproom at the bottom of the stairs. Ché sat and stared at the food with a soft spin to the world around him. For a while he forgot who this girl was, sitting next to him. Yet their legs were touching, and she seemed not to be bothered by it, so something existed between them, even if he couldn't recall what it was. In his other hand, a hazii stick hung smoking from his fingers. He drew it to his lips, trembling. Inhaled, feeling each and every grain of the hazii weed scratching down the back of his throat.

'Exhale, you idiot,' said the girl as she took the stick from him, her cheeks bulging with food. He'd been sitting with the smoke in his lungs, not doing anything but staring into the guttering flame of the candle in the middle of the table.

Ché exhaled and sat back and looked at her. 'How beautiful you are,' he said.

She smiled politely, as though she'd heard those words a hundred times before, then returned to her food.

'You should eat,' she told him. 'It will do you good.'

He couldn't face the thought of eating just then. His neck was truly throbbing, and it dawned on him only slowly that it was more than mere head pains. *How long since I took the wildwood juice?* he suddenly wondered.

'They're coming for me,' Ché mumbled as he tried to rise to his feet, though the words were mashed by his useless tongue.

'They're coming for all of us,' he heard her reply.

His hand slipped from the table and he dropped back into his seat. He could no longer sit up straight.

He leaned forward to rest his forehead against the cool surface of the table, then turned it so that his cheek was pressed against it. Drool ran from the corner of his mouth.

He noticed that the wineskin was still in his lap. More drink was what he needed, he decided, and he straightened with a groan in the chair, and went through the laborious process of getting the Keratch into his mouth.

Before he could swallow it down, he was jolted by the sharp stab of the girl's elbow against his ribs.

Through his swimming vision he saw that someone now stood before the table, and another was closing the door behind them.

They were dressed in civilian clothing beneath thin cloaks, the cloaks parted at their waists, a pistol poking out from each of them aimed at Ché's heart.

All at once he was sitting upright in his chair.

'Mind if we sit?' enquired Guan, and took one of the chairs across the table while his sister did the same. Swan studied the food for a moment, plucked a small pastry and popped it into her mouth.

Curl was frozen in her chair. Swan flashed her dark eyes at the girl. 'Who's your pretty friend?' she asked sourly, and Ché wondered how he had ever considered this woman to be attractive.

He said nothing, for Guan was fixing him with a cold glare. 'I'd stop reaching for that gun if I were you,' the man said. 'I'm a whisker away from squeezing this trigger.'

Ché took his hand away from the wooden stock of the pistol in his belt.

'Hands on the table,' Guan told him. Ché laid the wineskin down, and his hands to either side of it. 'You too,' he told the girl.

Ché was finding it hard to stay focused on the Diplomat's face. It seemed to be leering at him in the dim candlelight of the room, shadows making pits of his eyes and a twisted gash of his lips. He could smell the water of the lake off him. Ché's eyes flickered to Curl's hands on the table. They were trembling. He blinked, focusing on the man's face again.

'Well, say something, won't you?' prompted Guan. 'Why don't you explain to us why you turned traitor?'

His silence was making him angry, Ché could see. He allowed a corner of his mouth to curl up, taunting him.

The man looked to his sister. She shrugged, helping herself to another pastry.

Guan raised the gun above the table and pointed it at Ché's face. His sister wiped her lips and swallowed the last of the pastry, then climbed to her feet. She went to the door, her pistol out, and waited there. She nodded.

Ché held a single finger up. *One moment.* It caused Guan to hesitate. Ché watched the end of the gun barrel through the flickering candle flame. He leaned forward.

Ché pursed his lips and blew.

The Keratch in his mouth jetted through the flame, igniting it in an even greater fire that roared across the Diplomat. The gun went off with a shocking bang. Guan toppled backwards with his clothes on fire, and Ché heaved against the edge of the table and flung it onto its side after him.

He lurched to his feet, staggering for balance as he turned to the window, the smoke of the flames making him gag. He yanked open the curtains and tried to pull the shutters open. They refused to budge.

Swan was kneeling over her brother, trying to put out the flames.

Ché grabbed Curl's wrist while she stood there locked in panic. She tried to resist him as he pulled her to the window, managed to jerk her arm free from his grasp. 'They'll kill you too!' he snapped at her, then turned for the window and charged the shutters with his shoulder.

They sprang open easier than he had expected, and with a cry Ché tumbled out through the window, landing on his back on a slope of soft lakeweed. Curl landed on top of him, and they both slipped and spilled down the slope towards the water's edge.

They stopped themselves just in time, and helped each other roughly to their feet. Ché held his hand over his eyes against the blinding white daylight.

A gun fired from the window. Neither saw where the shot went.

'Who are they?' Curl demanded. 'I don't understand!'

'This way,' Ché said, and set off at a rambling jog towards the nearest boardwalk.

The streets were empty of civilians. They ran as fast as they could, but he kept veering to one side as though the ground was tilting beneath him, so that Curl had to keep him straight. They ran until they were breathless, and kept on running. For a few moments it seemed as though the pulse in his neck was slowing ever so slightly. But then it hastened again, and he knew the two Diplomats were on their tail.

'Where are we going?' Curl wanted to know, angry more than frightened now.

But Ché had no answer for her. He was too busy vomiting as he hobbled along the boardwalk, stabbing a finger down his throat whenever his gag reflex needed prompting, trying to empty his stomach of alcohol. 'We should seek help,' she shouted, with an arm around him, more sure on her feet than he was. 'Find some guards!'

'No soldiers,' growled Ché with the bile scalding his breath. He kept running, leading them into the western district of the city. He tried to load his pistol on the move, but struggled getting the cartridge slotted into it. Curl swore and took them from him, loading the gun as she glanced behind her. 'They're coming,' she panted.

He looked back. His vision was a sickening wash of tones and forms. Squinting through it, trying to focus, he saw that Swan was on the left side of the street and Guan on the right, hugging the frontage of houses with their pistols held low. The upper half of Guan's clothing was a burned and ragged mess. Swan jabbed a finger across the street. Guan nodded and took a side street, where he disappeared from view.

Ché reckoned they should be near the house by now, for the street looked familiar to him. Not wanting to be outflanked by Guan, he turned them right into an alleyway and ran along it, then left so they were heading west again. He turned and aimed the pistol as Swan looked round the corner of a wall, ducked her head back. He stood waiting but she didn't present herself again.

'Go,' he said, and they started off alongside the walls of thatch that ran along the left side of it, screens for back gardens.

Again he turned and aimed half-blind at Swan. She ducked aside just as he fired.

A squad of Red Guards came into view, turning towards the sound of the gunshot. Curl staggered up to them before Ché could stop her. He hung back as she spoke, pointing back towards their pursuers. The men saw Swan and spread out as they moved towards her position.

Ché tugged Curl's sleeve, jerked his head for her to follow him. Slower now, both of them spent, they jogged along the street, Ché looking left and right for a sign of Guan or the house.

Something flapped in a breath of wind.

It was his cloak, dangling from the upstairs window where he'd hung it out to dry.

They went over the thatched wall at the back. Ché fell and rolled across a surface of wood chippings. When Curl helped him to his feet, he led her through the garden, around the edge of the house to the front.

'Here,' he said with his neck pounding, and they went inside and closed the door behind them. Ché drew the night bolt. The house was just as he'd left it. He pounded up the stairs and into his bedroom, where he pulled out his backpack and rummaged for the vial of wildwood juice. He shook a drop of it onto his tongue. The girl stood in the doorway, watching him.

Ché went to the window. He stood to one side of it and glanced out.

No one in sight.

Cautiously, he drew his cloak inside, felt that it was bone dry.

He pulled Curl into the room and closed that door too, then sat down on the bed with his pistol and fumbled to reload it. He snapped it together and waited there with it in his hands. They could hear loud snoring from the room next door.

The beat of the pulsegland seemed to be diminishing. He wasn't sure at first, but then, after an endless time, he grew more certain of it.

At last he sighed with relief.

'We're safe now,' he said, and flopped back on the bed with a groan. His head was still reeling.

'Are you sure?'

He nodded.

'You want to tell me who they were?'

'Old friends,' he tried. 'I owe them money.'

'What are you, a thief?'

Ché rose awkwardly and went to the window again and looked out, but still he couldn't see anyone out there. When he turned back towards her, she was trying to get the door open to leave.

He was across the room in three strides. Curl gasped as he snatched her wrist. 'Wait,' he was about to say, but before he knew it they were pressed against the closed door, their breaths hot in each other's faces.

And then they were kissing, and tearing at each other with their hands, all thoughts flown in passion and need.

CHAPTER THIRTY-FOUR

The Gauntlet

A Greyjacket fell in the darkness as Halahan jogged past him, dead before he even hit the ground. Halahan scrabbled through the debris of a storehouse, and stopped next to Sergeant Jay where he squatted behind an upturned wagon, ducking down next to him. Archers to either side of them were firing wildly over the barricade that stretched across the street. He took a quick glimpse over the wagon, saw bright flashes of gunfire and the streak of shots through the night.

Shapes flitted through the rubble of the gatehouse, bent low as they ran. Beyond them, through the siege-shields on the hastily finished bridge, more figures were massing for a second wave of attack.

'Where is he! Did you send another runner?' he shouted into Jay's ear. The staff sergeant nodded, then looked through a gap in the wood, staring grimly at swarms of Imperials crossing the bridge.

An explosion made the sergeant duck next to him; grenades tossed ahead of the assault.

Halahan looked up at the surrounding buildings. Riflemen and archers were firing down with everything they had now. In the night air over the lake, cannons roared at each other as skyships engaged.

Somehow, the fire-positions in the shattered buildings along either side of the gatehouse had fallen. Now, reports were coming in of enemy units trying to flank the second line of defence. Halahan suspected Commandos, using stealth to swim in from positions on the bridge or from the shore itself. They seemed to be attacking all along the southern edge of the island, if the crackles of gunfire were anything to go by.

Halahan scowled as he saw Red Guards and Specials falling back into the road from a side street they'd been defending. Next to Halahan, an archer stood and shot at an Imperial clambering up the opposite side of the wagon. More were bounding up it, howling like wild dogs, with the wagon shaking under their weights. Red Guards on both sides of him pushed forwards, their chartas licking out; a man's insane face glared at him before toppling backwards beyond sight.

He swung to look back along the street with a curse on his lips, but then he saw the great dark bulk of Creed striding towards his position, the general's bodyguards jostling around him. Halahan ran to meet him. The general's face was red with passion as he shouted over the noise. 'They're attacking all along the south with rafts and swimmers. How long can you hold here?'

'Hold? Does it look as though we can hold?'

'We have two thousand men still in the city, Colonel. You must give us time to get them all out.'

'I'm aware of our problems, General. But I'm telling you, we can't hold here any longer.'

Creed looked up, as they all did, at an explosion rippling through the sky to the east. A skyship was disintegrating in brilliant tumbles of fire.

'Fine, then,' Creed shouted. 'Pull back in good order, but slow them as much as you can. I'll have a boat waiting for you all.'

'Is that a promise, General?'

They stared hard at each other for a moment, both angry, both wanting to shout in other's faces for no other reason than the need to vent their frustrations. But then Creed's expression softened, and Halahan saw that he held out his hand. Halahan clasped it and shook hard.

'I'll see you there,' he told him.

*

It was obvious that Principari Vanichios knew what he was going to say before he even spoke the words.

Creed said it anyway: 'It's now or never, old friend. We have to go.'

The Michinè laid his hands against the parapet and stared south across the city. From their vantage on the citadel's highest tower, they could see the entirety of Tume spread out around them. Gunfire crackled along the streets to the south. A few buildings burned, trailing banners of fire in the breeze that blew in from the east. Soldiers were streaming back in disorder, heading for the Central Canal, where the last ferries were preparing to leave.

'Will you get all your men out in time?' Vanichios asked him.

'No,' Creed admitted heavily. 'Some pockets are trapped in the south-west. We can't break them out in time.'

'And the rest. You have room for them?'

'We're improvising. There's still a place for you and your men if you want it.'

The man's stare slid away from him. Flames bobbed in his eyes. He had nothing more to say on the matter.

For a moment, Creed thought of pinning his great arms around Vanichios and dragging him from his ancestral home by force. But there would be no dignity in that, not for this man. He was Michinè. Without dignity he was nothing.

In the east the sky battle was still raging. He could see coughs of fire lighting up the hulls of the skyships, broadsides hammering each other.

'I did not think I would be this afraid,' came Vanichios's quiet voice.

Creed flinched. He felt like a villain, deserting him like this.

'Farewell, my brother,' he said at last, and placed a hand on the man's shoulder.

Vanichios did not look at him as he left.

*

Ash shivered beneath the blankets, his eyes swimming with phantoms of colour. He had long ago drawn the curtains over the window of the bedroom, yet still the moonlight leaking in around the edges was too much for his closed eyes, so that he kept his head covered while he coughed and sputtered in his fever, and felt as though the whole bed was spinning.

In his mind, the distant gunshots were only the sounds of maize husks popping on a fire. He was half dreaming of the drinking house of his home village of Asa, the room hot with the fire burning in the hearth, the black pot above it tended by Teeki as the warming maize clattered within it and filled the smoky room with its aroma.

He was sitting alone in a corner, eyeing his step-uncle across the room with a growing sense of hatred.

Ash had been sitting there all evening, getting quietly drunk like the old regulars at the bar, mulling over the rice wine that was their nightly respite from the world. His own burdens had refused to lighten, though. Even now, he did not wish to return home to his young wife and child, and all the responsibilities that they represented.

They had lost another of their breeding dogs to the shaking disease that morning. Ash had no idea how they were going to find the money to replace it, nor even how they were going to repay the debts they already owed.

The more he drank, the more he thought of running away and leaving it all behind him. This was hardly the life he'd imagined for himself, not when he'd been growing up as a youth on his family farm, watching his mother and father work themselves into the ground trying to meet their own rising debts and taxation. Ash had dreamed of striking out on his own when was old enough, of earning his way as a soldier, a sailor, anything but this.

And then he'd fallen in love, of all things, and had married, and settled down . . . so that in the blink of an eye, it seemed, here he was, trying to drink away his burdens like his father before him.

Ash stared at his step-uncle across the room, brooding. Lokai was headsman for a dozen villages within the outer ranges of the Shale Mountains, a tax-collector in regal clothing, appointed by an official of the overlord Kengi-Nan. He doubled as the local moneylender too, lending back to the villagers his own skim of their taxes at extortionate rates.

A useful man to have in the family, Ash would have thought. Yet his step-uncle was obsessed with increasing his wealth, and with the power over others that it gave him. When it came to money, he seemed little impressed by ties of blood.

Lokai was enjoying himself tonight. In the midst of the banter with his henchmen, he deigned to acknowledge Ash's piercing glare. The man stared with a pipe in the corner of his mouth, his head tilted back just enough to look down his nose. Even from here, through the smoky atmosphere of the room, his eyes seemed to be laughing at him.

Ash had no idea why he suddenly snapped just then. A drunken intuition perhaps. A sense that in those mocking eyes lay knowledge that warranted such a reaction from him, even if he was ignorant of what it might be.

Ash saw the man's eyes widen as Ash lurched to his feet, stumbled drunkenly across the room towards Lokai.

He slurred words he did not fully understand himself, while his step-uncle struggled to rise and his henchmen around him did the same.

A table scattered. Lokai rolled to the floor with it, the drinks spilling everywhere, a flash of blood on the man's face.

Ash's knuckles stung as he roared over his sprawling form.

Men grabbed him from behind. He surged against them until he was spent of breath and grew still in their arms. He stood there heaving for air as he glared down at the man.

'You think yourself something special?' his step-uncle demanded from the floor, holding a hand to his bloody nose. 'You think because you have my pretty niece as your wife, because you married your way into a better family than your own, it makes you someone?' And he slapped off the helping hands of his henchman as he staggered unsteadily to his feet. 'You're nothing but a fool,' he snapped. 'And your own wife makes you the greatest fool of all!'

Silence in the room. The words so incongruous to Ash that it took several moments for them to sink in.

'What are you saying?' came his thick voice.

The man was in full flow by then. 'What do you think I'm saying? When you needed money, the year you were wed, to buy your damned dogs. You think I loaned you those coins freely? I had my way with her by way of a down payment.' He paused then, to look about at the other men standing there gaping. 'Aye, I did that, and there isn't a damned thing any of you dare say about it.'

He drew a breath to say more.

Ash realized that the tin mug he had been drinking from was still clutched in his left hand, the contents gone from it. He lunged forwards without warning, breaking free of the men's grasps as he swung the mug with all his might, a black rage upon him.

When they dragged Ash to his feet, his step-uncle was lying on the floor with his face caved in like a bowl. Blood was bubbling from a hole at the very bottom of it. The man's left foot kicked a beat against the planks of the floor, and then he gasped and died as they all stood there watching.

He's murdered the headsman, someone muttered.

Ash fled into the darkness of the night.

He looked up, found himself staring at a harsh square of moonlight.

It was the bedroom window, with the thin curtains hanging over it.

A figure sat silhouetted in the chair, picking at the wood of one of its arms.

'Ché?'

The figure leaned forward in the chair. Ash heard the wood creak.

'It must have been hard, hearing that news about your son.'

Nico.

A strange thrill filled Ash's stomach, like the fear of falling. He found that he couldn't speak.

'I'm sorry,' said Nico. 'I don't mean to pry.'

Ash rested his back against the headrest, feeling how the pillow was wet where his face had been lying.

The memory faded slowly in his mind, though he could still smell the popping maize in his nostrils.

'Not as hard as losing him,' he rasped, and blood pumped in his throat.

'You miss him.'

'I think of Lin every day. As I think of you.'

'What do you think about?'

'You, or my son?'

'Your son.'

'*Ach*,' Ash said in frustration.

He felt the urge for a drink, recalled he had already finished the wine he'd found in the kitchen.

'I think of his eyes, like his mother's. I think of how he gave his spare tackbread to his friends in the leanest days on the trail. I think of him chasing the girls before he even knew what he was chasing them for. I think—' and he stopped himself there, on the brink of something reckless.

'I think of his death,' he said in a whisper.

Ash saw it then, as though he was there in the Sea of Wind and Grasses. He saw the dust of the tindergrass engulfing the clash of battle. The Heavy Wing of General Shin emerging from behind the lines of the Shining Way, betraying the People's Revolutionary Army for a fortune in diamonds, when victory was finally within their grasp.

A rider bearing down on his son, felling the boy with a single stroke. Hooves trampling over his body as though he was nothing but a discarded sack of clothing.

'What is it?' said Nico in the silence.

Ash clutched the sheet he lay upon in his fists, needing something to cling to.

'You wish to hide things from me, even now?'

No, Ash thought. *I wish to hide them only from myself.*

He looked at the shadowy form of his apprentice across the room.

'I did not love him,' came his cracking voice. 'For a time, at least, I thought I did not love him as my son.'

'You thought he was not yours.'

Ash gripped harder. It came to him then that it hardly mattered whether he suppressed the memories of how he'd behaved towards the boy. He'd still be here, still living with the shame of it.

'After I heard what my wife's uncle had to say, I treated Lin unkindly.'

Unkindly, he reflected, as he listened to himself in disgust.

No, he'd been a bastard to the boy, plain and simple. For the few years they had spent together in the cause before he had died, Ash had treated his son with a cold and satisfying indifference.

'I'm sorry, Nico,' he said.

'For what?'

'If I was ever unkind to you also. If it seemed I did not care for you. I am not good with . . . these things at times.'

The figure watched him in silence.

'Please, now, I'm tired,' he told it.

And he lay down again, and slowly pulled the blanket over his head, and waited until he knew that Nico was gone.

*

The ferries approached the mouth of the Chilos in single file, borne by the quickening current of the lake and the banks of oars that splashed through the dark waters. Drums sounded from within them, beating slow and steady beats for the benefit of the oarsmen labouring to increase their speed.

Halahan stood in the fortified wheelhouse at the stern of the boat next to General Creed, who peered through the gap at the top of the wooden screen that sheathed the gloomy space. Behind, other officers swayed to the gentle rocking of the boat, reeking of sweat, saying little. Koolas the war chattēro was wedged in a corner at the back somewhere. The boat's captain, a middle-aged woman with a pipe in her mouth like Halahan, manned the wheel herself, squinting too through the gap before her, a pair of borrowed Owls wrapped around her eyes. The mood was a sombre one. None of them knew if they were going to make it through.

The captain spun the wheel hard. The boat turned sluggishly, heavy in the water with so many men cramming its weatherdeck and the deck below.

'Here we go,' she murmured as they swung into the river mouth, and she rapped her boot-heel against the floor three times. Someone shouted a command beneath their feet. The rhythm of the drummer picked up pace. The oars splashed even faster. Halahan listened to the first smattering of shots hitting the wood all round them.

A flare went up, illuminating the scene like a noon sun. More shots rained in. Arrows arced through the air towards the boat. Some were aflame. Riflemen on the deck opened up in reply, his own Greyjackets and regulars mixed in with archers.

Halahan turned to the screens fixed across the left side of the wheelhouse, and craned his neck to look behind them. He saw the other ferries bobbing over the wash of their wake, the churned waters of the Chilos aglow with blue fire. Each of the boats towed lines of improvised rafts, with men hunkered down behind what feeble protection they could find. They were falling already, picked off by the snipers along both banks.

'*Fear is the Great Destroyer,*' someone was chanting over the riotous clatter of shots. It was Koolas, Halahan saw in the bright wash of flare light that speared through the slits in the screens. He was chanting the prayer of Fate's Mercy.

They would need it, Halahan thought, as he glimpsed the dark shapes of cannon on the eastern bank, and men struggling to aim them.

'*Be without regrets, like straw in the gale.*'

He realized he was holding his breath, and glanced to Creed to see how he was faring. The general's attention was fixed on the river ahead of them. His face was still a grimace; he looked as though he wanted to tear something apart. His left hand was clenching in a fist.

They were passing the mouths of the cannon now.

'*Be as the empty pail in the rain.*'

Halahan waited for them to fire. He tried not to think of all the men crammed below deck; what would happen to them if the ferry's hull was holed and the boat went down.

The riflemen on the weatherdeck were firing fast, replying to the gunfire from the shore. The shooting rose in pitch until it was all one deafening sound.

'*Be as the stream that courses always to its source.*'

They were past the cannon now. Halahan released his breath and swayed back on his aching feet. He looked behind again.

The second ferry was less fortunate. A spume of white water rose from its left side, falling as a shower of hissing droplets. The boat listed to its side, taking on water. Shouts rose from its decks.

Men were rolling clear of the rafts, and holding on as best they could as they tried to stay low in the water.

The firing on the weatherdeck was dying down.

Halahan saw that they were through the gauntlet, even as he heard the cannons fire again behind.

It was clear on either bank here, dark until another flare went screeching into the sky.

In the wake of their boat, corpses of men were floating after them.

'I'll make them pay for this,' Creed muttered to no one. 'Kincheko and the rest of the Michiné. They'll pay for this.' And the general gripped his left arm as though in sudden pain, and ground his teeth in silent fury.

—CHAPTER THIRTY-FIVE—

Waking Up in Tume

Ash awoke feeling better than he had done in weeks. His chest seemed less constricted, and he was able to breathe a deep lungful of air without feeling the need to cough it back out again.

He touched his scalp and winced at the painful lump there.

Tume, he told himself. *I'm in Tume.*

His bladder felt as though it was about to burst. *Up*, he thought, and rose swiftly from the bed, his bare feet slapping down against the cool boards of the floor. He reached beneath the bed and dragged out the chamber pot, and sat there making water as he scratched his armpit and yawned.

There was a tin of ground chee in the kitchen, he recalled. Ash stood and swayed for a moment, a little light-headed. He felt as weak as a kitten.

He trod across to the window with the chamber pot in his hand. He threw the curtains aside and squinted against the flood of daylight, then fumbled half blind with the window latch until he pushed it open. Fresh air tumbled into the room, cold and rancid. He inhaled it deeply, feeling his sinuses clearing instantly. Another yawn split his face wide open. His bones cracked as he stood there naked and stretching.

When he opened his eyes he caught a glimpse of movement in the street below. A Mannian soldier was ambling past the house, picking over the lakeweed of the island shore.

Ash pressed himself against the wall out of sight. He counted four heartbeats before he chanced another look outside. The man had passed beyond view.

Ash ran for the door.

'Whuh!' Ché exclaimed as he cleared the young man's bed with a single bound.

Ash peered through a gap in the curtains there. A squad of Imperials were marching along the street, crossbows over their shoulders. Further along, more soldiers were ransacking the houses of the neighbourhood, piling goods onto carts, breaking and wrecking everything else. All across the city, columns of smoke tilted into the sky.

'You're recovered, then,' came Ché's thick voice from the bed.

Ash rounded on the young man. A girl was lying naked in the bed next to Ché, and she sat up and rubbed her sleepy eyes. Ché's face held the pale tint of someone who was soon going to vomit.

'Anything you would like to tell me, Ché?'

'Like what?'

'Like why there are imperial troops walking past in the street outside?'

Ché rolled to his feet and rushed to look out the window. His face grew even paler.

'You did not notice the fall of the city. You were too busy having sport.'

The Diplomat scratched his fingers through the stubble of his hair. 'I was drunk,' he said, defensively, and then he held a hand to his stomach, and belched. 'I see you slept through it well enough yourself.'

Ash handed the pot to Ché just in time, and Ché retched into it loudly as he held it to his mouth. He spat, looking down at what he was using, then gagged again and rushed to the door with it still in his hand.

His retching faded down the stairs.

The girl was peering at Ash with bloodshot eyes, marvelling over his body. He supposed she had never seen a naked black man standing before her before.

'Morning,' he said to her with a nod, and strode off to fetch his clothes.

*

'I don't believe this,' Curl was hissing as she scrambled under the bed for one of her boots. 'I need to find out what's happening out there. *Holy kush!*' she exclaimed as her head came up with the boot in her hand. 'What if they've all left already?'

Together they dressed in a hurry. Ché watched the girl as she watched him.

He was suddenly aware that he would probably never see her again. It seemed a great shame. They had connected in their time alone together. Even though he hardly knew her, Ché had felt comfortable enough to drop his guard a little, to be more his real self. Laughter had come eagerly to his lips; affection to his touches. For the first time in his life, he'd wanted to please more than be pleased.

She was remarkable, and he wanted more of her.

'Last night,' he said quickly as she made for the door. She paused, breathlessly, and turned back. 'Last night,' he said again, but then faltered, unable to find the right words. He shook his head lightly. 'Thank you.'

She placed a hand on his face. 'No need. It was fun.'

'Wait!' he called after her as she stepped through the doorway. He grabbed his pack off the floor. Something skittered away from his foot, though he paid it no mind as he hurried after her. He was still reeling with the pain of his hangover.

She was already at the front door of the house as he came hobbling down the stairs.

'Curl, wait! You're not thinking straight. Your people must be gone by now.'

'You don't know that,' she said with her hand on the door handle. 'They could still be holed up in the citadel. I have to find out, at least.'

He pressed his palm hard against the door. 'If they were still holding the citadel,' he commented, 'we would be hearing the sounds of fighting.'

She ignored him, and stubbornly tugged at the door while he pressed to keep it shut. She cursed him then, looking tearful.

'This is your fault!' she hissed with her fists clenched.

'My fault? If you hadn't forced so much drink down my throat, I dare say I might have noticed what was happening.'

'Me? Force drink down your throat? Are you—'

'*Hush*,' exclaimed Ash as he bounded down the stairs with his sword in his hand. He glared once at Ché as he darted past into the kitchen.

Through the front door, Ché suddenly heard the gate rattle open.

Curl looked at him in alarm.

In silence he drew her after him into the kitchen. The old farlander was already halfway through the open window. Ché bundled Curl through it after him. She was still annoyed enough to slap his hands away in indignation.

Even as he scrambled out behind them, he felt the windowframe quiver in his hand as the front door crashed open.

They crouched down in the back garden, and listened to the scuff of boots inside the house, and the sound of a few gunshots to the south. 'I told you,' whispered Curl. 'They're still fighting somewhere.'

Ché ignored her as he loaded his pistol. Ash motioned with his hand, then set off for the back gate. They followed.

A squad of imperial infantry were breaking into a house at the western end of the street. A zel-drawn cart sat in the middle of the boardwalk with a single soldier slouched against it, smoking a cheroot. A few captured civilians stood leashed behind the cart; young men, their heads hanging in resignation.

Ash waited until the soldier's head was turned the other way, then led Ché and Curl in the opposite direction. He pressed against a fence as he chanced a look north into the next street along. He turned to go that way.

Curl ignored him and took off south towards the sound of fighting.

'Curl!' Ché hissed after the girl. But she didn't look back, let alone stop. 'Curl!' he tried one last time, and perhaps it was the concern in his voice, for she glanced back then, and flapped her hand for them to follow.

The farlander simply shrugged when he looked at him. Together, they set off after her.

'You Diplomats,' panted Ash by his side. 'You are softer than I imagined.'

*

She was a fast runner, and by the time they'd caught up with her Ché was feeling sick again and Ash was gasping for air. They ran along a row of tenements, large blocks of wooden buildings with narrow alleyways in between them. A squad of Imperials ran past the end of the street, not looking in their direction.

At the mouth of an alley, they crouched down on the boardwalk and listened to the sporadic pops of the guns. A Red Guard jogged past their position. Curl was about to call out to him when Ché clamped a hand over her mouth. She jerked it free in anger, was about to curse at him when a trio of imperial soldiers charged past in pursuit.

'Look,' whispered Ash.

Across the street and to the right, in a small stand of trees circling a stone cistern, a shape rose from the shadows and stepped carefully into daylight. A Special, blackened with soot. The soldier glanced after the running soldiers, then began to run in the opposite direction, past their location.

Ché was too slow this time. 'Hey!' Curl called out before he could stop her.

The man spun around in alarm, but he lowered his knife when Curl waved her hand at him and he saw her leathers. He came across at a sprint and hunkered down next to Curl, looking calm and measured as he inspected them in turn. Blood covered his blackened neck and hands. Ché did not think it was his own.

The Special's attention lingered on the old farlander the longest.

'Morning,' Ash said with a nod.

The man jerked his head by way of a response.

'What's happening?' Curl asked outright. 'How did the city fall so quickly?'

He glanced at Ché and Ash again, then back to the girl. 'I won't ask how you missed it.'

Curl scowled at him.

'They finished the bridge last night while we were still evacuating. Sent in Commandos too, across the water.'

'How many got out?'

'The army? Most of them, along with Creed. I've a feeling we're the only ones left in the city, those of us trapped here in the south-west.'

'Is there a plan? A way out?' Ché asked him.

The man leaned to spit on the boardwalk, then regarded him with thin eyes. 'The word was passed after we lost the southern fire-positions. They'll be trying for a pickup tonight, at midnight. Skyships.'

'From where?'

'There's a marina on the south-west point of the

island. We were told to rendezvous on one of the warehouse roofs. It's where I'm trying to get to now.'

'In daylight?' It was Ash, as cool as the man was.

'Reckon I can make it on my own, if I'm careful. Have you water?'

Ché passed him his own flask.

'My thanks,' said the Special as he wiped his lips. He nodded again. 'Good luck to you,' he said as he tossed the flask back. Then he glanced along the street, and without another word took off along it.

Curl rose as though to follow him, but Ché snatched her wrist and held her back.

'You heard the man,' she said. 'We have to get to that marina.'

It was Ash who spoke some sense into her. 'You think the three of us will make it in daylight without being seen? He said midnight. We must wait until it is dark when our chances will be better.'

'He's right,' added Ché, and she stopped struggling in his grasp. He released her.

'What *are* you?' Curl asked the old man suddenly.

When Ash would not respond, she looked to Ché instead.

'It's a long story,' he told her. 'Now come.'

*

Ash darted through one of the back doors of the tenement building, his head darting left and right. They both hurried to keep up with him.

They went through the door and up a series of steps to the third floor, the uppermost floor. Ash entered one of the open doorways into a small apartment. He inspected the ceiling of each of the three small rooms while Ché and Curl waited in the hallway, keeping watch. The old farlander returned and strode back down the hallway, still examining the ceiling.

At last he stopped by a window. He opened the shutters and peered outside, then hopped up onto the sill.

As they looked on he jumped again and caught hold of the eaves of the roof. He tried to pull himself up; gasped and could not manage it.

'Give me a hand there,' he said as he dangled in front of the window.

Ché tucked his pistol into his belt and offered his cupped hands as a stirrup. With a grunt the old man was up.

'You next,' said Ché to Curl, and helped her to do the same before climbing up himself.

On the sloped roof, Ash was tugging free the wooden tiles and setting them to one side. Ché stopped and scanned the streets surrounding the building.

When he turned, Ash was gone and a hole in the roof had replaced him. Ché ducked his head inside and saw a small dark attic space beneath the eaves. He dropped his backpack down to Ash, helped Curl down after it, then climbed down. Carefully, he settled his feet on one of the beams of wood that ran across the top of the plaster ceilings below, between the old straw stuffed flat in the wide spaces.

Ché held his nose for a moment, resisting the urge to sneeze. 'No trapdoors in the ceilings. No access. I like your thinking.'

Pass me down the tiles,' Ash told him, and then he laid the tiles out across two beams so that they would have somewhere to sit.

They sat in silence while motes of straw danced in the beam of daylight. What water they had was shared around equally. None of them had anything to eat.

Ché held his head in his hands, feeling sorry for himself. His hangover seemed to be worsening, if that was possible. He felt as if he was dying. 'If you still intend to kill me, old man,' he said, 'I'd advise you take your chances now.'

The farlander surprised him with a smile. 'What was it, Keratch?'

With a nod he replied, 'It was forced on me.'

'You were the one who kept asking for it,' Curl snapped.

Ash tutted, as though admonishing two children. 'I am told that in old Khosian, Keratch means a serious injury to the head.'

'Yes,' said Ché. 'That sounds about right.'

The farlander studied Curl in the shafts of light. 'You look a little young for this.'

'I'm seventeen,' she told him crisply. 'Old enough for most things, don't you think?'

He seemed to agree. 'Well, Curl, I am Ash,' and he held out his hand. She shook it, tentatively.

Ash stood and poked his head out through the hole in the roof, resting his arms on its edges. Below him, Ché fumbled through his pack until he found his covestick, then poured the last of his water from his flask across it and scrubbed his teeth in the gloom. 'How are you?' he asked Curl from around the brush, hoping to break through her frostiness.

'I could do with using that after you.'

'If you don't mind sharing,' he said. He looked to Ash. 'Anything of interest out there, old man?'

Ash said nothing. He seemed to be fixated on something in the distance.

Ché spat and offered the covestick to Curl, then hobbled over to Ash to poke his head out too. He followed his gaze through the rising pillars of smoke, focusing on the citadel that reared up at its very heart. 'Tell me what you see there,' Ash said.

'A flag, flying from the citadel.'

'What kind of flag.'

Ché squinted. The light was good today, the sky a clear blue. He felt a jolt of shock pass through him.

'I thought you said she was dead,' Ash remarked drily.

Ché glanced down to see if Curl was listening. He bit his lip, adjusted his footing beneath him on the beams as he pondered for a moment.

'It could be a ruse of some kind,' he said quietly.

'Perhaps they don't wish to announce her death just yet. Or perhaps she's dying even now.' He shook his head.

The Rōshun grunted. His gaze remained fixed on the distant flag on top of the citadel: white in colour, a black raven upon it, flapping in the wind like a challenge.

—CHAPTER THIRTY-SIX—

Prisoners of War

The pit was ten feet deep and covered by a screen of wooden bars. Looking up from its filthy earthen floor, the sky was a circle of brilliance that held aloft the occasional bird, tilting its wings in a wind they couldn't feel. The men craned their necks to watch that circle. There was nothing else for them to see down there, save for each other; sad battered reminders of where they were, and how they suffered.

It was their third day of captivity. Each wore a grubby one-piece suit of yellow finely woven cotton, with buttoned flaps they could release when they needed to relieve themselves. They were shackled hand and foot. All of them bore bruises, cuts, internal injuries.

Bull had just spat a mouthful of water onto the floor, and was staring at a rotten tooth he had plucked from his jaw.

'Here,' he whispered, and passed the skin of water to his old comrade in arms.

Bahn failed to respond at first. He was staring at the opposite wall of earth and far beyond it, his face a filthy smear but for his reddened eyes, and the purplish swelling of his cheek where a gash had inflamed the skin. He had a hand resting on his outstretched leg, and it was trembling badly. His other hand was pressed against his growling stomach. They were all underfed and hungry.

Bahn had complained of not being able to hear in his

right ear, so Bull nudged him, and the man turned his head slowly, and looked at the waterskin, then looked at Bull. He returned to staring through the wall.

Weakness rode through Bull like nausea. He tossed the waterskin to the staff sergeant, Chilanos, instead, who refused to speak either, only offered a flicker of gratitude with his eyes. The next man along took it from him when he was done with it. This tepid water was all they had by way of luxury; they each sipped it like fine wine.

For three days now, the small group had been deprived in every way that mattered. They weren't permitted to talk, though they did so anyway, surreptitiously, when boredom finally dulled the edges of their fears. Neither were they left alone to sleep. Their guards would drop small stones on those who had their eyes closed. At night, men would come to urinate on them as they huddled down in exhaustion.

For a while, Bull had searched amongst the soldiers that often stood above them, trying to spot the giant tribesman who had saved him. He wanted to shout up at him, '*Look – look what you saved me for!*' but there was no sign of the man, and he knew he must have died of his wounds.

Every so often, a squad of imperial hard-men would descend on a ladder into the pit, and would choose one of them seemingly on a whim, and would lay into him with their wooden staves. At first they had tried to protest these actions. But each time they did so they were beaten just as brutally, until even Bull could take no more of it, and it made more sense for them to simply sit there, and listen.

Humour was what Bull used in the bleakest of times to help them through it; when one of them was crawling across the floor after a beating; when one of them was standing over the bucket pissing blood.

After three days of this the world had begun to take on a strange sheen of transparency, as though Bull could poke his fingers through into something other and unreal. The smell of the pit had become unbearable, for they shared a single bucket to relieve themselves, and it was only emptied every morning. Bull handled it better than the other men. He was, after all, long inured to the privations of captivity. In a tangible way he became their rock in a storm-tossed sea.

Even now, as a rattle over their heads made Bull squint up at the dark crisscrossing of wood across the pit, dirty faces turned towards him for assurance.

The guards were untying the door to the pit. They flung it open and dropped the ladder down.

He would make a fight of it this time, he decided, if they chose him for a hiding.

Four soldiers climbed down with their heavy staves and studied the men blinking up at them from the floor. The oldest saw Bahn staring at the wall. He pointed his stick at him. 'Up!' he snapped.

Bahn paid him no heed.

The other soldiers grabbed Bahn and forced him to his feet, his shackles rattling. With his eyes blinking rapidly, they shoved a sack over his head and tugged him towards the ladder.

Bull struggled to his own two feet, sliding his back up against the earth wall. 'Where are you taking him?' he rasped.

'No talking!' shouted the older soldier, and he lashed into Bull with his stave. Bull grabbed him with his shackled hands, managed to strike his face with his forehead. He was content enough with that, seeing the blood flowing, and he rode the rest of it through in his usual manner as they lashed out at him, Bull listening to the thud of the blows, refusing to go down as though it somehow mattered, as though he was back in his pit-fighting days, forced against the wall without even a decent defence left to him.

He did go down, though, eventually. He fell to the ground and bared his bloody grin at them, while they bundled Bahn up the ladder, the man making no effort himself as he was manhandled through the opening like a sack of potatoes.

Chilanos opened his mouth and began to sing as they closed and locked the pit after them. It was *The Song of the Forgotten*, the familiar words loud and stirring in the depths of the pit.

Bull scrabbled up onto his knees with his shackles clinking. 'Tell them what they want!' he shouted. 'You hear me, Bahn? Tell them anything they ask you!'

*

Sparus was an unhappy man as he descended the spiral steps that wound down through the rock of the island upon which the citadel stood.

Creed had escaped, there was no doubting that now. The Principari of Tume had said as much, taunting him with the news even as the Michinè lay dying of his wounds.

And now this latest news, that the Matriarch's condition was worsening.

Sparus could feel it all begin to unravel around him, this crazy-fool invasion inspired by the plans of his predecessor Mokabi. Even the fall of Tume meant little to him in terms of success. Unless they pushed hard for Bar-Khos now, it could still turn disastrously wrong for them – for him.

More than ever, he wished he had refused the command of this expedition. All those years on dusty foreign campaigns, climbing the slippery rungs of promotion to achieve what he had once thought impossible, the position of Archgeneral of Mann. And now this chancy mess that was the invasion of Khos, with the reputation of a lifetime staked on its outcome. How would he be remembered in the records and the history books if it all went wrong here?

It made him rage just to think of it.

Deep beneath the citadel, the Sunken Palace was a complex of large chambers, brightly illuminated by crystal lanterns hanging from countless candelabra. It was walled on the outer edges by great sweeping windows of thick glass, where Sasheen's honour guards stood at attention. Past them shimmered the clear waters of the lake, shadowed by the overhanging weed-raft of the city, where fans of light spilled through the open canals. From any window, shoals of distant fish could be seen darting in and out of the daylight. Bubbles rose up from the gloomy lake bottom, some bursting on the surface above, others rolling and bobbing along the underside of the lakeweed itself.

'Ah, Archgeneral. A word with you, if you please.' It was Klint, coming to stand before him.

'What is it, physician?' he asked the man, without patience.

Klint beckoned him to an empty chamber, a lounge with reclining seats and old portraits on the walls. The man licked his lips and looked around to see if anyone was listening.

In a hurried hush: 'I believe the Holy Matriarch has been poisoned.'

'Poisoned? How?'

'Her wound. I believe the shot was coated in a toxin.'

'Are you certain?'

'You can smell it in the wound, if you have the nose for these things. And her symptoms – at first I thought it was blood poisoning. Now,' he shook his head, 'I can see it's more than that. It looks like black-foot spore.'

Sparus closed his eye for a long moment. *So here it is*, he thought. *The disaster you've been waiting to happen.*

'I didn't think the Khosians used such things,' he said, and smelled the man's sickly perfume as Klint drew closer.

'They don't. Only the Élash produces such toxins. And only our Diplomats make use of them.'

Archgeneral Sparus narrowed his eye and studied the man carefully. 'You're suggesting one of our own people did this to her?'

A precise shrug. 'I'm a physician, nothing more. I can only report my findings.'

Sparus rubbed the bridge of his nose with his grimy fingers. It didn't make sense to him.

'Can you save her?'

The physician looked at his feet. 'It's hard to say. I'm treating her with Royal Milk, but the Milk itself . . . Our only supply of it is in that jar with Lucian's head, and she is tetchy about me using it.'

'Never mind that fool Lucian. Use as much of it as you need to. You have my authority on that.'

'Thank you. But even so. The Milk is old, used up, not much good for anything more than preservation. We need a fresh supply, and even then . . . Black-foot you see, it's used by Diplomats because Royal Milk has such little effect on it. *King's Worry*, they call it.'

Sparus felt patronized by the physician's assumption of his ignorance. He contained his frustration, though, focusing on the problem at hand.

'What if you had a fresh supply of Milk?'

Klint shook his head sadly. 'I suppose we could dispatch a skyship to Zanzahar, or Bairat. But I doubt there's time for that. She's failing fast now.'

'Have you told her any of this?'

'No. For now I think it's best that she remains rested.'

'Physician. If she's dying, she should know of it.'

'Yes. But perhaps it's best if we do not tell her how.'

He assented to that, seeing the sense of it.

'I need to see her.'

'Yes, of course. You'll need to follow some precautions, however.'

Klint led him towards the Royal Chamber. They passed the priestess Sool, the woman looking lost here in the depths of the rock. In the anteroom, the physician offered Sparus a silk mask to tie around his mouth and nose. It smelled of mint, and something much harsher than that.

'Is it contagious?' asked Sparus from behind the mask.

'It's known to be. Especially when it has taken hold. With such things it's always best to be cautious.' The man gave him a pair of sheep-gut mittens to wear.

In the main sleeping chamber, Sasheen lay on the bed with the sheets crumpled over her shivering body, lit by nothing more than the blue flickering light of the lake beyond the curving window. She was feverish and panting quickly. Sweat glistened on her face, which was inflamed like her arms and hands. A smell of bile hung strong in the air.

'Matriarch,' said Sparus as he stopped by her bed.

Sasheen blinked, confused for a moment. She focused on him weakly. 'Sparus,' she rasped, and tried to move, but gave up after a single effort. 'I'm told I should not touch anyone. For fear I might catch something in my weakened condition.'

Sparus hesitated, then placed his hand on top of her own. Her skin felt hot against the sheep-gut that encased his own. It held a vague tint of blueness to it, as did her lips. The dressings on her neck were stained with patches of yellow.

The doctor busied himself around her. With gloved hands he checked her pulse and inspected the lesions on her body. When he lifted the bedsheets fully back, Sparus could see the blackness of her feet.

Dear Passion, he thought in surprise, realizing then how far gone she really was.

'What have you to report, General?'

He cleared his throat from behind the mask. 'We're still encountering some pockets of resistance in the south-west of the city. We should have them cleared out presently.'

'And Romano?'

'He complains he has not been allowed to enter the city yet with his men.'

'Does he now?' she breathed, and even in her condition he could see the rise of her anger. She gasped a few times, drawing the breath she needed to fuel it. 'Let him complain. I will not risk allowing him into Tume with his men. He knows I am vulnerable. I would only be inviting a coup.'

Sparus bowed his head, keeping his thoughts to himself. He found it difficult to look at her. Already, his head was playing out the possible outcomes of his position now. Romano, with the backing of his family, was the strongest contender to be the next Patriarch of Mann. If Sasheen failed to recover, if she died here in Tume, Romano would declare himself Patriarch, never mind any successor she might name. He would demand to lead the Expeditionary Force himself, for the glory of taking Bar-Khos.

He could have it, he decided, if it meant Sparus could return to Q'os with his reputation intact. But he wasn't certain even that was possible now. Romano would call for another purge, and Sparus could very well be at the top of the list.

I could approach him with an offer of loyalty now, he thought, and wondered who he could entrust with such an errand.

Sasheen was studying him closely, her gaze darting about his face.

'I'm dying, Sparus, aren't I?'

She sounded like a young girl, her voice frail and breaking.

Look at me. I plot my own survival even as she lies here fighting for breath.

'There's hope,' Sparus tried. 'We're sending for a fresh supply of Milk.'

Her head settled back on the pillows. 'Then make it fast. I can feel it worsening with every breath I take.' She tilted her head to one side, watched the physician Klint unscrew the jar containing Lucian's head. Within it, Sparus could see the man's preserved scalp, the level of milk having been reduced that far.

'Be sparing with it,' said Sasheen as the physician lowered a small ladle into the jar.

Klint came to her and poured some of it into her open mouth. At once, her lips grew less pale, and colour returned to her face.

'Let him stay out,' she instructed him. 'Next to me.'

Klint looked to Sparus as though he had any say in it. The physician removed the head from the jar and settled it on the bedside table next to her. His eyes were closed, and they flickered behind their eyelids as though he was dreaming.

'Let us talk later,' Sasheen said gently as her own eyes closed too.

'Yes, Matriarch,' he replied, then turned and left the room with the physician following him.

Sparus felt relieved to be gone from there. 'Keep her condition to yourself,' he instructed Klint as they removed their masks and gloves. 'And no mention of poison either.'

He strode for the stairwell that would take him up to daylight, his thoughts in disarray.

*

'She's dying. She has a matter of days at most.'

'You're certain of it?' Romano demanded.

The physician Klint tried to hide his annoyance. 'Of course. They have sent for more Royal Milk, though I doubt it will arrive in time to do much good.'

General Romano digested the news with a thrill of excitement. His uncle had been right all along. Give it enough time, enough patience, and all things came to those who desired them.

He looked down at the red-faced physician before him. 'Your assistance shall be remembered.'

'Thank you,' replied Klint with a bow of his head. 'I must return now, before I am missed.'

'Then go,' drawled Romano.

He watched the man climb onto his zel, and kick the flanks of the animal harshly until it was cantering back towards the Tume bridge.

Beside Romano, his second-in-command's expression was as sombre as it always was. 'It's time, then,' Scalp said in his rough voice.

'It would seem so.' He showed his teeth in a feral smile. 'I hope that bitch suffers to the very last.'

The tent was open on one side, and as they stood there with the rotten breeze in their faces, taking in his men and the lake and the island city that floated upon it, Romano felt restored in every way he could be, his doubts scattering like so much chatter. How strange life could be at times. At home in Q'os, he hardly stood a chance of usurping the Matriarch. Now here he was, in Khos of all places, at the very point where the throne was to be lost.

'What of the Archgeneral?' Scalp asked by his side.

'Sparus is no fool. He will be looking out for himself now. Once she's dead, I'll demand his loyalty and that of the Expeditionary Force. With the army mine, I can take Bar-Khos. No one will be able to dispute my claim as Holy Patriarch then.'

'If we wait much longer we might lose our chance at taking the city.'

'*Tsk!*' exclaimed Romano. 'Don't bring me down just yet. Let me cherish this a while.'

'Still,' said Scalp. 'We must be swift.'

'It can't be helped, I tell you. We play a larger game here, even if your narrow mind can't grasp it.'

Romano, Holy Patriarch of Mann, he tried in his mind for size.

'We could at least start making some preparations.'

Romano sighed. He wanted to be rid of the man now, so he could celebrate the news properly with his entourage.

'Very well. Approach the captains and other lower officers. Offer them promotions if they side with us. Anyone who refuses an immediate answer, mark for the purging.'

CHAPTER THIRTY-SEVEN

Parting Ways

They slept off their hangovers for most of the day, waking occasionally to the odd sound of gunfire in the distance. Curl lay on the tiles they had placed over the beams of the attic, with Ché pressed against her back, an arm across her body to keep her warm.

The old farlander remained outside on the roof, perched in the shadows of a chimney stack, watching the citadel and the streets below.

Curl was hungry, and thirsty too since they had run out of water. Venturing outside was beyond her, though. She'd panicked enough when they had heard noises from the rooms below them; a door closing, a rattle of glasses. She hadn't moved, staying silent as a rat in hiding.

Ché fidgeted against her in the fading light that filtered in through the hole in the roof.

'Have you fleas?' she asked him.

'Why?'

'All your scratching.'

He stopped moving. She could feel the ruffle of his breaths against her neck.

'It will be time to leave soon,' he murmured in her ear.

Curl nodded. She had been trying not to think of it. She felt safe here in this hiding space, at least as safe as she could be given her circumstances.

'I'm frightened,' she admitted.

He held her tighter, though it wasn't what she needed just then. Curl needed a stiff snort of dust, and some hard liquor to wash it down with.

'Aren't you afraid?' she asked him, turning her head slightly.

'No.'

How strange, she thought.

'You still haven't told me anything about you. I recall it was me doing most of the talking last night.'

'Amongst other things. And no. I'm not much of a talker.'

'You don't *want* to tell me, is that it?'

A heavy breath. 'It's better this way, trust me.'

Curl rolled onto her back, her hipbone sore after lying against the hard tiles. Through the hole in the roof she saw an evening star glimmer in the darkening sky.

She turned her tired eyes on Ché.

'So, do you still think I'm beautiful?'

'I'm sorry?'

'Yesterday, when you were drunk, you told me so.'

'Well, the important word there would be *drunk*.'

She feigned annoyance, and turned to roll away from him. Felt his hand rest on her shoulder and gently pull her back.

'Curl, if there were a thousand beautiful women standing naked before me, you'd still be the one to catch my eye first.'

'Oh?'

'Oh.'

'So that's all that matters to you, pretty looks and a firm body?'

It was Ché's turn to scowl. His expression softened, though, with the flicker of a smile. 'No,' he said. 'Not with you.'

He seemed to mean it.

A scrape sounded from overhead, and the old farlander's face appeared in the hole. 'Ché,' he said. 'A word with you.'

Curl watched as the young man climbed to his feet and stepped over to speak with Ash. She sat up and dusted herself off. Thought suddenly of a hot bath and a warm meal in her stomach.

The two men were arguing over something in equally hushed tones. Curl waited, staring at a web that hung in the shadows of the beams, a fat spider sitting in the middle of it, fishing the air for flies.

Ché's voice rose louder. 'She might already be dying, you old fool. You'll get yourself killed, and for what?'

'*Because I must*,' hissed the old man.

They were both quiet for a moment, both angry. Ché glanced down at her, and Curl pretended to look elsewhere.

Ché offered the man an outstretched hand. The farlander hesitated, then took it. They shook, and as Ash withdrew his hand Ché grasped his wrist suddenly. 'It's settled, between us?'

The old man studied his face.

'I think, at least, that we are not enemies,' he said.

'Then that shall do,' Ché replied, releasing his grip.

Ash glanced once at Curl, and then swept out into the twilight.

When she stood next to Ché, she saw the farlander walking lightly over the rooftop with his sword in his hand. A pair of imperial soldiers were drinking from a cistern in the street below. As they continued on their way, Ash began to stalk them.

At the end of the roof he stopped, looked down at a street they could not see. Gently, he laid his sword down, then plucked two tiles free, one in each hand.

He held his hands over the edge of the roof, as far apart as he could, then brought them together by an inch, judging something. He whistled down at the street.

Released the two tiles at the same time.

In an instant he was scrabbling down the slope of the roof.

'Ash!' Ché called out to him.

The farlander stopped and looked back. 'What?'

'May you find your peace, old man.'

Ash swung himself off the edge of the roof, and then he was gone.

*

'Who are you?' demanded the old priest an inch way from his face.

It was the thousandth time his interrogator had asked Bahn that question. For the thousandth time, Bahn told him who he was.

'Bahn,' he panted at the floor. 'Bahn Calvone.'

It hurt when he talked, the wound in his cheek inflamed and tender.

'And what is your rank?'

Bahn felt his hair being tugged back so that he faced the old priest. The man's skin was creased with deep wrinkles, though it was scarred too from acne he must have suffered as a youth. 'Lieutenant. Of the Khosian Red Guards.'

'Yes,' soothed the old priest, stroking his face. His vile breath made Bahn want to gag, to turn away. 'But who are you?'

It was hot in the confined space of the tent. A brazier smoked near the far wall, and sweat beaded Bahn's forehead. 'I don't understand,' he sobbed.

The priest smiled and glanced at the Acolytes stationed behind the chair Bahn was strapped to. The Acolyte released his hair so that his head lolled forwards again, and he could see the bare earth of the floor. Through his eyelashes, he watched as the priest turned his back on him, his withered hands reaching out to the small table, across the vials upon it, the folded papers, the blades.

'Are you a traitor?' asked the priest without turning from the table.

Bahn felt a burst of fire in his stomach. He was going to be sick, he thought, right here at his feet.

'Are you a traitor?' repeated the man.

A fist struck the back of his head.

Bahn tried to focus. The sweat was pouring down his face now, mixing with the blood in his mouth. 'No,' he rasped. 'I'm no traitor.'

'Oh? So you would never be a traitor to your people?'

'Of course I wouldn't!'

The priest turned around. In one hand he held a slip of folded paper, and in the other a delicate curved blade. 'Yet all men are traitors.'

He leaned towards Bahn's face, and his thumb opened the folded slip of paper. Bahn drew back, his breath caught in his chest. He watched as the priest pressed his lips together and blew once across the paper. A fine white dust engulfed Bahn's face. In his panic he sucked in a breath and the powder with it, and his mouth instantly went numb.

Colours, dancing on the edges of his vision. White light flickering in the midst of a gathering darkness.

Bahn lolled his head back, his body going slack. Hands steadied him from behind.

'Now,' came the distant voice of the priest. 'Tell me again. Who are you?'

*

Ché looked up at the hole in the roof. It was twilight outside, and the sky was a deepening shade of violet. Thick banks of smoke were rising into it as more of the city burned around them. The air seemed to be growing thicker with the smell of it. It was starting to sting his eyes.

They were out there somewhere, the Diplomats, circling around the area. He could feel their presence as a faint tickling sensation in his pulsegland, a kind of itch that could not be scratched away. It had been that way since the sun had first begun to set, after he'd discovered that he had left the wildwood juice back at the house – though it had grown no stronger since then.

What are they waiting for? Ché found himself wondering.

'Those fires are getting closer,' he announced, and Curl nodded, looking at his hand but not at his eyes. He was playing with her fingers as she sat before him, and she with his.

He watched her with affection. There was something

vulnerable about this girl, behind her wit and her determined manner.

'We should be going,' he said, and tugged her hand.

She looked at him at last, and he could see her steeling herself for the task ahead, the streets that needed to be negotiated if they were to make it to safety. Ché helped her to her feet as she held a hand to her mouth and coughed. The smoke was thickening.

They both stood there looking out, mouths hanging open in wonder.

To the north a few streets away, an entire row of buildings was alight; a line of fire that crackled and sparked and rose higher as it gained purchase on walls and furnishings, spreading through the buildings towards them. To the left it was the same, a street burning; to the right too. He and Curl seemed to be standing at the centre of a gathering inferno.

'I don't understand,' said Curl, twisting her head from side to side.

Ché clambered out of the hole and scrambled on all fours up the slope of the roof. He coughed and covered his mouth as he looked south, his eyes reflecting flames.

'Water,' he called down to Curl. 'We have to reach the nearest water!'

*

It wasn't far, he saw. He could see it through the smoke as they rounded the corner.

'This way,' Ché said from behind the cloth that wrapped his face, and took off towards the walls of the spa, his eyes scanning to left and right. He knew without looking that she was following behind.

They ran through a plaza of long tables and benches, with a lattice of wooden poles over their heads from which hung paper lanterns, each one slightly aglow from the burning structures behind them. Their boots pounded loud against the planking. Ahead, the structure of the public spa stood low against its fiery backdrop, its walls

round, steam pouring from its open top as though it
too was on fire. Ché spotted movement in the street
beyond it, between the sheets of flames that were dying
buildings.

'Hey!' Curl swore as he grabbed her and forced her
down behind one of the tables.

He released her so he could look over the table. Nothing now. No sign of the figure he had just seen. Ché
glanced around and took in the plumes of smoke and
flying sparks getting closer, and tried not to let them
spook him.

'Come on,' he said, and he was up and jogging again,
pistol in his hand now.

From their left came a blast of noise. One of the lanterns disappeared before his eyes.

Ché swore and ran onwards while trying to spot the
source of it. Another blast sounded, and a table flew into
the air just as they were passing. He veered to the right
and cleared the plaza, bursting through a sheet of cloth
hanging in his way. The rear of the spa loomed right in
front of them; before it, squat huts belching steam.

'I think someone's shooting at us!' Curl exclaimed as
he guided her through he door of one of the huts, into
its clammy darkness. He slammed the flimsy door shut
behind them, and a fist-sized hole appeared in the wall
at the level of their heads.

Ché was on the ground in an instant. 'Get your head
down!' he hollered, pulling Curl to the floor. In the next
moment the hut erupted with the violence of a storm.
Chips of wood spat across the darkened space as portions of the walls imploded.

'*Do something!*' she screamed at him from her foetal
position on the floor.

'I'm doing it!' he yelled back from beneath the cover
of his own arms.

He felt shards of flying wood stabbing into his flesh.
His body had taken over, trying to preserve itself at the
expense of its arms and legs.

The violence diminished for a moment. Voices shouted outside.

Ché slithered across to one of the holes in the wall and peered outside. A dozen figures were approaching the hut. They were clad in heavy fire-suits, their heads fully covered and their eyes shielded by glass, bending awkwardly to reload heavy weapons that by the size of them could only be hand cannons.

Ché wiped his face clear of sweat. He sniffed the steamy air, foul with sulphur, scented a trace of something else within it, something familiar. He glanced behind him. In the gloom of the hut he could see a basket of laundry at the back of it. His eyes searched the floor in between.

They started to fire again, whoever they were. Curl screamed as Ché slid across to a handle on the floor and heaved open a trapdoor, revealing a square hole in the lakeweed below, a wooden board slanting into it, ribbed for scrubbing clothes. He felt a sting of pain in his ear, another in his back. She shrieked louder.

'Curl!' he shouted.

'What?'

'Are you hurt?'

'What?'

'We're leaving!'

She stared down into the black bubbling water of the lake and cast him a round-eyed glare. 'Are you crazy?'

Ché was already struggling out of his backpack. He slid into the water, warm like a bath.

'Just hold onto me and kick as hard as you can. I think there's a canal to the south of us. It can't be far.'

She was terrified, he saw. It struck him that he should be frightened too.

She plunged into the water and came up sputtering. 'South?' she shouted. 'How can you tell which way is south?'

'I'm guessing,' he told her. 'Are you ready? Deep breath now. Go!'

*

The old priest and caretaker Heelas removed the cloth mask from his mouth and nose and inhaled a deep breath of the Tume night air.

Such a stench, he thought sourly. It reminded him of Q'os in the deep summer, when the reeking Baal's mist would sometimes cover the city, except this was much worse than that.

Still, at least he was away from the inner chamber and Sasheen's sickly scent of death, and out of the depths of the citadel. Heelas had always loathed being in the vicinity of illness as much as he feared the enclosure of spaces. His worst fear had always been the cool tunnels of the Hypermorum, where they laid the dead to rest. His worst nightmare was of being dead himself, and of being interred there for an eternity.

She's dying, he thought once more as he crossed the drawbridge of the citadel and stepped onto the central plaza. *Sasheen is dying.*

He had left the Matriarch in her chamber, alone save for the gruesome presence of Lucian next to the bed. What a couple they made, he had thought as he'd closed the door behind him in relief. It was hard to picture them both as they once had been: two lovers struck by each other's dazzle. For a time they had been inseparable, she and her dashing general from Lagos. Sasheen had even spoken of having children with him, of building a family retreat in Brulé.

His head down, Heelas walked with his hands in his sleeves, ignoring the bows of passing priests, all of them men and women without status.

Heelas stopped by the canal and looked down at the loose rafts of lakeweed and the debris of wood still floating there. He saw a splash, though failed to see the fish that made it, only the soft ghost light in its wake.

The lesser priests would not be bowing their heads to

him after she died, he reflected morosely. He would be lucky if Romano merely had him *chitted*, his nose removed, and cast him out on. Always it went that way when one ruler was supplanted by another. The old inner circle was cleansed to make room for the new. His whole life, everything he had worked towards – gone.

'My pardon,' said a voice as someone bumped against him.

Heelas turned in anger and instantly felt something sharp press through his robe and against his stomach. He was much too long in the tooth to wonder if it was anything but a knife.

An Acolyte's masked face hovered close to his own.

'Where is she?' came a deep voice from behind it.

'Who?' he asked, playing for time.

'Sasheen. Where is she?'

Heelas held up his hands. 'How would I know? I'm only a courier.'

'*Put your hands down!*' hissed the man. 'I see how you strut, priest. Now stop lying to me and answer my question, or I will kill you now, here, where you stand.'

Heelas straightened. *So it comes to this*, he thought. *A knife in the belly and my nose filled with the smell of rotting eggs.*

'You think you can frighten me?' he said. 'I can see your eyes, farlander. You intend to kill me anyway. Do it, then,' and he struck his chest loudly. 'I'm ready.'

A hand lashed out to grip the front of his robe, pinning him there on the spot. The knife popped through the robe and into the skin of his stomach. It stayed there, a finger's width inside him, as he felt warm blood trickle down into his pubic hair, his thighs.

Heelas blanched. The pain was nothing, and then it was everything.

Caretaker Heelas had been through his share of personal Purgings over the years. He knew how to handle pain by now, and so he did, summoning his will and forcing himself to relax into its waves.

'If I shout, I can have a dozen men here within a moment.'

'Then shout.'

Heelas looked about him. Priests and Acolytes came and went across the lantern-lit space. Over by a far wall a firing squad was dispatching some of Tume's Home Guard survivors. More soldiers milled around one of the nearby warehouses, where they were offloading a munitions cart, carrying away boxes of grenades and other explosives. He could call for them, certainly, but he would only be dead all the sooner.

What does it matter. She's dying anyway.

'You can't reach her,' he said, coolly. 'She's in the Sunken Palace. In the heart of the rock.'

'Describe it to me.'

He did so, all the while thinking how strange it was, what the mind and body will do to hold on to its life for even a single precious moment longer.

The flesh is strong, he reflected.

Just as he finished, the man struck him three times in and out, as fast as a snake striking. He walked away even as Heelas folded onto his knees, his hands clutching his torn and bloody stomach.

'Help me,' Heelas gasped, but no one heard him.

It was too late for help; he toppled sideways to the ground.

With his head resting against the boardwalk, he gasped and looked at the specks of grit scattered across it like rocks in a desert.

An ant was working its way through that landscape. He watched it twitch its antenna towards him for a moment as he lay there dying, and then it continued on its way.

*

Ché thought she was dead when he dragged her body out of the canal and laid her down against the lake-weed. Curl sputtered, though, when he pressed hard against her stomach, then rolled onto her side and coughed.

'Are you all right?' he asked her.

She wiped her mouth, taking a moment to find her voice. 'I think so.'

Across the canal the street was a roaring inferno. Curl sat shivering as they watched it, and he held her in his arms until she began to settle.

The itch in his neck was more a constant throb now. He looked about him, at the buildings on this side reflecting the light of the fires, the narrow street choked with the debris of looting.

They're close.

'You need to go now,' he said as he helped Curl shakily to her feet, the water running clear of their clothing.

'What about you?'

'There's something I must finish before I can join you.'

Her forehead furrowed, and she glanced along the empty street.

'You'll be fine,' he told her. 'Just be careful.' Even as he spoke he felt a sudden twist of guilt at letting her go like this.

'Here,' he said as he shoved the pistol into her hand.

'I've never used a gun in my life.'

'And you won't have to now. It's waterlogged. Needs taking apart and oiling again. If you get into any trouble, just point it and use it as a threat. Here, take this too.' He took the belt of ammunition from his waist, and buckled it around her as she watched him. 'You'll look more the part wearing this. Remember, just use it as a threat. Don't try firing it, understand?'

'Of course. I'm not an idiot.'

'Then go,' he told her softly.

Curl stood there, out of her depth and trembling. He drew a finger down her cheek, and when it reached her chin he tilted her head up so that their eyes met.

She grasped the finger and held it before her. 'You look after yourself, Ché, do you hear me?'

He liked the sound of her speaking his name.

'I will.'

Their kiss was a brief one, something awkward about it; two strangers parting ways.

She backed away from him, then walked off into the night.

Ché was alone once more.

*

Guan's sister stared open-mouthed at the firestorm before them, her eyes catching the flames within their gaze. She was swaying slightly, as though to some inner rhythm of music.

A rifle banged somewhere in the distance. An officer broke free from the line of soldiers to investigate.

'Where is he?' asked Guan impatiently, scanning the row of open markets that remained the only section they hadn't set on fire.

'Give it time. Our men will flush him out.'

'If they're not trapped somewhere in there with him. I tell you, we should have seen something by now.'

Guan was starting seriously to doubt this plan of theirs. It was too messy, more of a spectacle than anything practical. Better if they had just gone in alone to deal with Ché. But, as so often happened, he'd allowed his sister to persuade him otherwise.

They were holding hands, as they sometimes did; as they had done since their childhoods. She squeezed as though to reassure him.

Along the street stood a thin line of soldiers, faces wrapped in scarves like their own, all of them staring through the empty markets at the banks of flames and smoke piling into the night sky. In the streets behind, a second ring of soldiers lay hidden and waiting.

'You think he deserves any of this?' he asked his sister.

'And what's deserving got to do with anything?'

'Even so. He's one of our own.'

Cold air against his palm as she released it.

'You voice these concerns now? After he's deserted? After he's shown himself to be the traitor we practically accused him of being?'

Guan knew it was useless to argue with her. Besides, some truths were strong enough to stand on their own.

'You're thinking they'll do the same to us, after all of this is over.'

'Why wouldn't they? We know as much he does.'

'Yes, but by doing this we prove that we can be trusted. This is good for us, Guan, I can sense it. They need the likes of us for their dirty work. Whoever they are.'

'Let us hope that you're right.'

It was hard to see far with the grey haze filling the air. Something raced from the stalls with a carpet of flames on its back. The nearest soldiers levelled their crossbows and fired.

It was a dog on fire, yelping and biting at the flames as it ran. It convulsed as the bolts struck it and rolled to the ground dead.

Swan swore under her breath. Sourly, she said, 'These people. They just leave their dogs behind them to die.'

Not for the first time, Guan looked to his sister with something approaching wonder at how her mind worked. Twins they might be, sometimes able to finish each other's sentences, or read each other's thoughts, yet some kink was in her that he did not seem to share.

He was about to remind her gently that she should have no problem with burning dogs if she had no problem burning people, when his neck throbbed once, and then again more powerfully.

Guan clutched a finger to his neck as Swan did likewise.

'Get ready,' he told the soldiers in front of them. 'He's coming out.'

They aimed their crossbows while his sister drew her

pistol. Minutes passed as smoke tumbled out from between the stalls. The pulse grew ever faster in his neck.

Still there was no sign of anything. The crossbows began to sway in the men's hands.

'He should be close enough to see by now,' Swan said, raising her gun towards the markets.

Guan remained still. There was something wrong about this. Ché should be almost on top of them now.

'You don't think—'

He spun around, and his sister did the same a moment later. They both looked along the street in both directions, at the houses that lined the opposite side and their darkened windows.

Guan drew his own pistol, stepping to one side as he did so.

'Swan,' he said, and together they retreated into the shadow of a wall as deeply as they could.

—CHAPTER THIRTY-EIGHT—

The Art of Cali

They would never stop hunting him, Ché knew. Not unless he dealt with them first. And so he stalked them from the rooftops, closing in on their position even as they withdrew along the shadows of a wall.

They had alerted the soldiers to his presence, so that the men scanned about them and pointed their weapons one way and then the other. Ché stayed low, on the dark side of the sloping roofs, making sure not to skyline as he went. More soldiers were to the left of him, lurking in houses and garden plots; he saw the odd glint of steel, heard a cough. He could only hope that none of them spotted him.

Swan and Guan were retreating towards a temple at the end of the street, the lake visible just beyond it.

Clearly, they didn't like the prospect of being targets for sniper fire.

It was a shame he had no working gun.

The temple rose up at the end of the row of rooftops. A two-storey living annex lay dark and silent next to it. The twins stopped to speak with a squad of soldiers, and the men spread out along the houses. Ché heard doors being kicked in beneath him, rough searches of the rooms.

He squatted down and watched the two Diplomats look back to scan the street, the windows, the rooftops, and then step inside the temple. They left the door open.

He hung from the edge of the roof and dropped down into the alley between the houses and the temple. A glance in both directions, and then he was skirting around the back of the building, where the annex spread out into a small garden, using a low wall for cover. A window flickered in the structure; a candle brightening inside.

He padded over to the far end of the annex with the lakeweed soft and slippery beneath his feet, leaving the noise of the soldiers behind him. The gunfire to the south had risen in pitch since he'd last paid any attention to it. Curl would be there somewhere now, or so he hoped, making her way to the rendezvous.

How strange, he thought. Being here in Khos, in Tume, on this simmering lake, trying to kill a pair of my own people; hoping, too, that one of the enemy makes it out in one piece.

He noticed how the word felt wrong to him now: *enemy*. Something childish to it.

Over the lake another flare went up. He closed his right eye to preserve his night vision and waited until the flare had fallen. There was a window up there, and a tree leaning towards it.

In the gathering darkness, Ché took his knife out and clamped it between his teeth, then climbed up the rough bark of the tree until he dangled from a branch facing the window. He saw nothing but a dark room and an open door; a corridor beyond it bleeding soft light from where it turned a corner.

There was no time for subtleties, Ché decided. Take them out hard and fast, and hope he was the last one standing. His old sparring trainer in Q'os had been right, he reflected, as he reached out to open the window. The Rōshun training of cali was in him whether he wanted it or not. Advance and attack was its creed. Boldness and speed and recklessness.

If only he had a sword with him, never mind a working gun. All he had was his single knife.

Improvise, Ché thought, and he swung in through the open window and landed with the ease of a cat.

He clasped the knife in his hand, saw a chair. He picked it up and swung it hard against the wall. The crash was loud enough to stir the dead.

Quickly, Ché stepped through the scattered debris of the chair and snatched up a chair leg without stopping. The end of the leg had snapped off sharp and jagged. He improved the point with a swipe of his blade as he entered the hallway; shaved another slice off as he strode towards the corner.

They were waiting for him as he ducked his head around it, two figures with pistols aimed from the cover of opposite doorways.

Ché ducked back as a bullet ricocheted off the wall. He cut a final slice from the chair leg to finish its point, then stepped partly out and launched it with all his strength at the figure still aiming its gun at him.

The gun ignited and a sudden pain punched into his thigh. Ché tottered on his other leg, slumped against the wall for balance as the figure toppled out into the corridor. It was Guan, with the chair leg poking from his left cheek. His feet were scrabbling against the floor for purchase.

He saw a shadow flicker across the fan of light on the floor, and he tossed his knife into his right hand.

He launched it even as Swan came out of the doorway again and fired her pistol.

Ché fell backwards with his head ringing and a pain searing along the side of his skull. Swan was down too, holding the hilt of the knife sunk deep into her hip. The woman was crawling to her brother.

'Oh no,' she was gasping.

Since Ché was still breathing, he ignored the scalp wound and clutched his leg instead to probe it with his trembling fingers. The bullet had passed cleanly through the flesh on the side of his thigh. It had missed the bone, and blood flowed slickly from the ragged hole. He could barely move the numbed limb itself.

It was the first time Ché had ever been shot. He'd been expecting it to be much more of an agony.

He tugged at the sleeve of his tunic until it tore free, and used it to tie a tourniquet at the top of his thigh. He tried to stand. Ché hissed with the sudden shooting pain of it. Tried to see through the rising waves of nausea.

The Diplomat Swan was dragging her brother back into the room she'd emerged from. She paused as she strained to reach the empty gun lying on the floor. Ché managed a single step towards them, and Swan gave up on the gun and pulled Guan inside.

Ché stopped short, sucking air for a moment as Swan kicked the door closed behind her.

With grim determination he staggered to the door and tried to bend down to retrieve his bloody knife lying there. His head spun as warm blood dribbled down his face. His boot was filling up too. He tore off his other sleeve and used it to tie a wad of cloth against the wound itself, cinching it tight. For a moment he thought he might pass out.

'Come out!' he hollered, the knife heavy in his grip.

Grunts and muttering from within.

Ché steadied himself. Pushed a sticky hand against the door to swing it open.

The room was deserted, though a candle sputtered on

the mantelpiece above a hearth. Ché leaned further out. Another door lay open in the room. A trail of blood shone across the floor and through it. He limped inside and pressed his back to the wall, then slid around it towards the other doorway. A quick glance inside revealed a bedroom. Guan lay dead on the floor, his legs and arms spread-eagled. The stick of wood stood tall and unnatural from his face.

A creak behind him.

Ché was quick enough to get a hand up to the garrotte as it slipped around his throat. It bit deep into the edge of his palm, and he pushed back as hard as he could, hopping on his good leg as he shoved Swan backwards across the room. Swan crashed into something, a heavy wardrobe that clattered with hangers and open doors while they both struggled in its wooden embrace.

The woman's hot breaths hissed next to his ear, charged with fury.

Ché tossed the knife once to turn it around in his grasp, then struck it into the Diplomat's side. Once, twice, until Swan shifted and threw him sideways. Ché fell, and together they crashed through a table.

Swan managed to grip his knife hand as they rolled across the floor. With her other hand she maintained the pressure of the garrotte. The wire dug into his hand and the sides of his neck, blood spilling everywhere. '*Is this what you want?*' Swan hissed in her hatred for him. '*Is this what you wanted, you kush?*'

Ché's hand was a lifeless thing shoved between his ragged breathing and the garrotte's worsening constrictions. He could barely see, barely breathe.

He reached his free hand back, felt his fingers press against her face. He hooked his thumb and scooped it viciously into her eye. The woman's grip loosened a fraction.

Ché roared and pushed against the white-hot pain from his hand as he forced the garrotte off him.

He staggered to his feet as Swan did likewise, grasping a spilled chair for support and then the mantelpiece above the hearth. He turned just as she lashed out with the garrotte. The end of it wrapped around the hilt of his knife and she jerked it from his grasp. It was hard to stand now. Swan was doing little better. Her eye was a black mess running with blood.

A blow struck his cheek, stunning him. Ché shook it off as he blocked another punch, then another. He came out of his stance seeking a target, only to find her straightening with the knife in her hand.

Back he staggered, hopping again on his good leg as she dragged her own wounded limb across the floor after him. The knife was poised in her hand. It was a sliver of steel shining in the candlelight just beyond the range of his stomach. He shook his head to clear his dulling vision. Sweat scattered off him.

Ché backed through the door of the bedroom with Swan slowly closing the distance. She lunged at him suddenly. He was only just quick enough to sweep the blade aside. His foot caught against the prone body of Guan and he tripped backwards, shoving Swan to the side as he fell.

Gasping, he pushed himself off the floor again as Swan did the same. He managed to get a knee under his weight, then flailed his good hand around until it grasped the bed. Up, onto his feet, grunting and straining from the effort, seeing Guan's body lying there. His balance lurched around a spinning point. His vision receded until he teetered in the darkness of his own head. He bore down on it, applying focus, seeing a crack of light appear like a doorway.

He came through it, and saw Swan coming at him with the knife.

A desperate sidestep, a slippery grip of an arm and a foot outthrust to trip her. They fell hollering towards the floor with Ché riding her down with all his weight.

The stick of wood shot through the back of the woman's neck with a crunch of teeth and bone. She quivered once, as though in a delayed shock, then lay there perfectly still.

A soft whine of air escaped her lungs as her body deflated.

Ché gasped for a breath and rolled himself clear. He lay for some moments with his remaining energy flooding out of him, his mind beyond thought or reason.

He had the shakes when he finally regained his feet. He looked down at the two dead Diplomats. Swan was sprawled with her face pressed against her brother's, their bodies extended in opposite directions. They looked as though they were two lovers kissing.

'*Here I am!*' Ché spat at them with a hard slap to his chest.

*

In the shadows by the side of a minor canal, Ash finished his preparations and listened to the sounds of revelry in the distance. He observed the tall mansions on the opposite side of the canal, where priests walked past lit windows in suites they had made their own. Above the rooftops of the fine buildings, the rock of the citadel rose into the night air. Sasheen's flag was still flying up there.

A window opened, and a woman threw the contents of a chamber pot out into the water. Someone was singing in the room behind her. Ash maintained his stillness, confident that he was hidden by the shadows, until she withdrew again and closed the window, cutting the song off in mid-chorus.

Quickly, he removed his clothes and placed them in a neat pile beside his weaponry. Next to them sat a small wooden keg filled with blackpowder; a mine he'd appropriated from a Mannian munitions cart.

Goosebumps rose on Ash's skin from the caress of

cold air, and he rubbed his arms and legs to generate some warmth. His breath was visible in the shimmer of lantern light cast across the black surface of the canal.

The lakeweed had been shorn here to create the vertical sides of the waterway. Beams of wood shored them up further. He sat on the boardwalk at its edge then gently eased himself into the lukewarm water. It felt good against the tensions of his muscles, the abrasions on his skin, so he simply rested there for a while, near delirious with the relief of it. Beneath his feet, down in the depths of the clear water, he could see the distant glimmer of lights. He kicked to stay afloat, watching the brilliance of them between his toes.

When he felt ready, he rose up and grabbed the mine and pulled it into the water with a splash. He shook his face clear and checked the line of fuse that hung from a tarred hole in the bobbing keg; it floated out across the surface and up to the boardwalk above him, where it was tied around his Acolyte body armour, and then to a heavy portable reel fixed to the boardwalk by a knife-blade, where the rest of the fuse line was tightly coiled.

He pulled on the line of fuse until the armour toppled into the water with another noisy splash. It sank instantly, and a moment later pulled the mine down with it. Ash looped a portion of the fuse around his wrist while he breathed hard and fast. He felt the tug of the line against his hand, and dived beneath the surface, letting himself be pulled into the silent depths while the reel of fuse played out above him.

His eyes stung, and he blinked and forced them to stay open. His chest tightened as he dived deeper, drawing nearer to the rock all the time. The lights were bleeding from windows of thick glass far below, carved from the steep flanks of the rock the citadel stood upon. Ash kicked towards them as he dropped, pulling the line with him even as it pulled him. He knew he had one good chance at this.

He scattered a shoal of fish from his path, and then at

last he felt the weight slacken in his hand as the armour settled on the ledge of one of the windows. The mine slowly spun next to the glass. Ash uncoiled the line from his wrist and swam down. He chanced a look inside, saw a brilliantly lit chamber of couches and chandeliers; a priest talking to another; a pair of Acolytes next to a doorway.

Ash struggled to drag the armour to one side and the mine with it, so it would be less likely to be spotted.

His chest was bursting now. He kicked off for the surface, stars flashing in the edges of his vision. It took longer than the descent. He recalled his panic on the sinking ship; the weight of the world's water pressing him down.

Ash floundered when he resurfaced, gasping with lungs that still did not seem to be working too well. The noise of the city returned to his draining ears, and he looked about and was grateful to find the side street still deserted.

In vain he tried to pull himself out of the canal, found he couldn't manage it, couldn't breathe hard enough to restore his energy.

He settled himself in the water. Calmed his breathing and tried once more. Ash rolled onto the boardwalk wheezing for air. He sat up, rested his arms against his knees and let his head hang between them. He stared at the little pools forming where the lake water dripped from his skin.

A man cursed not far away. Shapes at the dark end of the street, someone relieving himself while others waited, talking drunkenly.

Ash looked at the line of fuse hanging in the water. All he needed to do was slice through it and toss it in the water and run.

The knife suddenly drew his attention, standing as it was with its tip buried in the boardwalk. Its blade was stained dark with the blood of the priest he had murdered the previous hour.

How many had he killed now in his pursuit of retribution? he wondered with a start.

He couldn't recall; had lost count somewhere along the way; had made them something less than human, faceless, without worth. The two camp followers he had felled during the battle – simply to be clear of them – were nothing but vague impressions now, save for the crisp sound of a kneecap breaking.

Ash had come so far. In his revenge he had climbed a high pinnacle into rarefied sky, forsaking the Rōshun order as he did so, the only home left to him, the only way of life where his anger had remained leashed by their code and by the better part of himself.

He felt as though all this time he'd been climbing upwards without a single glance behind him; and now, turning back to look, all he could see were corpses heaped along the steep track he'd been following; and past them all, Nico with his boyish laughter and a mother's fierce love for him, and far beyond his apprentice, way down at the dim beginnings of the trail, his son Lin, throat-singing with the other battlesquires, and close by a whitewashed homestead struck by sunlight, his wife waiting for a husband and son who would never return.

The summit was almost within his reach. All he had to do was cut the fuse.

Sasheen deserved to die. All of her kind deserved to die.

With trembling fingers, Ash reached for the knife and plucked it free.

*

When Sasheen woke, the first thing that she saw was Lucian staring at her intently, and for the briefest of moments she thought they were lovers again, wrapped in each other's arms.

But then she saw that he was only a severed head perched on the bedside table. She remembered how he had betrayed her, and her heart sank into bleakness.

'I never wanted this, you know,' she told him now.

His lips parted, spilling a dribble of Royal Milk down his chin. But he said nothing, only watched her.

'I never even wanted to be Matriarch. It was my mother's desire, not my own.'

'*I. Know,*' came his wet belching voice, and he glared with hatred in his eyes.

How to make him understand? The pain he had caused her, the loss of faith in the one person she'd thought she could finally trust. Sasheen had wanted this man like she had wanted no other, and he had cast her aside for the sake of his foolish insurgency and the fame that went with it.

'I'm dying, Lucian,' she told him.

He seemed pleased at that, for he smiled.

Even now he could hurt her.

'Do you remember the time we spent together in Brulé?'

'*No.*'

'Of course you do. You hardly stopped talking about it. You said we should retire there. Grow olives, like simple peasants.'

'*I. Was. A. Fool.*'

'You were anything but a fool, Lucian. That was one of the things I was attracted to, most of all.' Wistfully, she said, 'We were a good match, you and I.'

Sasheen could see it now, her life as it might have been, had she only found the courage to spite her mother's wishes, to renounce her position as Matriarch, to live a simple life of luxury with her lover. What had it gained her, any of this? Only a lonely death in the damp innards of a rock; a few scratches in the memory of Mann.

'I only wish . . . I only wish . . .' and she closed her eyes, and felt a wetness on her cheeks, and an ache in her chest as if the whole awful world was standing upon it.

She fought for a breath, wheezing hard until sweat beaded her skin. She gasped, blinked to focus on Lucian again. Beyond him, through the glass of the window, the waters of the lake were a black nothingness waiting to engulf her.

'What do I do?' she panted, lost in herself. 'I don't know what to do.'

His stare possessed all the force of a thrust knife.

'*You. Die.*'

*

A sudden flare lit the night sky over Ash's head. Of their own volition his eyes were drawn to the brightly lit ground.

Ash saw, stretching out from the base of his feet, how he ended in shadow.

He faltered.

For long heartbeats, he stared down at the knife and the fuse wire held in his shaking hands. *A strange fellow*, came the words in his head. Nico had said that once, about the Rōshun Seer.

Why did that come to his mind now?

The Seer had cast the sticks for them before they had set forth on vendetta to Q'os. He had told of a great shock in store for him, and of the paths that would face him beyond it.

After shock, you will have two paths facing you. On one path, you will fail in your task, though with no blame and much still to do . . . On the other, you will win through in the end with great blame, and nothing that would further you.

Great blame, Ash reflected. *Nothing that would further you.*

He blinked. Tears stung his eyes. His hand dropped to his side, and the knife clattered to the ground.

The flare faded, taking his shadow with it.

CHAPTER THIRTY-NINE

Rendezvous

Curl stood on the rooftop of the warehouse while men scrambled up the rope-ladders onto the waiting skyship. The vessel was badly damaged, its hull scorched by fire and its rigging in tatters. Another ship was already climbing into the air in a sluggish lift-off, turning in a long curve towards the south with its deck crammed with soldiers.

It was the second run the ships had made since she had arrived there. Greyjackets and archers manned the edges of the roof, firing down at the imperial forces moving in on their position. More enemy forces were converging along the marina. It was clear it would be the last trip out before the building was overrun.

'Who are you waiting for?' asked a passing Volunteer, a man so haggard in appearance he could have been twenty years old or forty.

'A friend!' she shouted over the noise of the gunfire.

'Girl, we have to go now – there isn't time to wait.' And he tried to pull her towards the ship.

'Let go of me!' she yelled in his face, breaking free from his grip. He looked startled for a moment, but then he gave up and ran for the ship.

Curl scanned the skies and could still see no sign of enemy skyships. She took a few steps closer to the edge, to look down at the surrounding streets and the marina, at the Imperials closing in. Some Khosian troops were still filtering towards the warehouse, many sprinting for it, others in squads performing fighting retreats.

Where are you, you idiot?

Curl didn't know what to make of this man whom she had only just met, yet he seemed to pluck all the right strings within her. Certainly their lovemaking had been memorable in the long hours they had shared together, free-spirited and playful when not intensely passionate. Beyond that, though, who was he?

He was a mystery, and a dangerous one at that, she sensed.

Curl was well aware of how she'd fallen twice already for such men in her life. She was beginning to suspect that it was a trait not entirely good for her, for in hindsight they had both been selfish bastards.

Yet this was war, and she found that it was true what the soldiers said. War created exceptional circumstances. You felt a responsibility to live recklessly and fully, only too aware that you might never see another sunrise.

As though proof of this, her heart suddenly leapt when she glimpsed his face on the edge of the roof. Ché was being helped along by a female Volunteer.

'Ché!' she yelled as she ran to meet him. He was drenched in blood, and barely conscious. 'Ché?' He lifted his head and tried to focus on her.

Get me out of here, his expression said.

Curl threw his free arm over her shoulder and helped the Volunteer drag him towards the ship.

One of the small scuds took off from the roof. Another fired its tubes, manoeuvring into the empty position. Men backed away to give it room.

'Any sign of the old farlander?' he croaked.

Curl shook her head. 'He'd better hurry, wherever he is, if he wants to get off this island.'

The young man wheezed as though in laughter. 'That old bastard? He'll have a way out of this. He's likely gone already.'

*

Ash charged the war-zel straight towards the front door of the house, slapping its rump hard with his sheathed sword.

He ducked low in the saddle as it burst through the door and clattered along the wooden floorboards of a hallway, hearing the shouts of pursuit behind him even as his mount bore him out through an open door at the back.

The animal snorted and took three great surges across an open yard. Ash kicked hard to urge it on, and it vaulted a fence with a leap and landed on the other side. The zel stumbled once, recovered its footing, then skirted a deserted plaza as crossbow bolts whined through the air from behind them.

Ash glanced back. Saw men pouring over the fence and riders emerging from the side streets around it.

The gunfire was closer now. He wasn't far.

The animal's flanks were bright with lather, its breath rasping in its throat. It felt good to be riding like this again, with the wind in his eyes and a recklessness in his blood like a reminiscence of youth.

'Come on!' he encouraged as the zel skipped over a mound of scattered baskets, took a street on the other side of the plaza with its hooves thundering along the boardwalk. He could see the marina at the end of the street now, its long quays supporting wooden poles with lit lanterns, entirely deserted of boats.

A cannon boomed, the sound of it rumbling along the street.

They emerged from the street right into a squad of imperial infantry. The zel burst through them without slowing. Ash spotted a warehouse to the right along the waterfront, with a skyship hovering over its broad roof lit by flashes of gunfire.

Men were sprinting over the roof towards the ship, climbing rope-ladders dangling from its hull. It looked familiar to him, that vessel. He squinted and saw the wooden figurehead on its prow. It was a falcon in flight.

I don't believe it.

He yanked the reins and aimed for the building as he kicked for speed. With the zel racing beneath him, he glanced at a scud to their left circling the marina, firing rounds of grape-shot. A smatter of plumes rose up from the nearby water, splashing down on the boardwalk as they charged along it. Ash shook his head dry and looked for a way onto the roof. He spotted a stairwell on the side of it, a few men still clambering upwards. He wondered if Ché and the girl had made it.

Suddenly the zel screamed and pitched forwards.

Ash spilled from the saddle and rolled on the hard boardwalk with his sword still in his grasp. He leapt to his feet and looked back at the animal as it reared on its side. Blood ran from a wound in its flank. He saw the Imperials racing towards him.

Ash turned and sprinted for his life.

*

The skyship was starting to move under its tremendous load of rescued men, the propulsion tubes burning ever louder along its hull. Below it, the warehouse roof was in the final stages of being overrun. Some Khosians hadn't made it. They were making their last stands back to back.

Men still dangled from the rope-ladders of the rising ship. One fell off, landing amongst a group of Imperials, who stabbed and hacked at him in a frenzy. Soldiers shouted down at their comrades who clung desperately to the ropes with their legs kicking air, reaching their hands out to them.

Ché sat with his back to the starboard rail while a medico tended to his leg. Curl crouched next to him, not seeming to mind the odd bolt or shot that clattered against the hull. The girl had her arm around him. Her touch felt good to him; warm and vivid. He did not want to look at the rooftop below.

'*Look!*' Curl suddenly shouted, pointing down to the warehouse roof.

He turned his head to see what she was pointing at.

It was Ash, stopping short as the ship nosed away.

'*Trench!*' the old man bellowed.

Ché struggled to his feet. He pushed away the medico as the man cursed and tried to hold him down.

'We can't just leave him,' Ché snapped frantically, and looked around for someone to shout at, to tell them to turn back. But he could barely see beyond the heads of the men pressing around him, and he knew in his sinking heart that it was useless.

In impotence, he turned back to watch.

They were high enough now for the entire warehouse roof to be framed in his vision. The streets around it were alive with Acolytes and soldiers, the rooftop itself an island awash with them.

In their midst, the lone farlander's black skin was a stark contrast to their white robes.

Ché saw the old man's blade glitter silver in the darkness, the Rōshun stepping into the spaces he was cutting through their masses.

'Merciful Mother,' Curl said, and she gripped the wooden pendant around her neck.

Ché barely heard her over the roar of the tubes. The ship banked sharply towards the far shore, and the lone figure of Ash grew smaller in size, a dot that vanished amongst them.

*

Ash's instincts took over. For a time his attention was focused so intensely on what he did that no part of him was aware of his own self in the midst of the carnage. He knew no fear, nor conscience, nor even spite, as he moved freely without distinctions of mind and body and blade in a performance of one, weaving their patterns as he ducked and darted and killed in a gradual movement towards the very edge of the rooftop.

Around him his opponents fell shooting blood – without feet, hands, arms. They fell without heads. They fell with their stomachs unravelling into their cupped palms. They fell in silence as though asleep. They fell in shouted protest.

They did not stop falling.

'Back!' Ash snarled as he spun from the edge of the roof, his feet tottering dangerously over the side.

'Back!' he spat again with a shake of his blade, gore sheeting off it.

They listened, at least enough to hesitate, to pull up short. Ash gulped down air as men joined them with crossbows, a few pistols. He wiped the blood from his face, spat it from his mouth. Every part of him drenched in it.

They panted and eyed the crimson-soaked vision with something approaching awe.

A soldier pushed quickly to the front, an officer by the tattoos on his face. 'Who are you?' the man enquired.

He sounded genuinely curious.

Ash took in the ragged assembly around him, the crossbows and guns aimed at his body. They looked scared, most of them. Scared and tired.

'Drop your weapon,' ordered the officer. 'Do it now, or die.'

Ash thought it over for a moment, then straightened from his fighting stance and lowered his sword. A flight of geese were crying somewhere in the night sky. He looked up, but couldn't see them for all the clouds. He felt the breeze run across his face like a breath from the World Mother. His expression softened.

'You should know,' he said, looking up at the officer as he sheathed his sword. 'That I would take my own life first.' And with the guns and crossbows aimed squarely at his chest, he did the only thing left to do.

Ash jumped.

CHAPTER FORTY

Lonely Ends

It was the water that saved him, not only in breaking his fall but in helping him escape.

Flush with the success of his supreme dive from the warehouse roof, Ash swam beneath the surface until his lungs were burning from lack of air. When he resurfaced the Imperials took some pot shots at him, but he ignored them, and submerged again, kicking hard.

He swam in that way until he was clear of the marina, and continued to swim along the littoral of lakeweed until the sights and sounds of their searching faded away behind him. It grew darker as the clouds massed even thicker overhead. For a time he lay on his back and floated there as the sickness of exhaustion slowly diminished.

Out over the lake the flares continued to rise and fall. It would be risky, trying for the far shore; snipers were no doubt watching the surface for signs of escaping Khosians.

What are you worried about? he asked himself. *In your condition you'll most likely drown first.*

Ash trod water and breathed calm breaths until he felt ready. He looked back at the island city. He looked at the far southern shore.

The old farlander began to swim for it.

*

It was raining now, and the fat drops were bursting against the surface all around him, the chorus of it deafening his ears to all else. The water seemed aglow wherever the drops collided with it.

Ash spat and chanced a look ahead. His last strokes had brought him past the dark mouth of the Chilos while the current had tried to sweep him into it. He could see fires on both sides of the river mouth, and lanterns strung along its banks, throwing their light across it. Men hunkered down next to upright rifles, gazing out at the passing flow.

He kicked and swam on, long past the limits of his endurance. Only his will kept him going now.

The shore here was a flat and treeless floodplain. Ash squinted through the falling rain, saw a glimmer of flames surrounded by the glowing canvas of a tent. Other tents too were clustered across the floodplain. Riders ambled back and forth in the darkness, huddled in their cloaks as they watched the water's edge.

His limbs were starting to cramp badly now. He could hardly breathe for the fire in his lungs. Ash knew he was going to drown if he stayed in the water any longer. He turned for the shore, paddling like a dog now, his body numb and almost useless. The fall of rain masked any sounds that he made. He felt mud beneath his hands and he scrabbled at it desperately, relief flooding him for a moment. On all fours he crawled out of the water onto a beach of silty mud, and lay for a long time catching his breath.

When he at last rose to his knees he looked left and right along the shore. He was facing a vertical bank of earth topped with straggly grasses, and the beach of mud ran up into deep runnels carved through the bank, water running out of them.

He heard something jingle in the darkness, and lay flat against the mud as he stifled a cough.

A soldier stood on the bank staring outwards. Ash pressed himself deeper into the mud, waited until the man turned away and disappeared in the darkness, calling out to someone beyond.

Quickly, Ash scrabbled up to one of the runnels in the bank. He looked into it, seeing nothing but blackness. Felt the chill of the water running out over his hands.

As he began to slither along the chute, mud splashed into his mouth and his nostrils and his eyes. It covered him and it filled him, until he became one with it, a creature of dirt, a thing still living, still fighting, because it did not know any other way.

*

She was dying, and the reek of her poisoned body was enough to make the eyes water.

Even with his mask on, it filled Sparus's mouth with saliva and made him want to spit. He looked down at the panting form of Sasheen, her swollen features, her blue lips. He looked at the head of Lucian sitting silently on the table, and its jar now empty of Royal Milk.

'Matriarch,' he said, quietly.

Sasheen stirred, fluttered her eyes open. A wheeze escaped her parted lips. He waited a few moments for her to focus on him.

'We have trouble,' he told her plainly.

'Romano,' Sasheen replied with a sigh.

'He's making his move. His people have been approaching the lower officers of the army with offers of promotion if they will support his claim for Patriarch.'

Her eyes blazed with sudden anger. 'I'm not even dead yet.'

Nor was Anslan, he recalled, *when you slit the Patriarch's throat in his bedchamber.*

She fluttered her hand, beckoning him closer. Her anger was robbing the breath from her, and she spoke in a whisper.

'And you, Sparus. Has he approached you yet?'

The Archgeneral faltered, taken aback by her bluntness. He supposed she had little time now for subtleties.

'Yes,' he confessed, his head low. 'He has asked for my support.'

Sasheen glanced at the head of Lucian. His eyes were closed, but Sparus had the sense that the man was listening to everything they said.

'He sees his chance,' added Sparus. 'You have not yet named a successor.'

'I care not . . . who takes my place in this. Only that it should never be Romano, or one of his clan.'

'Holy Matriarch,' tried Sparus, and he used her title quite intentionally. 'If we contest his claim it will divide the Expeditionary Force in two. We will be stalled here in Tume fighting amongst ourselves. For the sake of the campaign, we must have this settled now.'

'You forget yourself, Sparus. There is more at stake here than this venture in Khos. Listen to me. Kill Romano if you can, but do not concede to him.'

'He would be dead already if it was possible. Our Diplomats are still missing though.'

'Sparus!' she spat, and her hand lunged out to clutch his wrist. He felt the burning heat of her touch through his mitten. 'You will not give him this army. I command this of you. You have been loyal to my family. We have been friends, have we not? Did I not raise you to the position of Archgeneral? Now do this one last thing for me.'

Civil war, thought Sparus with sudden dread. It had been fifteen years since the last real conflict within Mann. He'd lost his father in it, and his brother. They had both died at his own hands.

Now she wished to plunge them into another one.

What she said, though, struck a chord with him. She *had* promoted him to Archgeneral, and her family had aided his career even long before. And in return, all they had ever asked of him was his loyalty. For a fighting general, it was the most important thing for him to have pledged.

Sparus gave a solemn bow of his head. 'As you wish,' he whispered, and she released her grip of him, and settled back into the pillows as though her work was done.

*

Sasheen knew she was near the end now. Her eyes were no longer working as they should be. All was a watery motion of lantern light and shadows unless she blinked and made a conscious effort to focus. Her lungs struggled over every shallow breath that she achieved. She could smell her own flesh rotting off her bones. Not long, she thought.

'*My son,*' croaked a voice, and then she realized that it was her own. Sasheen could see him now, young Kirkus. He was pouting at her, sore at having to have his head shaved every morning by his retainers. *But then I couldn't do this*, she told him, and kissed him on his gleaming head. He flinched and feigned annoyance. 'My son,' she said again.

Her breathing stopped for a moment. Sasheen hung there in paralysis, drifting, and then her lungs took in another trickle of air. For a spell her eyes cleared, and she saw around her the bedchamber of the Sunken Palace, and that she was alone.

They have all abandoned me in my weakness, she thought to herself. *Already scheming for their place in the new order.*

Only the head of Lucian remained now. He watched her in silence, his gaze full of rapture.

Sasheen tried to speak. Had to cough and force the words from her mouth, much like Lucian.

'We die together, then.'

The room was darkening. She floundered for a moment in her mind.

'Rest well, Lucian,' she whispered. 'I have missed you.'

Lucian said nothing. In the warm light of the crystal lanterns, his eyes suddenly glistened.

CHAPTER FORTY-ONE

Lines in the Dirt

The bronze bells of the temples were marking the turning of the hour as Creed splashed a handful of the Chilos over his aching frame. He listened to the droplets falling back into the sluggish flow, then pinched his nose and ducked beneath the surface, out of sight.

Dong ... Dong ... Dong he heard as he came up again with a gasp.

The general stood in one of the stone bathing areas built along the western bank of the river, where the temples rose above the waterline. Downstream were the fort and permanent camp of the Hoo, several times larger now that the army had returned from Tume, along with the many refugees who had fled here. People were washing themselves all along the twin banks of the river, though Creed was alone here, at his own request. He needed some time to himself today.

He felt better than he had during the night, when he'd found it hard to breathe for a while, and had become light-headed and nauseous. It had been bad enough that those around him had noticed the discomfort he was in. The medicos had been called for, and they had listened to his heart and taken his pulse, concerned at what they heard and felt.

Rest, they had told him as sternly as they dared. *You must rest and regain your strength. You have pushed yourself too hard.*

If only he had could afford the time for some rest, Creed thought. He had a defence to organize before the Mannians began to move again. Too late to save Tume, the reserves from Al-Khos had dug in to the north of Simmer Lake at the head of the Suck, hoping to hold off any raids beyond their lines. The main imperial force, though, would be heading south towards Bar-Khos. They would wish to avoid the physical barrier of the Wind-rush, which meant they would be coming here, to Juno's Ferry. And it would be soon.

Meanwhile, the defences of the Shield would have to be reinforced with what men he could spare.

And then, there was still the matter of the Michinè to deal with.

Creed felt his hackles rise at the mere thought of the painted noblemen. They had caused him the loss of Tume in their quibbling, the loss of men. At least, the Principari of Al-Khos had, and no doubt his brother too, Sinese, the Minister of Defence, so recently enraged at the powers that martial law gave to Creed.

He would start with them first, he thought. He had the power now to arrest anyone in Khos on matters of treason. He could march a squad of guards into the Defence Minister's chambers and have him taken away by force if needs be. The rest of them could throw their tantrums while their vaunted peer rotted in a cell and a case was made against him and his brother, and anyone else implicated in delaying the arrival of the Al-Khos reserves.

It was time, he knew. Time for a reckoning.

His heart was thumping fast; a tightness creeping across his body like the night before.

Let it go, he told himself, breathing it all out of him. *Make the most of this peace while you still can. They're right and you know it. You're pushing yourself too hard.*

It was a truth that he needed to remind himself of at times. That he was still only human.

Such a strange thing to have to remind oneself of, he would have thought once upon a time. Not now, though. Creed was the famous Lord Protector of Khos, after all, the man as strong as a bear, the general who had stood for nearly a decade with his feet astride the Lansway, fighting the Mannians for every inch of ground. How could he not fall for his own growing reputation, when everyone he met in the streets treated him with a kind of awe, and when they needed him to stand tall so that their own fears could be diminished. Creed carried himself like a warrior king of old because that was what he felt himself to be.

Yet in the end, behind all the bluff and bluster, he was still Marsalas Creed from the High Tell, and all else was merely glitter. He was an ageing man who dyed his hair to maintain its black lustre; who seldom doubted himself only because the alternative was to unravel at the seams; who ground his teeth so badly when he slept that he was forced to wear a tiq gum shield to preserve them.

If he was their saviour, then it was only because he was good at what he did.

For a moment, he sensed the presence of old Forias's ghost looking down on him from above; the previous Lord Protector of Khos, that ancient Michinè who had blathered and delayed while the Mannians gradually overwhelmed the Shield. Forias had died in his sleep with a slow poison coursing through his bloodways, killed by an agent of the Few.

It was for your own good, he told the man now. *How else were we to save the city?*

He sensed the silent accusation cast back at him. Creed shrugged it off like an argument that could never be settled.

He sluiced another handful of the river over his broad chest, washing his skin in the mystical waters of the Chilos. This morning was simply for living, for enjoying the moments of the day. Creed lay back in the river and swam like that for a while, looking up at the clouds and the sky, the sounds of distant laughter in his ears.

A scrape of a boot against stone caused him to turn around, his head just above the surface. Halahan stood there with his expression sombre.

'What is it?' sighed Creed.

'Urgent dispatch from Bar-Khos. From General Tanserine. I thought you'd want to know right away.'

Creed felt a tingle in his arm. A premonition of bad news.

He struggled to his feet, feeling the mud squeeze between his toes.

'Kharnost's Wall is close to falling. Tanserine requests that we send him what reinforcements we can.'

It was hard to breathe all of a sudden. Creed raised a hand to his chest, where a great weight seemed to be settling.

He tried to speak, had to pause and try again.

'Any word – of League reinforcements?'

'Still inbound. Marsalas, are you all right?'

'I'm fine,' he grunted, and he waved Halahan away, for the man was unbuckling his swordbelt as though he meant to come in after him.

Pain like needles shot through his veins and he knew that he was anything but fine. His legs gave out from under him.

Creed dropped beneath the surface, barely aware of the hands that reached out to grab him, or the shouts of concern muted through the womblike embrace of the water. He felt bubbles rushing past his face while all of life collapsed down into a single moment of intense pain, and then he knew no more.

*

They agreed to a parley on neutral ground the morning after Sasheen's death, in a tent hastily erected not far from the bridge that led into Tume. Alone and unarmed, Sparus and Romano came face to face in the cold light of day.

Romano was exultant this morning. Sparus could see it in his eyes.

The Archgeneral himself felt only lingering sadness.

'What will you do with her?' Romano asked with a smirk.

Sparus refused to allow the anger to show on his face. There was too much at stake to make this a personal matter.

He took a deliberate breath before he answered. 'The mortarus will preserve her body, then we'll have it flown back to Q'os.'

'Perhaps you should be on that ship also.'

Archgeneral Sparus removed his helm and held it at his waist. 'You are not having this army, Romano.'

A look of genuine puzzlement came over the young man's eager features. 'Why ever not?'

'Because it was the Matriarch's final command to me.'

'Ah,' he replied, and began to pace in front of him. 'I knew she would try to wreck my chances. Yet I wasn't certain that you would follow her command, once she was gone and it no longer mattered.' And he looked to Sparus, a question left open for him. 'It will be civil war otherwise.'

'Romano, if you wish to declare yourself Patriarch then do so. I won't stand in the way of that. Return to Q'os with your men and seize the capital if you can. And while you do that, I will carry on to Bar-Khos and take it for us all.'

It seemed Romano had already thought of that. 'My claim will be a stronger one if it comes from the ruins of Bar-Khos. I need the Expeditionary Force, Sparus. I need it for myself.'

'Then it is war,' Sparus told him plainly. 'Unless we can think of some other way out of this.'

Romano gave a flick of his eyebrow, and stopped his pacing a few feet before him.

Sparus tensed, sensing the sudden change in the atmosphere.

He looked into the man's eyes and saw it in an instant – Romano intended to kill him, here and now.

It was a soldier's reflexes that brought his helm up to

strike at Romano even as the young man was lashing out with his hand. Sparus jerked back, his helm crashing across Romano's head as the young general's fingertips brushed past his face.

Poison! he thought, as he jumped back another step and brought a hand to his cheek. Lucky. The man's nails hadn't broken his skin.

'Guards!' Sparus hollered as he backed out of the tent, glaring at the young man across the empty space. 'You will die for this,' he promised him.

'We will see,' replied Romano, then turned and fled.

—CHAPTER FORTY-TWO—

Dining with the Natives

When the family of Contrarè saw him walking along the riverbank towards their hut, caked from scalp to foot in hardened mud and with his fierce eyes staring, his sword in his hand, they stopped what they were doing and opened their mouths agape as though he was some bog monster come to pillage them. In an instant they had taken flight into the trees.

Ash could hardly blame them, for he knew what a sight he must be. As he picked his way along the bank of the Chilos, he whistled an old tune so they would know at least that he was human. When he came to the small clearing before their hut of sticks and leaves, he stopped before the smoking fire, with the pot of boiling fish stew hanging above it, and sat down with a weary groan and helped himself to it.

The forest folk failed to reappear, though he knew they watched him from the undergrowth. He heard one of them knocking rapidly on wood. Moments later, the signal was returned from deeper within the forest.

To placate them before they started any trouble, he rummaged around in his filthy trousers where he fumbled with the drawstrings of his purse. At last he produced a coin from it, a whole golden eagle, and held the small fortune over his head so they could see. 'It is yours,' he called out, and carefully laid it down on a wooden chopping block that stood in the dirt nearby. 'I will not be long here. Just passing through.'

He felt that was enough to buy him a little time. He went to the water's edge and stripped off his stiff clothes and scrubbed himself down with handfuls of leather-leaves, using their rough undersides as he hummed a tune from Honshu. He washed his clothes next, almost rags by now, and let them dry in the breeze as he sat on the bank and watched the waterfowl cluck and preen themselves in the water.

There were two canoes tied to the shore. When he was dressed and ready to leave, he stepped into one carefully and laid down his sword and picked up the paddle. He sat and nudged the boat out into the flow.

'My thanks!' he called out to the people as he held up a hand.

The breeze played noisily through the bushes. The trees creaked overhead.

*

They both woke at the same time, and lay there beneath the blanket, blinking at each other bleary-eyed and dirty, the sounds of the camp all around them.

'Good morning,' Ché said with a smile, and Curl smiled back at him.

He watched her roll onto her back and stretch, then sit up and look about her. She took a sniff of her leathers, wrinkled her nose. 'I need a wash,' she announced.

He limped down to the river with Curl helping to support him. His wound had been cleaned and stitched the night before, though it still hurt enough to make him pant. Together they washed naked in the river, Curl drawing the eyes of the men there, soldiers and civilians alike, until Ché scowled at them, and they made their interest less obvious.

He'd heard of the spiritual properties of the Chilos. And even though he hardly believed in such things, he dunked himself anyway, and tried to make himself believe there was truth in it. All the while, he wondered what he would do with himself now, what he was even doing here with this girl he'd grown fond of so quickly.

Afterwards, they helped themselves to breakfast in one of the military mess tents that had been set up amongst the encampment. He saw Curl look about her for faces she knew. She talked to a couple of them, asking after a few people by name, pleased when she heard they still lived.

Together, they took their wooden platters outside and sat on a mound of grass to eat their plain meals of hash and beans.

'What is that thing?' he asked Curl as she absently fingered the wooden charm about her neck.

'This?' she said, noticing herself playing with it. 'My ally.'

'Yes?'

'It looks after me,' she explained.

Ché gave a tilt of his head. Lagosians had some strange notions, he reflected. But then that was a little rich, being a Mannian himself. 'Do you miss it?' he asked her.

'What?'

'Your home.'

She looked at him over her plate of food, her brow furrowed.

'I'm sorry. That was stupid of me.'

He was surprised to hear the word come so easily from his lips. He could not recall when he had last apologized for anything.

Ché did not feel entirely like himself today. An odd

contentedness had come upon him, as though for the first time in his life he was precisely where he was supposed to be, and all was fine with the world. He had dreamed of his mother in the night. She had spoken about many things he couldn't now remember, yet he recalled how she had smiled, and how the warmth shone off her like sunshine. His heart had swelled with it, and he had thought, *How ugly the world is without these connections between us.*

And then he had awakened, to find Curl blinking at him next to his side.

'What about you? Do you miss it?' Her tone said she was still annoyed with him.

'Home?'

'Yes.'

He shook his head and realized it was true. He didn't care if he never saw Q'os again.

'And where is home, Ché?'

He hesitated, and then the lie that formed got tangled in his lips somehow, so that he said nothing. He was weary of secrets and the burdens they had become to him. This was a day for new beginnings.

'Ché?'

He placed his platter on the ground, wiped his hands on his knees.

'What is it? Why can't you tell me?'

'It's just . . .' He met her eye then.

Curl seemed to see into him, for her expression hardened. 'No,' she said, shaking her head. 'Not you.'

Still he couldn't find the words. Her face twisted in anguish. When Curl spoke, it was as though some invisible creature was trying to throttle her. 'You're one of them? A Mannian?'

Ché glanced about to see if anyone had overheard her. When he looked back, he felt the gulf that suddenly existed between them, the sudden loss of their connection, like a candle flame snuffed out.

What have I done?

Her platter fell to the ground. She walked off quickly towards the mess tent.

'Wait,' he suddenly called after her. 'Let me explain!'

She went inside. He watched with dread in his stomach as a group of Specials rushed from the tent, Curl walking behind them.

'On your feet,' one of them ordered.

Ché had eyes only for Curl. He knew he could still make her understand, if only she would look at him.

'*On your feet, Mannian,*' growled another, catching the attention of others nearby.

The man kicked Ché hard in the ribs, and he spilled over onto the grass. He caught a sight of Curl, her back turned to him, walking away with a hand covering her face.

And then they laid into him with all their fury.

—CHAPTER FORTY-THREE—

Courage of the Dead

Bull dreamed of his younger brother Kurtez, though in the dream Kurtez was a gangly boy again, shy and overly sensitive to the world, and Bull still the overbearing full-grown man.

They were in the warren slums of their Bar-Khos childhoods, where Bull had first learned to fight and to enjoy it, being chased by a gang of unseen pursuers and their whoops and their war cries. In the dream, Bull told his younger brother to keep running, while he stopped and turned to face the baying mob, putting his scarred and massive body in their way to save him.

When he awoke, startled, he found himself curled on the wet straw floor of the pit, shaking from the cold and drenched by the rain that fell from the night sky overhead. A soldier stood over the pit, a long jabber in his hand that wobbled as it he held it down through the wooden bars. He was poking Bull hard in the ribs to rouse him.

'No sleeping,' said the man, and he sounded annoyed at having to remind him of this vital rule of life.

Bull scraped himself up and leaned his back against the earthen wall, where rainwater was trickling down into the hole. The soldier moved around the edge of the pit, poking each of the prisoners in turn. Grunts and snorts of surprise sounded in the blackness.

Bull thought of his dream, of the face of his brother.

Kurtez had left a note when he'd taken his belt and hung himself from the rafters of his room. He couldn't live with being cast aside by Adrianos, he had written. And seeing him strut around with his new lover.

It was that note that Bull had stuffed into the mouth of Adrianos as the man lay there dying. There had been no mention of it at his trial. Perhaps the family had removed it to cover their own sense of shame.

Another jab against his shoulder made him look up. The guard had made a circuit of the pit, and had returned to him.

'No sleeping.'

Bull was still shackled. His cramped and abused body was a study in every shade of bruise. Still, something snapped in him. He grabbed for the end of the jabber and yanked it from the surprised man's grip. He clamped his other hand around it and shoved hard so that the end of it struck the man's mouth. Bull rammed it again and again into his face.

The man's foot slipped on the crumbling edge of the pit, and he went down, sprawling face first across the bars that caged them in, the wood creaking against his weight. Bull wiped his face clear of rain and aimed the swaying jabber carefully. He cracked the man a final time on his temple, knocking him out.

'Chilanos!' he hissed in the darkness and the rain as he struggled to his feet. 'Give me a hand up, man.'

But Chilanos was silent, and Bull recalled the fellow had lost the ability to speak after his last interrogation with the priests.

'Bahn!' he tried, though he wasn't sure why, for Bahn was as far gone as the rest of them. '*Calvone!*'

A rustle of chains sounded next to him.

'Help me, damn it!'

He was surprised when a hand reached out and grabbed his overall, and Bahn hauled himself to his feet.

Good man, he thought. *Good man!*

He could hardly see his old comrade in the darkness, only the vague shape of him. Bahn bent down and grabbed at his foot until Bull lifted it and placed it into the stirrup of his hands. '*Now,*' whispered Bull, and he hopped with his other foot as Bahn strained and grunted to lift his great bulk.

Bahn managed to raise him by a few feet, his arms shaking and his back braced against the wall. Bull grabbed out for one of the wooden bars. He missed and fell back down as Bahn's strength gave out. The soldier was starting to stir above them.

'Once more,' Bull told him. 'Come on, you bastard!'

They tried again, and this time Bull managed to grab one of the slippery bars. The wood creaked some more, sagging a little as it took his weight. Raindrops were blinding him.

'*Hold steady,*' he hissed down at Bahn, and fumbled with the leather straps that held the door shut, blinking to see anything while the face of the soldier looked down at him from a few feet away, his eyes rolling white in his head. The straps were slippery in his fingers. He cursed and tugged and tried to free them.

A loop of leather came free, and then before he knew it the rest of the bound strap was unravelling from around the bars. He pulled it clear and dropped it into the pit.

Bull shoved at the door and it swung open. He hung

there long enough to catch a breath, dripping with water, no strength left in him.

'Push,' he said down to Bahn. 'For the love of Mercy, push now!'

*

Bahn was dreaming; he was sure of it.

They were walking through the camp of the Imperial Expeditionary Force in a torrent of freezing rain. Bull was up front, dressed in the armour of an imperial soldier, a slight limp in his gait. The others shambled after him, arms supporting each other, their eyes wide and staring at the neatly ordered rows of pup tents they passed by, at the soldiers hunkered down inside them.

Over their shoulders lay Simmer Lake and the island of Tume, the city brilliantly lit tonight. The camp sprawled around the shore not far from where the bridge ran onto the land. Bahn could see earthworks over there, near the bridge. They had heard fighting over recent days, gunshots and men riding past in haste. At first they'd hoped and prayed for it to be a rescue mission, but no one had come for them.

From the overhead mutters of their captors it had sounded as though the Mannians were fighting amongst themselves. Still, it offered the prisoners a respite from their torments. The beatings had stopped, and the regular interrogations and the drugs. It was as though they'd been forgotten.

For Bahn, it had been a time for brooding, of coming to terms with the knowledge that he was dead now in this nightmare of a pit, and was simply waiting to be buried. He'd found a measure of peace amongst the despair of their situation. Had found that you could face your own impending death and come to terms with it, almost welcome it, for the end of all your earthly petty troubles that it would bring.

And now this; this dream of stumbling along at the

rear of the chain of men, with the sheets of rain blinding him and his shackles biting into the open sores of his skin.

They walked and walked with the reek of their foulness preceding them, passing through the camp unchallenged, shuffling clinking past the gleaming eyes of soldiers as they watched Bull leading them, the soldiers looking miserable and spent and uncaring.

In front of Bahn, the man called Gadeon uttered a strange mewling noise from his throat and began to stagger away on a different course. Bahn grabbed him, slipping in the mud in his bare feet as he pulled him back in line.

'Stay with us, brother,' he whispered. 'Stay with us now.'

'We should go back,' said the man frantically. 'They'll punish us for this when they find us gone. They'll call us traitors again or worse.'

Bahn felt ashamed to see the man so broken; then ashamed that he should feel that way at all.

What have they done to us? he thought, listening to the man gabble in fright. *What have they done to our minds?*

Gadeon stopped all of a sudden, and he turned on Bahn and seized him with his clawed hands. 'Are they letting us go?' he asked loudly, almost shouting. 'Is that it?'

Someone shushed for him to be quiet. 'Tell me, Bahn!' he shouted. 'I can't go on if they—' Bahn clamped a hand over his mouth and nose. The man struggled, suffocating.

For a moment Bahn held on grimly, wanting him only to shut up and die.

A hand seized his arm and pulled it free. It was Chilanos. He pushed Gadeon ahead of him and back into line, following the man with an arm across his shoulder.

Bahn stumbled after them.

Yes, he thought to himself. *They're playing with our heads. They're making us dream this night, and when I wake I'll be back in that hole, waiting to die.*

He looked about him, and realized they had left the camp behind them, that they were stumbling out onto the open plain. The darkness there like an embrace.

Bahn bumped into the back of Chilanos, for the man had stopped dead in his tracks. He peered ahead through the rain and saw that Gadeon had stopped too, and the man before him. Bahn staggered forwards around them, not wanting to stop now. He saw the dark form of Bull with his hand held up for silence. The big warrior's head was scanning slowly left to right.

'Halt!' came a voice through the darkness ahead of them, and then the sound of footsteps squelching through mud. 'Declare yourselves!'

Steel rasped against leather. Bull vanished into the night.

Two blades struck each other. Another shout sounded from their left. 'Sound a report!'

Footsteps running towards them. 'Report, I say!'

This is real, Bahn thought. *This is no fantasy.*

'*Go*,' urged Bahn to his comrades in a sudden rush of panic. He grabbed a man and shoved him forwards into the darkness. '*Go*,' he said again, trying to get them all moving. They started to run for it, the whole huffing shambling group of them.

They passed Bull in the darkness. The man whirled away from something and waved them on.

'Sound the alarm!' a man was hollering. 'Sound the alarm there!'

The men gasped as they splashed through the gully of a stream. They helped each other to their feet and up the other side of it. Bahn fell and swallowed a mouthful of muddy water. Rain splashed off the flowing stream. Retching, he got to his feet and clawed his way up the other side.

He turned back for Bull. The man stood on the bank of the gully silhouetted by the campfires. His back was to them, a naked sword in his hand.

Someone was trying to tug Bahn along. He turned and followed in a hopping skipping run. They ran until their hearts were fit to burst and kept on running, scattering into the night like phantoms.

—CHAPTER FORTY-FOUR—

A Mother

Smoke tumbled from the chimney of the cottage and from the roof of a rundown shack at the back. Against the side of the cottage rested a lean-to of rotten planks, its floor strewn with hay that had spilled out into the muddy yard where chickens pecked at scattered corn. At the edge of a fenced enclosure, an old zel ambled lazily, chewing contentedly and swatting its tail at the late autumn flies. Beyond, in the far distance, the southern mountains rose with silver falls of water shining on their flanks, catching sunlight.

Nico's mother bustled from the kitchen doorway. She selected a few small logs from a pile that leaned against the whitewashed wall of the cottage, then made her way quickly to the smoky shack with the dirty hems of her skirts dragging across the ground. Her red hair was tied back this morning; it shone with a deep lustre.

Ash saw her as walked up the dirt track, and stopped as though he had walked into a wall. His heart started hammering inside him.

He came up to her as she left the smoking shack, wiping her empty hands.

'*Oh!*' Reese exclaimed and clutched her chest in fright. She relaxed as recognition came to her. She glanced behind him for Nico, and her face tightened when she failed to see him.

'Mister Ash,' she managed.

'Mistress Calvone.'

He could see her taking in his ragged, unkempt condition. A tension was slowly settling upon her pretty features. 'My son. Where is he?'

Ash's eyes closed of their own accord, wanting to spare him from her distress. He lowered his head in shame.

'No,' she whispered in realization.

How could he say what needed to be said? Ash forced himself at least to meet her stare.

'The boy . . .' he began, and it took all the force of his will to continue. 'Miss Calvone. I am sorry. He is gone.'

'No.' She was shaking her head, a hand clutching at her throat; her skin had flushed a vivid crimson.

Ash fumbled with the small clay vial of ashes about his neck until he held it outstretched in his hands. He saw how pitiful it looked. More pitiful even than the urn of ashes he had given to Baracha for safe keeping. But it was all he could offer her, and he had a need just then to give something of her son back to her.

'I . . . I am . . . deeply sorry.'

Reese glared in horror at the tiny vial as though he held a stillborn foetus in his hands. In that moment, it was true self-loathing that possessed him.

She slapped the jar from his hands and it went spinning across the yard, where it struck the wall of the cottage and shattered into pieces. Reese launched herself at him, swinging her fist across his face. It was a solid blow and he swayed from it, and then her rage fully unleashed in a torrent of punches and kicks.

'You promised!' she screamed over and over again. 'You promised you'd protect him!'

Ash didn't try to stop her, not even when she blindly grabbed at a spade and laid into him with the full weight of its metal head. He fell, sprawling in the dirt with his hands raised over his face. Vaguely, he was aware of the torrent of words rushing from her mouth, words of accusation, every one of them justified, each one true.

He could barely see with the blood coursing into his eyes. He heard the shouts of a man, felt strong hands grabbing him. Ash blinked his eyes clear, saw the looming face of Los peering down at him. Reese sat on the ground amongst her piled skirts, sobbing inconsolably, slapping at the earth and wrenching handfuls free with her fingertips.

'You'd better leave, old man,' advised Los, his hands helping Ash to his feet.

Ash stood and swayed on the spot. He wanted to say something to her, try in some way to lighten her grief. But he knew there was nothing in all the world he could say that would do that.

He left her in pieces, like the clay vial scattered in the dirt.

*

Clouds gathered overhead, darkening the autumn sky with a promise of more rain. Ash passed carts on the road laden with goods or families; individual travellers carrying packs on their backs; herds of livestock driven by dour, pipe-smoking herders. By early afternoon he crested a rise of ground and saw the Bay of Squalls and the city of Bar-Khos spread out before him.

It felt as though it had been years since he'd visited this besieged city of the Free Ports. Yet it had only been a handful of months ago when he had stopped here with the *Falcon* for its much-needed repairs, and encountered Nico for the first, fateful time.

A stiff sea breeze blew across the rugged edge of the coast, beyond which heaved the white-capped waters of the bay. He could see the Lansway running out into the bay, with the dark walls of the Shield shrouded in a haze of smoke, brief flashes in the midst of it that were the belches of cannon fire.

Of all the cities to be returning to, he thought. *It should be Nico coming back here, with a few scars and a dozen stories to tell, not you.*

Ash plodded down the busy road towards the eastern gatehouse. To his right lay the city skyport with its fluttering windsocks and sprawling warehouses. Half a dozen skyships lay berthed on the ground with their envelopes deflated, repair crews swarming around them.

As the gatehouse grew nearer, he could hear above the noise of the traffic something different now – the distant din of battle on the Shield. They could all hear it, everyone who was trying to get through the bottleneck of traffic at the open gates, where each cart was being checked by a soldier before being allowed through.

Ash was carried through the bustle without inspection into the streets within.

*

It began to rain as he made his way towards the heart of the city. Life seemed to be carrying on as normal beneath the distant crash of artillery fire, though the atmosphere was more tense than before, more agitated. Several times he passed someone shouting in anger with their tempers unravelling.

With money from his purse he bought a paper bowl of rice from a street vendor, and was wolfing it down even as he turned away. He walked on through the Quarter of Guilds then through the Quarter of Barbers, coming out at last into the wide thoroughfare that was the Avenue of Lies. The street was less busy than usual. People scurried by under their paper umbrellas or sheltered beneath the dripping eaves of buildings, glumly watching the covered carts that passed, carrying wounded soldiers, and dead ones.

From a small bazaar, Ash purchased an oiled longcoat and a wide-brimmed hat woven of grasses, which curved all the way down to the level of his eyes. Properly garbed against the weather, he next sought out an apothecary, for the air had grown heavy with the press of clouds, and in turn it had brought a return of his head pains. He heard the relief in his own voice as he bought a fresh supply of dulce leaves from a pair of brothers in their little shop in a narrow side street, interrupting them in the midst of a quarrel. Stepping out of the place he stuffed one of the leaves into his mouth. He tasted the bitterness of it, and chewed some more while the pain refused to diminish. Ash took four more of the leaves before his head began to lighten, not dwelling on what that might mean.

Ahead, through the mists of rain, he saw the Mount of Truth rising up above the flat roofs of the district. He turned away from the sight, heading into the alleyways of the Bardello, the little enclave of musicians and poets and artists, finally stopping outside a wooden building that leaned out badly over the cobbled street, its windows shuttered and dark. A metal bracket was fixed over the door, where a wooden sign should have been hanging, sporting the picture of a seal on a neck-chain.

Ash looked about him to make sure he was in the right street. Mystified, he tried the door and found that it was locked.

'Hermes!' he shouted out and pounded his fist against it.

After a moment he heard feet shuffling and the sounds of bolts being drawn back. The door tugged open, and Hermes the agent poked his head around and squinted up at him through a thick pair of spectacles.

'Ash!' hollered the tiny man with his eyes widening in surprise. 'You old dog! Is it really you?' And he opened the door further and beckoned him inside.

'What is left of me,' Ash replied. He stepped into the dim dusty space of an empty room, a few chairs arranged around the walls beneath sketches of the bay. Birds were squawking loudly from the neighbouring rooms. 'What is going on here? Why are you closed for business?'

The man looked up as though he had just been struck across his face, blood flushing to his round cheeks. His eyes blinked and watered behind the glass of his spectacles. He cleared his throat, wiped a strand of curly hair from his forehead. 'You mean . . . you don't know?'

'Know what?'

Hermes wrung his hands in some distress. Ash didn't like how the agent was staring at him; as though Hermes was staring at the ghost of a dead man who had not yet been told he was dead.

'Come,' Hermes said gently – much too gently – and led Ash by the arm towards the inner door. 'You should sit down first. Let us go and sit by the fire, shall we?'

*

Hermes liked birds more than people, and every room of the house seemed filled with cages of the screeching, flapping creatures. Ash sneezed more than a few times as he listened to what the agent had to tell him. His hands gripped the arms of the chair ever harder as he listened. Hermes sat opposite, in his own armchair specially crafted for his small frame, the light of the fire washing over him. Despite the heat, Ash felt chilled to the bone.

He still could barely believe it.

'I wasn't certain what was happening at first,' the agent was telling him. 'I was waiting for a batch of fresh seals to be sent, but nothing came through. No seals, no carrier birds, no letters. After a while I sent a letter to Cheem myself, through one of the usual blockade runners that we use. Still I heard nothing from Sato. That's when I truly began to worry.'

He paused to take his spectacles off, to wipe his eyes. *Gone*, Ash was thinking. *All gone.*

'Last week, I finally received a letter. It was from Baracha. He told me to cease business until I heard from him further. He wrote that Sato had been attacked by the Imperials, that they had put it to the torch. Killed all they found there. Apparently he was away at the time. When he returned he found everything in ruins. That's what he said, Ash. That's how he put it. *In ruins.*'

'Survivors?' Ash heard his distant, impossibly calm voice ask in reply.

'He didn't say. I don't think so. Oshō, though . . . he said that that Oshō had been slain in the fighting.'

Ash closed his eyes, while all around him the birds called out and rattled around in their cages.

Ché, he thought. *They used what he knew to find us.*

For the longest of times he could not move, could not even speak.

—CHAPTER FORTY-FIVE—

Bilge Town

The forest was a world within a world, his mother, the Contrarè, had liked to say.

As he staggered into its outer treeline, dripping wet from his river crossing and with the rags hanging off him, he sensed the difference in the air, the change of scents in his nostrils, the softening of light as it fell through the high canopy, and realized that it was true.

He ventured onwards, deeper into the Windrush until his legs would carry him no further. He collapsed onto the soft floor of leaves and dirt and slept a dreamless sleep of oblivion.

When he awoke, Bull knew he could go no further without first regaining some strength. He set about making a camp for himself not far from the trickles of a wide, shallow stream. He burned deadwood that was wet and smoky, moved a large log in front of it for a seat. For food he ate berries and caught what fish he could with a sharpened stick, even chanced the mushrooms that looked familiar enough to his city eyes. Nuts too, of all kinds, were in abundance, though they lay heavy in his stomach if he consumed too many.

When he fell asleep those first nights on a carpet of soft moss, with the stars shining through the leaves over-head, and the trees surrounding him like the walls of a home, he knew the world beyond the forest was dimin-ishing in his mind, its troubles and conflicts no longer his own. He was at peace at last in this quiet, lonely place of his mother's people. He wished never to leave it.

On the fourth morning of his convalescence, Bull was wakened by a sharp stab to his side, and he sat up to find a group of male Contrarè gaping down at him. Warriors, by the looks of their painted faces, striped green and black from ear to ear, and the crow feathers and bone charms adorning their long dark hair.

'*Chushon! Tekanari!*' One of the men demanded as he jabbed his spear at him again. The warrior seemed the youngest of them all.

Bull grabbed the shaft of it and plucked it out of his grip.

At once, a dozen spear-tips were pressing against his flesh.

'Whoah,' Bull told them as he held up a hand. He tossed the spear back into the hand of the startled warrior.

'Calm down. I'm one of you, see?' And he gestured to his face as though it was obvious.

The men glanced at the young warrior. They wanted to kill Bull here and now, he could see.

With graceful movements the young warrior planted the end of his spear in the earth and plucked at the knees of his trousers to bend down before him. Tenta-tively, he grasped Bull's face and turned it one way and then the other. He studied the sharpness of his cheeks, the swarthy complexion of his skin. He peered closely at the horns tattooed on his temples, and nodded his head in appreciation.

'Then welcome home, brother of the tribes,' the young man said in rough Trade, and helped him to his feet.

*

Ash wandered through the rain, lost and aimless. His mind had sunk into his feet, and he released himself to the feel of the hard rounded cobbles against the soles of his boots, letting them take him wherever they would.

Hermes the agent had offered him a room to stay in for as long as he needed it. Numbly, Ash had thanked him but declined, and had left the man standing at the front door with the birds shrieking behind him.

'I'm not certain what I do now, Ash. Are we finished then? Is it over?'

Ash had only waved a silent farewell.

He didn't realize he'd been walking south towards the Shield until he sniffed the scents of fish and seaweed and brine, and looked up from beneath the brim of his dripping hat, and saw the Sargassi Sea and the calmer waters of the east harbour before him. The countless ships that sheltered there bobbed and rocked in the gentle swell, while gulls wailed forlorn and hungry, sweeping back and forth through the sheets of rain. Men with fishing rods sat on stools along the waterfront, clad in hooded ponchos to protect themselves from the weather. Their demeanours were calm and patient as they chewed on tarweed or smoked from clay pipes.

To Ash, just then, they looked like the most contented men in the world.

The Shield was visible from here above the huddle of All Fools. The Lansway it stood upon stretched out across the water into a dull obscurity. He could see little of the ongoing assault itself out there; just plumes of smoke rising from the outermost wall, and the occasional flash of fire. The scene was muted, the sea breeze carrying the sounds elsewhere into the city.

Pressing onwards, he came to a busy junction overlooked by inns and merchants' storehouses. The junction was the scene of a vagabond street market. Fancy carriages attempted to force their way through the crowds, which were mostly street vendors, brash prostitutes, the occasional gang of roaming urchins. A hill rose steeply ahead of him into leafy streets and high, marble mansions fronted by spike-topped walls, an enclave of Michinè and wealthy common-born. The Congress of the council could be found up there, he recalled.

Ash saw little point in going that way. He carried on along the seafront, the road curving out to skirt the base of the hill. After a row of rowdy taverns and sleep-easies, the road eventually petered out into a shingle track, with the hill on his left fronted by limestone cliffs.

The coastline here was a narrow, windswept strip of rock between the cliffs and the sea. Shanties had been erected amongst pools of brackish seawater that plopped and shimmered in the rainfall. Ash meandered between the shacks, stepping over the occasional crab or bundle of seaweed. The flimsy domiciles were propped high on stacks of flattened stones, and wooden boards ran between many of them.

He'd heard of this district in his previous visits to the city, though he had never visited before. The Shoals, the city-folk called it, due to the tides that swamped it in heavy weather. It was said to be the poorest district of the city, the place where people landed when they could fall no lower. Many penniless sailors came here and waited for news of ships hiring men. They had their own name for the place.

They called it Bilge Town.

Ash smiled without humour, wondering at the irony of his life.

The area stank of running sewage and rotting fish. Picking his way along the rocks, he risked straining his neck by looking up to the very top of the cliffs. Seabirds were spinning in the updraught rising past the Michinè villas, where orchards overhung the crumbling edges of limestone. Kings had once lived up there. For a thousand years they had lived in the Pale Palace with their families and courts, ruling over all of Khos.

Ash slipped on something beneath his heel and caught himself just in time. He looked down at a sour apple, fallen from one of the high overhanging trees of the orchards, smeared flat and brown beneath his boot. A gust drove the rain into his face. Ash shivered.

He headed towards the cliff face, where the rocky shore rose sharply and the shanties huddled together more densely than they did below. The shingle paths wound between dwellings both small and weather-worn, leaning against each other for support, clinging to the slopes all the way to the face of the cliffs. In the cliffs themselves, within depressions in the chalky face of stone, structures were perched in enclaves that seemed impossible to the eye. High above them caves had been carved out, connected by ladders and swaying gantries.

He trod upwards along a path that switchbacked between shanties and the occasional two-storey structure. Women hung clothes out to dry beneath stretches of tarpaulin, their heads and shoulders wrapped in shawls, faces reddened by the wind. Babes cried indoors. The street children chased after dogs or skipped to odd chanting rhymes, or struggled with bulging waterskins up the slopes. There seemed to be fewer men than women, he noticed.

Already the ache in his head was returning, despite the leaves still bundled in his mouth. His eyes swam with a kind of fog, and Ash blinked hard to try and clear them. He took more of the dulce leaves, and stood for some moments until his vision cleared a little, though the pain remained, stabbing his forehead to the beat of his heart. He began to feel sick with it.

He stopped a local – an old, hungry-looking, grey-haired man carrying a straw umbrella – and asked where he might find some room and board. The old man looked at him curiously, but was helpful enough. Ash followed his directions, climbing ever upwards.

*

The Perch was a ramshackle establishment that occupied a shallow ledge on the cliff wall. The sign above the door swung creaking in the wind, as old and decrepit as the rest of the long, narrow building. The flaking picture showed a rat squatting on a sea-tossed barrel, its own tail clamped in its mouth in apprehension.

Smoke was billowing from the taverna's central chimney. Laughter could be heard from within.

Ash pushed through the doors into the taproom. A squall of rain followed him in, causing the lantern light in the dim, smoky space to flicker against the walls. A few heads turned to appraise the newcomer.

'Shut that door!' shouted a man behind the bar, a fat bald-headed man with thick tattooed arms. 'You're letting the cold in, man!'

Ash pushed the door closed, warped and ill-fitting in its frame, and shook his coat dry as a pool of water gathered at his feet, soaking into the rushes that covered the floor. It was hot in the narrow room. A log fire crackled fitfully in the hearth. Ash removed his hat and stepped to the bar, trailing water.

The proprietor was playing a game of ylang with a woman sitting on a stool and wearing an expression of boredom. The man moved one of his black pebbles across the board, and looked up at Ash as he approached.

'What can I get for you?' he asked.

'Cheem Fire, if you have any.'

His eyes brightened. 'Then you're in luck. I probably have the last case in the whole city.'

The bottles were hidden behind the bar in a locked

strongbox chained to the floor. The proprietor fumbled with a ring of keys that hung from his belt, then unlocked it and removed a bottle with an exaggerated show of care. The cork squeaked as he pulled it free with his teeth. He swirled the contents of the bottle, allowing the aroma to waft into his flaring, hairy nostrils.

'Only the finest,' he purred as he trickled out the tiniest of portions into a glass tumbler, chipped but reasonably clean. He was about to add some water into it when Ash held his hand over the glass.

'And leave the bottle,' Ash told him.

Suspicion, suddenly. 'It costs half an eagle for a bottle of this stuff. It isn't watered down already, you know.'

The coin skittered across the bar, turning every head in the room.

The proprietor licked his lips. He took the gold eagle and hefted it for weight. His tongue poked out and he dabbed it against the coin.

'Very good,' he proclaimed with satisfaction. He left the bottle where it stood and took out a chisel and small mallet from beneath the bar. The eagle, like all eagles, was stamped with two deep lines across its face, one crossing the other so as to divide it into quarters. He aligned the end of the chisel with one of the lines and pounded once, hard, with the mallet. The coin broke in two. He scooped up one half, returned the other.

Ash swirled the contents of the glass for a moment, took a sniff, then downed it.

The swarthy woman was studying him with her kohl-lined eyes. She looked Alhazii, he saw. Her eyes seemed overly fascinated with his skin.

'What brings you to Bilge Town, stranger?' she asked of him, and her voice was deep and rich, and it made him think of dusk.

'My feet,' he said, and threw the fiery liquid to the back of his throat, and refilled his glass to the brim.

*

Ash hired a room for the night, a dreary upstairs cubicle barely large enough for its dusty bed, where he left his sword and nothing else. He went back downstairs, and sat in a corner of the taproom with his bottle of Cheem Fire, where he began the slow but appealing process of drinking himself into the ground.

He spoke to no one all that long evening, and the look of him told them all to leave him be. The Cheem Fire soothed the pain in his skull, but most of all numbed him to himself. When the proprietor finally called for time, Ash found himself unwilling to climb to his empty room just yet. The drink had made him melancholy. He knew he would find sleep difficult, and would dream of things he would rather not be dreaming.

Ash finished off the glass in his hand and banged it down on the table. He took the bottle with him as he gathered his longcoat from the cloakstand and put on his hat, then tugged the door open.

Outside, the rain had turned to sleet, and the wind was tossing it about so that it stung as it struck his face. It was bitterly cold even with the coat fastened tight about him, and the hat tied firmly to his head. The tide was washing in with the high swells, and much of the lower Shoals was submerged in a foot or so of churning water. Ash clutched his bottle of Cheem Fire and staggered down through the dark shingle street towards it.

He tracked along the water's edge, negotiating the shacks that perched in his way. Once or twice he stumbled, had to catch himself before he fell into the surf. He walked until the dwellings petered out, and the slope ended at a bluff that ran down into the sea.

He sat on the flattened top of a boulder with his feet dangling above the lapping waves and the rock smooth and chilly against his haunches. He stared out at the wildness of the sea, watching the sleet falling as though from nowhere. In the distant darkness, the Lansway stretched towards the far continent, and the great walls of the Shield stood tall and black. Explosions flickered across the scene occasionally, their low grumbles reaching him a moment later.

Ash wondered how much longer they had left to them. It certainly felt like the end now, though perhaps that was only his own end he was sensing.

In ruins, Ash. In ruins.

He could not stop thinking of Sato, and all those who had been slain when the Mannians had struck; most of all the few surviving comrades from the People's Revolution, men who had shared the same fate of exile as himself.

It should be fury he was feeling now. Yet all he truly felt was despair and isolation, a mood only deepened as he watched the bombardment against the far walls continuing. Once this city fell like Sato, the island would fall too, and then the rest of the Free Ports would be starved into submission. The darkness would finally have conquered the flame.

Strange, how only now he felt such a bond of solidarity with these people, now that he had lost everything to Mann, now that the Khosians stared defeat in the eyes. But then, perhaps it was not so strange. He had been the same with Nico. Unable to open up to the boy, to invest himself in what he could never bear to lose again. Like everything else that had ever mattered in his life since being cast from the old country.

He saw the full awful waste of his life, and could hardly bear it.

We should have joined the Few, when they first began writing to Oshō.

We should have chosen a side.

Ash made a toast to the people of Bar-Khos, and drank deep.

The old Rōshun sang sad drinking songs from Honshu as he worked his way through the rest of the bottle. He steadily grew wearier and drunker and colder, and all the more dull-headed for it. At last, the bottle produced only a single drip against his tongue.

Ash clutched the empty bottle to his chest. He spoke into it.

'Hello,' he said in a mocking voice that was deepened by the echo from the glass. 'I'm stranded. Nowhere to go. Send help. More drink.'

With a few moments of concentration, he stuffed the stopper back into its neck, hefted the bottle, and flung it as far out as he could.

His eyelids drooped. Tired. Time for bed.

Ash lay down on the rock and curled himself into a ball. He began to snore.

The falling sleet grew worse.

*

In his dreams Ash climbed the valley towards the monastery of Sato, the slope growing steeper with every step that he took.

He pushed on, trying to hurry, keen for a glimpse of his home amongst the forest of mali trees shivering in the wind.

He couldn't see it at first, even as he grew closer. Panic filled him as he rushed headlong through the trees. At last he stopped before a great mound of smoking ashes.

He could not comprehend it, that scene.

It must be a mistake, he thought. *In my old age I've gone and hiked up the wrong valley*.

He could feel the soft fall of ashes against his face, strangely cold, and against his lips, as tasteless as ice.

Ash squinted, peering closer at the ruins.

From the centre of the mound of ashes, a single young mali tree was growing. Its bronze leaves were shaking in a gust he could no longer feel. Already, around it, as Ash looked on, the wind was scattering the ashes to nothing.

*

A figure picked its way through the falling sleet. It carried a bundle of driftwood in its arms, and occasionally it stooped to gather up another branch or a broken length of planking left stranded by the waves. The figure stopped when it came across the huddled form of a man curled on the rock. He was shuddering, and moaning something in his sleep.

'*Hmf*,' Meer said, and nudged him with a toe.

The sleeping man groaned louder and shifted in his sleep.

'An old fool farlander,' he muttered. 'You'll die of exposure sleeping out here on a night like this.'

Meer sighed, dropped his armload of wood, and with effort hoisted the man from where he slept and slung him over his shoulder. He adjusted the weight of him, then turned and went back the way he had come, past the bluff of rock, further away from the shacks.

*

Ash had to stop waking up like this, stiff necked and in a place he did not expect.

It was early morning, judging by the pale daylight that filtered in from behind him, casting a bluish tint to the smoke that rose from the small fire in its hearth of rounded stones. He was lying on a reed mat, and was covered in his longcoat with his head resting on one of his boots. It was a cave, this place; manmade, by the looks of it. The curving walls were covered in sky-blue plaster, though the plaster was damp and flaking in many places to reveal the naked rock behind.

A shrine, thought Ash. It looks like a shrine.

Some possessions were piled against the opposite wall: a wooden begging bowl, a canvas bag, a gnarled stick, a neatly folded blanket, a pile of parchments pressed within a canvas binding, an ink pot, some candles, a large jug.

Ash crawled to the jug and peered inside.

Water.

He drank half of it in one tremendous gulp, spilling even more of it down his tunic. He grunted as the frigid water crashed into his stomach and tried to come back up.

A scratch of footsteps caused him to look over his shoulder.

'Ah, you're alive, then.'

The words stomped through his head with every syllable, making Ash wince.

The speaker was a monk, it appeared, for his head was shaven and he wore a black robe and sandals on his feet. Forty years of age perhaps, but with the glittering, fascinated eyes of a youth.

The monk dropped an armful of wood beside the fire. He hiked up his robe to reveal white, powerful legs, and squatted by the fire to poke some life back into it with a stick.

Ash crawled to the entrance with his eyes squinting against the daylight. He was high in the cliff face here, staring out at a grey sea feathered with white. He looked down. A ladder ran down to a narrow path at the bottom of the cliff.

He inhaled the sea wind and tried to clear the fog from his head.

'How did I get here?' he asked as quietly as he could.

'Eh? You flew in last night, like a leaf tossed by the wind. Gave me quite a start, I can tell you.'

Under different circumstances Ash might have appreciated this man's sense of humour. Instead he ignored it, and sat up and began the slow, awful process of pulling on his wet boots.

'What is this place, a shrine?' He gasped for air, one loose boot still facing him.

'Yes,' the monk replied, looking about the dismal space. 'Very old, I think. I was told there was once a bronze statue here of the Great Fool. It stood right there where the fire is now.' The monk wiped his hands together, held them out for warmth. 'The local people, they say they used to leave offerings and prayers written on rice paper. And then the statue was stolen one day, and it took them a long time to raise the money for another. That one they chained to the floor. But it too was taken by a thief.'

The monk kneeled on the floor with spine erect, right hand resting in his left: the position of chachen meditation. 'When I moved in here last winter I took the statue's place. And here I sit, every day, waiting to be stolen.'

Ash grunted, and with a final effort managed to pull on the other boot. He exhaled with relief, though the boots were cold and wet and little comfort; and then he looked at the slimy laces, overly complex just then, and he blinked with dismay. They would have to do like that, he decided.

'My name is Meer, by the way.'

Ash barely heard him. Memories were flickering through his head. He could recall singing on a rock, and throwing the empty bottle into the sea, and curling up to sleep. It had been falling heavy with sleet last night.

'Thank you, for bringing me inside last night.'

Meer nodded, a smile in his eyes. 'You are from Honshu, are you not?'

Ash nodded, noticing how he used the real name of his homeland.

'Then I hope you can tell me about that country some time. I have never been there, though I would dearly like to see it. I'm a traveller, you see.'

'Yes. When I have the time.'

'You are going somewhere?'

Ash looked up from the flames, struck by the question. He was not sure of the answer. What was left for him in Cheem, if the monastery was gone, and Oshō and Kosh and the rest of them?

'I do not know,' he said aloud. 'I thought I would be returning to Cheem, to my home there, if I could find a boat to take me. Now, though . . .' and he shook his head.

The monk was peering through the rising smoke, his expression suddenly keen. 'Cheem, you say?'

'Aye. What of it?'

A shy smile. 'Nothing,' he told him, shaking his head. 'I should tell you, they were talking about you this morning in the Perch, when I was doing my rounds with my bowl. They said a rich farlander with a sword had come to drink away his sorrows. They thought you had thrown yourself into the sea last night.'

'I am sorry to disappoint them'

'They were only showing their concern for you. The people are like that here. You know, I thought at first you were only hungover from drink. But now I have had a proper look at you, I think you are truly unwell. Is there something that afflicts you, my friend?'

'Yes. The curiosity of others.'

'I'm sorry,' said Meer. 'I don't mean to pry.'

The words struck a chord with Ash. He was being rude to his host, he could see. He might be dead from exposure if it weren't for this generous stranger.

'I have an illness,' he admitted. 'My father died from the same thing, after the pains in his head grew so bad he could not see. It grows worse in me.'

'I see. Then perhaps I can help you with those head pains. I know of a few remedies. I could make a special brew of chee for you, if you like?'

He nodded, not entirely convinced.

'But there is something else, no?'

'What do you mean?'

'Something that troubles your spirit, I think.'

Ash tried to calm his thumping heart.

'It is hard to talk of this, yes?'

He could only nod. Something was building within him. Something needing to be released.

It took Ash a long breath before he could speak. 'I lost someone,' he said at last. 'A person close to me.'

With feeling, Meer nodded. Just then he reminded Ash of Pau-sin back in his home village of Asa, the little monk who would listen to the villagers' problems without judgement, only sympathy. He had a way of drawing out words from the heart too.

'Yes?' prompted the monk.

'Now, all that is left of the boy are ashes scattered over a chicken yard, and in a jar I gave to someone for safekeeping. Most likely, the jar sits next to a pile of rubble that was once my home.'

Meer considered his words. Ash had not the vaguest notion what he was thinking.

'I see. You don't believe you can go on any longer, with so much grief inside you. You think life is not worth living if it's to be as terrible as this.'

Ash could not look away from the man's steady gaze.

'This is why you wish to drink yourself to death.'

He wondered if the man was a Seer. Some had the knack without any training at all.

Ash watched as the monk stepped to the entrance of the cave and sat down next to him with his legs dangling over the edge. The wind ruffled the folds of his black robe.

'Those waves down there. Do you see them?'

A cough to clear his throat. 'I am not blind yet.'

'Sometimes, when I hear of such a thing as this, I am reminded of how those waves are very much like ourselves, only that they live much shorter lives. I watch them come rushing for the shore and see how they tumble in equal creation and destruction, so captivating to my eyes. And I see how it is the force of the wind riding through them that keeps them alive. It borrows the water of those waves so it may pass its force through them. How many laqs, I wonder? How far have they travelled from the distant storm to reach here?'

Ash was listening with his full attention, his hangover momentarily forgotten. The dull sea made the monk's eyes a dark green. They turned to regard him now.

'You wish to hear this? I'm not boring you?'

A shake of his head.

Meer looked back out at the sea.

'You see, I watch as they crash against the shore and fizzle out to nothing. The end of their journey; the end of their existence. And it becomes clear to me, in those moments, how their end is what makes them complete. It's what gives them meaning, what gives their life form. What would that be, if they simply surged around the oceans of the world without ever ceasing? What is creation without destruction? Something bland and uniform and unchanging. Something truly dead.'

Meer leaned back and breathed deeply, as though returning to himself. He looked once more at Ash with his vibrant eyes, surveyed his expression to see how much Ash comprehended.

He seemed to decide that it was not enough.

'I will tell you something,' Meer said. 'In the end, death is a gift of life. I know: it's a hard thing to appreciate when you lose those you love so fiercely. But without death we would not be alive. Those you have lost would not have lived at all.'

Ash moved to squat in front of the fire, his back to the monk now. They were fine sentiments, these words of Meer. Yet they were still only that: words and ideas. They did not dispel his suffering.

'I will tell you this also. Call it an advance for all the stories you will tell me of Honshu.

'When I visited the Isles of Sky, I saw how the people lived. They are almost immortal there, did you know that? They have ways of sustaining life, even of cheating death itself. But I thought, ultimately, their longevity brought them much harm. They seemed inhuman to me. Even with all their miracles and wonders, they lived in great boredom and listlessness. Worse, much worse – they could no longer see the poetry in the world around them, so buried in themselves had they become.'

Ash turned around slowly, a single eyebrow raised in disbelief. 'The Isles of Sky?'

'It's true.'

'I thought only the longtraders of Zanzahar knew the way.'

Meer shrugged. 'Maybe when you tell me of Honshu, I will tell you more of my own tales. How does that sound?'

Ash opened his mouth, closed it again with a snap of teeth.

Meer was wrong about sharing his burdens. He felt even worse now than he had only a few moments before. He groaned as he staggered to his feet and threw the longcoat over his shoulders.

'Thank you, again,' Ash said, and left for the comfort of his room and a long hot soak in a tub.

*

The regulars were talking of the war the next afternoon when Ash finally rose from his bed, and stuffed some of the leaves into his mouth, and went downstairs to find himself a drink.

Against the bar he sat on a stool with a half-finished bottle of Cheem Fire, and played a game of ylang with Samanda, the dark Alhazii woman he had seen on his first night here, and who turned out to be the proprietor's wife. Lars, the proprietor, seemed much infatuated with his young wife. He rarely complained at the fact that she refused to do any form of work about the inn.

'I sleep with you, that is work enough,' she replied the one time he bordered on criticism, and he lowered his eyes, and skulked away, muttering.

Ash scratched the bites from the bedbugs and listened to the gossip of the men around the room. They were talking of the latest rumours, of how the Matriarch had died from the wounds she had gained in the battle of Chey-Wes.

Ash longed for it to be true. He barely listened as they went on to describe how the imperial invaders were fighting now amongst themselves; how the defence of the Shield was going badly, how Kharnost's Wall was about to fall.

Ash lost the game of ylang, his mind no longer on it. Drunk and in need of a walk, he excused himself and took his bottle with him and went outside. Dead leaves covered the pathways, piled in drifts against buildings, making for treacherous walking. The wind was jagged with cold today. It certainly felt as though winter was arriving early.

Near the edge of the Shoals, close to the waves, he spotted Meer the monk sitting beneath a raised lean-to close to the sea, with a group of children gathered around him. Ash stopped, and lowered his bottle of Cheem Fire to watch.

The monk was holding up a slate and a stick of chalk. He was teaching the children how to read, and they were laughing, making a game of it.

Ash felt a semblance of peace as he gazed at the scene. He walked a few steps further onto the rocks and hunkered down with his bottle, still within earshot of the group, just out of reach of the hissing spray of the waves.

A fishing boat was out there in the heavy swell, struggling towards the harbour, its sails flapping in tatters and its crew straining with oars against the current. A hard business, thought Ash.

He settled into himself. Thoughts fluttered like falling leaves, glimpsed then gone.

A flake of snow ensnared itself in his eyelashes. He blinked it away and looked up at the clouds. More snow began to tumble down.

'Look, children, snow!' he heard the monk exclaim from behind.

The children instantly forgot their lessons and chased him over the rocks, overjoyed at the flakes of ice floating from the sky.

The wind felt cold on Ash's teeth as he smiled.

*

The monk approached him as dusk was falling, a long
fishing pole in his hand.

'You look hungry, my sad friend.'

Ash's stomach made an audible noise in reply.

'Follow me. We'll catch some fish and enjoy a supper
together.'

He agreed, and together they found a flat spot next to
the lapping water as the stars emerged, slowly populat-
ing the night sky with their shingle of light. Meer cast
his line as far out as he could, then hummed a tune as
they waited.

'I thought the monks of Khos did not eat the flesh of
fish,' Ash said after a while, drawing his gaze from the
eastern sky, where constellations were rising.

Meer drew in the line slowly, then tossed the hook,
weight and float back out into the water. He sat down
again.

A minute passed before he spoke. 'I have a confession
to make. I'm not really a monk.'

Ash saw that he was serious.

'You've heard of fake monks before?'

'Of course. Since the war only monks may beg for
coin.'

The monk who was not a monk exhaled loudly. 'I
find it a useful way to live, whenever I'm here. It suits
me best.'

'So why tell me this?'

'Because it's no secret. If anyone asks me directly I
tell them. And most people here don't care what you
are. I've helped them when I could, unlike a great many
of the monks you'll find on this island, locked away in
their high sanctuaries. I must tell you. Even in my few
months at the monastery, I thought most of them were
more concerned with dogma and politics than with the
Way.'

Meer glanced at Ash then, sideways, as though trying

to read his reaction. 'Besides, as soon as spring arrives, I'll be leaving again to travel abroad.'

'But I have heard them talk in the Perch of how you keep a vigil in the shrine every day, meditating deeply.'

'*Pah*. They call it what they wish to call it. In the shrine I merely sit and watch the world turning.'

Ash saw the irony in that. In the native tongue of Honshu, the meditative act of *chachen* meant simply to sit in stillness.

He watched the man and pondered.

'I was coming to see you later,' Meer admitted. 'I've been talking with some friends in the city. Concerning your situation.'

'*You have been doing what?*'

'I can get you to Cheem, if you want it.'

'Oh? And I suppose we are flying, like a leaf on the wind?'

Meer showed him one of his quick, boyish smiles. 'I have a friend who owns a boat.'

Ash's expression clearly said it all.

'It's true,' Meer chirped.

'And tell me. Why would you go to all that trouble, simply for an old farlander like me?'

'Because we'd want to come along with you. To Sato.'

Ash's hand reached for his sword, though it grasped at nothing. He had left his weapon back in his room.

'Who are you?' he asked coolly. 'How do you know of Sato?'

The man shrugged and held out his hands in a gesture of openness. 'I am who I say I am. And a little more. All you need to know, in this moment here and now, is that I'm a friend to you, Ash. And that I have certain other friends. People who would dearly wish to have words with the Rōshun order.'

'There is no more Rōshun order.'

'Why not? Because the Imperials attacked it? Yes, we have already spoken to several of your agents in the Free Ports. They all said the same as you. Still, there might be survivors left in Cheem. If there are, we would like to make them an offer.'

Ash was on his feet now, though he could not recall standing.

'You are with the Few?'

A modest twitch of the head.

'Trust me – we only wish to talk with your people. And in return, I may just be willing to help you.'

'Help me? With what?'

Meer stepped forward to set a hand on his shoulder. He looked Ash straight in the eye.

'With your loss, my friend.'

—CHAPTER FORTY-SIX—

The Bunker

Deep beneath the Temple of Whispers, old Kira, mother of Sasheen, stepped from an elevator into an underground tunnel lit by gaslights, and saw that all but one of the carriages had already departed.

She boarded the remaining one, the carriage sitting there with its wheels on the rails and the driver diligently avoiding her eye, the team of zels sniffing and snorting in impatience. With a hard tug on the cord she rang the bell, and the driver, a slave with a complexion made pasty white from lack of sunlight, lashed his whip across the backs of the zels, and they were away.

Deep within her own heart a fierce fire was burning. With the bland concrete walls flowing past her, and the harshness of the lights interspersed with identical lengths of gloom, she stoked it with memories of her daughter, and her grandson too, young Kirkus, both of them gone now.

It had been Kira, in her capacity as a handler within the Section, who had given the order to the Diplomat

Ché concerning what was to be done in the event that Sasheen was captured, or ran from battle. An order that had needed to be given, as it always had been when a Matriarch or Patriarch had taken to the field; an order she had been commanded to pass on herself.

And now it had come to pass. Her daughter lay dead, poisoned by a Diplomat's bullet.

Oh, Sasheen, she thought, and couldn't help the grip of loss that seized her thin frame.

Her direct bloodline would end with her own passing. Others within the family of Dubois, her half-sister Velma and her get, would take the helm of the family's falling fortunes.

Her thoughts turned to the Diplomat still at large in Khos, the one who had clearly shot her daughter through the neck. Ché, the young man with his Rōshun ways. A deserter, if the vague report from the twins was in any way accurate.

Kira wondered how utterly she could destroy him.

It felt like hours, rocking from side to side as the carriage rolled along the endless track of rails, always downwards towards a never-changing vanishing point. Time to linger on things, to allow her emotions to slowly ebb into numbness and her mind into random thoughts.

She was jolted as the carriage came to a halt, and saw that they had arrived at their destination. The air was stale here, so deep beneath the catacombs of the Hypermorum.

Kira stepped out and walked to the heavy iron door in the wall. Even as she approached, a priest stepped out from a cubicle to open it. He bowed low as she stepped through the raised threshold into the small chamber within, which was cylindrical, its sides glassy smooth, so that she felt as if she was standing in a bottle. Another round iron door plugged the end of it.

Darkness, as the light slowly faded to nothing. A hiss as a fine spray covered her, smelling of pine trees and the sea.

'Your pass, please,' came a voice from all around her. 'Eight-six-oh-four-nine-nine-one.'

The inner door cracked opened. Kira stepped through into the light beyond.

*

The bunker was a tomb for all those who had been buried there alive; the iron doors were there to keep them in as much as others out.

The priests and slaves who lived down here would never see the sky again. Some had volunteered for this half existence, but for most there had been little choice in it. The dry, filtered air that fluttered through its rooms held an atmosphere of hopes abandoned and desires forever repressed. Quiet chatter came from the pools and salons and cages of the harem. Silence from the libraries and map rooms. Singing, even, from a boy standing naked on a pedestal in a marbled hallway, his words a celebration of the jealousy of lovers.

Kira stood beneath the strips of gaslights that made it as bright as day in there, surrounded by friezes on the leather-faced walls of forest hunting scenes. It smelled of dampness in the waiting chamber, and of decay, even with the fresh scents on her clothing and skin.

Four others stood in various postures around the room. Octas Lefall was there, famous uncle of Romano, leaning on the mantelpiece of a decorative hearth while he stared down his long nose at her, looking as though he was pleased with the news of the Matriarch's death. The rest were over by the bar, conversing quietly in whispers.

Kira returned the stare of Octas with one just as icy. She would afford him no small victories today by an outward betrayal of her emotions.

They all fell quiet as a set of double doors clattered opened. Quickly, they gathered in a line and fell to their knees, their heads bowed low.

The high-backed chair creaked as it was wheeled through by a burly male priest. The man sitting in it had his eyes closed behind a pair of gilded spectacles. He was naked beneath his half-open silk robe, and his ancient withered skin was covered with the blotches of liver spots and the odd wiry white hair. His bald head rocked slightly as the chair stopped before them. His bearer retreated from the room and closed the door.

Nihilis snapped open his eyes.

Through the thick spectacles, the watery orbs were oversized and spiteful.

'Kira,' he snapped, and his voice sounded as worn and scratchy as his one hundred and thirty-one years warranted. 'Your daughter lies dead in Khos. My condolences for your misfortune. May she be remembered for her strengths and not her many weaknesses.'

Kira bowed her head even lower, if only to hide her sudden flush of rage.

He rang a tiny bell that sat in his lap. The tips of his fingers were coal black.

Another priest entered, and strode silently across the plush carpet to hand him a crystal tumbler filled with Royal Milk. Nihilis smacked his lips as he took a sip from it. Colour washed into his face, and he straightened. The robe parted further to reveal the silver spikes in his nipples, the mass of piercings in his genitals.

She watched him from beneath her eyelids, loathing him as much as she feared him.

'So. What is to be done now? It seems we have an empty throne requiring an occupant.'

Octas Lefall cleared his throat first. Lefall was as old as Kira, had been there too during the Longest Night and the subsequent rise of Mann. 'My nephew intends to lay his claim once he has wrested control of the Expeditionary Force in Khos. He is a stronger candidate than any other, and all here know it. We should notify the Archgeneral to accede to his command. Let the transition be a smooth one. Let them get on with the business of taking Bar-Khos.'

'A predictable sentiment, Octas. As always. And what do the rest of you think of this?'

'I would support such a motion,' commented Chishara of the Bonnes. 'The longer this war continues, the longer it costs us all dearly.'

Hart, of the coal-rich Chirt clan, looked to Chishara in surprise.

'That may be,' Hart responded loudly. 'But there are others who intend to make a rightful claim to the throne. My son is one of them. He should be given his chance.'

A snort of derision came from Lefall, who snuffled it with a swipe of a finger down his long nose.

'You wish me to give the nod to spirited Romano,' Nihilis said to him. 'Yet that is hardly our way, is it? No. We must see if he is fit enough to rule first. If he wins through in Khos, *then* he may have my consent. If not, we shall see who rises from the infighting here in Q'os, and I shall decide then if they are right for it.'

'But, lord,' said Chishara. 'If we allow them to dither, we may lose our chance at Bar-Khos.'

'Oh, the Free Ports will fall all right, have no doubts on that, Chishara.'

Kira found that her attention was drifting. Her fists were clenching tight by her sides. She could feel her fingernails biting into her palms. A fierce bitterness had possessed her, a sense of shame, even, at this lessening of her daughter before them all; at the lessening of her own position.

Look at the harm you have caused our family, she spoke to her daughter. *We are losers now. Our star falls and our force diminishes. You were meant to win, my child! You were meant to conquer!*

Beyond her, in the greater world, Chishara was glancing at Lefall as she made to reply. 'It is not only that, my lord. There is the expense of it. Last week, my annaliticos informed me that if the war continues for another year, it will have cost us more than we can hope to recoup from the islands over twenty years of occupation.'

Nihilis waggled a finger at her, as though at an impudent child. Indeed she was the youngest of the gathering, barely beyond fifty years old. 'The defeat of the Free Ports means much more to us than merely what we can profit from their wheat and ores.' He paused to drink again from the tumbler of Milk. Savoured the taste of it for a lingering moment. 'Yes, I see that you are interested now, all of you. Kira, tell them of this clever plan of ours.'

Hostile faces turned to observe her. Stares that accused her of their lord's favouritism, because she had once been his casual lover.

'Of course,' Kira croaked, gazing straight at Nihilis now. Her knees were starting to hurt, kneeling like this. 'A plan, I should add, first endorsed by myself and my daughter.'

A tight-lipped smile stretched his wrinkled features, and his head nodded in subtle acknowledgement.

To the others, she said, 'We project that the Free Ports will have fallen within the year, once we have dealt with Bar-Khos. When they do fall, we will be free to turn our attentions to the problem of Zanzahar and the Caliphate.'

A rolling of the eyes from Lefall. Kira chose to ignore it.

The words tumbled from her lips of their own practised accord. 'At that point, we become their sole customer for blackpowder. With the war over, we will cut our demand for blackpowder to almost nothing. We will do so under the guise of a temporary consolidation of our accounts. At the same time, we will manufacture a famine in Pathia, or another of the southern lands, so that the price of our wheat will soar. We will be forced then, or so it will seem, to raise our tariffs in the wheat that we sell to Zanzahar, and which they are reliant upon.

'Within a year of these double blows to their economy, Zanzahar will be experiencing a period of deepening crisis. Conditions will be ripe for a coup against the

House of Sharat. We will make certain of that. We will manufacture the coup ourselves, with players of our own choosing, using our Diplomats to back them. Zanzahar and the Caliphate shall fall without a single battle. More importantly, their monopoly on trade with the Isles of Sky shall be ours. And with it, the only known source of blackpowder.'

They were all blinking at her as though she was speaking in tongues.

'Are you quite serious?' exclaimed Chishara, forgetting herself in the heat of her temper. 'We stand on the verge of finishing the Free Ports here, and already you wish to gamble with all that we will have gained? What if the Caliphate realizes our true intentions? They could call an embargo on our heads, choke us of powder whilst feeding it to whatever insurgencies they can foment within the Empire.'

'You fear for what we might lose,' interjected Nihilis, lifting a finger again. 'That is always your weakness, Chishara. Better if instead you embraced all that we could gain from this.'

'So it's settled, then,' asked Lefall. 'We're going ahead with this?'

Nihilis craned his head back so as to scrutinize the man better. Kira gazed at the startling redness of her master's lips, the tip of his tongue, the fleshy rims of his eyelids.

'Do you have enough chattel, Lefall? Enough to satisfy you, I mean.'

Lefall chanced a subtle smile. 'One can never have too much, my lord.'

The vivid tongue of Nihilis probed the air for an instant.

'Then there is your answer, is it not?'

Friends with Boats

It was a sound like no other, the roar of a skyship's burning tubes. It filled the air while blanketing all other noises, so that after a while, when the ears had grown used to it, it became a kind of silence.

Ash pressed forwards against the rail as the skyship began a slow circle above the monastery grounds. His grip tightened as he looked down on the small woodland of mali trees with their copper leaves covered in snow, and the stark black rectangle of ruins that lay at the heart of them like the stamp of some wrathful deity.

Amongst the thinning outskirts of the woodland, canvas tents stood in a sprawling camp with smoke smearing from their metal chimney pipes.

'All gone, you said,' remarked Meer the monk. 'You recall?'

Ash could only stare in astonishment.

He heard a cane rapping against the decking as Coya came to join them both.

'My spirits lift to see that there are survivors,' he remarked, cheerfully, and then turned towards the captain of the ship, standing on the quarterdeck with his pilot. Both of them were discussing where they should land.

He rapped his cane loudly against the planking, trying to be heard above the burners.

'Quickly now, Ronson. Bring us down!'

*

Ash jumped to the ground even before the ship had touched down on the snow, and a moment before the ship's boys vaulted clear to tether the ship with stakes and ropes, their clothes and hair blowing in the wind.

Around him, the high mountain valley lay beneath a carpet of white. A pica called out from somewhere, cackling to itself as though at some dirty joke. He stood for a moment, watching the outlines of the distant, heaving tents. He stroked the hilt of his sheathed sword with his thumb.

A few hesitant steps, and then Ash was striding towards them with his blood already starting to rise.

He heard voices suddenly raised, people arguing, as he neared the closest tent, its sloped roof bulging with snowfall. Ash stepped around to the entrance. At the same moment Baracha stepped out with a scowl on his tattoo-covered face.

The big Alhazii froze in surprise, a curious display of expressions passing across his face – surprise, anger, confusion, and then, at last – relief.

'You old bastard!' he exclaimed, and seized him by the shoulders and shook him before Ash could respond.

Behind Baracha, he saw Serèse and Aléas sitting on rough cots inside the tent with playing cards in their hands, their mouths gaping. 'Ash!' they both exclaimed, and rushed to greet him.

Warmth filled his body as they embraced. At last he broke clear of them, uncomfortable with their open displays of emotion. He nodded to the stump of Baracha's left arm, wrapped now in a leather binding. 'It healed well, then?'

'Aye, well enough. Itches like the damned, though.'

Yes, thought Ash, and was reminded of Oshō and his own missing limb, scratching at a wooden leg that his memory still thought to be flesh.

All at once they started to talk across each other. Ash waved their questions aside. 'Tell me,' he said, unable to contain himself any longer. 'The urn I gave you, is it still safe?'

'Of course,' rumbled Baracha. 'I gave it to Aléas to look after.'

Aléas went and drew the urn of ashes out from beneath his cot. Relief flooded Ash so entirely that for a moment his body trembled.

'Come,' said Baracha. 'We must bring you to the others!'

*

'You heard what happened, then?' Baracha asked over his shoulder as he led the way.

'From our agent in Khos.'

'We lost half our people in the attack. When Oshō realized the situation was hopeless, he ordered everyone he could down into the watching-house. The Mannians left without knowing they were even there.'

Ash stopped with his boots deep in the snow. He could feel fines of ash in his nostrils now.

'Oshō. How did he die?'

Baracha paused for a moment before he turned to face him.

'We found him at the gates surrounded by the others. They made a last stand there, so the rest of us could make it down below.'

'And Kosh?'

'He's thinner than he used to be. And drinking more than ever.'

'He lives?'

'Come see.'

It was more than Ash could have hoped for – another steamy tent, and Kosh sitting on a cot talking to a group of apprentices.

His old comrade opened his mouth wide, then hurried across to him, his eyes sparkling. 'You're alive,' he breathed in Honshu, and he grasped Ash with an outstretched hand, as though to confirm his existence.

'It's good to see you, old friend,' Ash said as they embraced. 'Damned good to see you all.'

*

In the largest tent of the camp, the remaining Rōshun gathered in raucous excitement. Even the Seer came down from his shack to join them, and greeted Ash kindly.

There were twenty-four survivors in all, many of them apprentices or the youngest Rōshun of the order. It had mostly been the older hands who had stood at the gates and fought to buy them some time. He saw Stretch of the Green Isles there amongst them, and wily Hull, and the two Nevarēs brothers, sitting together as always.

They stoked the fire in the central pit higher as the wind howled outside. Alcohol was produced and enough food for a feast. It seemed they were well enough stocked. Baracha explained they had been bringing up supplies from Cheem Port, while they waited for the return of those few Rōshun remaining in the field so that they could decide on what to do next. Opinions were still divided. The younger survivors wished to declare vendetta against the empire of Mann, never mind that the Rōshun code forbade such a thing. Others, like Baracha, thought they could rebuild elsewhere and carry on, if only a safe location could be found.

Ash wondered how many remained to be swayed.

When Meer and Coya finally arrived, Ash stood quickly to introduce them. Meer smiled, while Coya, stooped over his cane, nodded in greeting.

'These are friends,' Ash told them all. 'They have come to make us an offer.'

Around the tent the Rōshun shifted uncomfortably.

'And what is this offer?' Aléas asked him.

As Coya opened his mouth to speak, Ash shook his head. 'Not here.'

And he stepped outside, knowing they would all follow him.

*

Ash stopped before the ruins with a thousand impressions numbing him. For a long time he simply stared across it, this rubble that was the burial mound of his home, his friends.

Behind him, he heard the Rōshun gather.

'*Tell them,*' Ash barked over his shoulder.

He didn't listen as Coya began to address them. Instead he bent down and studied the particles of ash dancing and racing in the breeze. He closed his eyes for a moment, and when he opened them again, he stabbed his splayed fingers into the surface of ash and rubble, and drew them out again slowly.

Ash drew his fingers along his skull, down his face, all the way to the bottom of his neck. Only then did he turn to face the gathering.

'Where are you based?' Baracha was asking Coya. 'Where do you work from?'

'From the Free Ports, mostly.'

'So you are Mercians then?'

'Most of us. Though by no means all.'

'And explain to us again, what it is that you do?'

Coya tilted his head and looked to Meer. 'We fight against . . .' the monk began, then spread his arms apart, suddenly awkward, and brought his hands together in a clap. 'Concentrations of power, I suppose you could say.'

'And the Mannians?' asked Aleas, keenly. 'You fight the Mannians?'

'Of course.'

Kosh spoke up then. 'So you want us to come and work for you?'

Meer sniffed a breath of air, looked at the sky above their heads for a moment. 'No,' he said. 'We wish to ask if you are ready to choose sides yet.'

'You have us wrong,' spoke up the old Seer in his quiet voice. 'Rōshun do not choose sides.'

'Then perhaps it's time you became something else,' replied Coya. 'Something new. All things change after all, do they not?'

Ash watched the Rōshun closely, the wind tugging at their hair and their robes, the boughs swaying all around them, spilling snow. They sensed he was waiting to speak. One by one they turned and gave him their attention.

'Sato was built by exiles fleeing from defeat,' he said to them all. 'Now we find ourselves exiles once more.'

He stepped forwards, so that he stood in the midst of them. He met the Seer's gaze. 'Do we run again, and hide?' he asked of the gathering. 'Or do we honour those we have lost here, by fighting for something that is worthy? Even if we must choose a side in doing so, even if we no longer remain Rōshun? Well I tell you now. It is what I would have us do.'

The wind gusted, and a stream of fine ash sifted across the surface of trampled snow around their feet. He saw their heads turn to the ruins of Sato, knew in that moment which way their decision would fall.

Ash walked away then, for the rest was only talk.

*

In the large tent that evening, the Rōshun sat around the fire with the canvas sides buffeting in the wind to celebrate the reunion of old friends, their talk loud as Ash and Kosh sat together watching the flames.

Kosh produced a bottle of Cheem Fire, forcing a groan of surprise from Ash's throat.

'I purchased it in hope of your return,' he said in Honshu. 'Let us enjoy a drink for old times' sake.' He was still bright eyed, still patting Ash occasionally. Kosh seemed a different man from when Ash had last talked with him. He could see it in the slackness of his skin, the lines carved even deeper than before, his gaze less intent, his voice subdued. Something in Kosh had broken in some subtle way.

It grew hot in the tent, with so many bodies pressed together and the logs flaring into flames. Ash relaxed into it all like a steaming bath.

'Tell me,' said Kosh. 'The Matriarch. Did you—'

Ash shook his head.

'Good. Then we'll speak of it no further. So then. You think we should trust these Mercians?'

'They're good people. And their offer is a sound one. We can help down there, in the Free Ports.'

'I thought we'd seen the last of lost causes,' said Kosh drily, and he looked across at Coya and the laughing monk, his drink forgotten for a moment.

Give him time, thought Ash, knowing his old friend only too well.

'You should hear the monk's stories,' he tried, watching Meer too. 'He has travelled far.'

'Further than us? Surely not.'

'He tells me he's been to the Isles of Sky and back.'

'That far?' replied Kosh with a grudging nod of his head.

'The old Seer has a tale himself,' Kosh said. 'You recall Ché, our mysterious disappearing apprentice? He says the man came to him on the night of the attack. That he saved his life by hiding him away.'

Ash gave him a startled glance. 'A strange tale,' he replied. He took a deep drink, felt the burn of it deep in his stomach. He wondered what the young Diplomat was doing now, whether he was even still alive.

He was surprised to find that he wished him well. His mind felt clear at long last. His heart open.

Ash took in the gathering of Rōshun, noticing the absences within the group, those they had lost, men he had shared half his life with here in the cold mountains of Cheem.

'I thought you all gone,' he confessed.

'Aye, well we were luckier than we deserved. I'm sorry, by the way. I was grieved when I heard of your own loss. The boy deserved better than that.'

Another long drink.

'It isn't finished yet,' Ash said, and he leaned closer so that Kosh could hear him against the noise of the celebrations. 'There may be a way, my friend.'

'A way?'

'Of bringing Nico back.'

Kosh studied him carefully for signs of illness. He blinked, not knowing what to make of his words. 'I don't understand what you're saying.'

'Meer knows a way. If we agree to join them, he will show me how.'

'And you really believe such a thing can be possible?'

'No, not here. But in the Isles of Sky . . .'

'A way of raising the dead? Please.'

He knew how it must sound to his old friend. He offered an awkward smile.

'You're leaving us again,' Kosh realized with a start. 'After all your talk of helping the Free Ports, you're leaving again.'

'Only for a while. But it will be easier now, knowing I may at least have something to return to.'

Kosh poured him another drink, thinking it over. He shook his head fast as though dispelling all the thoughts in his head, then raised his mug and clinked it against the one in Ash's hand, some of the Cheem Fire sloshing out onto their hands.

'With heart,' he declared.

They both leaned back, content to share each other's companionship in silence.

Meer was telling his tales by the fire next to Coya and the Seer. The men were drunk already. They all were drunk already.

Baracha sat next to his daughter, talking with her freely. Aléas laughed at something, his mouth opened wide, looking to the young apprentice Florés to share in his delight.

Ash settled back in comfort, his eyes gazing deep into the flames. For a moment, in his mind, he thought he heard another young man's laughter, the memory of it, at least.

He tilted his head to one side, in hope of hearing it again.